Bye Bye Oscars

John Sheffield

Acknowledgements

I am fortunate to be a member of the Atlanta Writers Club and its literary critique groups, and of the North Point Barnes & Noble critique group. I am grateful to my late wife, Dace, and to Vicki Kestranek, Carolyn Robbins, and Maree and John Stephens who have read and reread *Bye Bye Oscars*, and patiently helped me to refine it. I am deeply indebted to Anne Kempner Fisher for her thoughtful advice.

The wonderful cover art was produced by Janice Stewart at janicestewart.com. The cover was produced by Jason Sheffield.

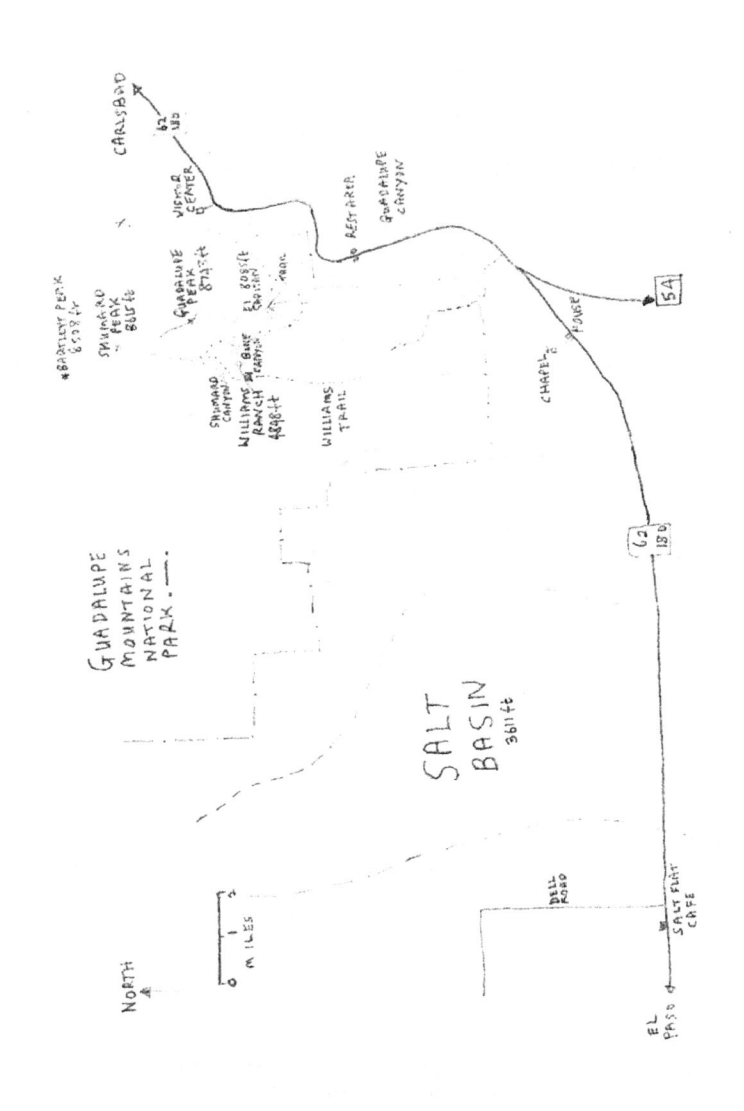

1.

Amarillo, 1978.

"What do you mean, you've lost the fucking hydrogen bombs?" the shift superintendent tried to shout, but the sound from his tightened chest came out as a gasp. "The last I heard you'd pulled into a rest area." His free arm shook and knocked over his coffee cup. "Why couldn't you contact the security van?"

His assistant at the Department of Energy's Pantex weapons assembly plant, looking startled, left the bank of TV monitors and came over to the control desk. With his hand over the mouthpiece, the superintendent said, "Charlie, get hold of the plant manager, then we're going to have to tell DOE. Now!"

He activated the speaker phone so that Charlie could hear the excitable driver on the other end. "Okay, calm down. What happened to the truck?" He moved his chair back to evade coffee dripping onto his lap.

"I-40's a sheet of ice," the driver said. "When we couldn't see the car behind us, we reckoned it'd crashed. So we pulled into this rest area."

"So, what happened?"

"We were just about to do our regular call in, when these two guys came over and asked if we could help them start their pickup."

"Don't tell me." Thee superintendent sat up straighter. "You didn't both get out, did you?"

"We were only trying to be helpful." The driver's voice faltered. "It's real bad out here. Snow's drifted across the interstate. Ice—"

"What about procedures? I don't give a damn if the weather was bad."

"They had a gun."

"So do you."

"They were drunk, and we were scared they'd shoot."

The superintendent slapped the desk." Jesus Christ!"

Charlie approached the desk. "Manager's on the way."

The superintendent nodded, indicating the spilt coffee and motioning at a Kleenex box. "Okay. What happened next?"

"They tied us up and left us in their pickup." The driver said adding. "It was full of empty beer cans, and must have broken down…oil leaked on the snow."

"So you let a couple of drunks get the…. What's the use?" Exasperated, the superintendent paused again. "How did you get to a phone?"

"We're in the patrol car you sent to look for us."

"How long before he came along?"

"At least an hour."

"Oh shit." The superintendent turned to his assistant, who had started to mop up the coffee. "Did you put out the alert, Charlie?"

"Yes. The FBI, police, and Highway Patrol have the info that a truck's missing. I didn't tell them anything was in it. The manager's trying to get hold of DOE."

The superintendent pictured Sheldon Marsh, the officious DOE official who oversaw the shipping operation. "Sheldon's going to blow a gasket." The superintendent glanced up to catch assistant grinning. "It's not funny, Charlie."

*   *   *

"Why'd yer turn off, Hector?" the skinny, unshaven passenger in the truck asked in a slurred voice.

"Best get off I-40, Jimmy," the driver, Hector, said. "Highway Patrol." He ran a hand through his mop of black hair. "I need a *cerveza*."

"Me too," Jimmy replied. "What the hell's that lighted thing I saw under the dash?"

"Beats me. Some kind of electronics." Hector reached over and tried to remove the device.

"Let me." Jimmy reached behind the seat. He pulled out a metal tool box, opened it, removed a hefty tire iron, and beat on the device until the light went out.

"Better get rid of that damn radio phone, too," Hector said, ripping it out. He opened the window and threw the phone onto the side of the road. "Wonder what's in back?"

"Could be food or TVs." Jimmy pushed the toolkit under the seat.

"We'll check later."

"Where we going'?"

"Carlsbad. There's no beer around here."

"Then El Paso, like before?"

"Nah. Presidio. I've got relatives there. When we've transferred the stuff to my uncle's van it'll be easier to get it across the border."

"We're getting good at this," Jimmy said.

"*Si, si mi amigo.* That's two trucks we've stolen. Good thing the pickup packed up." The truck fishtailed slightly as they rounded a bend. "*Madre de dios,* this ice is a pain in the butt."

* * *

"Sorry to get you out of bed, Sheldon, but we've got a big problem," the Pantex Plant Manager said into the phone. "Our shift superintendent just informed me that a couple of drunks have stolen one of our trucks," He rubbed his forehead in a vain attempt to clear a massive headache. *It was tough enough being a contractor running a DOE plant, without having on-site DOE staff permanently second guessing you and protecting their rear ends.* "There were two nukes…. You'll tell your Albuquerque office and DC."

While he listened to the Sheldon, the plant manager stared at the multiple television screens in the shift operations center. "Better you contact them…. No, don't count on Air Force spotter planes. I don't think they could see anything in this weather and it's already dark." He paused. "Our best bet is to pick up the locator signal." The manager noticed the superintendent shaking his head vigorously. "What's that? Why's it stopped?"

"Sheldon, the shift superintendent says the signal's gone off," he said into the phone. "God help us. But at least, they can't get into the back of the truck. That's for sure." He envisaged the multiple security devices that would activate if the hijackers tried to open the door.

"I agree. We'll meet in your office first thing, but it'll take time to get Highway Patrol and FBI to the site.

*   *   *

"Hector, did you notice that jerk-off looking at us strange-like when we got the beer?"

"Yeah, we better get off this road. Been here before. Turn in ten miles or so."

"Watch out," Jimmy said as they passed a diner at the Carlsbad city limits. "There's a cop car."

Hector put his foot down, glancing repeatedly at his mirror. After a while, he said, "Think somebody's following us. Turn's coming up soon. I'll get onto 62/180."

"Where's it go?" Jimmy asked.

"Whites City," Hector said. "Small place. Shouldn't be a problem. Then Guadalupe Park, and on to Presidio. Better slow down. God, this road's bad. He held his hand out. "*Cerveza, por favor.*"

As they drove into Whites City, a police car with flashing lights overtook them. Hector clipped the rear of the car, spinning it onto the sidewalk. "Truck seems okay. To hell with slow," he muttered.

They left Whites City behind and soon came up to the Guadalupe Mountains National Park. Hector steered with his right hand, clutched a *Dos Equis* in his left, and belted out Wichita Lineman in a scratchy voice.

As the road curved to the left, Jimmy tried to take a mouthful of beer. The truck skidded. "Watch it, Hector," Jimmy screamed. "I knows what I'm doing, Jimmy." Hector started another verse. The truck fishtailed again. "It's fucking ice," he said. "I am a lineman for the…oh shit!"

*   *   *

The old man leading two burros looked up as a crashing sound came from an arroyo behind him. He put his head down and let his wide-brimmed hat take the brunt of the driving sleet as he headed back up the arroyo. The sleet abated as he reached the crumpled remains of a truck lying just short of a large tree. One body lay beside the crushed cab, another was trapped inside. The bodies' necks were twisted.

"Dead," he said, without checking further.

The truck had split open on impact, spilling its contents—two wooden crates. He went over to the nearest one, bent down and lifted an end. "Heavy," he muttered. "Need my hoist."

He tied his lead rope to a wing mirror that still remained intact, and removed a pulley arrangement from a saddlebag. He stood on the truck's hood and tied one end of the hoist to a thick branch that projected to the side of the truck. After an hour or more of wrestling with the crates he managed to lash one to each of his burros. He stood back and studied the nearest crate. The writing on the box read DOE-B-61- followed by a string of numbers and letters. Near one end was a yellow square with a strange black clover-leaf design in the middle.

He scratched his head. "I can add em to my stash," he mumbled. "Cops'll never know what happened. In this weather ain't no one goin' to find that truck fer days. Have to ask the reverend if they're worth anything." He headed off into the cold mist that had settled into the arroyo.

2.

Albuquerque, 2004.

Sebastian Agincourt sat back and scanned the photographs hiding the peeling paint on the walls of his office. Those were the days: helping a drunken Errol Flynn out of nightclubs. Agincourt glanced across his desk at his scriptwriter, Lance Dupree, a slim man in a lime-colored jumpsuit. "I like the general idea of your rewrite of *Bye Bye Oscars*, Lancie; terrorists nuke the Academy Awards ceremony," he said. "And you say you have a backer who suggested it? But, my God, here we are in 2004. It's been sixteen years."

Lance tilted his head, and fiddled with his blond ponytail. "Why not?"

"Okay, let's assume we do it," Agincourt replied. "Can I film it here in Albuquerque?"

"I don't see a problem. As I told you when I talked you into moving here, one crappy urban area looks like any other these days. And God knows Albuquerque's got plenty of crap."

"Good." Agincourt stroked the straggly Van Dyke beard that peeked out from a fold in his chin. "It's been too long since my last movie, but I wish you'd tell me who he is."

Lance looked at his feet. "I don't know. This all came—"

"Hold on," Agincourt snapped, eyes narrowing. "There's another catch?"

"Only a little one…our unknown angel has a suggestion for the leading man."

"Are you going to tell me?"

"He wants us to use Chuck Steak," Lance replied warily.

"Who the hell's he?" Agincourt shouted.

"Up till now he's used the stage name, Charles Innocent."

"Wait a minute. I've seen him in something." Agincourt stood up and waddled around his office. "Mid-twenties, sanctimonious religious crap and can't act. Right?"

"He's reformed," Lance sniggered. "Wants to do mild porno."

"God help me. Any choice?"

"Not if you want the money."

"You won't tell me the name of Mister Moneybags?"

"Don't know. This all came from Chuck. He loves the original movie and thinks the reviews were shit."

"Another example that those damn critics didn't know what they were talking about." Agincourt pointed at framed yellowing newspaper columns hung next to a lurid poster that depicted a voluptuous blonde, standing on a red carpet, recoiling from a fishy-looking creature. Large red letters, dripping blood announced Lola Paramour and Bogdan Mirnov in Bye Bye Oscars, director Sebastian Agincourt. Not an Otto Preminger or a John Houston production, he knew, but comparable to those of Roger Corman, whom he admired and copied.

Agincourt peered closely at the columns, which he kept to remind himself how stupid and unfair the critics were. He'd shown them. Three of his movies still brought in money. Not just *Bye Bye* but also *Atomic Bactrian Camels of the Mohave*, and *Alien Ghost Riders of the Purple Mesa*; all still shown late Saturday nights on college campuses.

Agincourt read, "The jellyfish look like mutant trash bags as they chew up the carpet and a chunk of the audience before returning to the sea at Venice Beach.

"I preferred this one," Lance said. "Lola Paramour is never shy about hiding her bushel under a light." He paused. "Which reminds me, Chuck wants us to use Monique von Minx for the female lead. I'll let you explain that to Lola. Wait a sec."

Lance reached in a folder and held out a photograph. A drop of water fell onto it from an overhead air vent. "How the hell your air conditioning system leaks water, even when the heats on, is a mystery to me," Lance muttered, his voice rising as he added, "You need to get that damned system fixed, Bas. Haven't you heard of Legionnaires disease?"

Agincourt ignored the question, shook the water off and scanned the photograph. "That her real name?

"Course not," Lance winked. "I invented it.

"Hot babe." Agincourt smirked "She'll do fine."

"Hoping to get to first base, Bas?" Lance asked, wide-eyed. "Planning another screen test on your couch?"

Agincourt returned to his chair without reacting. "Do you intend it to be a thriller or a comedy?"

"Both. It's a black-comedy-thriller."

"Okay then, if I like the script and Chuck brings the cash." Agincourt looked up at the wet spot on the ceiling. He'd have to get it fixed, but later when he had some spare cash. He hoped this new backer could solve a lot of problems. If not, maybe it was time to move again. Downtown Albuquerque was encroaching with new buildings and the rates were soaring. "I'm still not quite sure. Read me a scene so I can get a feel for the way you see the movie going."

"I think you'll enjoy this part, Bas," Lance offered smugly. "I'll just do the dialogue and a little bit of description. In this scene, Monique is forcing Chuck to tell her how much he's screwed up. They'll be using their stage names in the movie."

"Why?"

"Makes it easier for Chuck to remember who they are."

"A male Marilyn Monroe, who can't learn more than one line at a time." Agincourt sighed. "Just what I need." He glanced at Lance. "You're not kidding, are you?"

Lance shook his head.

"That means I'll have to get a stand-in, doesn't it?" Agincourt looked pensive. "I'd better get an advertisement out.... More money. I can't afford to pay much. It'll be difficult to find someone. Dammit, I hope that Chuck can find the funds."

"We don't have to tell him yet," Lance said. He opened his folder, found a page marked with a flier for a fancy restaurant in Santa Fe, and read from the manuscript:

"MONIQUE: *raises the riding crop*. What did you lose?

CHUCK: *face shows fear*. Nothing much.

Thwack! The riding crop hits the thighs of the bronzed, muscular man handcuffed to the bed, moving the line of welts closer to his most treasured possessions.

CHUCK: *screams*. You bitch. Why did you do that?

MONIQUE: *sneers*. Because you've been a bad boy.

CHUCK: It wasn't my fault.

MONIQUE: Oh, no? Tell me what happened.

CHUCK: I only parked the Hummer for a minute at Starbucks to get a vanilla-almond mochachino with extra whipped cream and cinnamon.

MONIQUE: And when you came out someone had opened the rear door?

CHUCK: Yes.

MONIQUE: Was it locked?

CHUCK: I, er— *Thwack.* Ow! No, it wasn't.

MONIQUE: And what did they take?

CHUCK: The Kalashnikovs—

MONIQUE: "And?"

CHUCK: The grenades, bows and arrows...rocket launcher, small arms, air-to-air missiles. *He pauses. The look on her*

face tells him she doesn't believe he's finished. He continues.
Flame throwers, anti-tank guns, and...I think that's all.
MONIQUE: *raises the crop.*
CHUCK: Okay, okay. I admit it. I lost the hydrogen bomb.
MONIQUE: What the fuck do you mean you've lost the hydrogen bomb? Where are we going to get another one?
CHUCK: *plaintively.* Where we got the last one?
MONIQUE: You think that Pakistani guy will still deal with us when he hears what happened?
CHUCK: He seemed nice enough.
MONIQUE: Do you remember what he called us?
CHUCK: He said we were like camel drool in the underpants of Osama bin Laden."

Lance stopped reading and looked at Agincourt. "What do you think?"

"It has promise, Lance," Agincourt replied, glancing at the photograph of Monique von Minx. "What the hell. I'll do it.... Wait a minute. Put out an advertisement for a double for Chuck ... brief summary of the new plot, and a photo of Chuck. As to pay, say something about industry standard."

"You want *Hollywood REPORTER* and *Variety*?" Lancelot asked.

Agincourt rolled his eyes. "One should be enough."

* * *

Lancelot walked a hundred yards from Agincourt's building before pulling out his cellphone. Painful working with Sebastian, but at least the stupid bastard had bought in to the plan. He dialed and waited. "Orlando—" He held the cellphone away for a moment. "Sorry, I'll say Bishop Orpheus next time. Anyway, he bought it," he said, then listened for a couple of minutes. "Don't worry. He's far too eager to have a new movie to figure out your motive." He listened again. "He's also got money problems and I'm concerned he'll move on again. So we need to keep him in Albuquerque. As to how much you'll have to fork out, don't worry about it. Sebastian may try to con you but he does everything on the cheap. Oh, and he'll take Chuck and Millie. But he insists on a stand-in for Chuck." He listened intently. "I agree, when he turns up, I'll check him out." He put the phone away and headed to his car.

3.

New Braunfels, Texas, 2004.

Fred Schwarzmuller flicked through television channels in the den of his parent's house in New Braunfels, Texas. He had been stuck there since losing his engineering job in Austin, when the company downsized. He prayed that something would come out of his applications for work in Dallas and Houston. He could handle that work. Best would be that long shot, the strange ad from Homeland Security that referred to technical qualifications and acting experience. That combined his field of electrical engineering, and his private passion, acting? The interview in Austin had gone well, he thought, though some of the questions were weird.

"Mailman's been, Fred," his mother said, pointing out of the window at the receding mail van. "Can you…?"

She didn't finish. Fred was already running down the drive that led from the white, forties ranch house to the country road. He returned, brandishing unopened envelopes and a letter, the torn envelope trailing precariously out of the back pocket of his jeans. "I got the job," he announced triumphantly, and read, "January 10, 2004. Dear Mr. Schwarzmuller: This letter is to inform you that you successfully completed the interview and test, and are being offered a position in Homeland Security in Los Angeles. Starting salary—"

"Los Angeles. I'd hoped they'd want you to go to Dallas." His mother's voice wavered and she looked down at her knitting.

Fred continued. "If you accept, we would like you to report for duty in February. On acceptance we will send further details. You may contact us by email." Fred glanced at his mother's bent head, leaned over and gave her a hug. "It's not that far, Mom…only a couple of hours by plane."

"A mother's allowed to worry. I've heard about Los Angeles…gangs, drugs. It's not like New Braunfels. What about those other letters?"

Fred opened them and glanced at their contents. "An advertisement for the hearing impaired…should I give it to Dad?"

"Put it on the hall table. Maybe he'll pick it up after work and take the hint. Now that I'm not at the store, I worry about whether he always understands what the customers want. What else?"

"A rejection, and an offer from an oil company in Houston to work on a rig in the Gulf."

"Oh, my heavens. What are you going to do?"

"Homeland Security. I bet it wasn't just my engineering degree. My acting experience must have impressed them." Fred spread his arms. "Think of it…Hollywood, film stars, beaches."

His mother looked up, smiling despite the tears that had welled up. "I bet they don't have Moon Pies."

"They'd better, or you'll have to send care packages." Fred hugged his mother again. "I've got to send that email." He bounded up the stairs.

4.

Los Angeles.

Eugene Kowalski sat in his office at Homeland Security in Los Angeles, scanning the advertisement his secretary had clipped from *Variety*. Sebastian Agincourt planned to remake his absurd movie, *Bye Bye Oscars*, with a nuclear weapon replacing the mutant alien jelly fish. *You've got to be kidding*. But policy was to follow up on anything where nukes were mentioned, however absurd. However, this one had seemed different and he'd decided to investigate. Fortunately, Agincourt needed a stand-in for the lead actor, a Chuck Steak. Not unusual but the first sight of the actor's photograph had made the hairs on the back of his neck stand up.

Gene picked up the photo and took a second one from a folder lying on the desk, and stared again at the two men in the pictures. The actor had an uncanny resemblance to the Reverend Orlando Jenkins he had met back in the seventies, during his hunt for two stolen hydrogen bombs. Gene ran his fingers idly through his thinning gray hair as his gray eyes scanned the photograph of the second man who, in turn, resembled Steak, one Frederick Howard Schwarzmuller—about the right height, close to six feet with a medium build, could lose a little weight, brown hair that could be dyed blond, contacts to make his eyes a paler blue, but most important, he had a technical background and acting experience. Gene had offered Schwarzmuller the job.

Gene put both photos in the folder and picked up a sheet of paper that gave Schwarzmuller's background. Frederick's parents, who owned a country store, were the descendants of German immigrants to Texas in the 19th century. Frederick was the second of their three children.

Frederick had good grades in high school and had been active in the band and amateur theater. He was fairly good at sports, although he failed to make the first team in football or baseball. No mention of basketball. One up for the old man, Gene thought, remembering how the game had gotten him into Notre Dame. Character not so clear; a reputation for being flippant, named class clown in high school, but that might match what he'd found out about Chuck Steak—what a ridiculous name. Reasonable grades at the University of Texas in Austin. Some work experience; unlucky to join a company that downsized soon after. At age twenty-four, Fred was seven years younger than Chuck, but that didn't matter for this job. Typical of the younger new recruits to Homeland Security's Nuclear Task Force, Schwarzmuller was inexperienced; he'd need training—lots of it. Anyway, he wanted someone new to take over the hunt for those stolen bombs.

Gene scanned the old photographs of the Guadalupe Mountains National Park in West Texas that covered one wall of his office at Homeland Security in Los Angeles. The picture of sunlight reflecting off the face of El Capitan evoked memories of what had happened some twenty-six years earlier. He reached across his drawer and picked out a tape. The label on the cover said telephone conversation, Pantex, Amarillo, February 1973—Copy 3. He pulled out the tape and plugged it into the player on his desk.

"What do you mean you've lost the fucking hydrogen bombs?" The words echoed around his office.

He smiled a wry smile. The panic stricken opening words of the plant shift superintendent at the Pantex weapons production facility in Amarillo always had that effect on him, when he listened to the tape of the telephone conversation. But it hadn't been funny back then, when a snow storm had caused the driver of a truck carrying two hydrogen bombs to pull into a rest area on I-40 in New Mexico.

Gene switched off the tape and sat back. From that moment on the problems had escalated. It had taken an hour for a New Mexico Highway patrol car to find and release the Pantex employees and put out an alert. The search, following incorrect information, had focused on roads going north. It turned out later that the hijackers had managed to disable the locator electronics. In fact, the hijackers headed south on back roads and, helped by the bad weather, had succeeded in reaching West Texas.

Their luck ended when they slid off the road at an icy bend and crashed into an arroyo on the southeastern edge of the Guadalupe Mountains National Park. They died instantly. A day later, the local police spotted broken bushes and a break in the fence on 180/62 as it dipped below El Capitan. They found the truck at the bottom of an arroyo, hidden from view. Its security systems ruined and the cargo had spilled out.

The local police concluded that a James Buchanan, known as Old Tex, had found the wrecked truck and removed the bombs. At the time, Gene worked for the FBI in El Paso. His orders were to find Buchanan. An expert informed him that the weapons had been shipped without their trigger. It was highly unlikely that anyone could get them to work at their full capability. Nevertheless, they could be used to make cruder dirty bombs.

Gene sat back and thought about how he had left El Paso early on February 14th, 1978 to join the search team's advance party. He had driven 80 miles east to Salt Flat close to the Park. Most of the few original buildings were in ruins, but the Salt Flat Café remained open for the locals and the occasional tourist going to or from the park to the east.

On his way in, he bumped into Corporal Collins who was in an army search party looking for what they had been told was a lost missile. Subsequently, Collins had helped him look for the bombs. Gene recalled seeing the valuable Indian artifacts in the café that Buchanan had traded for food and supplies. Most of all, he remembered travelling down the road to the Lord's Redeemer Chapel where Old Tex was supposedly a parishioner of the Reverend Orlando Jenkins.

Gene had nearly missed the unmarked road, but just in time noticed a small house by the junction with a chapel in the distance; a low white building with a corrugated iron roof—hot in summer, cold in winter. Beyond the chapel, low hills covered in scrub led to a towering mountain escarpment, flanked by the imposing 8,000 foot peak of El Capitan some six miles to the north. Kowalski retained a vague image of a scruffy graveyard behind the chapel, with one new grave covered by a tarpaulin and sporting a heavy-gauge metal tripod and pulley arrangement. He closed his eyes and recalled what had happened next; a scene he had gone over in his mind again and again over the years...

As Gene parked next to a battered Chevy truck, a tall man wearing a worn denim jacket, jeans, and dusty scuffed boots came out of the chapel.

"Reverend Jenkins?" Gene called out.

"Yes, sir, and you are?" The reverend's voice was surprisingly deep coming from such a gaunt figure.

Gene flashed his badge and held out his hand. "Agent Kowalski, FBI."

The reverend's startlingly pale blue eyes narrowed, as he brushed his long blond hair back from his face, then clasped the Bible he was holding with both hands, avoiding the handshake. "Come inside, sir," he said. "My wife and I were consulting the Good Book."

He turned and led Gene into the chapel. An unwashed odor trailed the reverend, causing Gene to put a hand to his face. A worried-looking, woman in a blue gingham dress and threadbare coat, buttoned at the top, was waiting inside the door. She held a small boy on her hip.

Gene noted that another child was on the way.

"My wife, Sarah," Jenkins said. "You can wait in the truck, dear. Agent Kowalski and I need to talk." He emphasized the word "agent."

Gene decided not to hold out his hand again. He nodded his head and said, "Pleased to meet you, ma'am."

She nodded uncertainly and edged out of the door.

"You're welcome to stay, ma'am. It's very cold out there."

She ignored his suggestion and left.

"What do you want, Agent?" Jenkins asked, motioning for Gene to take one of the twenty or so seats situated around the walls of the chapel.

Gene took a chair near the door, hoping the fresh air would tone down the smell. "The army had a missile malfunction and it landed somewhere north of here. You probably saw the trucks."

The reverend's eyes widened. "Yes. What's that got to do with me?"

"We think that James Buchanan, a member of your congregation—people call him Old Tex—may have seen something."

Jenkins raised the Bible, briefly hiding his face. "Old Tex. Saw him two Sundays ago. He was headed for Pine Spring. You might look around there."

"Near the park, then. Anywhere in particular?"

"Can't say, really. He covers a lot of area."

"Doing what?"

Jenkins laughed derisively. "Looking for gold. I told him he'd find more gold in heaven, God willing."

Gene concluded he was not going to learn much from Reverend Jenkins. "I may have more questions later. How can I contact you?"

Jenkins did not look happy at the prospect. "House by the road."

"Telephone?"

"No." Jenkins stood and led Gene outside.

Probably no running water either, Gene thought, wrinkling his nose. "If you think of anything, you can contact me through the park headquarters. I'm going there now to meet up with the search party." At the door, he pointed at the new grave and asked casually. "Someone local die?"

"Not yet," Jenkins replied, then continued, his voice rising. "Blessed are the meek, for they shall inherit the earth. Blessed are the poor. Those who defy God's will and those who arrogantly cling to false belongings will *weel the frath* of the Lord."

Weel the frath. That didn't sound pleasant. "May that never happen to you, Reverend," Gene said. "Thank you for your help."

Some weeks later, Gene had returned to ask the Reverend Jenkins more questions. His house was empty, and the tripod and tarpaulin were gone. An empty hole remained. None of the locals knew where the Reverend had gone. Gene had tried to track him down, but he had disappeared off the face of the earth; a loose end that Gene still worried about. As to the other loose end, James Buchanan, it was resolved quickly. His body was found by the side of Route 54. He had been hit by a car or truck.

Despite searching for more than a year, the team failed to find the bombs. Officials from the Department of Energy and the FBI informed the appropriate, closed congressional committees about the problem. The Administration supported downplaying the event, not wanting anything to confuse the mid-term elections. Later, DOE announced that they had found the remains of a missing weapons delivery truck, and added that it was fortunate it had been returning from a delivery and had been empty.

The troops had found a recently dug area near a trail outside the park, and Gene remained convinced that one bomb had been found and removed by who…by whom? He chuckled, remembering a rap on the knuckles from Miss Swenson, his tough old schoolteacher in Minnesota. Removed by the

Reverend Orlando Jenkins, likely, but Gene had never been able to prove it. And Jenkins was long gone from Salt Flat to some place Kowalski had not discovered. Unfortunately, few people in the FBI had believed his theory, particularly his superiors, and he'd been persuaded—ordered—to stop working on the case. After Carter lost to Reagan in 1980, most of the political appointees with knowledge of the case moved on. The few senior permanent staff remaining preferred to accept the lie that the stolen truck had made its delivery and had been empty. Decades later, he'd left the FBI and took a managerial job in Homeland Security. Gene returned to completing the set of lectures for the next two days.

* * *

The following day, Gene Kowalski waited in the office of Mrs. Rogers, administrative assistant to his boss, James B. Wheaton III, a political-appointee. He glanced at his watch; thirty minutes past the time of his appointment to brief Wheaton on the missing nukes. He flicked impatiently through the pages of an out-of-date Time magazine, not really taking in what it said. He decided that Wheaton must have been trained in techniques to put down subordinates. Gene dumped the Time and reached for a hunting magazine.

Then Mrs. Rogers' phone beeped, and she said, "Ambassador Wheaton will see you now."

"About time," Gene muttered.

She raised her eyebrows but did not reply.

Gene knocked before opening the door to the inner sanctum, a large room with a commanding view of downtown Los Angeles. The large American flag on a pole, occupying one corner of the office, was flanked by portraits of the president and vice president. Gene tried to avoid looking at the prominently displayed photographs of Wheaton and other important political figures. Without raising his head, Wheaton, sitting behind a large antique desk, waved him to a chair and continued reading a report.

Gene looked at the neatly cut, graying blond hair of the man at the desk. Ambassador. That said it all: six months in some fetid part of West Africa, screwing up the country, and now ambassador for life.

"Would you like me to come back later?" Gene asked after a couple of minutes had elapsed.

Wheaton raised his head and placed the report neatly in front of him. "What? No, no, Kowalski. We need to talk." He tapped the report. "A most fascinating description of advances in anthrax detection." He rested his elbows on the desk and clasped his hands together. "This business of the movie, Oscar something or other. I hear that you are looking into it." Wheaton unclasped his hands. "Why?"

"The FBI couldn't find anything peculiar about the movie, but I saw a face in an advertisement for the movie that reminded me of someone I met in the '70s when I was involved in investigating that missing nuclear weapons fiasco."

"Remind me." Wheaton touched his fingers together, beautifully manicured nails forming the apex of the steeple.

"Twenty-six years ago, a truck delivering nuclear warheads was hijacked in New Mexico, and—"

"Yes, yes, I've heard about it." Wheaton's brow tensed. "But it was returning from a delivery…empty. Right?"

"That was the story put out, Ambassador. Unfortunately, not so, and by the time our people found the truck, the warheads were gone."

Wheaton put his hands palms up on the desk, and said, "I see. Probably rusted by now."

"In the dry air of the desert?" Gene shook his head. "In my view, they remain the most dangerous potential source of nuclear weapons materials."

"I dealt with a case like that in the embassy." Wheaton glanced at a photograph of a white colonial building on the wall. "Someone stole ammunition from our armory. I questioned all of them. The cook looked guilty as hell. I fired him."

"So you found the ammunition?"

"Not the point, really. Teach them a lesson. I'm sure the bullets have rotted by now."

Gene struggled to hide his irritation. "Ambassador, I believe that one of the bombs was found and removed."

Wheaton, looking annoyed, retorted, "I remember now. The people in authority didn't believe that. His brow furrowed in a manner apparently designed to show that he was applying all of

35

his intellect to the new weighty matter. "Nevertheless, you may continue at a low level for the moment." He picked up the report and started reading. "You may go."

"Thank you, Aa...," Gene caught the word 'asshole' in time, "mbassador."

5.

Fred Schwarzmuller arrived at the Los Angeles Headquarters of Homeland Security for the second day of a briefing on nuclear security. At the building's entrance, handwritten signs marked "Nuclear Briefing - 2" directed him to that afternoon's meeting room. A notice stated that everyone entering had to show identification, and hand over all their writing materials and recording equipment before they would be allowed to go in.

"Can I take this in?" Fred asked, indicating his paper bag.

"Let me look." The guard peered in. "Moon Pies, that's a first. Why not?" He motioned for Fred to enter.

Fred scanned the room, most of the fifty or so seats were taken. He focused on a pretty blonde sitting near the front and sat next to her. Talk tapered off as Eugene Kowalski strode to the podium. Behind him, a screen started a slow descent between photographs of the president and vice president on the left, and a large flag on the right.

"Welcome back," Kowalski said. "Yesterday afternoon, I explained what we meant by the terms fission and fusion." He bent to peer at the podium, looking over his glasses, and pushed a button. His first slide appeared showing the definitions. He read the words on the screen pointing at each one with his laser pointer. "To recap:
* In fission, heavy elements like uranium and plutonium are split, releasing energy.

* In fusion, light elements like heavy hydrogen and lithium are joined together—fused to release energy."

Heads in the audience nodded, encouraging Kowalski to continue. "In this talk, I'll describe how these two sources of energy are combined in a hydrogen bomb, but I will not give engineering details."

A man in a police uniform raised his hand. "Can you recommend something to read?"

"Good question. What you're going to hear is unclassified and may be found on the Internet, like a lot of material on how to design a bomb." Kowalski shrugged, showing his disapproval. "Another useful source is the book." Kowalski pushed a button on his remote and a picture appeared on the screen. The new one showed a sketch of a bomb; from *Megawatts and Megatons* by R. Garwin and A. Charpak written underneath.

"It looks like a bomb. It ticks like a bomb. My God, it is a bomb," Fred whispered to the blonde FBI agent sitting next to him. She made a tut-tut gesture with her fingers. But she was smiling, Fred noted.

Kowalski looked hard in their direction before saying, "This cartoon is taken from the May 1999, congressional Cox Report. It shows the guts of a multiple, independently-targetable, re-entry vehicle (MIRV) with its 300-kiloton hydrogen bomb: more than ten times the energy of the bomb dropped on Hiroshima."

A coastguard officer raised his hand and said, "Sir, from the scale in the caption, that thing looks about six feet long. I'd heard that nukes were smaller."

"You're looking at the whole re-entry system, captain. Those two spheres inside a roughly cylindrical tube are what counts." Kowalski moved his hands apart and flapped them at chest level to indicate the size.

"Then, take the primary. That's the sphere on the left. Look at the circle marked plutonium. Drat…battery's gone dead in the laser." Kowalski picked up a wooden pointer and tapped the area on the screen. "If you use the scale, the plutonium sphere appears to be maybe the size of an orange."

Fred raised his hand. "Big orange or small orange, sir?"

Kowalski smiled bleakly at his audience. "Yes," he said, receiving a few titters.

The blonde nudged Fred in the ribs. "That'll teach you."

Fred grinned. He suppressed an image of his ex-girlfriend who was back in Austin. Even though their relationship cooled off when he lost his job, she had, nevertheless, wanted to come to Los Angeles. Since arriving there, Fred had been on the lookout for her successor.

"The point of showing you this illustration is to make it clear that a device, particularly if it consists only of the primary, can be quite small." Kowalski looked at his audience to see if there were more questions. No hands were raised so he continued. "Staying with the primary, you can see that a beryllium reflector surrounds the plutonium sphere. Its purpose is to reflect neutrons back into the core, allowing less plutonium to be used. An outside shell of high explosives is used to compress the beryllium and plutonium and achieve criticality."

"I worked with explosives in the Gulf when I was in the army," a police officer said. "How do they get the explosive to go off symmetrically?"

"Multiple detonators, focusing, and good timing," the lecturer replied.

"How many detonators?" Fred asked.

"Enough," Kowalski said, receiving louder applause. "No engineering details. Remember?"

"You're a good straight man," the blonde commented dryly. She was not smiling.

"Note the words deuterium and tritium on the cartoon," Kowalski said. "The fusion of these heavy isotopes of hydrogen is used to boost the yield of the primary. The X-rays from the primary are trapped in the metal cylinder. Its shape is designed to spread them uniformly around the sphere on the right—the secondary."

After a pause to take a sip of water, he continued, "The secondary is shown as a sphere of uranium with lithium-deuteride inside. Neutrons from the primary explosion convert some of the lithium to tritium. Rocket action, due to the X-rays boiling off the outside of the secondary, compresses the uranium sphere. Shock waves converge on the center, heat the fuel and you get fusion...Boom!" He smacked the pointer on the podium. "The total explosive yield can be, let's say ten times that of the primary."

"How sensitive is the yield to getting everything right?" a naval officer asked.

"Good question, Captain. You may have read Clancy's book, *The Sum of All Fears*. The terrorists get hold of a lost Israeli weapon and let it off in Denver. Because they didn't replenish the booster gases, the yield is reduced so much that the secondary fails to go off."

Fred raised his hand.

Kowalski looked at him with a resigned expression. "Yes?"

"Fred Schwarzmuller, sir. How about protection against misuse? I've read that you have to use special codes."

Kowalski's expression changed to one of interest. "Ah, Mr. Schwarzmuller, at last an appropriate question. All the U.S. weapons require a code to allow the trigger to be activated; however, the danger remains that, if someone with knowledge got hold of one, they would dismantle it and reuse the pieces. Even the primary alone would equal Hiroshima or Nagasaki"

"What about foreign weapons?" an FBI agent, who Fred had met in the lobby, asked.

Kowalski nodded. "A mixed bag, sir, but there remains the same possibility of using the 'pieces-parts.' I should add that dismantling one of these devices can be hazardous, precisely because of the high explosives."

"So we should keep an ear open for unexplained explosions?" Fred asked.

"Yes, sir. And carry a Geiger counter."

The blonde dug Fred in the ribs again. "What's in the bag?" she whispered.

"Moon Pies. Want one?"

She looked surprised and shook her head.

"I'm sure you have more questions, and I'll be happy to answer them at the end," Kowalski said. "Now let me move on to sources of weapons and weapon material."

He put up a second slide showing a map of the world.

"Other than us, Britain, France, Russia, China, India, and Pakistan are known to have nuclear weapons, and it is generally assumed that Israel does, too. We believe that the weapons that were located in the former Soviet Republics have been returned to Russia. But I'm sure you've heard that a fair amount of weapons grade material remains, and we are concerned about its security."

A second coastguard officer raised his hand. Kowalski nodded toward him. "I'd heard something about South Africa, sir?"

"They admitted to having produced a few, and informed the world that they had dismantled them. We don't see them as a threat, although they clearly have the knowledge."

"Mr. Kowalski, I've heard rumors that we may have lost a weapon or two. Can you tell us something about that?" an army officer requested.

"Certainly, sir. This is one of the biggest problems. I mentioned that Clancy's novel was predicated on the existence of a lost Israeli bomb. You may also recall the attempt to raise a sunken Soviet submarine, and the case of a U.S. bomber crash in Spain. There have been rumors that the British mislaid a bomb. A British reporter remarked sarcastically that there was a building on Salisbury Plain with the sign, 'Hut: Nuclear Weapons for the Storage of.'"

"You're joking, aren't you?" the blonde FBI agent asked.

"I hope so, ma'am," Kowalski replied. "The bottom line is that, with your help, we will investigate every mention of nuclear weapons, however absurd it may sound. And I heard of a real winner recently. That concludes the briefing. Come up here if you have further questions."

Fred joined in the applause and whispered to the blonde, "I hope I get that one."

"Good luck." She raised her eyebrows.

"Do you want to come for a coffee?" Fred asked.

She grinned. "Does that invitation include a Moon Pie for my boyfriend?"

"I, er...not really."

"Maybe you will get the real winner." She held out her hand. "Nice meeting you."

Fred shook her hand and watched her neat backside sashay out of the meeting room.

"Where I hope to send you on assignment, Mr. Schwarzmuller, you'll have plenty to ogle," said a voice from behind Fred. "Your file says you did some acting in college, and are still a member of the Screen Actors Guild?"

Fred turned to see Kowalski towering over him. "Yes sir, I've done amateur theater in Austin, and one summer I toured with a small group putting on plays across the Southwest…schools, town halls you know the kind of thing."

"That simplifies things. Let's talk. My office in twenty minutes. Upstairs, Room 315."

"Mr. Kowalski asked me to see him," Fred said to the plump, smiling woman seated behind a desk that sported a signed studio handout of Marilyn Monroe.

"He'll be ready in a few minutes, Fred. I'm Gene's administrative assistant, Linda Holmes," she said. "Would you like coffee?"

"Please. Cream and two sugars."

Linda poured his coffee.

"Is it okay if I eat something?"

"Sure." Linda glanced at the paper bag with curiosity.

"Moon Pies." Fred held out the bag.

"Let me have a look." Linda reached into the bag and pulled out a pie, and read the label. "Enriched flour, corn syrup, high fructose corn syrup, sugar, partially hydrogenated...you've gotta be kidding," she said.

"Chocolate, marshmallow sandwich," Fred replied. "It's real good.

"Thanks, but no. I'm watching my weight." Linda dropped the Moon Pie toward the bag.

Fred caught the pie and nibbled on it as he looking around, spotting two more photos of Marilyn. "You like Marilyn Monroe, don't you?"

"How did you guess?" Linda giggled. "Don't you think I look like her?" She primped her curly brown hair and struck a pose.

Fred grinned. "Amazing resemblance."

At that moment a red light blinked on Linda's telephone. "He'll see you now. Go on in."

Kowalski wasted no time when Fred entered. "Have you heard of Sebastian Agincourt?"

Fred started toward the swivel chair in front of the desk.

"GSA junk for show. Take that wooden one. Not comfortable but it won't fall apart.

"Okay, Fred said, swapping the chairs. "Agincourt, sure. A bunch of B-minus movies." Fred laughed, and the chair creaked ominously. "I read an article somewhere that described him as the poor man's Ed Wood, without *Plan 9 from Outer Space*."

"Agincourt does have cult hits like *Bye Bye Oscars*," Kowalski said. "You seen it?"

"Local movie-theater in Austin used to put *Oscars* on as a late night show. It's nearly up there with the *Rocky Horror Picture Show*." Fred glanced around the sparsely decorated office with its austere furniture, wondering if he'd got into the right business to be a success.

Kowalski interrupted his thoughts. "Well, he's doing a remake with terrorists and a lost hydrogen bomb."

"Great. But a hydrogen bomb wasn't in the original. The Oscars crowd was absorbed by mutant jellyfish." Fred looked puzzled. "It sounds like a quick job for the local FBI."

"Their agent didn't find anything. He saw some of the script, and concluded that the whole setup was crazy. The plot described in the script has an ending showing a newspaper headline, *Nuclear Explosion Interrupts Oscars*."

Fred chuckled. "Why are we interested, then?"

"I saw photographs of the people on the set. One of the faces looked familiar. Kowalski paused. "Linda said she sent in the classification forms, and you got your clearance, right?"

"Yes, sir. They interviewed me at home."

"Well, the photo took me back to my first job for the bureau, when I was hunting for two stolen bombs." Eugene Kowalski sighed and glanced at the photo of El Capitan. He continued as if speaking to himself. "It was a long time ago and it may all be in my imagination. Certain people here think I'm nuts to take this movie seriously. Mind you, they didn't believe my theory of what happened to the bombs."

Fred shook his head in disbelief. "You mean someone actually stole nuclear weapons?"

Kowalski's head jerked around. He reached into a drawer, took out a bulky folder, and removed several photographs. He handed them one at a time to Fred. "This picture shows one of the trucks that the Atomic Energy Commission used in the 1970s to transport weapons from the factory to bases around the country. A truck was hijacked in New Mexico by two guys—drunks likely—looking for a ride. The security vehicle trailing the truck had crashed. The men tied up the driver and guard and drove off. They had no idea what they had stolen. Murphy's Law ensured that the truck's tracking device had gone AWOL, and the winter weather caused poor visibility. By the time the driver and guard freed themselves and contacted authorities, the truck was miles away to the south. Here's what happened."

The succeeding photo showed the battered parts of the truck scattered over a stream bed. "The hijackers lost control on a bend, and crashed at high speed into a deep arroyo in the Guadalupe Mountains State Park in west Texas. Those are two bodies beside that tree. For the arborist in you, that's the bottom half of a big tooth maple the truck hit." He added dryly, "I leave it to you to work out how the tree managed to grow in that Godforsaken location."

A second photo showed the smashed rear end of the truck. "Shee-it," Fred muttered, exaggerating his Texan accent.

Kowalski ignored him, and went to a side wall which held a map of the Guadalupe Park area. Fred joined him.

Kowlalski indicated a cross, which showed where the truck had crashed at the base of El Capitan. "The recovery team found the tracks of a couple of burros. There were signs that someone had used a pulley on the one tree limb left to lift the crates onto them. Their tracks petered out after a few hundred yards. Days later, one of the search groups found the burros wandering beside Route 54, more than twenty miles south. We searched for tens of miles in all directions except up the escarpment. Nada."

"Did they find out who owned the burros?" Fred inquired.

"That was easy. James Buchanan, Old Tex, was well known in far west Texas. He prospected for gold that wasn't there, and spouted quotations from the Bible. He sometimes attended a fundamentalist chapel near Salt Flat, southeast of the park. His pastor, a Reverend Orlando Jenkins, was somewhat helpful in providing information."

"Did they ever find Old Tex?"

"Yes, they did." Kowalski returned to his chair. "His mangled remains were found a day after I got there…on Route 54. We reckon he had been chasing his burros and got hit by a car or truck. It seemed obvious that Old Tex had hidden the bombs? The Army and FBI teams scoured the area for months, but we never found them."

Fred, feeling he should ask questions to make a good impression, said, "What happened to the Reverend Jenkins?"

"After a couple of months, the FBI transferred me to Cleveland. Jenkins left the area shortly afterwards. I did some research but eventually gave up on finding him. Other work took priority.

Kowalski turned to the final photo, and hesitated before proffering it to Fred. "This is a photograph of one of the bombs. Their serial numbers are in the caption." He paused and took a deep breath. "Fortunately, the weapons were shipped without their trigger mechanisms. But, if someone managed to obtain or build a trigger, one of those nukes, assuming the secondary went off, would cause near total destruction out to about three miles from the blast center. Any images you have of what happened at Hiroshima and Nagasaki doesn't come close to showing what these modern devices can do at full power. Without the proper trigger, they could still be used to make cruder dirty bombs. Fred, this scares me more than all of the other potential sources put together. Those nukes are still out there, somewhere."

Fred scanned the photos again before placing them on the desk. "Does the public know?"

"No. We put out a story that we were looking for a crashed missile." Kowalski replaced the photos in the folder, and put it back in the drawer. After rummaging on his desk, he handed a second set of photos to Fred. "These are from the Oscars' movie set.

"Which was the face that interested you?"

"Not yet. I want your unbiased opinion after you've had a chance to study everyone."

"What will I do?" Fred asked.

"First, you'll report directly to me. I'm going to send you to Albuquerque to work on the movie. More of that in a minute. First, do not discuss this assignment with any other employees. Only Linda and I will know what you're doing. We can't trust the political appointees not to leak information."

Fred put his hand to his mouth to hide a grin. This was going to be great. Undercover agent Schwarzmuller rides again. But something was missing. "How do I get paid?"

Kowalski smiled bleakly. "The normal way, at the end of the month."

"What about travel expenses?"

"You'll be getting a job. You work it out with Agincourt. I don't want to have Accounting seeing travel claims."

"Oh."

"Fred, you'll be getting paid for two jobs."

It sounded okay. What the hell. "What will I be doing?"

Kowalski indicated one of the photographs. "As to how you fit in…their male lead, Chuck Steak, behaves like an idiot. My local source says that Agincourt's desperately looking for a stand-in to do the simple stuff, like park a car, walk through the right door. I think I've got it fixed through the Lou Cohen Agency for you to do the job. As you can see, you could look like Steak if we straighten your brown hair and dye it blond. And you can act. His eyes are a much paler blue than yours. We could use contacts, but that probably doesn't matter. I doubt you'll be doing close-ups." Kowalski grinned. "Judging by the names of the other actors, we may need to call you Fred Sirloin."

"I'll stick with my own name, thanks." Fred paused. "Incidentally, when I did acting I used a stage name. Frederick Howard Schwarzmuller's a handful and I didn't want to be mistaken for 'Arnold'." Fred flexed his biceps.

"Hmm. Not likely," Kowalski grunted. "Probably better you don't use your real name. What do you go by on stage?"

"My mother's maiden name. I'm Fred Howard."

"Let's stick with that. I'll get our people to fix you up with a phony I.D. and a new social security number under that name." Kowalski glanced down at the photographs.

"Do you suspect Agincourt of being involved," Fred asked. "Like he's got a real bomb?"

"No, no. I'm sure he's clean. I've spent a lot of time researching him. Of course, his real name's not Sebastian Agincourt. It's Liviu Malinauskas. His parents came from somewhere in Eastern Europe. He attended high school in the Bronx. Got interested in movie-making and went to Hollywood when he was twenty. As far as I can tell he was a gofer for anybody who'd put up with him. But, from being on the film sets he learned enough about the trade and had enough contacts to set out on his own. His first success came when *Bye Bye Oscars* was a hit on college campuses. Having found a formula that worked he's continued with it. He's known for conning backers, but gets support because his movies don't cost much and make a good profit."

"What's he doing in Albuquerque. It's not exactly the movie capital of the world."

"Good question. As far as I can tell, he was frustrated with what he viewed as a lack of recognition in Hollywood. There may also have been an expense issue. I've heard that someone offered him a deal for a building in Albuquerque." Kowalski scanned his notes, before continuing. "There's one other thing you need to know. During the last twelve years, two people with critical weapons knowledge disappeared from Department of Energy facilities: The first one from the Pantex weapons manufacturing facility near Amarillo; the second, a couple of years ago from the Sandia National Laboratory in Albuquerque." Kowalski shrugged. "We have no clue as to what happened to them."

"What exactly did they do or know?"

"How to assemble and disassemble a weapon, and the Sandia guy was a trigger and safety systems specialist."

"So, if some group has the bombs and can pick these people's brains, they can make them work?"

"That's the concern. Now, before you go, you'll need some training in self-defense. How fit are you?"

"Not bad. I run about ten miles a week, and work out at a gym when I get the chance." Kowalski pulled a notebook from his pocket and turned to a dog-eared page, adding, "Do you know how to pick a lock?"

"Never had the need."

"Well, you may now. Also you need more training on the bomb. What to do if you come across one, and what not to do."

"Which is?"

"Don't try and disarm the thing. It may be booby-trapped."

"Could I blow it up with something?"

"Possibly. A weapons designer once told me that hitting it with an anti-tank shell could prevent there being a spherical implosion of the primary. Symmetry is absolutely essential." Kowalski shrugged. "An M136 AT4 high-penetration projectile can go through up to 50 or 60 centimeters of armor. Of course it would still make a hell of a mess, and scatter plutonium and uranium around."

Fred pictured himself, the cartoon super hero, aiming at the bomb. "Kerpow!" he said.

"What?" Kowalski stared hard. "You'll be going to the FBI Academy at Quantico for that extensive training I mentioned: physical, combat, forensics, disguise, and learn how to pick a lock. We'll get you a set of tools."

Fred grinned. "Like Bond. When do I get to meet Q?"

"More like one of the Three Stooges." Kowalski said. "Don't get carried away. And let's hope you don't get to use your new-found skills."

6.

Seven weeks after Lance Dupree brought Sebastian Agincourt the proposal for the remake of *Bye Bye Oscars*, Agincourt's crew was shooting the end of the scene that Lance had read. The set was downstairs in the abandoned warehouse that housed Agincourt's office: a building purchased two decades earlier in downtown Albuquerque with profits from the original *Bye Bye Oscars* and the subsequent success, *Atomic Bactrian Camels of the Mojave*.

Agincourt's voice showed desperation as he said, "If Chuck would concentrate for a minute, we could continue."

"I'm scared of what Monique's going to do with that whip," Chuck complained. "And the air conditioning's not working again."

"I'm getting it fixed," Agincourt said irritably. "Monique'll be careful. Won't you, sweetie?"

Monique smiled and flicked the riding crop.

"Enough. Chuck, get back on the bed," Agincourt snapped. "Let's take it from where Monique says, 'Did anyone know you had the stuff in the Hummer? Who did you tell?' Ready Lancie?"

Lance patted the camera.

"Action!"

MONIQUE: Did anyone know you had the stuff in the Hummer? Who did you tell?

CHUCK, *simpering*: Only Achmed.

MONIQUE: Which Achmed, you buffoon?

CHUCK: Achmed Paddy Cohen.

MONIQUE: So you only told someone who's reputed to have connections to Al Quaeda, the the IRA, and is a renegade Mossad officer.

CHUCK, *squirming*: I didn't know he was Mossad.

MONIQUE, *raising the crop*: Idiot, you didn't connect Cohen to him being Jewish?

CHUCK: I thought he wore that funny little hat because he was having a bad hair day.

Thwack!

CHUCK: Ow! You hit it, Monique.

Chuck brought his knees up to his chest. "I need medical attention!"

"Cut! Cut! You didn't have to hit his p-thingy," Sebastian Agincourt scolded Monique. "Chuck, get back on the bed. It's still in one piece. Monique, be more careful next time."

"What next time?" Chuck whined.

"We've got to do something to keep the audience's attention away from that piece of dead meat. Any suggestions, Lancie?" Agincourt said.

"Perhaps Monique could arrange for a boob to pop out," Lance suggested, brushing a speck of dust off his purple jumpsuit.

"Why not ask me to drop my pants, Lance?" Monique muttered. "I'm not a porn star."

"Yet." Lance smirked, cowering in mock fear as Monique raised the crop.

"Enough already!" Agincourt shouted, rising from his chair and pacing. "We'll take a break. The next shoot's going to be the theft scene."

"Do you need me anymore, Bas?" Lance asked. "I've got to phone some folks."

"No. Well, yes. Have your guys finished the bomb?"

"Some parts. You want to see what we have?"

"Why not."

Lance turned around to speak to a small woman with straight brown hair, dark glasses, and a resigned expression. "Georgie, has that shop sent the n-thingy?"

Georgie nodded toward the back of the set.

"Georgina, be a pet." Lance sat back.

When Georgie returned, she was towing a cart with a scratched-up crate on it.

"Georgie, did you bring the screwdriver?" Lance pointed at the crate.

Georgie rotated and stuck her butt out, showing the screwdriver projecting from her back pocket.

"Open the damn thing, then," Lance screeched.

Georgie pouted, but did as she was told.

"Enough, children," Agincourt said wearily, walking over to the cart to look at the bomb.

"It's empty," he exclaimed.

"Sebastian," Georgie said condescendingly, "that's just the crate. They're putting the n-thingy together in the shop."

"Lance, why does the crate have DOE stamped on it?"

"Army surplus I guess, Bas," said Lance. "I'll get Carl Bates to paint some other words over it."

"Not English," Agincourt insisted.

"Any particular language?" Lance said.

"Yes, that shorthand stuff...Arabic, Agincourt said. "The man at that deli down the next block is named Ahmed something or other. He could help."

"You mean there really is an Achmed?" Chuck giggled, as he put his shirt on. "I'll bet there's a real bomb."

"Sure, lovey," Lance snapped, "and you're a real actor."

"Not fair," Chuck said petulantly. "How about some glitter and a happy face?"

"Whatever. I need a drink." Agincourt said, walking toward his office at the front of the building. "I need to look again at the shots of Chuck parking the Hummer at Starbucks."

"Yes, great leader." Lance stood and bowed. "Georgie, come with me, and then stand by the door. I've got to make a call. Don't let anyone through."

Georgie shoved her hands into the pockets of her tan Dockers and made a face. "What'll I tell them?"

"Tell them someone's painting the other side. I don't care. Then, take the n-thingy's crate back to the shop."

* * *

"Georgie brought the *sate* on the *cret*?" the man on the telephone screamed. "Is she trying to ruin everything? How did she get it?"

The man who had made the call ignored the mangled words. "I don't know, but I could find out."

"No, no. I'll be back in a few days. I'll deal with it then. I don't want calls on my cell connected to the church."

"Agincourt wants Arabic writing on the crate."

"Fine."

"There's this guy called Ahmed who could help."

"What! I don't want pagans in my church's workshop. Put a stop to that."

"Okay. Anything else?"

"Get that crate back!"

The line went dead.

7.

Sebastian Agincourt glanced around to see if the people he needed from the cast and crew of *Bye Bye Oscars* had assembled in the screening room adjacent to his office. Satisfied, he leaned forward in his seat and signaled to Georgie, who was operating the video projector. "Run the daily again where Chuck parks the Hummer," he ordered.

The daily, filmed from the roof of a Mexican restaurant, showed a yellow Hummer pulling into a shopping center parking lot, and trying unsuccessfully to park in a number of spots clearly marked, "Compact Cars Only."

"What were you thinking, Chuck?" Agincourt asked wearily. "Even drunk, Errol would have been able to handle it."

"You said to find the first empty space, not too close to Starbucks," Chuck complained. "And who's Errol?"

"Errol Flynn. What's the matter with these young people?" Agincourt shook his head in disgust. "In the same county, Chuck. Didn't you see that Hummer salesman showing you the spot we'd picked? Jesus Christ, look at the damn screen. In the old days, Clark Gable never had trouble parking."

The camera panned from the Hummer to show the salesman and Georgie waving frantically from the back of a pickup truck.

"Look at their dark glasses. For a moment, I thought they were terrorists," Chuck said. "And you shouldn't blaspheme."

"For...Pete's sake, it's a movie. The terrorists aren't real." Agincourt stood and paced.

"Monique is." Chuck's hands went down to his crotch, and he whined, "She nearly finished my career this morning with that da...riding crop."

"Pity she missed." Lance snickered.

"At least we finished that damn scene. But we'll have to shoot this one again," said Agincourt, thumping into his chair. "Thank God Lou's agency found someone who can stand in for Chuck. He'll be here this afternoon. What's his name, Lance?"

"Frederick Howard," Lance replied. "In this photo, he looks quite like Chuck, but handsome and younger."

"Up yours, too," Chuck mumbled. "I'm only twenty-nine."

"Which birthday are we talking about, Chuckie, a few years ago?" Lance sniggered.

"Enough, children." Agincourt looked at his watch. "We'll have to re-shoot."

"Sebastian, do you really think anyone would notice?" Monique asked.

"For Chr.... Monique, look where Chuck parked," Agincourt shouted. "Does 'Sam's Hardware' look like a Starbucks?"

"It starts with an S," Chuck volunteered. "And you're blaspheming again."

"If you don't like it, Chuck, go to your damn chapel and pray for me!" Agincourt snapped.

"It's not a chapel. Bishop John says it's a cathedral," Chuck complained. "And he's letting you use his workshop."

Agincourt's sighed. "Sorry, Chuckie, I'm stressed out."

Chuck look mollified until Lance said, "I heard that the Redeemer Fountain Cathedral sells sodas on the side."

"It does not. You're being sacrilegious." Chuck flounced away and plopped onto a chair.

Agincourt slumped in his chair. "Now look what you've done, Lance. We'll have to wait for this new guy."

* * *

For fifteen minutes, Fred circled a rundown area, in which many of the streets were named after metals. At last he found Antimony Street and saw a dilapidated two-story building on the left where the road stopped at railroad tracks. On the end wall was a faded picture of what appeared to be St. George about to lance a mutant alien jelly fish. Under it, someone had painted the words Agincourt Productions in fluorescent paint. Fred parked and as he searched for the main entrance, an athletic-looking woman in a pale blue track suit came out of a metal side door with a large dent in it.

"Showtime," Fred said to himself. Time to find out if Gene Kowalski was on to something or merely a fanatic about the lost nukes. He got out and walked up to the woman.

"This is the best way in." She held out her hand. "I'm Georgie. Sebastian doesn't like us to use the front entrance. It's for people with money. You're Frederick Howard, I hope?"

Her grip was firm.

"Nice to meet you. Do I really look like Chuck Steak?" Fred asked, wondering why Georgie wore dark glasses, and not realizing he was staring.

"Close enough." Georgie stopped, and tilted her elfin face. "I have weak eyes. Can't stand bright lights. Okay?"

She led Fred through the door and down a drab, dirty corridor to the set, where everybody was clustered around Agincourt. "Fred Howard," she said, when Agincourt looked up.

Agincourt did a double take. "Lance was right. You do look like Chuck. Same blond hair and blue eyes. I hope your—"

"I'll bet he's brighter," Lance interrupted. "Are you, Mr. Howard?"

"Most people call me Fred."

"How original." Agincourt sniffed. "If you work out, we'll have to get you a proper screen name. What do you reckon, Lance?"

"He's got a nice butt." Georgie, who had sidled up, patted Fred. "Firm, too. How about calling him Rock Rump."

Fred did not react. He was watching a beautiful woman with bright green eyes and long black hair coming toward them.

Georgie prodded him. "Your new name, Rock Rump."

"Oh, I see," Fred said as he moved away from the persistent drip coming from a stained crack in the ceiling. "But not in public, dear."

"Enough," Agincourt shouted. "Fred, I am Sebastian Agincourt, the director. You've met my assistant, Georgie. She fixes everything when the rest of them screw up. The lady," Agincourt emphasized the word, "whom you are staring at is our female lead, Monique von Minx. The gentleman in the puce-colored jumpsuit is our writer, cameraman, and artistic consultant, Lance Dupree. Our male lead, Chuck Steak, is sulking—"

"Am not either." Chuck emerged from behind a backdrop. "Sebastian, can Fred do the scenes with the whip? I'm scared of Monique."

"Give me a break, Chuck. What if his pecker's smaller than yours?" Agincourt asked. "Think what that would do for your reputation."

Lance grinned and moved closer. "Let's have a comparison."

Fred backed away. "I hope you're kidding. I only do clothed scenes."

"My, we are precious," Lance huffed.

Agincourt led the way off the set. "Lancie, it's your turn to get an H-thingy. We'll see you at Starbucks in an hour."

One and a half hours later, Lance walked up to Agincourt, who was sitting outside Starbucks nursing an iced coffee. "I've got a Hummer over there." He pointed across the lot. "But we don't have long. The salesman's getting nervous."

"I'll talk to him," Agincourt retorted.

"For Christ's sake, it's black," Agincourt exclaimed, as he walked toward the Hummer.

"Sorry, Bas. They were out of yellow H-thingies."

"It'll have to do."

The salesman leaned out of the window. "I've got to take this back. Now!"

"Good projection," said Agincourt. "It sounds like you've done some acting. I need a startled spectator. Could you spare a few minutes?"

"I'm not sure," the salesman replied warily. "What do you want me to do?"

"I'm Sebastian Agincourt. I'm remaking my 1981 hit movie, *Bye Bye Oscars*. This time, terrorists nuke the ceremony."

The salesman looked impressed. "I've seen *Oscars*. So—"

"You'll get billing," Agincourt said quickly. "What's your name?"

"Carlos Rodriguez."

Agincourt took a pen and scribbled on his notepad, saying, "Startled spectator—Carlos Rodriguez. You know, you look a lot like my good friend Ricardo Montalban."

"You know Ricardo?"

Agincourt clasped his two index fingers together. "Like that," he said.

"Does he really know him?" Fred whispered to Lance.

"Might have parked his car once or twice." Lance sniggered.

"Carlos, you see that empty space Georgie's holding?" Agincourt pointed and Carlos nodded. "You take her place. When Fred brings the Hummer up, you jump out of the way like it nearly hit you."

"Fred, take the Hummer onto the road, then come back through that entrance over there and park in this spot. Carlos will hold it for you." Agincourt looked at his watch. "Oh, and after you park, open the door, then duck down."

"Fine." Fred got in and fiddled with the key.

Lance minced up. "You can drive, can't you?"

"Funny," Fred said as he drove off.

"Lance, you're becoming tiresome," Agincourt grunted. "Chuck, get in the space with Carlos, and keep out of sight. After Fred parks and opens the door, come out as if you're the driver."

"Okay."

"Lance, did you tell the shop about the Arabic writing for the n-thingy?" Agincourt asked.

"They're working on it, Bas," Lance replied, pointing the camera toward the road.

"Here's the Hummer," Agincourt yelled. "Ready and action! Good, he's found the right spot."

"What the hell is Chuck doing now?" Agincourt yelled. "He's on the wrong side. Cut, cut!" He waved at Lance, and ran over to the Hummer.

"I thought he was going to back in," Chuck protested before Agincourt could speak.

"Fred, Carlos, do it again. Chuck, get it right this time."

Agincourt strode back to join Lance and Monique. "Lancie, is there any way I can talk to our backer? Chuck is killing me."

"You could ask, but...." Lance shook his head. "It's Chuck or nothing, he says."

"Shit." Agincourt banged the side of a car with his fist. "Monique, would you talk to Chuck. You've worked with him before. I swear I'll use Fred if he continues to screw up."

Monique sighed. "Okay."

"See if Fred knows what to do, sweetie." Agincourt patted her back. "Let's do it again. Action!"

When Monique joined him, Fred asked, "What's your real name?"

"You don't think Monique von Minx fits?" Monique chuckled. "First, Sebastian wants to know if you could do this scene if he needs you."

Fred watched as Chuck left the Hummer. "I don't have to walk like that, do I?"

Agincourt answered his question. "Cut!" he screamed. "Walk calmly from the damn Hummer, Chucklehead. Don't sashay. You're supposed to be macho, not a pansy."

"I wanted to be noticed," Chuck whined.

"Just walk," Agincourt said, quietly clenching his fists. "Do it again, again. Action!"

"What a joke," Monique whispered. "Promise you won't make fun."

Fred gazed earnestly into her eyes, and said, "Cross my heart and—"

"I'm serious." Monique grabbed Fred's hand.

"I promise."

"It's Mildred." She looked defiant.

"Is Millie von Minx okay?"

"Yes, but not in front of those jerks, and not the von Minx."

Millie turned to watch Chuck, and ignored the question.

"How about dinner tonight?" Fred asked casually. Seeing Millie frown, Fred started to edge away.

Millie touched his arm. "Okay, but nothing fancy. I'll meet you here at seven. Wait a second, I may have to do something first. I'd better give you my cell phone number. Call before you come here." She pulled a silver card case from her purse and handed Fred a card that read, *Monique von Minx, Actress. Most roles accepted.* The cell phone number was on the back. No address, Fred noted.

Millie pointed toward a row of small restaurants. "Mexican or Chinese would be fine."

"That's a wrap," Agincourt shouted at Chuck's back disappearing into Starbucks.

Carlos edged up. "Can I take the Hummer now, Mr. Agincourt?"

"Sure. Thanks for your help, Carlos."

"If you need a Hummer again, I'm available. I could be a terrorist."

"We'll look you up, Carlos."

Agincourt motioned for Fred to come over. "We'll go back to the office in a minute. You can sign some papers, so I can pay you. Incidentally, you'll need somewhere to live. I have some apartments off Juan Tabo near I-40. We can deal with that, too."

Hydrogen bombs with this crowd of weirdos. Is Chuck for real? Gene's got to be kidding, Fred mused as he walked to his car. But, at least it looked like he'd get a chance to play at acting.

* * *

The two men in lab coats looked up when they heard the key scrape in the lock. The shorter one with a swarthy face, faded, green eyes, and thinning hair spoke as the gaunt old man strode into the concrete-walled room. "Did you find anything, Bishop?" he asked.

"No, but I narrowed the possibilities. The new metal detector worked fine. And I've got the tools you need. Now, Carl, who let Georgie take that crate?" the bishop asked softly.

The two workers looked at each other nervously.

"Well?" His washed-out blue eyes were unblinking.

"We needed space to put stuff while we cleaned up the lab," Carl replied, scuffing a foot on the floor. "We put a few things outside. By the time we realized Georgie'd taken the crate, she'd gone."

The other man looked worried, brushed a hand across his black hair, and nodded.

"It's been days, Carl. You should've told me. I don't like hearing by phone, second hand."

"Georgie's an—"

"A what, Carl?" The bishop's face hardened.

"Nothing." Carl clenched his fists and placed them on the workbench. "It won't happen again."

"No, it won't." The old man paused. "How's the disassembly going?"

"Fine, we're taking our time. Can't afford a mistake," Carl said.

The bishop's face showed no sympathy. "You have to make another crate. Similar, so that Agincourt won't notice the difference. Check for something to use, like Army surplus. Add Arabic writing, but leave a hint of the U-S-A sign underneath."

"What for?"

"In case anyone who matters hears about what happened. Do it right away." The bishop walked to the door. "And I told you before, Agincourt needs a bomb. Fake something up with fins, Arabic, and a large electronic counter. If you don't know what it should look like, rent a movie—Bond, Schwarzenegger's *True Lies*, or whatever."

"I know what to do," the second man volunteered.

"Good. I'll see you tomorrow. Right now, I need to prepare my sermon for Sunday." The bishop's smile flashed, revealing uneven, white teeth between his white moustache and beard. "'Vengeance is mine sayeth the Lord.' An appropriate topic."

The thought of vengeance reminded him of a coffin in the crypt, and the occasion when that FBI agent had caught him by surprise those many years earlier. What was the man's name...? Kowalski. Yes that was it. Kowalski. He sat back on his chair and closed his eyes. The scene was still vivid...

He had watched Kowalski leave before going over to where his wife waited by the truck. "You go home." No need for her to see what he was going to do. "I have things to attend to."

After Kowalski's car disappeared down the highway heading north, he walked to the grave and removed the tarpaulin, revealing a closed, viewing coffin sitting at the bottom of a deep, wide, rectangular hole. A rope from the winch on the tripod connected to four short ropes that were attached to brass rings at the coffin's corners. He had hoisted the coffin to ground level then raised the viewing lid.

"Don't bury me again," the bearded man pleaded from the depths of the coffin.

He had showed no sympathy for the man's agony. "Tell me where they are."

"It's cold. I can't feel my fingers. Please untie my hands."

"No."

"For God's sake, Reverend, why are you doing this to me?"

"For God's sake."

The man's beard quivered as his teeth chattered. "I'll take you there."

"No, you'll tell me and I'll check for myself." He had started to close the open part of the coffin's lid.

"Please, please, don't." Tears ran down the dirty, sunburned cheeks. "They locked me in the dark in 'Nam. I can't take it."

"Nixon won't save you this time." His look remained implacable. "Are they in the main part of the park?"

"No, there'd be too many people when the weather clears." The trapped man closed his eyes. "What if I don't tell you?"

"You'll *ho to gell!*" He had shaken his head in irritation. "But if you tell me, I will release you from your pain."

"Where are my boys?"

No reason not to tell him. "I walked your burros south by 54. Now, you tell me where you hid the bombs!" He took hold of the lid.

The bearded face tilted. "One of 'em's a third of the way up the Williams Ranch trail from the gate. There's a bend and a lone salt cedar in a dried-up crick. Thirteen paces left, you'll find a pile of stones filling in a hole. Look under them. Then you'll come back and let me out?"

"Both weapons?"

"No. Water first."

"Then you'll tell me?"

"When you let me go." The trapped man blurted out, "I'll give you half my stash."

"What stash?" That had been a surprise. "No gold around here."

"Ain't gold." The beard parted showing stained teeth. "Water."

Better humor him. He took a bottle and dripped water slowly into the open mouth. "We'll talk when I come back." He closed the lid and started to winch the coffin down into the grave.

The sounds of sobbing filtered toward him through the air holes that he had drilled in the lid, interspersed with the muffled words, "I'll tell you."

The sobbing sounds were replaced by squeaks as he hoisted the coffin and opened the lid.

"Other side of mountains west of Carlsbad, but it's complicated. I'll need to draw a map."

He had made a quick decision and walked to the chapel, then returned to the gravesite and started to hand down the writing material.

"Can't do it like this," said Old Tex. "Need to sit up."

"Don't try anything, or I'll end it now." He had maneuvered Old Tex into a sitting position. He put the pad on the coffin lid and handed the pen to the old man, whose hands were still tied.

Old Tex grasped the pen and started to draw. A mess of jagged lines and illegible writing soon covered the paper.

"What's this?"

"Best I can do with my hands tied, Reverend."

He had been close to slapping the old man then reluctantly had untied the knot, moving away as the rope came off.

Old Tex rubbed his bony wrists before starting on a new piece of paper. When the map was finished he held it up

As he had grabbed for the map, Old Tex let it go. He had lost his balance, and fell onto the coffin. The tripod swayed violently and collapsed, dumping the coffin at an angle into the grave. The cheap coffin's box twisted and the lid fell off. The map fell with it.

"Got ya!" Old Tex screamed as he scrambled out, kicking him on the way.

Dazed from the blow, he lay among the pieces of the coffin, listening to a cackling sound and scampering footsteps. When he regained his senses, he saw the map by his feet. He stuffed it in his pocket and scrambled out of the grave. Old Tex had disappeared; gone to find his burros, likely. Dealing with him could wait. Agent Kowalski had mentioned going to the Park headquarters. Get the bomb first, while the search party was out of sight organizing what to do. With luck they wouldn't see him. If they did, he'd say that he'd remembered something Old Tex had said and was just trying to help. He had loaded the tripod and winch into his pickup and headed north on a track through the scrub covered dirt.

8.

Fred, who had been waiting outside Starbucks since six forty-five, cast an admiring glance at a pretty, brown-haired girl who had just parked her Toyota. She came toward him.

"It's me, Millie," she said.

Fred stared. "Sorry, I didn't recognize you. What happened to the black hair and green eyes?"

"A wig and contacts to fit Monique's persona," Millie replied, her hazel eyes twinkling.

"Either way, you both look great. Actually, I prefer this new version of you," Fred said reflectively. "Now to food. How about Mexican?" He pointed at *Mi Casa Su Casa*.

"Sure," Millie replied. "If you like New Mex-Mex."

"You don't sound overjoyed."

Millie took his arm. "It's just that I grew up on Tex-Mex."

"So did I. This New-Mex stuff ain't the same. Let's go Chinese."

A large painting of bamboo-covered mountains and pandas dominated the wall facing them, as they went into *Mrs. Chu's Szechuan House*. Ornate brass, wall lamps above each table pretended to compete with the fluorescent lights in the ceiling. Tinny, obscure music filtered through the room. A waiter showed them to a side table.

"Where were you in Texas?" Millie asked, after they were seated.

Fred looked up from the Chinese zodiac placemat. "Do people believe this stuff?" he asked, using the time to make sure his answer fitted the story he'd agreed to with Kowalski.

"What?"

"The zodiac stuff."

"I don't." Millie paused. "We were talking about Texas."

"Sorry. I'm from Austin," Fred lied, hiding the fact that he grew up down the road in New Braunfels; information that might have clued someone that his real surname was likely to be German. "I went to UT-Austin and struggled through electrical engineering."

"And now you're an actor?" Millie looked puzzled.

"Company downsized...first in, first out." Fred used the story he'd worked out with Kowalski. "This job came up.... Look, to be honest, what I wanted to do all along was acting. My Mom and Dad persuaded me to take engineering, so I'd have something to fall back on."

"Funny, the same for me." Millie laughed. "My Mom made me take office management...secretary really, but the minute an acting job comes up I'm off. Not so easy now that I'm stuck in Albuquerque."

"How so?"

Millie's face showed her unhappiness. "My Mom's not well. I need to look after her."

Fred closed his eyes, seeing an image of his ailing mother and his hard-of-hearing father. He'd not realized how much they'd aged in the time he'd been at college and working, until he'd lost his job and gone home. Maybe he should have stayed. No, he'd have gone crazy. But Millie, here was a nice girl. "You're nothing like Monique von Minx, are you?" he said.

"Didn't take you long to work that out." Millie giggled. "How did you find out about our little movie?"

"Someone noticed that I looked like Chuck. I got a call." Fred grinned. "God help me."

Millie laughed. "Don't say that in front of Chuck. He'll accuse you of blasphemy."

"You're kidding?"

"No, he's done religious movies for our church."

"What church?"

"It's out on I-40 East; Redeemer Fountain Cathedral." Millie picked up her menu. "C'mon, let's order, the waiter's coming over. How about this deal for two…tea, appetizers, soup, and a choice of one each from four entrees?"

"Sounds good to me." Fred put his menu down.

"I'll order General Tso's chicken and Szechuan beef. Okay?"

"Sure, and I'd like a Dr Pepper."

Millie ordered. The restaurant didn't have Dr Pepper. Fred settled for the tea. "What got you into this kind of movie?" he asked.

Millie laughed. "Typical story; too much competition in the mainstream. I did some advertising and religious stuff. That's when I worked with Chuck."

"What parts did you play?"

"The Virgin Mary, and Mary Magdalene without the Victoria's Secret gear."

Fred grinned. "So Chuck got you this deal?"

"Yes, he knows the backer."

"Who is it?"

"Chuck won't say."

The waiter delivered the hot-sour soup, tea, and spring rolls.

"Is he as dumb as he acts?" Fred asked.

"Chuck likes to jerk Agincourt's chain. Knows he can't be fired." Millie took a spoonful of soup. "I'm not sure. Boy that soup's hot." She grabbed her water. "He acted differently when he played Jesus."

"Why is he doing this, then?" Fred blew on his spoon before sipping the soup.

"Hot pepper, not hot, hot," Millie replied. "Beats me."

"Makes you wonder if the backer's the same guy who does the religious movies," Fred volunteered cautiously.

"Bishop Orpheus John? Not likely." Millie shook her head. "But Sebastian has a deal to use the workshop that the bishop uses for his movies."

"What does Agincourt need to have made?" Fred asked.

"The bomb for one thing, Fred." Millie laughed. "You should have been there a couple of days ago. Sebastian asked to see it, and Georgie brought in this empty crate. Sebastian hit the roof."

Fred bit into his spring roll, and said with a mouthful, "Why?"

"It was Army surplus and had U-S-A stamped on it. Sebastian expected Arabic."

Interesting. Could this crate have been what Gene had showed him in the photograph? "Where did it come from? Did it have a serial number on it.?"

"The prop-shop, and that's a weird question."

"Just remembering a movie I saw," Fred replied quickly. "Military stuff always has a serial number."

"I suppose." Millie finished her soup before continuing. "That's enough questions."

Damn, thought Fred, realizing he was coming on too strong. What had they said in training? "Try not to be obvious." He hadn't succeeded. "Sorry, Millie." Fred reached across the table and patted the back of her hand. "First date nerves, and it's the first time I've done a movie like this. I'm just curious."

Millie smiled, but pulled back her hand. "No problem. Tell me about yourself." She took a hefty bite of her spring roll.

"I grew up in Austin, and went to UT, naturally. It's a great party school, and I guess not bad for education, and football."

Millie pointed the index finger and pinkie of her right hand, and gave the hook-em-horns sign. "Go Horns."

"You a fan?"

"The Longhorns, no. Football yes. I was a cheerleader at UTEP. You were saying."

"Right. When I graduated I went to work for this start-up company. Two years later, it rapidly became a rundown company and I was laid off." Fred spooned rice onto his plate.

"What then?"

"Mainly waiting and waiting. You know...restaurants." Fred replied, ladling Szechuan beef onto his rice.

"Then this came up. Why did you take it? You must know Agincourt's reputation." Millie sounded serious.

"I could ask you the same question."

"*Touché.*" Millie looked rueful. "His stuff's pretty bad: *Alien Ghost Riders of the Purple Mesa, Atomic Bactrian Camels of the Mojave—*"

"I remember that one," Fred interrupted her. "He couldn't afford camels, so he put masks and humps on donkeys, and had electric sparks jump between their two humps. We used to watch his stuff at the fraternity house. After *Bye Bye Oscars* my favorite bit of crap was *Electric Razor Bloodbath.*"

"Shame on you. Many people consider that his masterpiece."

"It's certainly a piece of something." Fred chuckled. "What about his main man...er, Bogdan Mirnov. 'The actor of a thousand roles,' according to Agincourt's fliers?"

"He's upset because Chuck has the lead. But he still has a number of parts to play," Millie replied. "Did you know his real name's Francis Sykes?"

"No. What's he like?"

"Fine, when you get to know him." She grinned. "Lance calls him 'The man of a thousand roles—and only one expression.'"

"I reckon he's right. I wonder how he hooked up with Agincourt," Fred said, recalling Mirnov's numerous appearances in Agincourt's masterpieces.

"Probably same reason that Lance says that he did," Millie said with a little grimace.

Fred thought about the answer and concluded he didn't understand. "What was that?"

"No place for Gentiles."

"Lance's anti-Semitic?"

"Work it out for yourself. My guess is Lance got turned down so any times in Hollywood, he's bitter. Can't accept that maybe he's not a very good script writer."

"And Agincourt?"

"Same treatment, but I don't think he's anti-Semitic." Millie shrugged. "He's happy to work with anybody provided he can make his movies the way he wants to, and not pay them much."

They ate in silence until the waiter brought the fortune cookies, slices of orange, and the check. Millie extracted the piece of paper and crushed her cookie.

"You're not going to eat it?" Fred exclaimed.

"Got to watch my figure." Millie grinned and pushed the pieces across the table.

"It's sure worth watching." Fred looked appreciatively at the way the words on her T-shirt, 'University of New Mexico,' rose and fell.

Millie shook her head. "You go first."

"It says, 'If at first you don't succeed, learn to live with disappointment.'"

"That's...you're kidding me, aren't you?"

"Yes. Confucius says, 'A low neckline hides knobbly knees.'"

"Fred, be serious." Millie kicked him under the table. "Mine says, 'Believe and all of your wishes will come true.'"

Fred reached across the table and put his hand on hers. "I hope it works out."

Millie lifted Fred's hand off, glanced at the check, and said, "Let's pay. I need my beauty sleep."

"I'll do it." Fred reached for the check.

"No, we'll go Dutch. Seventeen each should cover it." Millie reached in her bag. "Incidentally, where are you staying?"

"Sebastian's apartments."

"Good luck. He offered that to me. One look was enough. Anyway, I had a place."

"It's cheap," Fred reasoned.

"Sure, and you give him back some of that miserable salary he pays you." Millie chuckled. "A lot of Sebastian's old stable of actors live there, including Lola and Bogdan."

"I haven't seen them."

Millie shrugged. "The rumor is that both of them like a wee drop occasionally. Bogdan's got like a suite near the pool, I've heard."

"I'll look for him." Fred paused, remembering a question he had meant to ask earlier. "One thing seemed odd. Does Agincourt deal with all the paperwork?"

Millie giggled. "Anything to do with money's in his safe. No one else knows the combination.

"The miser's touch." Fred tried not to show his relief. That would make it harder for anyone else to find out his new social security number, which he had been obliged to fill in on his employment form. He still worried that a knowledgeable person could work out that his identity was a fake.

"Nice evening, Fred," Millie said as they reached her car. She kissed Fred quickly on the cheek. "See you tomorrow."

She jumped into the car and drove off before Fred could say anything.

At least he'd got a date, Fred thought, but she'd pushed his hand away. Maybe she had been burned recently by someone. He hoped it wouldn't affect the beginning of a beautiful relationship.

9.

Before reaching the studio, Fred pulled into the parking lot of a shopping mall to call Kowalski. He got out of his car, remembering the advice that he should never assume that a car or a room hadn't been bugged.

"I thought I was on to something," he said as soon as Kowalski answered. "Agincourt got into a fight with his script writer, Lance Dupree, because the crate for the bomb had U-S-A stamped on it."

"You don't sound like you think it was the real thing," Kowalski said.

"No. Apparently, it was made up in a workshop Agincourt gets to use."

"This shop is where?"

"It's not really Agincourt's workshop. It's the bishop's."

"A bishop?" Kowalski sounded incredulous.

"Bishop Orpheus John. The shop's in back of his Redeemer Fountain Cathedral."

"Orpheus John, an unusual name." After a long silence, Kowalski continued. "Doesn't it seem odd to you that this bishop is letting his staff make props for a questionable movie?"

"Yes. Chuck Steak fixed it. He brought in the sponsor. Won't say who it is."

"Could the bishop be the sponsor?"

Fred scratched his nose with the phone. "I asked Millie. She said no."

"Millie?"

"Monique von Minx. Millie's her real name."

"Wonders never cease." Kowalski chuckled. "Check out this workshop and the bishop." Kowalski did not elaborate and hung up

* * *

Fred had to weave around overflowing trashcans on his way to the set. Over the sound of wind whistling through gaps in the duct tape that had been used to seal holes in the siding, he heard voices coming from Agincourt's office. He knocked, entered, and saw Sebastian slumped in his chair. Lance, Chuck, and Georgie sat across from his desk, looking like children in front of a teacher. Millie was staring out of the grimy window.

"We're trying to come up with something to show we're in LA," Agincourt said, looking older and tired. "I want more than stock movie footage."

"How about a street sign for Rodeo Drive," Georgie volunteered. "Lance could ask Carl to make one."

Agincourt sat up. "Not bad."

"Build that Chinese Theater place," Chuck suggested. "We could show a movie and eat Chinese food."

Agincourt buried his head in his hands. "Something simple."

Fred, who had been studying Agincourt's photos chimed in, "How about a copy of the Hollywood sign?" He pointed at a series of pictures showing the sign; the last had Agincourt and a busty, tousle-haired blonde posing at the base of the D.

Agincourt jumped up from his chair, waving his hands excitedly. "Fred, you've got it! The sign won't have to be that big. We could put it up on Sandia Mountain and use a telescopic lens."

"My idea's better," Chuck muttered petulantly.

"Let me borrow this," Lance said, lifting the photo from the wall. "Carl'll know what to do." He paused. "Oh, look what it says here. Double-De-licious for Lola. How charming."

"I wrote that," Agincourt said, looking smug.

A chance to check out the workshop, Fred thought, saying casually, "I'd be happy to help."

"I don't know if Carl would like that." Lance looked at Agincourt for advice.

"To hell with Carl, it's my movie, Agincourt snapped. "We're not ready to do the next scene anyway. Chuck's still learning his lines."

"It's not my fault, Sebastian. Lancie needs to stop using the dictionary." Chuck pulled a script off the table, and thumbed through the pages. "Listen to what I have to say, Achmed. Stop it with your bombastic impre-cat-i-ons! What's that?"

"It means curses," Lance said, shaking his head in disgust.

"Well, say curses, Lancie," Chuck giggled. "And bombastic sounds like bombs."

"Enough children! I need to work. Bogie was never this much trouble." Agincourt's expression highlighted his irritation. "Georgie, you take Lance and Fred to the shop. Chuck, go and play with your toys. Monique, you stay. I need to talk to you."

"Scr.... I don't like you, Sebastian. And I bet you never worked with Bogart" Chuck mumbled as he left the office.

"I need to go to the girls' room first," Monique said, winking at Fred, who had picked up the open script.

"I'd bring gas masks if I had them," Georgie said, following her.

"I wish. It's hard holding your nose," Millie replied.

When Millie returned, Fred commented, "It's odd. Bombastic imprecations wasn't on the page Chuck was looking at."

"Chuck likes to needle Sebastian," Millie said. "Tell me what you think of the workshop."

"And you can tell me what Sebastian wanted."

Millie made a face. "I know what he wants. He won't get it. See you later."

To Fred, the tone of her voice said, *and nor will anyone else.*

* * *

"Where's the workshop, exactly?" Fred asked as Georgie turned the pickup onto the interstate going east.

"Next to the Redeemer Cathedral," Lance replied. "And stop crowding me, Fred. Stuck between you and Georgie, I feel like wilted lettuce in a double hamburger."

They drove in silence for the next ten miles until Lance pulled off onto a side road. Rounding a bend, he pointed to his left and said, "You can see it now."

Fred stared in amazement at the towering white edifice that stood out against the scrub-covered hills. "It looks like one of those Mormon temples."

Lance laughed. "Bishop Orpheus John admires the Mormons, at least the tithing part."

"It must have cost a lot," Fred mused. "How do you start something like that?"

"No idea, but I suppose it's like financing for a movie," Lance replied. "I heard he came here from Amarillo. Most of his flock live in the pueblos. Maybe he got some of their casino money."

Leaving I-40, they followed a side road that led them to the cathedral. Imposing gates framed the view of the main building, which rose more than a hundred feet from the top of a knoll. Two-story buildings clustered against each side of the hill. Fountains flanked the wide steps that swept up to massive wooden doors at the front. Three gardeners were working on manicured flower beds that extended from the fountains along the hillside above the parking lot.

"Wow." Fred marveled. "It's as wide as it's long."

"The whole point," Lance chuckled. "Impress the natives. You should see the inside; heaven and hell in one building. Go to a service; organ, mariachis, and a celestial choir. It's a heck of a show."

Georgie drove the truck through a huge lot before parking at a lower level near the back of the church. She remained in the truck.

"Aren't you coming?" Fred asked Georgie.

Georgie curled her lip.

"Georgie and Carl don't get on," Lance volunteered. "The workshop's over there." He pointed at the first of two industrial buildings, nestled against the church's left-hand side wall.

"Larger than I expected and what's the other building for?"

"A movie set and storage, Freddie," Lance said as they entered the building. "I'll show you later. Orpheus John thinks big."

Lance walked up to the older of two men working on equipment. "Fred let me introduce you to carl bates. Carl, this is Fred. He doubles for Chuckie."

Fred held out a hand, which Carl ignored as he continued to copy Arabic letters from a book onto a khaki-colored crate.

"I hear you want a Hollywood sign." Carl said. "How big?"

"Big enough so that we can see it on Sandia Mountain from downtown," Lance replied. "Fred suggested it."

Carl glared at Fred. "You're kidding. The Hollywood sign's got to be at least forty feet high."

"Agincourt will photo ours using a telescopic lens," Fred said quickly.

"Better," Carl grunted. "With lights, I suppose?"

"Yes." Fred nodded. "I can help with the wiring if you like."

"Miguel normally does that." Carl pointed at a darker-skinned man working on a strange-looking contraption on a second bench.

Lance, who had been retying his ponytail, walked over. "What the hell is that?" he asked.

"Agincourt's bomb." Carl laughed without humor. "We're making it look as stupid as he seems to want."

Lance inspected the device. "I like the countdown clock-thingy. What's the bomb made of?"

"Old gas cylinder," Miguel replied. "Gives it weight."

"Is it empty?" Lance asked.

"Not quite," Carl replied as he joined them.

Fred noticed that Carl favored his left leg.

Carl, seeing Fred watching, muttered, "Combat wound."

"If we stuck a whoopie-sound-thingy on the cylinder, we could scare the hell out of Chuck," Lance mused.

"I'll get on it, Mr. Dupree." Miguel chuckled. "But I want to be there."

Fred, who had been inspecting the edge of what appeared to be the remains of a U-S-A sign on the crate, saw Carl watching him. "Nice work. I like the Arabic touch," Fred said, recognizing an opportunity to snoop, and adding quickly, "Lance says you have some great props in another building. Could I see them?"

Miguel looked at Carl. Carl nodded.

"Come with me," Miguel said.

As the two left the workshop, Fred glanced around, noting the assortment of machine tools. A large engine block sat on one of them. He noted the metal tracks that ran under a metal door in the cathedral's concrete wall.

A covered walkway led into the neighboring studio and storage area. Half the building was taken up by a sound stage and a green screen. "Lance was right; it's impressive," Fred exclaimed.

Miguel pointed beyond the stage. "Look over here," he said proudly. "Walls for the temple of Solomon, parts of the Tower of Babel, Noah's Ark. Carl and I made them."

"The Hollywood sign should be a cinch." Fred grinned.

Miguel smiled at the compliment. "I'll work on Carl," he said. "I could use some help."

A good start, Fred thought, wondering if he was wasting his time on this seemingly idiotic movie. "Thanks." He looked at Lance. "We'd better get back to the truck."

Georgie was not there when they reached it.

"Where the hell is she?" Lance muttered. "Oh." He turned to Fred. "I meant to tell Carl something. Back in a minute."

As Lance disappeared, Georgie emerged from behind the sound-set building. She jogged over to Fred. "Been waiting long?"

"Just got here. Lance'll be back in a minute. He needed to talk to Carl."

"About what?"

"Don't know."

"You doing anything this evening?" Georgie asked diffidently.

Fred scrambled for an answer. "Uh, yes, I'm meeting a friend," he replied, making a snap decision to try Millie again.

Georgie shrugged and walked with an exaggerated sway of her hips to the truck. The action made Fred look at her more closely. Older than me, but good body. Maybe, if things don't work out with Millie. He shook his head. Wrong reason; he had a job to do, and if he dated Georgie, it would just be to get information on the case.

As soon as Fred got back to his apartment, he telephoned Millie. Although she didn't exactly sound thrilled to hear from him, Fred mustered his courage and asked if she would like to meet for a drink and dinner. She said she had another commitment and hung up. Not a good sign. Disappointed, Fred went outside and called Kowalski.

"I saw the crate," Fred reported. "Wrong era, and probably an Army-surplus ammunition crate. The U-S-A sign was barely visible. Carl, the guy who runs the shop, was putting Arabic writing on it."

"Pity," Kowalski said. "You're sure it's a fake?"

"Yes." Fred paused, recalling what had caught his attention. "One other thing, sir. Metal tracks run from the workshop under steel doors in the concrete walls of the church's basement."

"Try to find out what's behind the doors. The tracks could be for moving coffins into the cathedral. Of course, that would be interesting," Kowalski added cryptically.

10.

Sebastian Agincourt wiped his brow with a large white handkerchief, and then pointed at the anxious-looking owners of *Mi Casa Su Casa*. "Chuck, we don't have long to shoot this scene. They want to set up for lunch. Go outside and come in again without acting like you're barging into a Western saloon. You nearly broke Juan's door."

Millie, dressed as Monique, stood with Fred and a waiter watching the scene from the corridor leading to the kitchen. "How did it go, yesterday?" Fred whispered.

"We did a few laps around his desk. I tired him out." Millie's voice showed her irritation.

"That's all?" Fred asked, thinking how cute she looked when she wrinkled her nose.

"No. He was pissed off, threatened to fire me." She looked at Agincourt with disgust. "I told him I'd talk to Chuck. Sebast'ard backed off."

"Good for you."

Millie turned to face Fred. "How about the shop?"

"Will you two stop chattering." Agincourt bellowed. "Gable and Lombard never acted like this. You set, Boggie?"

Burnoose-clad Bogdan Mirnov, playing Achmed Cohen, waved an empty Corona bottle trying to get the waiter's attention. He put the bottle down and nodded, his expression hidden behind a thick, black beard and moustache.

The waiter looked uncertain and stepped behind Fred. Agincourt raised his arms.

"Stop." Georgie shouted. "Bogdan's missing his hat."

"Sorry." Bogdan reached in his jacket pocket and placed a yarmulke on his head.

"Action!" Agincourt shouted as he turned the camera toward the door.

Chuck flung open the door, just managing to catch it before it bounced. He stood in the entrance looking at each table in turn, as if searching for Achmed.

"It's like a silent movie," Fred whispered to Millie. "Achmed's the only customer."

"Shhh," she said, grinning at him.

"Found you at last, Achmed," Chuck said

"I've been waiting for an hour." Achmed/Bogdan's thick beard quivered.

Lance looked down at his script. "I didn't write that," he whispered.

"Why did you steal our stuff?" Chuck said petulantly as he sat opposite Achmed.

Achmed glanced at his menu, and appeared to read from it. "Because my colleagues and I don't think you and Monique can pull off this stunt.

"You don't know our plan."

"Wrong." Achmed said. "You're going to nuke the Oscars." He beckoned more vigorously in the direction of the kitchen.

The waiter looked questioningly at Agincourt, who shrugged okay.

"I'd like some nachos and another *Corona*," Bogdan said.

"That's not your line." Chuck looked puzzled. "How did you find out?" He turned to the waiter. "If we're going to eat, I'll have beef enchiladas and a Diet Coke."

"This isn't scripted, Bas," Lance said, this time more loudly.

"*Cinema verité*. Live with it, Lance," Agincourt snapped, then signaled to Millie.

As she passed the waiter, Millie/Monique said, "I'll have a margarita."

"Action!" Agincourt shouted.

"I told Achmed," Monique said.

Chuck gaped. "Why did you whip me if you knew?"

"For fun." Monique raised her riding crop. "I like to see you squirm."

Chuck half rose from his chair, and was prodded back by Monique.

"Enough," Achmed growled. "Tell me the details of how you're going to get the stuff into the Oscars.

"I'm going to deliver them as costumes and props. I'll hijack one of the delivery vans they're expecting."

"And their security won't check?"

"Sure, but I'll hide the bomb, arms, and nerve gas in the props," Chuck said smugly.

"You'll have time to do that after you steal the truck?

"No, silly...." Chuck paused while the waiter delivered the beer, Coke, and nachos. "I'll already have hidden them in my own props.

"Like what?"

"A large gold Oscar statue and an MGM lion."

"You know they use sniffer dogs, Chuck?" Bogdan/Achmed's beard parted briefly as his mouth opened, showing whitish teeth between which he shoveled a forkful of nachos.

"So what?" Chuck said. "I'll pee on them."

Bogdan grabbed the Corona, threw the lime slice on the floor, and took a swig, before returning to his role. "That'll sure distract the dogs."

"Cut, cut, cut!" Agincourt put his hands to his face. "What are you doing, Boggie? I should have spotted it. No beer, you're Achmed, for God's sake."

"It's okay, Bas," Lance exclaimed. He's "Achmed Paddy Cohen. Most of his names are fine with booze, particularly Paddy."

Agincourt's hands went down. "Action!"

"So what. I'll—"

"We did that already, Chuck. Boggie, give him a lead," Agincourt pleaded.

100

Achmed put his beer down. "That'll sure distract the dogs."

"That's what I thought," Chuck said triumphantly.

Achmad sniffed disgustedly causing his beard to slip. He pushed the beard back into place. "Then the dogs will pee all over your pee, and security will check to see why."

The waiter came out with the enchiladas and the margarita.

Chuck did not respond, but picked up his fork and sampled a piece of enchilada.

Monique hit Chuck on the shoulder with the crop. "What have you got to say to that?"

"Say to what?" Chuck's words come out in a small shower of shredded beef.

Achmed gulped the remainder of his beer. "We need to get a sketch into the Oscars program that's a spoof of all the movies that have big explosions and fires."

The opening bars of *Happy Days Are Here Again* drifted over the set. "Who the hell's forgotten to turn off their damn cell phone?" Agincourt screamed.

"Sorry, boss," Fred said as he muted the sound. He glanced at the number showing on the little screen; the L. A. office had called.

"Don't do that again, or you'll be out of here." Agincourt scowled. "You're not needed now anyway, take a break."

"Sebastian, he said he was sorry," said Chuck in a surprisingly firm tone.

"Oh, what the hell. Stay," Agincourt retorted. "Boggie, repeat your line. Action!"

"We need to get a sketch into the Oscars program that's a spoof of all the movies that have big explosions and fires."

"Like what?" Monique asked.

"*Dr. Strangelove*, war movies, *The Wages of Fear*, *Gone with the Wind*—"

"*Towering Inferno*," Chuck said quickly. "But how do we get the bomb in, if we don't hide it?"

"As a bomb, of course," Achmed said. "But we'll make it look silly; fins, a large red countdown dial, and.... He looked across the table, adding, "Monique, if you're not going to drink that margarita, I'll take it." He reached for the glass.

Monique pouted and pushed the drink toward him.

Chuck giggled. "We could have a countdown, ten, nine, eight, seven, six, five—

"We get it, Chuck." Achmed took a healthy swig of the margarita. "Shit, that's cold." He put his head in his hands.

"I could lead all the stars in the countdown." Chuck frowned and stood up. "Wait a second. If I'm there, I'll go up with the rest of them."

Bogdan pulled his hands down from his face and succeeded in pulling his beard down, snagging his lower denture, which fell into remains of the nachos He quickly stuck everything back in place. "A true martyr, Chuck," he said.

"I don't want to be a martyr. Let Monique do it."

Monique placed the tip of the riding crop on Chuck's nose. "We'll do it together, sweetie."

"That's settled then," Achmed said. "Come to my place tomorrow, and we'll finalize the plans. It's off Sepulveda, 1270 Calle Rosa, apartment 6."

Agincourt spread his arms. "Cut! That's better than I expected. I'm going to use it."

"You're kidding?" Lance raised his hand to his forehead and pretended to swoon. "What about all the asides and food crap-thingies."

"As I said, Lancie, *cinema verité*." Agincourt reached over and patted Lance on the shoulder. "You can help with the cutting. It'll look good, believe me."

Lance shrugged. "Whatever."

Agincourt stood and pointed at Georgie. "Did you get the stills?"

"All done." Georgie showed him her digital camera.

Agincourt nodded, signaled the waiter, and bellowed, "I'd like the enchiladas combo. Plenty of sour cream, okay?"

"Why did you get a margarita?" Fred said when Millie joined him. "You didn't drink it."

"It's what Monique would have done. I don't drink."

"Oh. You got any plans tonight?"

"Sorry, I have to meet my...a friend. See you tomorrow." She walked away.

Nothing doing there, Fred concluded. Watching regretfully as Millie left, he did not hear the soft footsteps of the person who suddenly tapped him on the shoulder.

"Problems, Fred, can I help?" Georgie asked.

Fred thought quickly. "Just wishing I had more to do."

Georgie smiled sympathetically and squeezed his arm. "I'll talk to Sebastian."

"Thanks, Georgie. I appreciate it."

Georgie started to walk away, then turned and blurted out. "I'm barbecuing tonight, if you're interested."

Fred was embarrassed by her embarrassment and nearly said no, but remembered that it might be an opportunity to find out more about the movie. "Sure. Where do you live?"

"Calle del Rey, 335," Georgie replied. "Say six-thirty."

"Can I bring anything?"

Georgie nodded. "Sure, but for God's sake don't bring any of that Dr Pepper I've seen you drinking. Beer would be good."

Fred left the restaurant, went to his car, and called Kowalski's assistant, Linda, who had left voicemail on his cell phone.

"Hi, Fred. I just called to see if your paycheck came through," she said.

"Yes, thanks."

"How's the movie going? Have you been in anything yet?"

"Yeah. It's weird, but I got to drive a Hummer."

"Look after yourself."

"You and Marilyn, too." Fred heard a giggle as he snapped the phone shut. He reached for his package of Moon Pies, took one out, ate it and licked the remaining moist icing chocolate off his fingers.

*   *   *

When Millie opened her front door, her mother was waiting in the hall in her wheelchair. She put her book down, and said, "Did you have a good day?" as she turned the wheelchair toward the living room.

"We did a scene in that Mexican restaurant I told you about. It was fun," Millie replied, following the chair and preparing an answer for what was coming next.

"Was that nice young man, Fred, there?"

"Yes, mother."

"Are you going to see him again?"

"He asked me out, but I turned him down."

"In heaven's name, why?"

"Mother, we've been through this a hundred times. I can't afford to have someone sit with you, and I don't like to leave you alone at night."

"I can always call you. And Millie, if you don't do something about it, you won't have anybody else when I'm gone."

"I need to start supper." An image of Fred's smiling face flashed into her mind; a nice crinkly smile, warm blue eyes, not handsome but comfortable looking, not petulant like Chuck.

And she and Fred had a lot in common. Her mother was right. Next time Fred asked…if he did…she'd accept. "Okay, you've persuaded me."

*　　*　　*

Fred parked near the mailbox, neatly labeled 335 with Georgie's full name, Georgina Williams. Georgie met him at the door. She looked different. Tight jeans and an open necked shirt with the top two buttons undone, revealed a sexy figure that had been covered at work by her track suit. She still wore the dark glasses. "This sure beats Sebastian's apartments," Fred said, looking at the spacious patio with built in barbecue and hot tub in the backyard that they had reached through the little ranch house.

Georgie laughed. "I've lived there. Got out the first chance I had."

Fred, knowing that Sebastian didn't pay much, wondered how she could afford such a house. "Nice place."

Georgie seemed to have read his thoughts. "I inherited enough to buy it when my mother…er, died."

Fred shrugged and handed her the bags with two six-packs. "I'm from Texas. Lone Star beer, okay?"

"I'll survive. Cold mugs, or out of the can?"

"Beer mug."

Georgie went into the kitchen, and returned with two mugs and two cans. "I started the barbecue. Won't be long. Have a seat."

"How long have you worked for Sebastian?"

"Coming up on two years. I came in a couple of years ago, after his previous assistant, Penelope, suffered an unfortunate accident."

"*Bactrian Camels*, a masterpiece." Fred chuckled. "What happened to her?"

Georgie wagged a scolding finger at him. "She got electrocuted in her bath. Silly cow was using a hair dryer."

"Jeez.

Georgie tilted her head. "So what do you do for a real job?"

"Technician mainly," Fred said. "Whatever I can find. Acting's what I really like."

"I'd have put you down for a college boy," Georgie said. "Whatever. "I'll get the steaks. You bring out the salad. The baked potatoes are in the oven."

She returned from the kitchen with two huge T-bones, and silverware on a tray.

When she bent over to put the steaks on the barbecue, Fred noticed that the third button on her shirt was undone revealing perky boobs pushing out from a skimpy bra.

"Big enough for you?" Georgie asked pointing at the steaks.

Up until then, Fred had not thought about Georgie from a sexual point of view, but since Millie wouldn't play, what the hell. He made a point of looking at her cleavage when he replied, "Just what a man needs."

Georgie grinned. "I hoped you'd like them. So, why aren't you teching?"

"Company tanked and I was laid off."

Georgie pushed the steaks around. "What kind of company?"

"Light electrical stuff, supporting the electronics industry."

"Like stable power supplies, surge protectors?"

"You know about that?" Fred asked.

"Don't act surprised, Fred. Women can do engineering, you know."

"Where did you go?"

"Wisconsin." Before Fred could ask about what she had majored in, Georgie added. "I tried electrical and mechanical, even physics. It got boring. After I separated from my husband, I took off and crewed on ocean-going yachts for a time." She laughed. "My dad was furious."

"Disappointed, I'd guess. How about your ex-husband?"

Georgie gave a sly smile. "He wasn't in a position to complain."

"I suppose not." Fred paused, before asking, "You don't sound like you come from Wisconsin."

"Y'all joking." Georgie exaggerated her accent. "Southwest."

"Texas?"

"More or less. You can get me another beer." Georgie stopped the discussion.

Fred sipped on his beer while Georgie cooked the steaks. They ate in a tense silence. Afterwards, Fred helped Georgie clean up.

"How about the hot tub?" Georgie asked diffidently, when the last plates were stacked in the dish washer.

"Sure, but—"

Georgie smiled. "You can get in while I get the towels. I need to go to the bathroom anyway."

"Me first."

"Okay."

"What the hell." Fred chuckled. He took the cover off the tub, stripped, and climbed in.

When Georgie reappeared carrying two beer cans, she was stark naked, but still wearing dark glasses.

"You're tanned all over." Fred said.

"Not quite." Georgie turned and mooned him.

"How did you get those two scars on your thigh?" Fred asked, thinking bullet wounds.

"So that's what you were looking at." Georgie giggled. "Hunting accident." She handed him a beer can and climbed into the tub.

After they had played footsie for a while, Georgie said, "My glasses are fogged up, I can't see you anymore." She dropped her beer can on the patio, and sidled over.

"I'll take your glasses."

"No." Georgie stopped Fred's hand and pulled it down to her breasts. "They stay on or you leave."

"No problem." Fred wanted to ask why, but was distracted as he felt her nipples harden.

Georgie quickly moved on top of him, reaching down as she did. "Not as good as Chuck, but not bad," she said.

"What a compliment. You're not so bad yourself. You work out?"

"For protection." Georgie's mouth closed on Fred's and she bit hard on his lip.

"Ouch." Fred wiped his hand across his mouth and glanced at it. "You drew blood."

"Part vampire."

"One way to deal with that." Fred tipped Georgie over and dunked her.

She came up spluttering, holding her glasses on. "I like it rough." She reared up and slapped him hard.

"Damn you." Fred raised his hand.

Georgie took his hand and pushed on his chest. His feet slid on the slippery bottom of the tub and he went underwater. When Georgie showed no sign of letting him up, Fred used all his strength to get his head above the water.

"You could have drowned me," he cried out.

Georgie ignored him and climbed out of the tub. "I'm ready."

Fred gaped.

"It won't work in the hot water...lubrication."

Fred had a momentary concern that this woman was nuts, but he was ready, too. He stood and asked, "Protection?"

"I'm okay."

After he clambered out, Georgie led him onto a small grassy area. She wrapped her legs around him, grabbed his butt and pulled. They worked together feverishly. Georgie's mouth roamed around his neck and nibbled and bit. Fred managed to hold off until Georgie's moans became soft. As he finished, her hands shifted to his throat and she squeezed.

Fred wrestled her away and sat up. "You're crazy!"

Georgie, legs still wrapped around him, snorted. "Only a little. Want to spend the night?"

Fred, his head still throbbing, thought hard before answering. "Another time, I've got stuff I need to do." It sounded weak. He grinned and said jokingly, "I might not get out of here alive."

"That's a risk you'd have to take."

Fred saw that Georgie had managed to keep her glasses on despite their thrashing around. He pointed at them. "How do you do that?"

"Experience." She stood, threw him a towel, and wrapped another one around her waist.

When he got back to his little apartment, Fred stripped and looked in the mirror. Georgie's subtle and not-so-subtle squeezes and nibbles and slaps had left him looking like he'd been in a brawl. He was about to take a shower, but changed his mind and decided to go in the pool. After donning speedos, he swam a few laps lazily and then lay on his back looking up at the stars.

"Nice evening," a resonant, slurred male voice said.

Fred rolled over in surprise, breathing in as his head went under. "Sure is," he spluttered, coughing up water.

A rangy looking man in a loose-fitting black suit peered down at him. "You're Chuck's double, aren't you? I'm Bogdan Mirnov."

"Yes, Fred Howard. I didn't recognize you without the beard." Fred climbed out of the pool and grabbed his towel.

"I've got bourbon, or bourbon and ice. Anything else is up to you." Bogdan peered at Fred. "Come here a second. What have you been doing?"

"I fell over," Fred said quickly. "I don't think I need a drink, thanks."

"Fell over." Bogdan's voice rumbled. "You've been with Georgie. I recognize the wounds."

"You've been there?"

"Don't sound so surprised, young man. This old bow has made many a fine violin sing." Bogdan looked away as if remembering his conquests.

"Well said, sir." Fred applauded. "I didn't mean any...wait a second, the sheik in *Bactrian Camels*, right? You said that."

Bogdan bowed his head. "Caught out again."

"Georgie's always rough?"

"It seems from the marks on your throat that we're batting two for two. She tried to strangle me at my climactic moment," Bogdan said.

"I'll stay away."

"Will you, really? I'd go back for another shot if she'd have me." Bogdan reached down, grabbed the bourbon bottle and took a large swig.

A movement on the other side of the pool caused Fred to turn his head. "Who's that?" he asked, pointing at an elderly blond woman wearing a scarlet caftan and a hat that would have looked good at Churchill Downs on Derby Day.

Bogdan chuckled. "Sebastian's main squeeze, Lola Paramour."

"You're kidding. Wasn't she in the original *Oscars*?"

"Yes. Monique's role." Bogdan sighed. "She was a real looker, and generous with it. Want to meet her?"

"Some other time, Bogdan. I need my beauty sleep."

"Well then, leave me with my memories, young man." \

11.

The day after Fred's phone call, Kowalski received a message from Mrs. Rogers that Ambassador Wheaton wished to see him. This time he took a book to read, and had finished a chapter before he was summoned to the inner sanctum.

"Sorry to keep you waiting. It's been a busy day." Wheaton motioned to the chair in front of his desk

Kowalski, convinced that Wheaton did nothing useful, hid a smile as he sat down.

Wheaton held his hands, as if in prayer, and brought the fingertips up to touch his nose. "I have been considering this Oscars business. I hear through Franklin Jackson's contacts that this director...Agincourt I believe, has an arrangement with a Bishop Orpheus John's church to make props for the movie."

Kowalski noted the reference to Franklin Jackson's contacts, implying that his were not to be trusted. Jackson was one of a number of the religious right who had been drafted into Homeland Security by the ambassador and his cronies. He seemed to have no qualifications for the job, yet held a position slightly below Kowalski's. "Yes, Ambassador, he does. An FBI agent visited the shop," Kowalski lied, having made a snap decision not to tell the ambassador about Fred Schwarzmuller. "He noticed something interesting."

"What?"

"The workshop backs onto the basement of the church. There are metal tracks leading under the doors into the church."

"Obviously, so that they can wheel things in and out." Wheaton waved his hands dismissively.

"But what things?" Kowalski narrowed his eyes.

"Are you implying that Bishop John is doing something illicit?"

"I don't know, Ambassador."

Wheaton put his hands flat on the desk and leaned forward. "Kowalski, you should know that Bishop John is held in high regard by our administration—anti-abortion, NRA member, intelligent design. All the things that matter to you know who. The bishop is a generous supporter, fund raiser, and he has a huge congregation to influence."

Your people, not mine, Kowalski thought, but realized he needed to be conciliatory. "The bishop is not the focus of our investigation. The FBI assures me that they will be careful not to offend him. There are just a few things to check—"

"If there's the slightest hint of a problem I'll stop the investigation." Wheaton barked. "Now, what I want to know is why we haven't found those two lost bombs. They're radioactive for God's sake, and metal detectors have been around forever."

"We assumed that the prospector, Old Tex, loaded the bombs onto his burros and left," Kowalski said quietly. "We found the burros more than thirty miles away. Unfortunately, he was run over, apparently chasing the burros. We have no idea where he went between there and the crash site. Hundreds of square—"

"Yes, yes, I can calculate areas." Wheaton clasped his forehead then looked out between his fingers. "What did you do?"

"We searched for miles on each side of the most obvious trail from the truck to where we found the burros...south on Route 54." Kowalski could see that Wheaton was expecting more. "With metal and radiation detectors."

"Obviously, you looked in the wrong places."

"Not necessarily, if the bombs were buried deep enough or in a cave. We—"

"You checked for caves?"

"Of course, and for holes, and for signs of digging."

"And?"

"The weather was lousy with high winds and rain."

"I still don't understand why you couldn't detect radiation."

"You might want to read the 1950's classified Screwdriver Report, Ambassador. The assignment was to detect a cubic inch of hidden uranium-235 or plutonium being smuggled into the States."

"Why screwdriver?"

"Robert Oppenheimer, who headed the development of the bomb during World War II, was asked by a congressional committee how he would detect a nuclear weapon in a shipping container. His answer was, 'With a screwdriver.'"

The ambassador's face was blank.

"To open the container." Seeing that Wheaton still looked confused, Kowalski continued. "Plutonium and uranium-235 aren't that radioactive, they emit alpha particles at around five million electron volts. Five MeV alphas are easy to shield. A well-known scientist once commented that it would be hard to detect a bomb from more than ten feet."

"Surely, things are different now?"

"The Cyclops Project was one attempt to do better. I gather it wasn't a success."

Wheaton stacked reports, one by one, in front of him. "What are the options then?"

"Basically three: passive, by trying to detect radiation...too easy to shield; active, with X-rays, but it needs huge equipment; and active, with some penetrating radiation that leads to a signal coming back."

"Anything new?" Wheaton systematically returned the reports to their original positions, lining then up with the edge of his desk, and accidentally turning a framed photograph.

Kowalski glanced briefly at the patrician face and coiffured blonde hair of the woman in the studio portrait, *ambassador's wife?* before responding. "There is one new possibility using fusion neutrons." Seeing Wheaton's uncomprehending stare, Kowalski went on. "They are higher energy. Up to fourteen Mev if you use tritium and deuterium. They penetrate further."

"Get one. I'll deal with funding."

"I don't think they're commercial yet. Wisconsin or Illinoi—"

Wheaton flapped his hands in exasperation. "Get one. I have *work* to do."

"I'll try, Ambassador." Kowalski had difficulty suppressing his anger. Ambassador Wheaton—a worthy successor to a long list of embarrassing political appointees: including an ambassador to Italy who, during a trip in a glass bottomed boat, had inquired if he would be seeing the Italian fleet from WWII; and an ambassador to Indonesia who thought that Jakarta was in India.

* * *

When Fred entered the workshop, Carl was by the vertical mill removing the engine block that Fred had seen before.

He looked up briefly. "Oh, it's you again."

"I'm here to work on the Hollywood sign." Fred held out a drawing. "Lance gave me a photo of the original, and I've made a sketch of what Agincourt said he wanted."

Carl glanced at the picture. "How big?"

"We reckon about four or five feet high should do it."

"Put it on Miguel's bench," Carl said. "He'll be back in a minute."

"What's that for?" Fred asked, pointing at the engine block.

"Overhauling the bishop's limo," Carl replied as turned his back and covered the engine with a cloth.

On his way to Miguel's bench, Fred took a detour toward the large doors. The tracks in the floor were dirty, showing that they were not used recently; suggesting that this was not a standard route for coffins. A scratching sound warned that one of the doors was being opened. Fred stepped sideways, conscious that Carl was now looking at him. As Miguel came out of the church into the workshop, Fred observed that the tracks led into what appeared to be a concrete vault. The faint light reflected from metal surfaces.

"I said Miguel's bench," Carl growled.

"Childhood habit," Fred replied, tiptoeing back along one of the tracks. "Hi, Miguel, I'm here to work on the sign. I've made a sketch."

Miguel scanned the proposed sign. "How—"

"Four or five feet," Carl interjected.

Miguel took a ruler from the table and measured the drawing. "At five feet, that would make the letters four feet wide. Nine letters…allowing for a gap…an overall length about fifty-four feet. Better to drop to four by three. It won't waste as much material."

"Should we do them in groups?"

"You want to put it up on Sandia Mountain, right?" Fred nodded. "Better one at a time." Miguel made a sketch, and showed it to Fred. "Two five-foot horizontal L-bars for each letter, enough to give some overlap so we can bolt them together, if needed, plus two seven-foot vertical L-bars to complete the frame. Do you think that's enough extra height to stand the letters off the ground?"

"Sounds fine to me. What do you want me to do?"

"We've got some aluminum bars left over from making the Temple. Let me get some, and you can cut them to length."

When he returned with a couple of twelve-foot bars, Miguel took Fred to a power saw and handed him thick gloves and safety goggles. "Go for it," he said.

Miguel watched intently as Fred marked the cutting line and locked a bar onto the saw table. Apparently satisfied that Fred was competent, Miguel went back to his bench.

Fred, concentrating on his job, did not hear the door open, but did hear the sharp tone of the bishop's voice.

"Is this Howard?"

"Yes, Bishop," Carl replied. "Chuck's stand-in."

Fred glanced up to see a tall, austere-looking man with a mane of white hair, moustache and beard that framed startlingly pale, blue eyes approaching. The image of a biblical prophet, designed to impress his congregation, Fred concluded. An aura of Old Spice scent arrived with the bishop, insufficient to mask the body odor, but sufficiently powerful to cause Fred to blink.

Fred held out his hand. "Bishop John, it's a pleasure to meet you. I...." He stopped, seeing the puzzled look on the bishop's face.

"Is something wrong, Bishop?"

"Mr. Howard, you remind me of myself when I was young." The bishop shook his head. "Uncanny resemblance."

Fred tried to visualize the face under the hair, but could not see himself. "I'd like to see a photograph." He had the sudden thought that, if he looked like the bishop and also like Chuck, the inference was obvious: Chuck was the bishop's son, and that meant that the bishop could be funding the movie. Gene Kowalski had not been tilting at windmills. His assignment was not a joke. He took a deep breath.

"Some other time. Now, what are you making?"

"A model of the Hollywood sign. We're going to put it on Sandia Mountain and photograph it through a telescopic lens." The bishop stared in silence. Fred shrugged. "Make the audience think they're in Hollywood."

"Hollywood is a Sodom and Gomorrah. I will make it the subject of next Sunday's sermon. You should come, Mr. Howard."

The bishop's tone was so authoritative that Fred realized he had better turn up. "I'll be there."

"Good. Ten o'clock." The bishop turned to Carl. "I need to speak to you."

Fred watched the door close as they went back into the church. The scent of "Old Spice" hung around until the air conditioners changed out the air.

"I want to know more about that young man, Carl," said the bishop, later in the day. "Call our mutual acquaintance and see what he can find out."

"He is Chuck's double, Bishop."

"I guess I should have expected it, Carl. But it was like seeing a ghost."

12.

Fred arrived at the church early on Sunday morning, hoping to be there before the bulk of the congregation. His plan was to use the opportunity to find a way into the basement from the inside. But when he reached the cathedral at nine-thirty, the parking lots around the church were full, and he was directed to park in a cleared area across the road. On reaching the cathedral, he joined the stream of people ascending the steps, flanked by white-robed acolytes, to where the bishop stood in front of the open doors to the cathedral.

When the first acolyte said, "Welcome in God's name," Fred replied, "You, too." But the welcome was repeated on each step, and after hearing it from yet another inanely-smiling person, he had to bottle up a rude response.

As he neared the top, he saw that the bishop was not alone. On his right side was a Jesus, and on his left a Virgin Mary—Chuck and Millie.

"Come in peace, my son." The bishop put his hands together in a prayer-like gesture.

"Welcome in God's name," Chuck said, gazing past Fred.

Millie lowered her head and, peeking from under her cowl, winked.

Even in the open air, Fred could smell the bishop's overpowering scent. He wanted to say something, but the crowd pushed him forward into the church. When ushers tried to seat him, Fred declined saying he was looking for a friend. He started his stroll by the walls, with the hope of identifying a door to the basement. But the thought that the architect had done a clever job of using the hilltop site distracted him from his goal. Inside, the cathedral was nearly circular. About two thirds of the area was filled with semicircular tiers of seats that descended to a stage. Above the stage, gleaming, crystal chandeliers hung from the perimeter of a painted ceiling depicting heaven, apparently modeled on the Sistine Chapel.

A large altar, carved from a block of stone, dominated the back of the stage. Behind it, stained glass windows depicted Adam and Eve in the Garden of Eden. The red eyes of the snake appeared to be staring into what might have been an orchestra pit, but in fact represented the hell that Fred had seen in the church's brochure. Wide steps descended into this pit from the congregation. A steeper set of steps led back up to the stage—symbolizing that while the descent into hell is easy, the ascent is hard.

Fred found a seat in the top row on the left, only thirty feet from where the ornately carved wooden pulpit rose to half the height of the top seats. The murmuring of the crowded cathedral died down as the sound of organ music grew louder, signaling the appearance of the band on the opposite side of the stage. He counted three drummers, two trumpet players, and five guitars players, all dressed as mariachis. A white-robed choir followed the band, and spread out on each side of the altar.

Abruptly, the lights dimmed, the organist stopped playing, and a spotlight shone on the center of the stage. Fred half expected the bishop to pop up through a trap door. But the spotlight was a ploy, for it suddenly swung to the left and up to reveal the bishop with hands raised, standing in the pulpit. Fred contributed to the communal gasp that echoed throughout the cathedral.

The bishop posed for a second, then lowered his hands quickly; a signal for the organ, band, and choir to launch into an unusual, brief variant of Handel's Messiah. As the congregation joined in the hallelujahs, the bishop pointed to the back of the cathedral. A second spotlight highlighted Jesus and Mary as they walked down the center aisle, skirted the pit and stopped in front of the altar as the Messiah ended.

"Who among you has sinned?" The bishop's voice reverberated around the cathedral. He spread his arms wide, implying that no one could claim to be free of sin.

One by one men and women stood, until Fred, who was counting, reached twenty-three sinners from the congregation of maybe a thousand people.

"You must descend into the pit before you can be saved."

The sinners started their descent and Mary left the altar, and stood at the top of the steps from the stage to the pit.

"Kneel and repent." The bishop paused. Fred judged there had been more than enough time for repenting when the bishop continued. "The Virgin will escort you to the altar where you will give thanks to the Lord."

Mary went into the pit and led the sinners up to Jesus, who held a silver platter. Fred stared at the bizarre sight of people handing over cash and jewelry. He made a mental note of a couple of sinners, an elderly woman wearing a bright red, head scarf, and a tall man in a gray suit. As the sinners returned to their seats, the organist played the theme song from *Rocky*. Fred watched his picks to see where they sat, hoping to find one of them after the service so that he could ask whether the pit had a door.

"So shall you be saved," the bishop intoned, his sonorous voice rising. "Join the choir now, and while you sing consider whether others among you have a need to repent." His voice rose, "Psalm 25: *A Flea for Porgiveness*."

A Flea for Porgiveness? The congregation had not reacted to the spoonerism. Fred wondered if he had misheard.

One by one, sixteen more members of the congregation stood and made their way into the pit. At the end of the hymn, Mary led them to the altar. They were saved, and contributed to the cause with cash.

After the choir sang *Amazing Grace*, the bishop mounted the pulpit again. The church lights dimmed and he basked in the spotlight before gripping the edge of the pulpit and staring, fierce-faced at his congregation.

"Matthew 10:15: Assuredly, I say to you, it will be more tolerable for the land of Sodom and Gomorrah in the day of judgment than for that town." The bishop spread his arms, appealing to his congregation to name the town.

Fred heard Santa Fe and New York suggested by people sitting near him.

The bishop waited until the congregation quieted. "Hollywood is the modern Sodom and Gomorrah."

Fred wondered if the comment indicated why the bishop might support the destruction of Hollywood elite in *Bye Bye Oscars*? Or, did it show that the bishop was not the backer? In which case, why was he letting Agincourt use his workshop? None of it made sense.

Again the bishop's hands descended to grip the pulpit as he leaned forward and thundered, "Like those ancient cities, Hollywood is populated by a tribe of Israel and by homosexuals and communists." The bishop's face showed disgust. "Do not be seduced by their cunning, by their filthy gold. For every movie that illustrates the right path for fighting the forces of evil, for defeating the heathens, for protecting our children...for living a just and proper life...there are ten, no twenty, no a hundred...that enrich the pockets of these pornographers. We will battle them, and we will prevail!"

The bishop raised his hands and the choir sang a chorus of hallelujahs. Many of the congregation stood and joined in.

"Earlier, our fine Redeemer ensemble played Hollywood music, the theme song from *Rocky*." The bishop's voice rose again. "Am I guilty of *talling* into their *frap*?"

No reaction from the congregation, but there he goes again, Fred thought; a modern Reverend Spooner.

"No. *Rocky* inspires us to fight for what we believe in, to overcome our challenges with the help of God. It is garbage like *Hairspray* that perverts our children and leads them down the path to perdition."

Fred lost interest as the bishop droned on with a litany of appropriate and inappropriate movies, while the mariachis played the theme songs from those he approved. Fred returned to his original goal of searching for doors that might lead to the basement. He was jolted back to the service when the organ blared, and everyone erupted in a burst of hosannas and hallelujahs. Most stood, and the building echoed with fervent responses. Fred was drawn into the moment.

The bishop thundered over the final chants, "To protect you from the purveyors of filth, my staff, under my guidance, has prepared a list of suitable movies. This list may be purchased for only two dollars from my angels, who will now circulate in the aisles. Two dollar is a small price to pay for receiving God's guidance. I.... Tell us, sister." The bishop extended his hands, palms up toward a large woman who had stood in the front row.

She opened her purse and extracted two bills. "Thank you, Bishop, for guiding me and my family. We are blessed by your wisdom."

Her statement triggered a mass flourishing of money.

Some members of the choir, angels with fledgling wings, started their tour of the cathedral. The woman next to Fred sat down clutching her dollars. "Isn't he wonderful?" she whispered to Fred.

"Certainly different," Fred replied, trying not to show his disgust at the bishop's stunt.

The woman looked at him closely before turning away.

Fred reached for his wallet, and found that he had nothing smaller than a five. Fortunately, the angels provided change, he realized, although many of the congregation refused to accept it, and donated larger bills. When the angel looked as if she was going to put him in that category, he motioned for his three dollars.

The angel smiled sadly as she held out his change. "For the cause, sir."

"For my lunch," Fred replied, taking the bills.

After the angels returned to the stage, the spotlight, focused on the bishop, took on a reddish tinge as he continued his sermon. "You may be surprised to find the work of Stephen King in your list," he said, tilting his head. "Stephen King is included because he offers a warning that unbelievable evil lurks in every corner of our world. Yet, the activities of Satan are even worse than anything Mr. King could dream up. The atrocities perpetrated by the heathens in the Middle East, Vietnam, North Korea; this axis of evil that led to nine-eleven. We must remain vigilant."

Vietnam? A strange connection, Fred thought, wondering where the bishop was going with this theme.

"I admired Richard Nixon. He helped restore our country to a godly path after that pinko-liberal Lyndon Baines Johnson. But Nixon made one mistake." The bishop looked briefly at his congregation as if expecting information on what that mistake might be. He did not wait for an answer. "Nixon should have rained down the wrath of the Lord on those dens of iniquity, Saigon and Hanoi. After our brave troops were safely home, he should have rained fire and brimstone on those communists, those usurers, and those perverts...a nuclear holocaust."

The opening bars of *Mars* from Holst's suite *The Planets* resonated throughout the cathedral. The music faded into the background as the bishop continued.

"As the men of Sodom sought to ravage the angels sent by God to Lot, so do the moguls of Hollywood, whether it be in movies or on television, lure our young men and women to despoil them. That new abomination, *American Idol*. You heard it, *American Idol*, a false god and idolatry. I say to you, do not allow your children to travel to that despicable place. If misfortune has led them there, call them home." The bishop raised his arms in supplication. "Remember Genesis 15: 15:

When the morning dawned, the angels urged Lot to hurry, saying, 'Arise, take your wife and your two daughters who are here, lest you be consumed in the punishment of the city.'" The bishop waited for the music to crescendo before shouting, "Then the Lord rained brimstone and fire on *Godom* and *Somorrah* from out of the heavens. Verily, so shall it be with Hollywood...and with *Heverly Bills*."

The lights dimmed, the spotlight swung back to the stage, illuminating three, fully-armed troops bearing the flag. The organist and the mariachis played the *Battle Hymn of the Republic*, and the congregation stood and sang along with the choir.

The bishop, standing hand in hand between Jesus and Mary, raised their arms in a gesture that reminded Fred of a victor's salute after a boxing match. The congregation cheered, and the bishop, Jesus and Mary led them out of the cathedral.

On the way out, Fred kept the woman with the bright red scarf in sight. He gradually pushed through the crowd toward her. As he passed the bishop, Jesus and Mary at the top of the steps and started down between the acolytes, a voice called out to him, "Can you come in tomorrow?"

Fred turned to see Miguel dressed in a white robe. "I can be there in the morning...early. Have to leave by twelve."

"Seven-thirty," Miguel called after him.

Fred nodded, then faced a barrage of persistent *God be with you's*, waiting until he was halfway down the cathedral steps to move alongside his mark.

"Ma'am, I saw you go down to hell and rise out of it. I admire you for that. I have not yet had the courage," Fred said.

A smile lit the woman's worn face. "I go in place of my son. He...he has strayed from the church."

Fred put his hand on her shoulder. "I pray for your success."

"Thank you. If you have problems, you should consult the bishop," she said.

"Next time, I will try to have the courage to descend into hell. I'm nervous and it would help if I knew what it was like," Fred said.

The woman stopped and clasped his hand. "You shouldn't be. The walls are painted with flames, but you can still see heaven above. And then the blessed Virgin leads you out."

"I think I could go there," Fred said, adding casually, "I was worried that there might be a door leading further down."

"We're holding people up," said the woman as she released his hand. "I didn't want to put you off, but there is a door with a picture of Satan welcoming you to descend further."

Got it, Fred thought, as they reached the bottom of the steps. "I won't like going there but knowing will make the experience easier to handle." He smiled. "Good luck with your son."

134

The bishop watched Fred cross the road, and beckoned to Miguel, who was standing behind him by the door. "Find out what Mrs. Gonzalez was talking about with Mr. Howard."

Fred's cell phone rang while he was driving back to his apartment. He pulled to the side of the road, looked at the caller's number and answered, "Sir, I just left the cathedral. What a performance."

"Tell me about it."

When Fred finished, Kowalski asked, "You'll need to check out that door in hell. You've got the burglary tools from your training course?"

"Yes."

"Be careful. And one other thing, do you find it curious that this Millie plays the Virgin Mary during the service?"

"A bit. She told me it's a role she has in the bishop's movies. Maybe she's paid to do it." Fred absent mindedly lowered the phone, thought about Millie, and considered whether to tell Kowalski about Georgie.

"Are you listening?" Kowalski shouted, waking Fred out of his reverie. "Sorry, sir, I guess I could ask her."

"Don't be too pushy. Was there anything else?"

"Well, I had a date with Agincourt's assistant, Georgie."

"Find out anything?"

"You told me to act like someone in the business." Fred said, hoping he didn't sound too defensive.

"And...?"

"She's a bit rough."

"No drugs, I hope," Kowalski snapped.

"Nothing like that."

"Well, watch out. That's everything?"

"Yes. Oh wait. I met the bishop."

"Anything particular about him?" Kowalski sounded impatient.

Fred laughed. "Says I look like him, which suggests that Chuck may be his son. Oh, and when he gets excited, he mangles his words. What was it? The psalm, *A Plea for Forgiveness* became *a Flea for Porgiveness*."

"Are you sure?" Kowalski's asked sharply. "Absolutely sure?"

"Yes," Fred replied. "And he ranted against Hollywood and I'm sure he's anti-Semitic. So maybe he is the backer of *Bye Bye Oscars*; his way of getting at Hollywood."

"Anything else?"

"He smells. Tries to cover it up with Old Spice. Made my eyes water."

"Interesting." Kowalski laughed. "I only met the Reverend Jenkins once, but I haven't forgotten how he stank. Grew up poor, where a bath was a once-a-month event. Bet he hasn't changed. Good work, Fred. I need to check into this bishop's background. I'll get someone on it. Now, you be careful, y'hear?"

Kowalski hung up and went to a filing cabinet. He pulled out a worn manila folder, returned to his desk and scanned through the scanty contents. It contained everything he had been able to find out about the Reverend Orlando Jenkins: Born near Cleveland, Tennessee, 1933 to destitute tenant farmer, Orville, and his wife, Jane; dropped out of high school in 1938 to work for his father, despite a near 4.0 GPA. Orlando attended a congregation of snake handlers with his parents. Orlando joined the army in 1941, and was discharged in 1945 for insubordination after calling his Jewish captain a son of the devil. Activities between 1945 and 1963 were unclear, except that he obtained a mail-order degree in religious studies. Then he toured the south and southwest holding revival meetings in a tent; by then using the title "Reverend." In 1970, he married Sarah Jernigan, a devout Seventh Day Adventist, and settled in Salt Flat. He had a note mentioning the birth of a son in 1971 and, annotated with a question mark, a daughter in 1973. Kowalski added another note, saying that it looked likely that the reverend was now known as Bishop Orpheus John.

* * *

Two days later, Kowalski called Fred again, this time sounding angry. "Ambassador Wheaton found out from Franklin Jackson that I'd asked the FBI to look into Bishop John's background, and stopped it."

"Why?"

After a silence, Kowalski replied. "The bishop has connections."

"Did you tell him why you were interested?"

"No, and I didn't tell him about you. I pretended my information came from the FBI. God knows who the ambassador talks to."

"Bummer." Fred paused. Thinking about why the ambassador didn't believe Gene reminded Fred of a question that had bugged him since he had heard about the stolen bombs. "Gene, I heard that it took two or three days to find the truck. I thought they always traveled with a security vehicle following, and had a signal that would go off if anything went wrong."

Gene laughed. "I wondered when you'd ask how it could have happened. Unfortunately, none of those safeguards was a match for Murphy's Law. The convoy was on I-40 about eighty miles east of Albuquerque when the freezing rain started. The trailing security car went off the road, killing the driver and severely injuring the other armed occupant. Before passing out, he managed to contact the truck and tell them to wait. The truck driver pulled off into a rest area, and got out to check the truck. At the same time the guard got out to pee. They weren't expecting trouble. That's when the hijackers struck. Later, the hijackers' broken-down pickup was found abandoned in the rest area. A stack of empty beer cans indicated that they were most likely drunk, and looking for a ride. They had no idea what they'd stolen."

"But how did they get away?" Fred asked.

"They did something that confused everybody. The truck driver and guard, who'd been left tied up in the pick-up, saw them head west toward Albuquerque. But the hijackers must have taken the next road south, probably 285 to Roswell and Carlsbad, and then got on the road to the park."

"I still don't get it. It's got to be nearly three hundred miles. Say at least six hours in bad weather. And surely the police would have been looking for them."

"Murphy strikes again. It was two hours before the authorities believed what had happened. Then they started to check all traffic on the interstate between Santa Rosa and Albuquerque, and asked if anyone had seen the truck. A lot of the people had pulled off the interstate because of the bad driving conditions. Unfortunately, one person thought they had seen the truck head toward Santa Fe. So the emphasis of the search shifted to the north."

"They might have gotten as far as Roswell before the general alarm went out. Speaking of alarms, what about the one in the truck?" Fred asked.

"The radio alarm didn't go off until the truck crashed, and then only briefly. The hijackers never tried to open the back and look at the cargo. All hell would have broken loose if they had."

"Too bad."

"To cut the story short, they were spotted heading south on route 285 in Carlsbad by a cop who'd stopped for coffee and a donut. He ran out of the café, got in his car and gave chase. He got past them and they rammed him off the road. By the time he started after them again he was too far behind to see them pull off onto the park road."

"Murphy always wins."

"Hopefully, not this time," Gene replied dryly.

"So, do you want me to check on the bishop's background?"

"Too risky. I don't want to break your cover." Kowalski said and hung up.

For the second time, Fred realized that his assignment was not a lark. *Bye Bye Oscars* was not simply another Agincourt schlock movie. At the beginning he had concluded that Gene Kowalski was a nice guy, but with a touch of Don Quixote and Captain Ahab in his character. Fred had been happy to enjoy being involved and fantasizing about being a Bond-like character. Cold reality had now crept in and he realized that finding out what was happening in the cathedral could be dangerous. He reached for a Moon Pie, but put it down before opening the wrapping. He needed a beer.

13.

"No cars in the lot by the workshop, good sign," Fred muttered to himself. He had arrived early at the cathedral to have a chance to snoop. He parked and made a point of rattling the locked door, in case someone was watching. Getting no response, he idly walked around the workshop and soundstage building. At the back of the workshop he came across a white Lincoln, stretch-limo resting on wooden blocks, its rear wheels and brake drums removed: probably where the engine that he'd seen Carl working on came from. Farther along a concrete foundation wall rose some twenty feet up to the cathedral's main floor. What looked like air conditioning vents and a hole for the entry of a substantial power line were the only penetrations in the concrete. Walking on, Fred came to an extensive building that abutted the far side of the cathedral. A loading dock with double doors jutted from the two-story wall next to the cathedral. A sign announced, Office Deliveries Only. Further around the building he came across a sign for the Redeemer Fountain Kindergarten and Sunday School.

As Fred completed his circuit, Miguel drove up.

"You weren't here so I took a tour," Fred said as Miguel got out. "Impressive."

Miguel shrugged. "That's the idea." He walked a few steps then turned. "Enjoy the service?"

"I can't get over the inside of the cathedral...heaven and hell. Who thought of that?"

"The bishop, of course." Miguel unlocked the door. "You're curious about hell?"

Fred thought quickly, realizing that Miguel might have seen him talking to the lady in the red scarf. He nodded. "I was sitting high up on the left. Good view of heaven, but I couldn't really see hell."

"Hmm." Miguel continued inside and pointed at the metal bars stacked by the cutting bench. "Cut those to length. I'll start on the frames."

"Okay." Fred placed a bar in front of the saw and marked the cutting line. "On the way out, I asked this lady what hell was like." Out of the corner of his eye he saw Miguel look up. "Sounded interesting. Could you give me the grand tour?"

"Suppose I could." Miguel returned to assembling the frame for the H of Hollywood.

They had completed the frames for four letters by the time Carl arrived at nine. "Mornin'," he said. "Coffee ready?"

"Yes, and I've got some Moon Pies," Fred replied. He offered one to Carl.

"Can't eat them...diabetes." Carl poured coffee and added creamer.

"More for me." Miguel smiled.

At eleven-thirty, Miguel came over to Fred's bench. "Time for a break. I'll give you a quick tour."

Fred finished the cut on his bar, placed it in the stack, and then washed his hands. He was about to walk toward the door into the cathedral, when he saw Miguel leaving through the outside door. His hope of getting into the basement as part of the tour faded. "We'll be filming. I'll see you in a couple of days, Carl."

Carl gave an who-gives-a-damn look and flapped his hand.

"Don't mind Carl," Miguel said as they walked toward the cathedral. "He's always like that with everybody, except me and the bishop…but that's another story."

They reached the imposing front portal. Miguel opened a smaller door, inset at the left. "Want to see the organ?"

Fred noted that the smaller door had not been locked. "Sure."

Miguel led him up steps that spiraled to the left of the entrance. A vast bank of pipes soaring to the roof confronted them when they reached the organ loft. The keyboard faced the sidewall to the left of the main entrance. It gave a view of the altar and pulpit, so that the organist could respond to cues from the bishop, Fred assumed. He looked at the piece of sheet music on the stand, *We'll Meet Again*. After a moment, he remembered that this was the end theme music from *Dr. Strangelove*.

As they were leaving, Fred noticed that a bank of television monitors and a control panel for the cameras in the cathedral were located against the right side wall opposite the organ. Two of the cameras, mounted on each side of the stained glass window behind the altar gave a clear view of the stage and the ascent from hell. Fred suspected that the cameras recorded all the time, which meant that it would be difficult to break in through the door to hell undetected. Great. He chuckled nervously.

"Something funny?" Miguel asked.

"Nothing."

Miguel grinned. "Let's go to hell then."

The paintings on the walls of hell were in stark contrast to the blissful scenes depicted above them, with tortured beings engulfed in flames. Straight out of Dürer, Fred thought. The woman had been right. The door behind the descent showed a lurid-looking devil with horns standing sideways to usher any sinners to join him in hell.

Fred moved closer to inspect it. The handle and lock were made of what looked like black cast iron. The large keyhole implied that it took an old-fashioned key. "What's it like inside?" Fred asked, expecting to be told it was locked.

"Open it and see," Miguel replied.

Fred turned the handle. Behind the door was a broom closet. "Ah. The bishop has a sense of humor."

"Not really," said Miguel. "That was the architect's idea."

When they reached the stage, Fred moved toward the pulpit. Another question had been bugging him—how did the bishop suddenly appear in the pulpit, since it looked to be free-standing from the congregation's viewpoint. He decided not to ask Miguel, and quickly climbed the spiral stone staircase.

"Don't go...." Miguel's voice trailed off. He was too late to stop Fred.

When Fred reached the top, he discovered that the design was a very clever *trompe d'oeil*. A second, narrow staircase, inaccessible from the stage, angled down by the wall toward the basement.

Very clever, Fred thought. Grasping the moment, he placed his hands on the front of the pulpit. "Friends, Romans, countrymen, lend me your ears." His voice echoed around the walls. "I come t—"

"Shhh!" Miguel hissed. "Someone might hear you. If you've seen enough, I'd better get to work. When do you think you'll be back?"

"As I said, we'll be shooting tomorrow and probably Wednesday, so say Thursday morning."

"That'll work. Carl and I've got to finish up the fake entrance for the Oscar ceremony and take it to the Tijeras Casino, tomorrow morning. You and I can get the sign finished Thursday."

Driving back to Albuquerque, Fred tried to come up with a plan that would allow him to use the secret stairs so that he could explore the basement without being detected. He decided that if he arrived late for the Sunday service, there was a good chance the bishop wouldn't spot him. At the end of the service he could hide in the restroom near the front door. When the organist left he would disable the cameras—shades of *Mission Impossible*. Fred was starting to like this assignment again.

*   *   *

When Fred arrived at Agincourt's studio on Tuesday, Georgie was waiting for him.

"Sore?" she asked, a faint smile curling her lips.

"A little. You?"

"Yes. Thank you." Georgie scuffed a sneaker on the ground. "I've got two more steaks. How about tonight?"

"Let me take a raincheck."

"You can tie me up, if you want."

"Georgie, I'm not into that kind of stuff," Fred said adamantly.

"Too bad." Georgie, leading the way to the door, briefly pulled down the bottom of her jogging suit revealing the top of a red thong. "See what you'll be missing." She giggled and ran to the door.

For a moment, Fred was tempted, but he knew that her offer meant that she would want to tie him up. Entering the studio, he remembered his Security Training 101: "Don't get caught in compromising situations." He'd ignored it once, not again.

"Good," Lance greeted him. "We need you. Chuck's gone AWOL."

"What do you want me to do?" Fred asked.

Lance pointed at a group of people who looked like they might have come off an unemployment line. "We're rehearsing the arrival of stars for the Oscars' ceremony. Grab a woman and walk along the path marked on the floor until you get to Bogdan and Monique. They will interview you. Watch out for the puddles from that damn air conditioner."

Fred glanced up at the rusting framework of the roof; the engineer in him wondering idly what a good snowfall would do to it. "Is there a script?"

"Yes, but you don't need it." Lance raised his hands pleadingly. "Just pretend to have a conversation."

Taking the arm of an elderly woman at the front of the group, Fred said, "It's you and me, babe."

"¿Qué?" Looking nervous, she smiled but held on as they strolled down the pretend red carpet. Lance motioned for other pairs to follow them.

"Able to walk, I see." Bogdan sniggered.

"What does he mean?" Monique asked, moving sideways to avoid drips from above.

Fred said, "N-nothing much. I f-fell over."

Bogdan's eyebrows raised and he nodded in Georgie's direction.

"Oh." Monique said. "Who's your date here?"

Fred, surprised that she had sounded disappointed, didn't answer.

"For the camera, laddie," Bogdan muttered.

"Sorry. I think her name's Kay."

Millie looked irritated. "Well then, move Kay along, so we can chat to the next couple."

Agincourt tried the scene a number of times over the next couple of hours, explaining at the end, "While I've talked the Tijeras Casino into letting us use their foyer—the carpet's red—they're uneasy about us tying up the entrance for a long time. So we'll only get at most two shots at the location."

"Wouldn't making a movie be a big attraction?" Fred asked.

"Yeah, but they think people will be watching us and not gambling," Agincourt replied.

"Bet they use it in their publicity when the movie's a hit," Lance grumbled.

Agincourt shrugged. "I'm patient. Next time I need them, it'll go easier."

"Am I too late?" Chuck asked as he sauntered onto the set.

"What do you think?" Agincourt snapped, pointing to where Georgie was paying minimum wages to the extras who had walk-on parts, and taking their names, addresses, and contact phone numbers.

"Fred did a great job," Lance gushed. "Maybe you should be his double."

"Not funny," Chuck replied coldly. "Remember who's bring—"

"Chuck, come here!" Georgie interrupted him. "I need you to try on some stuff."

Chuck started to turn away as if he were going to ignore her, then his head sank and he went over, looking like a guilty child.

He's back in character, Fred mused to himself. If it were an act, then it might be so that nobody would take him seriously. If so, why? He edged toward Millie.

Georgie finished paying the extras, and led Chuck to the wardrobe room. Sounds of a vigorous argument filtered onto the set. When Chuck emerged, he was wearing a tight-fitting green suit with a frilly white shirt, paisley silk scarf, and high heeled green boots. He spotted Agincourt, and yelled, "I'm supposed to be a glamorous star. I look like a Cuban pimp."

"Get used to it," Agincourt replied. "I need you to stand out on the red carpet."

"You look just lovely," Lance purred. "Just think what the colorblind people are missing."

"Thank God I didn't have to wear that outfit," Fred mumbled to Millie.

"It can be arranged," Millie retorted, as she moved away.

"You're wasting your time there," Georgie whispered in Fred's ear. "She's got problems."

Fred tried not to show his irritation at Georgie's snide comment, and turned away. The evening with Georgie had been a mistake. He wished he hadn't upset Millie. He decided to ask Bogdan what Georgie meant.

"Gather round, children," Agincourt shouted. "Tomorrow afternoon, we'll shoot at the Tijeras Casino starting at one. Go with Georgie now and get fitted. Then come back here and show me what you've chosen. That includes you Fred, but you'll have to wear a wig. Can't have you and Chuck looking like twins."

Millie watched Fred and Georgie leave. Her eyes started to water, and she turned away so that no one would see. If only she had listened to her mother.

"It won't last," Bogdan whispered.

"What?" she replied, but knowing what he meant. But somehow she felt that Fred had been contaminated.

"Grow up, girl," Bogdan scolded. "You're acting like the heroine in a Harlequin novel."

"Why would I care?"

"Because you like him." Bogdan looked intently at her. "And you wouldn't want him to get hurt."

"Hurt. How?"

"Georgie's dangerous." For once, Bogdan's expressionless face showed concern. "Enough said. You fight back."

"I'll think about it," Millie said to his retreating back.

* * *

Clever, Fred thought, as he walked onto the red carpet with "Kay," the way Carl and Miguel had transformed the front of the casino to look like the Kodak Theater in LA. Further on he could see customers working banks of slots. He wondered if Agincourt would bother to keep them out of the picture. Loraine, the make-up artist, had aged him by using a gray wig and makeup. By his side, "Kay" looked surprisingly glamorous in a red gown that appeared to have been designed for a western movie.

"*¡Hola!* Rosita, Rosita," a small group of fans called out to Kay.

She smiled self-consciously. "*Mi familia*," she whispered.

Fred grinned and waved to them.

Chuck, now resplendent in a bespangled suit that had played an important role in *Atomic Bactrian Camels of the Mojave*, strutted in front. Fred wondered how Chuck had won the argument over the green outfit. Georgie accompanied Chuck, wearing her trademark dark glasses, cowboy boots, and a low-cut blouse. Her skirt that cut up might have produced three handkerchiefs gave Fred tantalizing glimpses of her backside. Lance, sitting in a wheel chair, manned the camera and followed Chuck and Georgie. The camera was always pointed at the modest number of extras who had been carefully positioned to provide "background."

Fred's instructions had been to carry on walking, while Bogdan and Millie interviewed Chuck and Georgie, but Bogdan, immaculate in an Armani tuxedo, motioned him to stop. When Chuck's interview was over, Bogdan grasped Fred's arm and said to the camera, "Greg Godfrey and his charming date, Kay, I think. Is an Oscar in the offing for you?"

"Uh, a good chance," Fred replied quickly. "Of course, all due to our wonderful director Sebastian Agincourt.... And the great script from Lance Dupree."

"Good luck, Greg," said Bogdan turning to Millie. "What do you think, Angelina?"

Millie looked at Agincourt for guidance. He motioned for her to play along.

"I hear that you and Kay are a serious item." Millie tilted her head and asked, "Any truth to rumors you'll be tying the knot soon?"

"We're just casual friends," Fred replied, nodding his head to where Georgie continued down the carpet.

Millie raised her eyebrows and turned to Bogdan. "Oh look, I see Lola Paramour and Tex Whittaker. Nice talking to you, Greg, and Kay." She walked away.

"Interesting discussion," Bogdan said blandly.

"Kay" smiled uncertainly and clung to Fred's arm. Other extras followed them down the red carpet, wearing a motley array of exotic costumes that had been left over from Agincourt's earlier movies.

By the time Agincourt yelled "Cut!" a large crowd of casino customers were hovering on the edges of the makeshift set.

Agincourt's eyes gleamed. "We'll do it again," he said. He called out to the crowd, "If you want to be in a movie, line up beside the carpet. Remember you're a crowd at the Oscars. Wave to the stars as they pass, and applaud the ones you like."

"What about the part where Bogdan interviewed Fred?" Lance asked.

"Keep it. Okay, Boggie?"

Bogdan nodded.

Fred worked out what to say to Millie as he and Rosita/Kay followed Chuck and Georgie down the carpet. Chuck turned and glared when Rosita's expanding *familia* erupted in applause as Millie finished interviewing him.

This time Fred escorted Kay over to Bogdan.

"Ah. Greg Godfrey and his charming date, Kay, I think. Angelina tells me that wedding bells may be rung soon." Bogdan stated casually.

"What? Uh, not likely." Fred replied, wondering what Bogdan was up to.

"Are you sure you and Kay aren't a serious item?" Millie/Angelina sounded serious.

Fred took Kay's hand. "She's a sweet girl but any romance is only in the movies." Fred smiled broadly and attempted to look roguish. "Now, if you're not available—"

"Oh look, I see Lola Paramour and Tex Whittaker," Millie interrupted him, pointing at the next couple on the red carpet. The camera and microphone followed Bogdan, who had taken the hint.

"Your moustache is coming unglued," Millie whispered.

"What?" Fred whispered back.

"Moustache. You look demented."

Fred pushed the straggling end into place. "Thanks. How about dinner tomorrow night after I finish at the workshop?"

"I'm not sure. I think I have to take mother somewhere. You need to move on." Millie joined Bogdan.

Agincourt made his cast do one more take, and then dismissed them. Rosita insisted that Fred should meet her *familia.* Apparently, they made up a quarter of the fans. When the introductions were over, Fred looked for Millie. She had sounded as if she might accept his invitation, but she had disappeared. Damn.

Someone poked him in the ribs. "You did great," Georgie said. "Wanna beer?"

Fred was about to say no, but frustrated with his failure to get Millie to come out, thought what the hell. "No bondage. Okay?"

"I was only joking," Georgie replied, looking shifty. "Follow me back to my place."

"I'll be home soon, mother. You didn't need to call me," Millie said. "We'll be in plenty of time for your appointment." She put her cell phone in her tote bag, and went back to the set, in time to see Fred head out of the door with Georgie. Her eyes misted again. Why did her family always get in the way? But she knew it had just been an excuse because she was angry about Georgie. The appointment wouldn't take more than an hour. Harlequin heroine Bogdan had said. He was right. Next time she saw Fred she'd be nice to him.

When Fred returned to his apartment, Bogdan was sitting in his usual place by the pool. He looked hard as Fred approached and sat down in a plastic chair. "I judge by your walk that you and Georgie have been doing the horizontal tango again," he said.

"Yeah. After Millie turned me down...again, Georgie offered me steak and—"

"Let me guess. Honey or hot candle wax?" Bogdan grinned.

"Neither. Cool Whip."

"Was it worth it?"

"I suppose so." Fred rubbed his neck.

Bogdan tilted his head. "Except for the attempted throttling, eh?"

"So she always does it?"

"Always, I can't say." Bogdan looked thoughtful. "You know I've often wondered if she ever went too far."

"You mean killed somebody?"

"Yes. Want a drink?" Bogdan proffered a bottle of bourbon.

"No thanks. If only...."

"If only Monique, or should I say Millie, would go out with you." Bogdan smiled wistfully. "She likes you, Fred."

"How do you know?"

"She was upset when she heard about you and Georgie." Bogdan shook his head. "I should have kept my big mouth shut."

"Then why does she brush me off?"

"I probably shouldn't tell you, but what the hell. Her mother's an invalid and has seizures. Millie doesn't like to leave her alone."

"What about work...and the church?" Fred tried not to sound suspicious.

"During the day, a neighbor drops in to check on her mother, and she's got a cell phone."

Fred brightened. "I'll try Millie again. Georgie scares me."

"And so she should." Bogdan smiled paternally. "Now, if you're not going to drink, leave me to my memories of the many uses for honey." He took a sip of bourbon and closed his eyes.

14.

"How are the other props for Oscars going?" Fred asked Miguel on entering the workshop on Wednesday morning.

"The bomb's over there." Miguel pointed to an open crate on a table near the door into the cathedral.

Fred wandered over to take a look. "Timer, fins, death's head, now that's a real bomb. Who designed it?"

"Carl. I did the painting."

Fred thought hard for a moment before deciding to risk a big question. He pointed at the door. "What's in there?"

For a moment, Miguel looked like he might not answer. Then he replied curtly, "Storage and, further back, the crypt. Enough talk. We need to finish the sign."

Over the following five hours, they completed the task in near silence, and then stacked the parts against the outside wall.

Back inside, Miguel called Georgie. "We're ready for Agincourt's truck," he said. "It's going to be hot up on the mountain. Get some drinks, too…water, Gator—"

"Dr Pepper, too," Fred pleaded.

"A bag of ice and Dr Pepper for the kid." Miguel hung up.

"Does Georgie always wear dark glasses?" Fred asked tentatively.

"I guess so. Why do you ask?"

"Just curious."

"Curiosity can get you trouble." Miguel was smiling, but his eyes were cold. "I forgot to tell her that Carl wasn't here. She probably won't come in. You'd better go outside and wait for her."

Fred went to his car, a gray '97 Dodge Avenger provided by Homeland Security, and brooded about whether Miguel had sent him outside to stop the questions. He flipped to a country western station and closed his eyes.

He was dreaming about mutant nuclear jellyfish, when a rap on the windshield told him Georgie had arrived. She was lying on the hood, her arms spread wide, and her tongue licking the glass lasciviously.

Fred hesitated for only a second before turning on the windshield washer.

Georgie jumped back, screeching in delight, "You bastard. I'll get you for that." She slid off the hood and stood a few steps in front of the car, waiting until Fred had gotten out before edging toward him. At the last moment, she adopted a karate pose and delivered a straight arm punch. Fred managed to parry the fist, and caught her in a bear hug.

For a second, Georgie went still, then ground her pelvis into him "We've got time for a quickie," she said.

"It's a church."

"Spoilsport. Who cares?" Georgie purred in a husky voice. "I got your Dr Pepper."

"Miguel's by the door watching," Fred said loosening his grip.

"How about Carl?" Georgie asked.

"He's in Santa Fe with the bishop."

Fred's thoughts, about whether this had all been an act for Carl's sake, were interrupted when Georgie stopped, turned and asked casually, "Where did you learn self-defense?"

Fred gave thanks to Kowalski for insisting he learn his cover story. "Some kids were bullying me at school. My dad took me to karate classes."

Georgie shrugged and continued walking.

When Fred told Sebastian Agincourt that the sign would be arriving shortly, the director left his office and began pacing outside the studio's front door.

"He's like a kid with a new toy," Lance said. "Bet you a dollar he wants to set the sign up right now."

"You mean here?" Fred asked.

Lance looked to the heavens. "On the mountain, silly boy."

"What about the lights? What about approval?"

"He bought a portable generator weeks ago." Lance chuckled. "We'll get it up and take the shots."

"And get it down quickly?"

"No, silly, leave it until the authorities complain."

Fred looked confused.

"Publicity."

"Oh. I hadn't thought of that."

"That's why you're a poorly-paid actor, duckie, and...." Lance pointed. "Here's the truck."

Agincourt signaled for Miguel to park his creaking Chevy truck next to the door, and called out, "Fred, I want to see one of the letters. Help Georgie and Miguel unload it."

They extricated the letter D, and placed it up against the back of the truck.

Chuck emerged from the studio. "Not bad. I still think the Chinese Theater would have been better."

Agincourt ignored him and studied the letter D from various angles. "Looks good to me. You can put it back, Georgie, then take the sign to the Sandia Peak Tramway station."

"Do you want me and Miguel to wait for you at the station?" she asked.

"Ye-es. There's a track up Sandia Mountain near the station. I sort of have approval to use it, but best we go together in case some officious employee decides to investigate. Fred and I will bring the generator." Agincourt scanned the group, finally focusing on Lance. "Lancie, I've decided we can't get a good shot from here. Set up the camera on the roof of *Mi Casa Su Casa*. Look for the white tanks above and to the right of the Station. We'll be up a bit higher. I'll call you on your cell when we get there."

Agincourt looked around. "Chuck, help Fred load the generator. It's inside the door."

"Sebastian, I don't do manual labor." Chuck pouted. "That's for the help...like Fred and," Chuck looked around to see the truck leaving, "Georgie."

"If you don't help Fred, I'll tell her what you said," Lance threatened and walked toward the studio.

"Bitch," Chuck muttered sulkily. "Come on, Freddie. You can take the heavy end."

Agincourt and Fred arrived at the Tramway station's lower parking lot around two, Georgie was waiting. Agincourt drove up beside her and opened his window.

"The track's off the upper lot," Georgie said. "It's got a padlocked post. Give me a couple of minute to remove it then drive on up to where you can't be seen from the station."

"Go for it." Agincourt closed his window.

Fred drove around the station and headed up the gravel track. He stopped and waited for Georgie and Agincourt, then led them up to the higher of the two tanks and parked.

"What do you want to do now?" Georgie asked when they all got out.

Agincourt pointed to the right where a saddle between two rocky crags loomed a couple of hundred feet above them. "You, Miguel and Fred unload the letters and take them up to that ridge. Set them facing downtown."

"Thank God we used aluminum alloy and not steel," Fred said, wiping sweat from under his cap, as he laid the last letter on a rough ledge, some hundred feet above the van.

"Experience," Miguel chuckled. "I always end up having to move the props. It's amazing how light a Tower of Babel can be when you put your mind to it. Of course, if there's a strong wind...."

"That happened?"

"In one of the bishop's movies, we had to catch the Tower before it blew onto I-40. You should have heard the bishop."

"What about this stuff?"

"No problems, Fred." Miguel indicated the posthole digger and pickax that Georgie had carried up. "We'll set the feet in the ground. Might as well start."

Fred and Miguel were concentrating on placing the second letter O in Hollywood, when Fred heard a grinding noise, and looked up to see the Tram on its way up to Sandia Peak. He waved back to the passengers gawking at them. "Good publicity," he said. "Agincourt'll—"

Georgie interrupted him and pointed down the hill. "Not all publicity's good."

Fred watched two men coming up the track from the Tramway station. "What do we do?" he asked.

"Rest for a bit, drink something, and then finish the letters," Miguel said. Unlike Fred he was not sweating. "Let Agincourt deal with it. Then we'll get the generator."

"Two guys, this could be fun," Georgie said, pointing at the men getting out of the Jeep. She unbuttoned the top two buttons of her shirt. "I'll give Sebastian a hand."

"Fred finished his Dr Pepper, and muttered, "God help them." He watched Georgie scrambling down the hill. Looking up he took in the view. "I wish I had binoculars, Miguel. I can see downtown, and the airport to the south. I know roughly where *Mi Casa* is, but it's too far away to pinpoint."

Miguel ignored him, and continued clearing surface rocks to make spaces for holes for the legs of the last of the Os.

They were busy installing the final letter—D, when they heard scuffling and grunting. Looking down, they saw two men lugging the generator up the hill.

Fred chuckled. "That Georgie's something else."

Miguel sniffed. "Don't underestimate Agincourt. I bet he made them an offer. Bet you a dollar."

"Oh, you mean like a part in the movie? You're on." Fred looked thoughtful. "Wait, I remember he did that with the Hummer salesman."

"Too late. Bet's on. I gotta finish the wiring."

A man named Mike introduced himself and his partner Luis as the two set the generator on the ground. "Mr. Agincourt said for you to connect this up and turn it on for ten minutes as a test," Mike said panting.

"There's a flat space I've cleared behind the H," Miguel said pointedly.

Luis and Mike looked at each other. Mike shrugged. "We got this far."

"Thanks," Miguel said. "Will we be seeing you again?"

"Mr. Agincourt asked us to be extras in an Oscar scene. He said Luis's wife and my girlfriend could be in it, too," Mike replied. "She loved the first *Bye Bye Oscars*." He winked. "I'll have a good time tonight."

Miguel held out his hand and made a gimme sign.

"Will it be okay with your company, Mike?" Fred asked.

"We can stall them for a bit. Agincourt suggested the publicity could be useful for the Tramway." Mike paused. "Maybe the manager will buy that. If not, I'll get that Georgie to talk to him." He winked again. "Come on, Luis. We'd better get back."

"Easy money." Miguel said, taking the dollar from Fred. "Come on. Let's get this thing connected."

Agincourt greeted Fred and Miguel after they had clambered down to the track. "Great work," he said. "Lancie's got some terrific shots. Fred, it'll be dark in an hour or so. We'll all go to the studio. You come back here and turn the sign on again for thirty minutes. Start at eight, okay?"

"You'll need a flashlight." Georgie added, looking as if she wanted Fred to ask her for one.

"I'll be fine," Fred replied, ignoring the hint.

Miguel raised his eyebrows and grinned. "Good luck."

Fred waited until the tram had passed on its trip up the mountain. He glanced at his watch; close enough to eight, he thought, as he switched on the generator.

"We've got thirty minutes to do it," Georgie said, appearing from behind a large rock.

"What the hell!" Fred staggered back, nearly losing his footing. "You've got to be kidding?"

Georgie pulled her shirt up and her jeans down.

"For God's sake, Agincourt's filming!"

"Can't see us. We're behind the sign." Georgie finished removing her clothes and knelt in front of Fred. "I'll make you feel good," she said, stroking up Fred's legs.

Got to get out of this, Fred thought. "I can't. It's the wrong time of the month." He moved away.

"Funny, funny, you chicken." Georgie sounded angry. She stood and lunged at him, fists flailing.

Fred grabbed her.

"Bastard, I could kill you," she screamed, going limp for a second until he was off guard, at which point she tried to push him down the ridge.

Fred held tight until she stopped moving, then scrambled away. "Are you crazy?" As he said the words, he understood for the first time that her roughhousing wasn't acting. She would have sent him onto the rocks below.

Georgie's elfin face, illuminated by light from the sign, turned bitter and ugly-looking. "Nobody turns me down."

Fred considered ways to get out of the mess. The thought that he might need Georgie's help decided his response. "Georgie," he said gently, "this isn't the right place." He held out his hand. "Friends."

Georgie took it and jabbed his palm with a fingernail. "Suppose so. Got a handkerchief?"

Fred rummaged in his pocket and handed her one. "I haven't used it."

Georgie shrugged, took the handkerchief, turned her head and removed her glasses, wiping them carefully. Fred got a brief glimpse of intense blue, before she covered her eyes.

"Hand me my clothes...please."

After Georgie was dressed, they sat and looked at the lighted outlines of Albuquerque, spread out below them.

"Doing anything Saturday?" Georgie asked.

"Visiting an aunt and uncle in Amarillo," Fred lied

Georgie grunted and turned away.

"Thirty minutes is about up." Fred went to the generator and turned it off.

Georgie recovered her flashlight. "Race you to the parking lot." She started down the ridge, squawking like a chicken.

Fred took his time following her, fearing an ambush. By the time he reached the lot, Georgie had gone.

On his way home, Fred pulled into a shopping mall and called Gene. "Reporting in, boss."

"And?"

"We finished the Hollywood sign and put it on Sandia Mountain near the Tramway station."

Kowalski snorted. "How did Agincourt get approval for that?"

"I don't think he did. Lance says Agincourt thinks it'll be good for publicity when the authorities complain."

"Clever. So, what else?"

"Georgie's still coming on to me. She's likes to play rough."

"Wearing dark glasses?"

"Yes, but when we were up on the mountain, she had to clean them. I think her eyes are blue." Fred heard the sound of papers being rustled.

"Dark or pale?"

"Pale, I think."

"Try and find out. I'll do some investigating, too."

"I don't know if it's any help, but she was at school in Wisconsin, Madison…took engineering."

"Thanks." Fred heard more paper rustling, before Kowalski came back on the line. "When do you plan to check out the church?"

"I got a tour of the cathedral from Miguel. I think I've found a way into the basement. I'm afraid that the cameras are on all the time, but I know where the control panel is. I'm going to try Sunday."

"Good luck, and be very careful," Kowalski said. "Remember, you are not James Bond."

"Sir, I don't feel like Bond," Fred blurted out. "Frankly, this whole assignment seems…nuts. I'm having trouble believing in a plot involving Agincourt and his merry men and women." Fred paused as the line went silent.

After a moment, Kowalski said quietly, "Mr. Schwarzmuller, hang in there. I have trouble believing it, too. But my experience tells me that there's something strange with the set up. Why would this bishop allow his workshop to be used to help make a semi-pornographic movie?"

"Good point, sir," Fred said. "But, if someone wants to blow up Hollywood, why wouldn't they simply take a bomb there and let it off when the Oscars ceremony is underway? As you told me, at full blast, that nuke would take out an area six miles in diameter. There's no need to be in the building."

Following a long silence, Kowalski responded, "I can't answer that. We'll discuss it again after you've checked the cathedral. In the meantime, remember, no heroics."

15.

On Sunday, Fred changed his appearance. He had not shaved for two days, and used a brown rinse on his hair, which he slicked down with gel. Uncomfortable cotton pads made his cheeks look plump. He left his so-called apartment, wearing thick-rimmed glasses and a battered denim baseball cap. A half mile from the cathedral, Fred parked his old Avenger on a side road in front of an abandoned country store. On a reconnaissance, he had decided that this place would allow him the best chance of getting to the cathedral without being spotted.

When his watch alarm beeped he started out on foot along the dusty road. By the time he reached the cathedral he was uncomfortably sweaty. No one was outside. He stood in the shadow of the Sunday school building until he judged that the service would be nearly over. Fred crept up a side path and in through the partially open front door. He was relieved to see the backs of a standing-room-only crowd, and to hear the bishop leading his congregation from the stage. Satisfied that the crowd had blocked the view of the cameras, he went to the men's room and waited in a stall.

Up to this point, his focus had been on stealth. Now, sitting on the toilet, he had time to brood about the risk he was taking, and his stomach was churning. Prompted by a queasy feeling after breakfast, he'd put a Lomotil pill in his pocket. Fred popped the tablet and swallowed with difficulty, wishing he'd brought a Dr Pepper.

Idle thoughts crossed his mind. Had this ever happened to James Bond? He pictured Roger Moore, battling SPECTRE and diarrhea...possible. Sean Connery...never.

After the final, musical crescendo, Fred heard the murmurs of the departing congregation. How long would it take them to leave? A few men came in to use the facilities. A couple of them stopped and chatted. An usher came around and told them to leave as they were going to close the cathedral down to save on air-conditioning costs. Curious, but thank God. Then there was silence. As he was about to leave the restroom, he heard someone approach. On his earlier visit he had noticed graffiti on the cubicle walls, and had decided on a cover story in case anyone questioned him. In fact, the words on the cubicles were harmless: 'Jesus loves me;' 'smile and God smiles at you;' and so on. He put on cotton work gloves, pulled some light sandpaper and a rag from his pocket, and went back into a stall.

"What *yer* doin?" the janitor asked, putting down his bucket.

"Bishop told me to clean these off," Fred replied, adding inventively, "Penance."

"Nobody told me." The janitor came over and studied the wall. "What'd you do?"

Fred made a drinking motion with his hand.

"Figures." The janitor seemed happy to find somebody worse off than he was, and started removing the plastic bags containing paper towels.

Fred made sure that the janitor had left before erasing the final graffiti. He sidled out of the restroom and walked with his head down to where the stairs rose up to the organ loft. Hearing no sounds from above, he ascended and went immediately to the control console for the security cameras. He studied the multiple TV monitors. They all showed the inside of the cathedral. He turned off switches until all the screens that showed the path to the pulpit were blank. Finally, he turned off the whole system. Fred listened for people sounds. Hearing none, he went into the nave and down into hell. The devil's face leered at him as he climbed to the stage and from there up to the pulpit.

For a moment, Fred had the urge to address the empty seats. No grandstanding, he thought ruefully. As he started down the tight, spiral staircase to the basement, the lights dimmed suddenly. Fred started in surprise. Soon after, a growing hum of electrical equipment filtered up from beneath him. The stairs ended in a corridor that went under the stage. Small elevators and trap doors dotted the underside of the stage, obviously designed for the bishop's grand productions. He paused again, listening to see if he had any company. No voices. Good.

The only other exit from the area under the stage was a door facing him. Fred tried the handle—locked. He considered his options for a minute, and decided to press ahead. He extracted the package of lock-picking tools from inside his jacket. He inserted the small leg of the L-shaped torsion tool into the keyway and applied a gentle downward pressure. He then selected what he guessed to be the right 'rake' from his kit, and inserted this slender tool. A couple of strokes of its gently curved end and the tumblers fell into line. His training had paid off and he was in. A metal staircase led down to the ground floor. Ahead of him, a recessed door looked inviting. He turned the handle—not locked—and pushed it open to see a line of four viewing coffins resting on cloth-covered tables. A sickly smell percolated out. Fred backed away quickly.

To his right, the corridor ended at a door to what must be the administration building that he had seen in his walk around the complex. He easily passed the door and found the back of a storage rack. The box-filled shelves hid the door. He went to the end of the rack and saw other shelves holding office supplies. The thought crossed his mind that this might be the best way in, if he had to come back. He retreated, locking the door behind him.

At the far end of the corridor he saw metal tracks and what had to be the workshop door. Three more recessed areas were visible in a concrete wall on his right. He walked toward them.

The first entrance had a metal frame covered with wire mesh—locked. Above it was a fixture with a pair of lighted panels. The red light shone. The companion green panel was dark. Fred could make out a high-voltage, step-up transformer, the source of a loud humming noise. Heavy electrical cables fed what looked like the back end of an accelerator. This equipment faced an area surrounded by concrete blocks and lead bricks. A large brown gas cylinder—deuterium—was mounted on the blocks. This setup, added to the cathedral's minimum electrical load, explained the need for the powerful external electrical feed he had seen. More important, it meant that Gene's hunch had been right. The bishop was making tritium to refurbish a nuclear weapon. He wasn't a pretend Bond any more, this was the real thing. He felt both elated and scared—a strange high.

Fred walked to the second room, which had a similar entrance, giving a view of the back side of two pairs of thick rubber gloves that were attached below a glass window. The area behind the glass contained handling devices and banks of chemical equipment. Fred recognized it as a glove-box for dealing with dangerous materials. To the left, a table held electronic circuit boards. He continued on to the final room. Its door was solid metal, and the tracks from the workshop disappeared under it. All the doors had been locked. A camouflage-painted crate sat on the floor to the side of the workshop door.

As Fred approached the crate, reaching for his camera, he heard voices and a scraping sound from the direction of the workshop. The stairs were in full view. Fred ran to the crypt, opened the door enough to squeeze in, and closed it behind him. The rancid smell near the third coffin made him want to gag as he edged his way to the coffin closest to the far wall. He slid under the table and pressed a handkerchief to his nose. The voices drew closer. When the bishop and Carl raised their voices, occasional words filtered through to him.

"...longer till we have enough?"

"...months...."

"Can you speed...?" The bishop sounded exasperated.

"No, too dang...."

"Dismant...."

"Finished."

"Good."

A pause before someone opened the door. Fred heard the bishop say, "Get on with the separation. I need to communicate with my flock."

The bishop came into the crypt and turned on the lights. Thank God the tablecloth hung nearly to the floor. Nevertheless, Fred turned toward the wall to hide his pale face and hands.

He heard the bishop's footsteps getting closer, and glanced over his shoulder to see the bishop's boots inches from his face. The squeak of hinges indicated that a viewing lid was being opened. Fred struggled to breathe quietly and not gag. For once, he welcomed the aroma of Old Spice.

"I must get you oiled," the bishop said. "I don't want to disturb you, old friend, even though you didn't tell me your last secret."

Fred heard the sound of a lid closing, and a second lid, further from him, opening. "May you rest in peace," the bishop intoned. "You told me everything we needed to know. Sleep well."

The footsteps moved away. The bishop's voice rose. "Unfortunate *dawn* of the *spevil*, you don't deserve to see the daylight ever again. Why didn't you tell me about your heart condition? Why did you die before telling Carl how the safety system works?"

Fred could hear the bishop banging on the coffin lid.

"Tell me the code!"

Silence.

"But you can't. No matter, Carl says you've told us enough for him to bypass the system, but at what cost? Your stench already tells me that you are rotting in hell."

The bishop moved toward the door and stopped at the fourth coffin.

"Who shall we put in you? Do the authorities have someone snooping around?" The bishop stood in silence for minutes before walking out and down the corridor.

Fred waited until he heard the door into the workshop close before crawling from under the table. He turned on his flashlight and carefully opened the viewing lid. A white shirt with dark stains covered what had been the chest. The hand and wrist bones lying across it were tied with cord. Gray hair on the skull showed the man had been older, maybe fifties, Fred thought. He took a photograph.

He studied the outside of the cheap, pine casket for clues, but found none. He moved to the second coffin; walnut with brass fittings. The lid was locked. He decided not to force if open. As he was about to move on, he noticed a label sticking out from underneath it. Most of the word 'Amarillo' was visible. He was about to investigate the third coffin when a sound from the direction of the workshop made him decide not to push his luck. He proceeded quickly under the stage, making sure the door locked behind him, and went via the pulpit and nave, up to the organ loft. Fred switched the cameras back on, and confirmed that they were all working, before edging out of the front door. He hugged the wall as he went down by the side of the buildings, and returned to his car using as much cover as possible.

Fred drove back to the motel and called Gene Kowalski.

"I got in," he said proudly, not waiting to find out who had answered the phone.

"Good for you," a woman replied, giggling. "I'm sure Gene will be very proud of you."

"Sorry, ma'am."

"I'll get him."

Fred gave a detailed account of his exploit, at the end of which Kowalski said, "You're convinced no one saw you except the janitor?"

"Only the janitor, and there's probably a poor view from the cameras when I came in and when I went to turn them off."

'Is the janitor going to be a problem?"

Fred who hadn't given him much thought, replied quickly, "I doubt it, sir. He didn't seem very bright."

"Good. Now tell me about the basement."

"One door facing the stairs, the crypt. I'll get to that. And three rooms with concrete walls leading to the workshop doors I told you about."

"How do you know?"

"The tracks from the workshop lead into the first room. Heavy metal doors. I couldn't see inside. One other thing." Fred paused. "Back in L.A., you showed me a picture of a shipping crate for a bomb. There was one like it on the floor. "

"Did you get the serial number?"

"Couldn't. I heard people coming."

"What about the other two rooms?"

"Wire mesh was on the doors so I could see in. The first has what looks like an accelerator."

"What do you think it's for?"

Glad that he had read the books that Kowalski had recommended, Fred said, "Judging by the deuterium bottle strapped to the wall, I reckon they're accelerating deuterium ions into a target to make neutrons, and bombarding lithium to make tritium."

"What I feared. Carry on?"

"The second room has a glove box, and from what I overheard when the bishop and Carl came in, I think it contain separations equipment."

"It would make sense. Separation for the tritium" Kowalski said.

"Yes, sir."

Gene sighed. "Most of the original tritium in the bomb would have decayed to helium. They would need to remove the helium and replenish the tritium. I'll get someone to check how much power would be needed to make the tritium at a high enough rate to be useful."

"Another thing, when I was going to the basement, the lights in the cathedral dimmed, and I heard the equipment start up." Fred said. "Scared the shit out of me. And when I left, the inside of the cathedral was warm. I believe they'd turned the air conditioning down. I think they're trading off the lights and air conditioning against the power for the accelerator. That way the load won't have a huge bump in it."

"I'll get someone to check that, too. Now, you mentioned hearing the bishop...."

"I was about to look at the crate and take photos of the labs...incidentally there's an area for building electronic circuits...when I heard voices. It sounded like the door from the workshop was opening. No time to use the stairs, so I went into the crypt and hid. God it stank!"

"And?"

"I could hear bits of a discussion between the bishop and Carl, I think. The bishop seemed angry that work wasn't going fast enough. He mentioned separation." Fred tried to remember more of the conversation. "I think Carl said 'dangerous,' but I didn't hear all the word. Oh! And the bishop said 'dismant,' and Carl replied 'finished.'"

"Dismantling, I bet. They've got a bomb there. Shit!"

Fred listened, expecting Kowalski to continue.

Silence.

"Sir, you there?"

"Sorry. Trying to figure out what to do. I need more ammunition, and I need to figure out how to get around Wheaton. Anything else?"

"Yes. There were four viewing coffins on the tables in the crypt. The bishop talked to them."

"Stank, you said. One of the bodies must have been a recent death. And he did what?"

"Called them his flock, and the skeleton above me 'his old friend.'"

"You looked in this coffin?"

"Yes. It contained a long-dead, older man. There was a label sticking out from under the second coffin. I could make out one word—Amarillo."

"Did the bishop have anything to say?"

"He seemed happy with that second one, but called the third, 'the *dawn* of the *spevil*.'"

"Any more photos?"

"No. The place stank, and I heard a noise. I got out."

"You did the right thing," Gene said. "It scares me to say it, but the coffins you looked in probably held the 'disappeared' technician from the Pantex Plant. It seems that the bishop may have may have moved to Amarillo after he left Salt Flat. I'll check that out."

After a moment's silence, gene continued, "I just realized something else. The other coffin may contain the remains of an engineer from Sandia National Laboratory, who vanished some months ago. As I said, given the stench, that poor guy may have died very recently. I need to find out what his field was."

Fred heard papers being shuffled.

When Kowalski came back on the line, he said, "Great work, Fred. I need to think. I'll call you back in half an hour."

Fred took the opportunity to remove his shirt, shave, and rinse out the dark coloring from his hair. His hair wasn't blonde enough yet, but it would do if anyone he knew saw him. He'd bleach it again later. The cotton pads had fallen out of the shirt pocket. He threw them in the trash and put on a fresh shirt, then watched TV until his cell phone beeped.

"I've decided what to do," Kowalski said. "First, I should tell you that the person I recognized in the photo of the cast and crew was Chuck Steak. He was a ringer for the Reverend Jenkins, now Bishop John. You were right in guessing that Chuck is the bishop's son."

"And you agree that would make the bishop the secret sponsor."

"I think so, and we need to find out exactly what he plans to do."

"Did the bishop have any other kids?" Fred asked.

"I don't know. Wait a minute. Chuck's got to be at least thirty, right? When I met the bishop, his wife was pregnant. Ready to pop, as I remember. So there should be another kid, about thirty years old."

Fred suddenly had the sad feeling that he knew who this kid was. He debated whether to say anything. This was not a time for secrets, he realized reluctantly. "I wondered about Georgie, but the way she acts doesn't fit with the bishop I've seen and heard. I guess it's got to be Millie…though she doesn't look that old. But she and Chuck help out the bishop at the cathedral."

"You don't sound happy?"

"I like Millie. Problem is she's not interested in me."

"Fred, in our business you've got to check everybody. Try again."

"Bogdan says that Millie doesn't go out much because she's looking after her invalid mother."

After a long pause, Kowalski mused, "If her mother is the reverend's wife I saw thirty-one years ago, I'm not surprised. She looked beaten down even then."

"I'll try and find out. Anything else?"

"Yes, I'd like you to get photos of the apparatus you saw."

Fred's stomach started to churn. "You mean go back into the basement, sir?"

"Your call, but we need more evidence. I'll get back to you when I've figured out what to do." Kowalski sounded tired. "Incidentally, let's stop this sir business. It makes me feel old. I'm Gene."

Fred turned the phone off, and ran to the bathroom. Millie's face flashed in front of him. He tried to focus on something else but failed. Surprisingly, after a while, he felt hungry. An image of a large steak replaced thoughts of Millie. Why the hell not! He'd heard good things about a truck stop east on I-40; a good place to waste some of the time until he checked out on Monday morning and returned to Albuquerque.

* * *

"This Monday, let us give our individual thanks to the Lord for a successful weekend," the bishop said to his assembled staff. After a minute of silence, he raised his head. "Amen. The contributions from our congregation exceeded my expectations. Thanks go to Mary Gimenez and our ushers for their efforts." As usual, the bishop did not give a dollar figure. And, as usual, nobody asked for one.

One by one, the bishop's staff reported on their areas of responsibility. Finally, the building manager made his comments. "Your exhortation to keep the cathedral clean seems to have worked, Bishop. Only a few gum wrappers and programs inside the cathedral, and very little trash outside. The crew picked up only one bag of trash. The far parking lot's another matter." He added diffidently, "Maybe you could say something next week?"

The bishop turned to his secretary. "Make a note. Anything else?"

"No, I don't think.... Wait a minute. I nearly forgot. The janitor said the man you had doing penance did a good job cleaning off the graffiti in the men's restroom."

The manager's look of pleasure at bringing the good news dissipated quickly as the bishop rose to his feet.

"What man?"

"I-I-I d-don't know," the manager stammered.

The bishop stood and raised his arms. "*Jell* the *tanitor* I want to see him in my office as soon as possible," he barked. "Then get Carl."

The bishop looked out of his office window, tapping the glass impatiently. When Carl knocked and came in, he turned slowly. "Carl, someone was snooping around yesterday."

"What makes you think that?"

"The janitor found a man cleaning graffiti in the men's room. This man said I'd given him the task as penance for drinking too much."

"And you hadn't?"

"Right. The janitor's useless. All he could say was a tall man with brown hair, a fat face, glasses and unshaven." The bishop started pacing in front of his desk, and added angrily, "Of course, to that dwarf everybody's tall."

"What do the cameras show?"

"Nothing useful. Someone came in near the end of the service, but you can only see his cap. He has his head down and the people standing at the back blocked a good view. Later, there's a moving shadow in the entrance. It looks as if someone went out the front door."

Carl pursed his lips. "Not good. What do you want me to do?"

"Go over the recordings and time them. You can use the length of the service as a gauge. I suspect that this man may have disabled the system while he snooped."

"Any ideas who?"

"From what my friend in Los Angeles told me, it could be the FBI. He swears that none of his people are involved, although one of his deputies is suspicious about me."

"What if your friend's lying...or doesn't know?"

The bishop stopped. "If you're right, it could be someone on the set."

"Fred?" Carl questioned. "Miguel says he asks lots of questions."

The bishop stared at Carl. "You're not saying that because of Georgie?"

"No. There's something about him that doesn't add up. Why's he doing this job?"

"He looks like Chuck. What's the probability Homeland Security would have an agent that resembles him? Anyway, I heard that he's doing it because he got laid off. Could happen to anyone."

"Do you want me to check him out?"

"No. I'll deal with it. But I'd like you to put alarms on every door into the basement." The bishop sat down behind his desk. "How's everything else going?"

"I told you yesterday. Slow but fine." Carl gave a sly grin. "We've got to be careful, or we'll all be going to heaven...or hell, faster than we planned. I'll check those recordings." Carl left.

The bishop worked on a sermon until the telephone rang forty-five minutes later. He picked it up and listened, his face hardening, before interrupting the speaker, Carl. "So, there's a small blip in the picture an hour after the end of the service, and you think forty minutes or so is missing. Damn him to hell!" The bishop prodded the off switch and dialed. "We had an intruder in the cathedral on Sunday. I don't know who, but it could be someone from the cast or crew of *Oscars*. Don't ignore anyone, but check on Frederick Howard."

The bishop paused, before saying, "I'm not joking...." "You heard what...?" "He went to Amarillo. I don't like the sound of that. Why'd he go...?" "To visit relatives...?" "Just check him out." The bishop slammed the phone down, and clasped his hands in prayer. "Lord, help me get through this challenge, so that I may slay the idolaters."

16.

"I called you on the weekend," Millie said, when Fred came onto the set, which represented the apartment of Achmed, the terrorist. "You weren't there." She sounded disappointed.

"Why did you call?" Fred asked, eying her Monique von Minx outfit, and caught off balance by her implied question. He tried to be gallant, saying, "If I'd only known, I wouldn't have gone out of town."

"Oh. Where were you?" Millie sounded as if she was trying to make conversation.

"To see my uncle and aunt in Amarillo. It's the first weekend Sebastian hasn't needed me. I just got back this morning."

Millie sniffed. "You didn't miss much."

"What happened?"

"We rehearsed the scene where the terrorists get together to make their final plans for blowing up the Oscars. Chuck kept forgetting his lines. Sebastian threatened to replace him with you."

"God, no."

"It won't happen. Chuck reminded Sebast'ard that he, Chuck, had brought in the sponsor. End of discussion." Millie looked as if this would be the end of their discussion.

Aroused by her sexy outfit and amazed that Millie had called him, Fred decided to seize the moment. "What did you call me about?"

"Nothing much.... I wanted to get your opinion on some things." Millie said, sounding as if the moment had passed.

"Happy to be—"

"Children, stop chattering." Sebastian Agincourt bellowed. "We've work to do."

"Dinner tonight?" Fred whispered as Millie walked away.

She turned. A smile appeared slowly on her face. She nodded.

Fred was pleased with himself until he remembered what Gene and he had discussed. Had the bishop told Millie to check on him? Damn job. His expression must have told Millie that something was wrong. Her smile disappeared. Fred attempted a grin. It felt phony. As Millie looked away, he noticed Georgie studying them, a quizzical look on her face.

Agincourt bellowed, "Take your places, children...and Bogdan.... Action!"

CHUCK, *slouching in a chair.* Achmed, you still haven't explained what sketch we're going to use to get into the Oscars. ACHMED, *takes a deliberated puff on his hookah before answering. Chuck looks impatient.* We're going to celebrate Sebastian Agincourt's masterpiece with a sketch about *Bye Bye Oscars*.

MONIQUE, *looking amazed at the ingenuity of the plan applauds.* Neat idea, but why do you think the organizing committee will agree?

ACHMED, *smiles, flashing an exaggerated set of teeth.* Money and blackmail always work.

CHUCK. Wait a second. *He looks pleased with himself.* Bye Bye Oscars doesn't have bombs. It has mutant jellyfish. What do you say to that?"

ACHMED, *after taking another deliberate puff on the hookah.* Exactly. The main jellyfish will remove its disguise, unveiling a terrorist. A second jellyfish will reveal the bomb hidden in a large Oscar statue.

MONIQUE. Brilliant. *She jumps up and does a provocative dance in front of Chuck.*

"You're standing between me and the camera, you bitch," Chuck leapt to his feet.

"Cut. Cut. Chuck, sit down!" Agincourt wipes his brow. "Boggie, take it from 'A second jellyfish.' Monique, jiggle your booty a little to the left."

Bogdan, who has been ogling Monique, looks around. "What?"

"Second jellyfish, Boggie," Agincourt said. "Action!"

ACHMED. A second jellyfish will reveal the bomb hidden in a large Oscar statue.

MONIQUE. Brilliant. *Monique jumps up and does a provocative dance to the side of Chuck.*

CHUCK, i*gnoring Monique, whines.* I suppose that would work.

MONIQUE, *giving a final flick of her hips.* Achmed, you look as if there's more.

ACHMED, s*miling evilly.* The terrorist will announce that this is an advertisement for the new *Bye Bye Oscars*. Then he'll do the countdown.

CHUCK, s*howing surprise.* The committee will accept that?

ACHMED. It's amazing what free cocaine, pretty girls...and prettier boys can achieve.

CHUCK. I've got to admit. It's a good plan. So, are you the terrorist?

ACHMED, t*akes two puffs on his hookah.* No.

CHUCK: *Looking worried.* It's not me, is it?"

ACHMED. No.

CHUCK, h*opefully.* Monique?

ACHMED, s*haking his head.* Sebastian Agincourt assisted by Lance Dupree.

MONIQUE: *Doubtfully.* Will they agree?

ACHMED. As I said, cocaine, girls, and boys. One way or the other.

"Hold it." Agincourt, who had been reading ahead of the action, rose out of his chair. "Lancie, come to my office now. We need to talk."

"I didn't expect that," Fred muttered.

"Nor did Sebastian. I told Lance, he wouldn't like it," a voice whispered.

Fred turned to see Georgie. "So you knew?"

"Chuck suggested it."

"You're kidding?"

Georgie shook her head. She appeared to be about to add something, when Agincourt and Lance reappeared.

"Slight change in the script." Sebastian motioned to Lance, who handed material to Bogdan, Chuck, and Millie. "Bogdan, you take it from Monique's last line. Action!"

ACHMED, t*alking in a wooden manner.* Sebastian Agincourt is very proud of his work. He's happy to do it.

"Cut!" Agincourt buried his head in his hands, and mumbled sadly, "Boggie that didn't sound enthusiastic. Do it again. Action!"

ACHMED, s*miling unconvincingly.* Sebastian Agincourt is very proud of his work. He's happy to do it.

CHUCK. So you and I don't have to be there?

ACHMED, w*ith an evil grin.* Right.

CHUCK. What about Monique?

MONIQUE. I'll be making sure you don't screw up again. We'll eliminate the Oscars once and for all, and the world will be a better place. Losing the genius of Sebastian Agincourt is a high price to pay. But he will die for his art.

Georgie prodded Fred in the ribs and made a gagging gesture with her fingers.

Fred smiled in agreement.

The ludicrous dialogue did not seem to concern Agincourt, who stood, beaming. "That's a wrap, folks. Now we'll rehearse the sketch that will be performed at the Oscars. There aren't many lines. Remember, Bogdan, you've got two roles. The final take will be at the casino this afternoon, where we'll have the dancers."

"Wait up, Sebastian!" Lola Paramour, dressed in red matador pants, stiletto heels, and a sweater that strained against her uplifted, historic boobs, strode onto the set and confronted Agincourt. "What about me?" she pleaded. "You're always giving stuff to Bogdan. I want my turn." She held a handkerchief to her face. Tears rolled down her cheeks cutting ravines in her makeup.

"Reminds me of the surface of Mars," Georgie sniggered.

"Put the onion away, Lolly. I've got something for you," Agincourt rose and clasped her hand. "We can rehearse in my office. The rest of you be back here by eleven."

Lola took the handkerchief and dabbed her cheeks. "Thank you, Sebastian," she said coquettishly, and weaved away, her ankle bracelets jangling.

"She's got enough metal down there to qualify for a chain gang," Lance said cattily in a stage whisper. "For Sebastian's sake, I hope she takes it off before they *rehearse.*"

By eleven-fifteen, the cast in street clothes had gathered on the set. Agincourt motioned for silence, and said, "We're going to act as if this scene takes place at next year's Oscar ceremony. I've heard that Sunny Jamaica will be emceeing, and I've asked Bogdan to play that role. Of course we don't know what Sunny will really say, but that doesn't matter for the moment. Go for it, Bogdan. Action."

SUNNY. And now, what you've all been waiting for. *He raises his arms.* Bye Bye Oscars!

Agincourt interrupted. "At this point a troupe of dancers looking as if they've come off the set of *The Ten Commandments*, will roll an oversize Oscar onto the stage. Some celebrity from the audience will make a comment. Lola, you're up. Action!"

LOLA, L*ola Paramour playing herself.* Show us the bomb! *A command echoed around the theater by the audience.*

SUNNY. Patience, children, all in good time.

The dancers perform semi-erotic gyrations to the Bye Bye Oscars' theme music. Chuck Steak, minces onto the stage. He is followed by Monique von Minx. They cavort in front of the Oscar statue.

AUDIENCE MEMBER. Ten, nine—
SUNNY. Wait for it, I have the honor."
Chuck and Monique cavort wildly around Sunny who moonwalks around the bomb pretending to start the countdown. Agincourt and Lance come on stage. They are followed by two mutant alien jellyfish.

Agincourt interrupted the action to say, "At this point the orchestra starts playing the *We'll Meet Again* song that graced the end of *Dr. Strangelove or: How I learned to Stop Worrying and Love the Bomb.* Action!"

The first jellyfish removes his disguise revealing an Achmed. But then Achmed removes his heavy beard and moustache revealing an alien. The second alien jellyfish pushes a lever on the back of the Oscar. It opens up to reveal a fake looking bomb with fins, a large red-lit, countdown clock, and a huge red button. The alien lunges for the button.
SUNNY, *grabbing the alien's arm.* It's my gig. Ten, nine—
AUDIENCE. Eight, seven, six, five..., *The alien starts to remove the cover from the second jellyfish.* four, three, two, one.
SUNNY. Bye Bye Oscars! *He pushes the button. A blast hurls clouds of confetti over the crowd. The scene switches to a family watching their television. They and the audience roar with laughter, not noticing that the alien has started the real countdown. After ten seconds the screen goes blank.*

As the scene ended, Chuck stormed up to Agincourt. "Sebastian, who's playing me?"

"You of course," Agincourt replied, making a screwing motion with his finger to the side of his head.

"I'm not going to get blown up. Let Fred do it."

"It's a scene from the movie, Chuck."

"I suppose so, but what if we get invited to the real thing?"

"Fat chance," Lance sniggered.

"A lot you know," Chuck retorted, adding coyly, "My backer thinks he could arrange for an Agincourt retrospective. Good for publicity."

Fred made a mental note to tell Gene about the possibility that, for once, Chuck had said something useful. It might explain what the bishop was up to, assuming he was the secret backer.

"You never told me that," Agincourt said, thoughtfully. "I like the idea. Maybe I could meet our angel and discuss it."

"I think that might be possible." Chuck flounced away, looking over his shoulder to say. "And I'll do the scene...but no real bomb. Right?"

"Right," said Agincourt, shaking his head. "All of you be at the casino by one. Carl and Miguel will have the props set up. Incidentally, Fred, you'll be the first alien. Go with Lancie, he'll give you a copy of the script and get you the alien mask and the Achmed-like beard and moustache to go over it."

"Okay, boss," Fred replied, before going quickly to Millie. "Tonight, same place as before?" he asked.

"Sure. Make it six-thirty, and we can decide where to eat, then. You'd better go. Lance's looking edgy."

As Fred followed Lance, he heard someone call out, "Chuck, I need to talk to you."

Fred turned to find Georgie right behind him. She gave him a sly grin and walked toward Chuck, wiggling her backside.

* * *

When Fred pulled up outside Mrs. Chu's restaurant for their second date, Millie was waiting. She started toward him the minute he got out of his car. She must really want to talk to me, he thought, or did the bishop send her?

Millie smiled warmly, but underneath the smile she looked apprehensive. "I wasn't sure you'd really come after I said no so often."

Fred shrugged. "No problem. Where do you want to eat?"

"There's a little Italian restaurant off Candelaria. Okay?"

"May I drive?" Millie asked. "I'm hopeless at giving directions."

"What did you want to talk about?" Fred asked as Millie drove to the restaurant.

"The remake of *Bye Bye Oscars*. It's weird, don't you think?" Millie said, glancing at Fred.

"How so?"

"Fred, you've only been with us a short while. It's changing all the time. Now I hear that the backer...whoever that is...wants it wrapped up next month."

"I hadn't heard that."

Millie pursed her lips. "Promise you won't tell anyone."

Fred nodded.

"When we started *Bye Bye Oscars*, I remembered I'd seen Lance at the cathedral a number of times. I asked him about it. He made me swear I wouldn't tell anyone, and he said that Chuck brought him a lot of new pages for the script."

"Does Sebastian know?"

"I.... Oh dang. I missed my turn." Millie pulled through a gas station and went round the block. "I need to concentrate. Wait till we get to Alfredo's."

Alfredo's was a restaurant built into what was a cleverly remodeled service station. Inside, the designer had gone wild with Italian scenes, plastic vines, strings of garlic and herbs, and empty Chianti bottles to disguise the building's origins. The hostess seated Fred and Millie under a gaudy painting of the Bay of Naples.

After giving the waiter their orders of steak *pizzaiola* and veal *romana*, Fred turned to Millie. "You were telling me that Chuck has been feeding parts of the script to Lance. Do you think he writes it?"

"Chuck acts stupid, but I'm not sure he's as dumb as he acts. He's not like that with the bishop. But write scripts? I don't see it."

"Who then?"

"The only person I can come up with is the bishop. He and Lance write the scripts for the religious movies I've been in."

"Lance?"

"He's very religious," Millie said.

Weird, but it added up with what Chuck had let drop on the set. Maybe the bishop had designed the movie as a vehicle to get the missing nuke into the Oscars ceremony. The movie was a rehearsal for the real thing.

"Interesting theory, Millie," Fred said, "and that would make the bishop the backer. Why do you think he's doing it?"

She shook her head. "I've asked myself that question many times. The only thing I can come up with is that it's all part of his hatred of Hollywood.... You've heard him at the cathedral, right?"

"Yeah."

"I just have this strange feeling," Millie said with a little shiver. "The bishop scares me. You haven't seen him really lose his temper—"

Fred had an instant image of the bishop's shoes as he screamed at the third coffin. "You mean like when he does one of his spoonerisms. I *san't cay* that I have."

Millie giggled. "Fred, you're awful." Her smile disappeared as quickly as it had come. "No. It's much worse than that. He gets quite vicious in the way he talks to people. Honestly, he sounds...insane. Then there's Chuck, and Georgie's pretty weird." Millie raised her eyebrows. "But you'd know that."

"You've got me there." Fred bowed his head, while trying to decide how far he could push her.

The waiter came to the table with two Diet Cokes, bread sticks, and house salads. When he'd left, Fred said, "Do you think the bishop's crazy? What if he really wants to get a *Bye Bye* sketch at the Oscars and blow it up?"

Millie looked startled for a moment. Then she chuckled, "You mean like dynamite? Be realistic."

"Good point. Maybe he just wants an opportunity to be able to preach at the ceremony. He could work his way into a sketch. Good publicity for the movie and for his church."

"You're probably right. It's not my business what he does with his money." She looked reflective, apparently wrestling with what to say, finally blurting out, "What about you, Fred? You don't fit."

"You're telling me," Fred responded quickly to defuse the comment. He wondered how she would react if he explained that he was "Secret Agent Schwarzmuller," and not just a scared country boy from rural Texas. The thought that Millie been sent to find out crossed his mind. "This is the weirdest set I've ever been on. Frankly, I needed the money. In a way I'm glad we'll be wrapping up because I think I've got a proper job lined up."

"Good for you. Where is it?" Millie asked casually.

"Back in Austin."

"Oh." Millie sounded disappointed.

Fred tilted his head, and said, "You told me you wanted to get out."

"Wishful thinking, Fred," Millie replied sadly.

"Sorry," Fred said, reaching across the table to pat her hand. Millie turned her hand and grasped his. *Good moment to find out about her.* "You've never said anything about yourself. Do you come from here?"

"No, I'm from Texas, too. Just outside…."

At that moment, the waiter brought their orders and Millie said, "Let's eat. I'm starving."

As they finished their entrees, Fred said, "Sebastian outdid himself. I thought we were going to have dancers dressed like ancient Egyptians."

Millie made a face. "That was the original plan, but he didn't want to pay for the costumes; hence the Aztec dancers who were already in the casino's show."

"I doubt anyone will notice the difference."

The waiter delivered the gelato they'd ordered. They took turns taking spoonfuls until the last little bit, which they clashed over before dueling to get half each.

"That last scene is strange, you know," Fred said. "The remake has the terrorists introducing a bomb that an original alien sets off, while Agincourt is in the scene. How the hell did someone come up with that, rather than simply redo the whole movie?"

"Simple," Millie replied. "It allows Sebastian to use old material with the mutant alien jellyfish. There's a scene that was done before you joined, where Achmed is brainwashed by the aliens. It's supposed to explain Bogdan's expressionless face."

"I thought he was always expressionless."

Millie raised her eyebrows. "Sure, but he doesn't know it."

"Okay. Let's assume they manage to get a sketch into the Oscars, probably the last scene, and the bishop wants to use the stage as a pulpit. Do you think the bishop will be able to persuade Sebastian to give up his role?"

"The bishop's very persuasive, but my guess is that he would oust Lance."

Fred nodded agreement. "Makes sense."

The waiter placed the check on their table. They shared the cost, went to Millie's car, and drove back to Fred's car, chatting about acting jobs they'd had.

Millie leaned across and kissed him quickly on the cheek. "I had a good time," she said.

Fred moved toward her. Millie held up her hand. "I've got to get home."

"Doing anything on the weekend?" Fred asked hopefully.

"I wish I could. It's difficult."

She sounded so unhappy that, for a moment, Fred was tempted to reveal who he really was. But an image of Gene lecturing him about not falling into a honey trap stopped him. "Maybe at church on Sunday?" he said as he got out of the car.

"I hope so. I really like you, Fred, but there are problems."

"The bishop?" Fred asked without thinking.

"What?" Millie shook her head, looked confused, and drove away before he could say anything else. As she turned onto the road, Fred saw her pick up a cell phone.

Fred drove home thinking that, despite Gene's warning, he could not see her being a part of blowing up the Oscars. He parked and took a circuitous path to his door to avoid the inevitable talk with Bogdan.

As he came through the door, Fred sensed that something was wrong. Glancing back, he noticed that the hair that he had licked and stuck in the door jamb was not in its place. Unfortunately, he'd been thinking about Millie and hadn't paid attention when he'd opened the door. He might have been the cause. Nevertheless, it would be worth checking all the traps that he'd placed.

The magazines on the coffee table were arranged in the pattern he had left. The sliver of paper stuck in a drawer in the kitchenette was in the correct place. His clothes on the shelves in the bedroom closet were just as he had left them. Wait a minute.

In the stack of socks, the dark blue and black ones were mixed up. Not the way they had been.

He stood for a minute absorbing the realization that someone had searched his apartment—someone experienced. This wasn't his James Bond fantasy. He could be in real danger. Millie could have set him up. What had she said?

"I think it would be easier if I drive." It had sounded strange.

And she was using the cell phone when she left him: Calling to warn her accomplice in case he was still in the apartment. Him, who? Chuck? Not likely. More likely it would have been Carl or Miguel. Well, they wouldn't have found anything. Homeland Security professionals had checked every single item that he had brought with him. He kept anything that might connect him to Homeland Security in a safety deposit box at his bank. His cell phone had been in his pocket, no numbers in its memory. Gene's address was in his head.

Fred sighed and went into the kitchen, got a beer from the refrigerator and settled in front of the television. He flicked through the channels, finding a rerun of *Get Smart*: If only real life were like that show. The truth was the bishop suspected him, and someone had been sent to search his apartment. Suspected him of what? The only possibility was the break in. Someone had noticed the time break in the tapes or, more likely, the janitor had mentioned the man cleaning off the graffiti.

Fred was tempted to call Gene, but decided to check for bugs first, sleep on it, and call Gene in the morning. He turned his attention back to the TV and flicked channels, hearing a commentator announce that there were ominous signs that a growing island in the Thera bay in the Mediterranean could lead to a catastrophic eruption—more devastating than a hydrogen bomb. "Just what we need," Fred muttered and dozed off on the couch.

* * *

"You didn't wake me up, my dear," the bishop said, looking at the clock on his desk. "I was working on next Sunday's sermon and lost track of time. What did you find?"

He listened patiently for a few minutes before interrupting. "So the bottom line is nothing ties Mr. Howard to the Feds. What about photographs and addresses we could check?"

He listened again, tapping his pen on the desk. "I see, only a photo of his parents, but no addresses. He's either clean or very careful. I'll think about what to do. You look after yourself, y'hear."

The bishop replaced the phone and sat back, staring at a photograph of a group of men that included Ambassador Wheaton.

17.

At ten the next morning, Fred called Gene Kowalski's office. Linda answered. "Hang on a minute, Fred, he's preparing for a meeting with the ambassador." When she came back on the line, she said, "He can give you five minutes. I'll put you through."

"How's it going?" Kowalski asked. "Find anything out about Millie?"

Fred sighed. "Unfortunately, yes. After she said she wanted to talk to me, we went out to dinner. Millie seemed genuinely worried about the movie. She thinks that the bishop has been writing a lot of the script, and may be feeding it to Lance through Chuck."

"How does Agincourt like that?"

"He doesn't know."

"I wonder what that means. Anything else?"

"Millie says she's scared of the bishop; feels there's something funny about the whole setup." Fred stopped talking while he considered what he wanted to say next. Kowalski remained silent. "I was tempted to open up to her a bit."

"My God, you didn't."

"No, and a good thing, too. When I got back to the apartment, I checked all my little traps. Nothing wrong except someone had mixed up my blue and black socks."

"You think Millie kept you away deliberately?"

"I don't know what else to think. She insisted I leave my car, and she drove us to the restaurant. As soon as she dropped me off, she got on her cell."

"Hmmm, seems like too much of a coincidence. You'd better be careful with her." Gene paused. "Anything more on the bishop's activities?"

He's angling for a *Bye Bye Oscars* sketch at the next Oscars ceremony." Fred added reflectively. "To be clear, the end of the movie felt like a rehearsal for the real thing."

"Fred, who would be in that scene?" Kowalski asked quietly.

"At the moment, the emcee, Sunny Jamaica, dancers, Chuck and Monique or their stand-ins, Sebastian and Lance, and alien jellyfish-slash-terrorists; the scene is confusing. One of the jellyfish hides the bomb."

"No bishop?"

"Not sure. I jokingly asked Millie, 'What if there's a real bomb?' She looked startled, and then added that the bishop might replace Lance and use the opportunity to deliver a sermon on national TV."

"That could be the reason the bishop's supporting this charade," Kowalski said. "So that he can shove his message in Hollywood's face. But would the bishop get himself blown up...? Fred, why did you say Sunny Jamaica? No one knows who's going to be emcee next year, let alone the one after."

"Apparently, Agincourt does know."

"But the movie isn't finished."

"That's what I thought. I was wrong. I'm going to be out of a job soon, unless I'm needed for retakes."

"That and the fact that someone searched your room, alters things. We don't have as much time as I thought. Don't search the cathedral again. It's too risky. I'll have to work out some other way."

"Okay," said Fred evenly, trying not to show his relief.

"Call me at home tonight. I hope to have made some decisions by then. In the meantime, find out how long Agincourt needs you. Tell him you have a job possibility. Take care." Kowalski hung up.

*   *   *

This time, Gene Kowalski had brought reports to read while he waited to see Ambassador Wheaton, but Mrs. Rogers ushered him straight in.

"Sit down, Kowalski," Wheaton said, motioning to a chair. "We need to deal with this quickly. I have to go to D.C. *The president* asked for *me* to brief him."

Wheaton wants me to congratulate him, Gene thought. Screw that. "Anything important?"

"Of course. Like the secretary and I, the president is concerned about the nuclear threat. I have decided to do something about those lost weapons in West Texas that everybody seems to have dropped the ball on."

"What exactly do you have in mind, Ambassador?"

"You were going to get one of those new-type detectors with improved penetrating capability that should make it easier to detect nuclear weapons. Have you got it yet?" Wheaton's tone of voice implied that he thought it unlikely.

"There's a company in Wisconsin that recently tested prototypes of a commercial unit."

"See if you can get one." Wheaton looked pensive. "Warn them that this is a security issue. Now, I had thought about doing a massive search. But, on further consideration, I concluded it would be better to keep it low key until we see how this device works." Wheaton clasped his hands together and rested his chin on them. "I want your best operative."

On the spur of the moment, Gene Kowalski decided that he needed to get Fred out of Albuquerque and this opportunity would do it. "The person to operate it would need the right scientific background. Fortunately, we have just the man—Frederick Schwarzmuller."

"I may need to see his—"

Mrs. Rogers knocked, poked her head around the door and said, "Limo's here, Ambassador. The driver says traffic is bad, and you need to leave now." She handed him a sealed envelope. "Your briefing material's in here."

"President's waiting. I don't have time. Go ahead with this Schwarzmuller." Wheaton said brusquely. "But I'd like to meet him." He crammed the envelope and some papers into his briefcase, and rushed out.

"Thank you for intervening, Mr. President," Kowalski said, bowing to the photograph on the wall.

*   *   *

"Gather around children," Sebastian Agincourt said to the assembled cast and crew. "I am both happy and unhappy to say that the shooting of the remake of *Bye Bye Oscars* is complete. Many of you will be moving on to other and, I hope, better things. Georgie has your final paychecks."

"I thought we still had scenes to shoot, Mr. Agincourt." Fred interjected, hoping for some confirmation about what he had worked out was happening.

Agincourt stroked his goatee, apparently to show that he was choosing his words carefully. "That had been my original plan, but I gather our backer would like to see it finished now. He feels that the timing will be better for releasing *Oscars*. While I still have to make the final editing, there is a rough cut of the complete movie. I'll screen it tonight at our farewell party, here at the studio." He looked at Fred as if expecting another question.

Fred hung his head.

"That reminds me, Fred," Agincourt continued, "Miguel will be here soon. Help him remove the Hollywood sign. City Hall's complaining. Anyway, we've got all the publicity we need."

"Do you want me to go with them?" Georgie asked.

"No. I want to talk to you, Lola, Boggie, and Lance in my office. I'll see the rest of you here at seven." Agincourt strode off the set.

Millie tapped Fred on the shoulder. "When will you be going back to Austin?" she asked.

"Not sure exactly, I'll have to check with the company. What are you going to do?"

Millie shook her head. "Back to being a temp-secretary, I guess."

"The bishop doesn't have anything for you?" Fred tried to make the question sound innocuous.

Millie looked surprised. "I don't think so. He hasn't mentioned another movie, and Sundays at the cathedral doesn't pay much."

Maybe I'm wrong about her being the bishop's daughter, Fred wondered hopefully. "See you tonight."

"Fred, I'd love to, but Mom's not been feeling well."

"I hope she gets better soon." Fred smiled. "I live in hope that I'll turn up and you'll be Monique."

Millie made a face, and left.

* * *

"May I speak to Gene, please?" Fred asked, trying not to repeat his previous mistake.

When Kowalski got on the phone, he wasted no time in saying, "I'm sending another operative to investigate the cathedral, starting with monitoring the power load. I want you to go to Madison, Wisconsin."

"Madison?" Fred exclaimed. "What for?"

"Two things that will get you out of Albuquerque. First, I'm concerned about this Georgina Williams woman. I want you to find out her original surname and what happened to her husband."

"You think she's connected to the bishop?"

"Don't know, but she sounds like a more credible candidate than your Millie. I had the FBI check Millie out. Her surname, believe it or not, *is* Smith...not Jenkins. She's twenty-four and she does live with her invalid mother."

Fred tried not to sound relieved as he said, "Make sure this operative knows the other way into the basement."

"Right. You can fill me in later. Now, after Madison, you'll be going to West Texas to look for the second bomb. You'll need a detector. There's a small company in Madison that has put together a portable, fusion neutron source and detector. They've agreed to let us borrow a prototype, provided that later they can use the fact that Homeland Security is testing it for publicity."

"Are we going to tell them about the bomb?"

"Hell no! They think it's going to Fort Bliss to look for unexploded ordinance on the firing range."

"I'll need their address."

"That can wait. Pack up as soon as you can and come to L.A.
"I'll give you all the information then. Oh, and the ambassador wants to meet you." Kowalski's laugh was hollow as he put down the phone.

* * *

Fred got to the cast party at 7:30. He weaved his way through the props from *Bye Bye Oscars* that were positioned around the soundstage in Agincourt's studio. The Hollywood sign, which he and Miguel had removed from the mountain, provided a lighted backdrop for a mariachi band. He headed toward the bar for a beer. Georgie waved to him, as he passed a margarita fountain. She was gyrating on the dance floor surrounded by the three Hummer salesmen who had been co-opted by Agincourt. Three women, holding margaritas, watched from the crowd by the bar. Wives or girlfriends Fred assumed by their resigned expressions.

As Fred reached down into the cooler for a *Dos Equis*, he felt a hand on his butt. "Cool it, Georgie," he snapped, standing up.

"It's not only Georgie who fancies you," Lance retorted.

Shit, Fred thought, as if he didn't have enough trouble. "I don't dance that way, Lance. I always lead," he said as he backed away.

"Fine with me."

"You know what I mean?"

"Unfortunately, yes." Lance shrugged and started to leave.

"Have you seen Millie?" Fred asked.

"Not—"

"I don't think she'll be here," Georgie interrupted. "I heard she had car trouble."

"Oh."

"Don't look so disappointed, Fred. Come on, let's dance." Giving him no time to argue, Georgie grabbed his beer, put it on the table, and dragged him onto the floor.

Fred held his right arm out and started to place his left around Georgie's waist. She ignored his move, and threw her arms around his neck grinding her body against him. Over her shoulder, Fred saw the three salesmen glaring. Their women, laughing, raised their glasses in a toast. Fred grinned self-consciously.

At the end of the song, Fred tried to extract himself. "Thanks, Georgie. That was great. First time I've done it in public with my clothes on."

The mariachis continued onto another song. "I'm not done," Georgie said, grinding harder.

Fred was saved by a tap on the shoulder.

"My turn," Chuck said.

"Bug off," Georgie retorted.

Fred dropped his arms and Chuck wrestled Georgie away. As he walked away to retrieve his beer, he heard Chuck speak sharply to Georgie, but he couldn't make out the words.

"I see you're having a good time," Agincourt said. He was holding a margarita in one hand and holding up Lola with the other. "That Georgie's a problem. Have you met Lola?"

"Only briefly." Fred, remembering a scene from the first *Bye Bye Oscars*, took her hand and kissed it. "An honor to make your acquaintance, ma'am."

"You're a fine-looking boy, and so gallant. Isn't he, Sebastian?"

"Good memory, too," Agincourt replied. "We must mingle. That reminds me, I haven't seen Millie."

"Georgie says she has car trouble."

"Odd. Give her a call. I'll pay for a taxi."

Fred took his beer, went into the parking lot and called. When someone picked up the phone, he said, "I hear your car's bust."

"You must want Mildred," a weak voice replied. "I'll get her.... Millie."

"It's not just bust," Millie sounded angry. "Someone let all the air out of my tires. How did you find out?"

Fred was about to say, Georgie, but decided not to tell Millie, nor to mention Agincourt's offer of a taxi. "Somebody at the party. Does that happen a lot in your neighborhood?"

"No. First time."

Fred remembered Georgie's self-satisfied look as she told him about Millie's car having a problem. No good telling Millie.

To hell with Georgie. "Agincourt was asking after you. You should come. I'll pick you up."

"I'm not sure."

"I've got a pump. I'll fix your tires."

"Well, I—"

Chuck heard her mother in the background say, "Mildred, you need to get out. Say yes."

After a moment's silence, Millie said, "Fred, I'll be ready by the time you get here. 324 Rio Grande Circle, off Alameda. But I can't be home late."

"No problem."

A short while later Fred pulled up alongside Millie's car, and connected his pump. He had just finished the second tire when he heard the door open.

"I'm Millie's mother. She'll be ready in a minute."

Fred looked up to see a small woman with bright green eyes, magnified by glasses, perched on the edge of her wheelchair. "I'm Fred, Mrs. Smith."

"You stay out as long as you like, Fred. Millie fusses over me too much."

"Mother!" said Millie, appearing behind the wheelchair. "Let Fred get on with the tires."

"We're having a nice visit," her mother replied, holding tightly onto the handbrake to prevent Millie moving the wheelchair. "Such a good looking young man."

Millie shook her head and walked back down the corridor. "Ready in a minute," she called out over her shoulder.

"She's needed a man in her life ever since my husband abandoned me, you know."

"When was that?" Fred asked as he started on the fourth tire.

Mrs. Smith put her hand to her forehead, and answered uncertainly, "It seems like forever.... I'm not sure. Millie would know."

"Know what?" Millie said, unlocking the brake and pulling the wheelchair back down the corridor.

"When your father left."

Fred heard a part of Millie's comment. "You're confused again, mother. He...."

"So, when did he leave?" Fred asked when Millie returned.

'Forget it, Fred. Let's go to the party," Millie responded sharply.

*   *   *

"Millie, I'm so glad you could make it," Agincourt said, rushing up to embrace her. "I'm going to miss our little *tête à têtes*."

"So am I, Sebastian," Millie winked at Fred over Agincourt's shoulder.

Lola peered at Millie, slurring her comments. "You look different, dear, and such pretty hair."

"She's the second best looking woman here," Fred said, squeezing Millie's hand and eyeing the subtle way her simple dress flattered her figure, after you, Lola."

Millie watched Lola totter away, supported by Agincourt. She giggled. "Fred, you are awful, but I feel better. What's Agincourt offering?"

"Other than the margaritas and beer, he's got food from your favorite restaurant *Mi Casa Su Casa*." Fred pointed to where tables next to the large Oscar statue overflowed with tacos, enchiladas, and steaming trays of fillings for fajitas. "I'm going to get a beer. What do you want?"

"Diet Coke, please," Millie replied. "I'll get fajitas for both of us and find a table."

When Fred sat down, Millie said, "Look at Chuck and Lance. Do you think they're an item?"

Fred glanced at the two of them gyrating suggestively in the vicinity of a sensuous dark-haired woman. "Nah. Chuck's just acting up as usual."

When Millie finished her last bite of fajita, she said, "That's better. Now, we can dance."

While they were sedately turning around the floor, Millie said, "Are you always so nice to women?"

"You mean Lola? I thought she needed a boost."

"And me?"

Fred pulled back and looked at her. "You're so beautiful I'm having a hard time not throwing you over my shoulder and taking you home."

Millie let go of his hand, looking quizzical.

"Sorry. It's the caveman in me."

Millie took his hand again and smiled. "You don't need to try so hard. I like you."

"But you wouldn't go out with me."

"I told you why. My mother," Millie said. "And then you started dating Georgie."

"I made a big mistake." Fred laughed. "But the only thing you and I ever do together is eat. I suspect there's more to dating than food."

"Georgie show you that?" Millie asked gently.

"Ha, ha. You know what I mean."

"Yes." Millie buried her head in Fred's shoulder. Her voice was muffled as she added. "It's too late. You're going to Austin and I'll be stuck here."

"I'll call."

Millie lifted her head. Her eyes were moist. "Promise."

Fred held her more tightly. "Yes." Out of the corner of his eye, he spotted Georgie edging toward the door. "Want to get out of here?"

Millie hesitated briefly. "Okay. I need to go to the ladies' room first."

"I'll see you outside."

Fred hurried after Georgie. He found her pacing between the rows of parked cars. She was still a distance from his Avenger. "Georgie," he called out, keeping a couple of rows of cars between them, "don't even think about it."

Georgie turned and glared. "You spoil all my fun." She held up a short screwdriver.

"It's not funny. Be a good girl and go back in and piss off the Hummer guys' dates."

Georgie hung her head like a guilty child, kicked a tire and edged away, turning to say, "I'd give you a good time. She won't do it, you know."

Fred didn't think so either, but he flashed a broad smile. "We'll see."

He watched Georgie head toward the door. She bent over and mooned him briefly. She was not wearing panties. Millie came out of the studio. They passed warily, like a pair of cats.

"What happened?" Millie asked when she reached Fred's car.

"Georgie was about to do my tires, too."

"You reckon she did mine?"

"That's my guess. Forget about it."

Fred opened the passenger side door. "I'll take you home, or…?"

"Home, Fred. I can't leave Mom for too long at night."

When Fred parked outside her house, Millie leaned over and kissed him passionately on the mouth. She pulled back the second he reacted. "I do know what to do, Fred, but I'm Millie Smith not Monique von Minx." She opened her door and got out.

Fred rolled down her window. "Will I ever get to go out with Monique?"

Millie smiled, cocked her hip, and struck a Monique pose. "That depends on whether you keep your promise to stay in touch."

"I promise," Fred replied sadly, thinking about the long drive to L.A. he had to make the next morning.

* * *

"Did you manage to follow him?" the bishop asked, when Miguel came into his office.

"Yes, Bishop."

"And?"

"He went to his bank and then onto I-40, but he didn't go east. He went west. I stayed behind him for about fifty miles."

"Interesting. So, he's not going to Austin."

"Maybe he's got another movie job in Los Angeles." Miguel suggested.

Bishop John stroked his beard. "Then why did he say Austin? There was nothing in his apartment, but I think we need to do some more checking on that young man."

"One other thing. Last night, he didn't park at the apartment."

"Another reason to check him out."

18.

A day and a half after leaving Albuquerque, Fred pulled into the underground parking garage of an innocuous-looking government building near the Los Angeles airport where he had received his briefing on nuclear weapons. He took the elevator to the third floor and went to Gene Kowalski's office.

"Long time no see," Linda said smiling from behind a blooming potted plant. "How were Albuquerque and *Bye Bye Oscars*?"

"Different."

"I saw it years ago. Crazy movie. I've got to see the new version. What did you do?"

"Looked for a guy driving a Hummer into a parking lot, and got interviewed on the red carpet."

"Is that all?"

"No. I was stand-in for the lead, Chuck Steak, and I helped build a Hollywood sign."

"Chuck Steak! You're kidding?"

"Not his real name. They used me for most of the rehearsals. Chuck wasn't very good at turning up on time."

"What an idiot."

"Kept me employed. See if you can detect which alien I am."

"They still have aliens?" She shook her head bemusedly.

"Aliens."

Fred pointed at the flowers. "What's the occasion? Should I have brought something?"

"Gene gave them to me for Marilyn Monroe day."

"I never heard of that."

"August fifth, four weeks ago, the day Marilyn died." Linda smiled. "After work, I went to the Westwood Memorial Park to put the flowers by her crypt. It's a little tradition with us; I take her flowers, and Gene gives me a potted plant. He says it's to show I'm more permanent."

"Nice. You mean she's not in Forrest Lawn?"

"No. It's a small cemetery. Come with me some time. There's lots of celebrities there: Natalie Wood, Dean Martin—"

"Thanks, but it's not really—"

"Roy Orbison, Jack Lemmon, Walter Matthau. I could go on."

"Sounds interesting. Some other time."

The red light flashed on Linda's telephone. "He's ready. Go on in."

Kowalski motioned for Fred to sit. "We've got fifteen minutes before leaving for the ambassador's office," he said. "I've lined up an agent for Albuquerque. You said you knew another way into the basement of the cathedral?"

"Yes. It's through a storage area in the administration building. I'll draw the layout."

Gene handed over a pad and pencil. After Fred had finished, Gene asked, "When's the best time for him to try?"

"During the service, I think. Nobody's outside." Fred shook his head. "But if they figured out what I did, they could be watching for that."

"Good point. Storage area, you said. Storage for what?"

"Office supplies."

'I'll talk to our man, and suggest he find a way to make a delivery." Gene typed a note into his computer.

Linda opened the door. "Mrs. Rogers called. Something's come up. You need to go."

When they reached the door to the ambassador's office, Kowalski turned to Fred. "Wheaton's an asshole. Be careful what you say. Oh, and call him ambassador." Gene opened the door to reveal the ambassador talking to Mrs. Rogers.

The ambassador looked up briefly and waved them toward his office. A few minutes later, he joined them. "What kept you so long?"

"Traffic. We came as soon as we got the message," Kowalski replied steadily.

"So this is...." The ambassador looked at his calendar. "Mr. Schwarzmuller."

Fred held out his hand. Wheaton ignored it and put down the calendar.

"Kowalski tells me that you're well qualified to look for these mislaid weapons." The ambassador clasped his hands together. "Exactly what qualifies you?"

"An engineering degree and physics courses I took at Texas, sir."

Wheaton unclasped his hands, picked up a file and looked down at the first page. Kowalski glared at Fred and mouthed Ambassador.

"I see that your transcript supports that statement. Tell me how you propose to proceed."

"Gene…Mr. Kowalski wants me to go to Wisconsin first to learn how to use a new type of detector. The company that makes it will loan us a prototype…, Ambassador."

Wheaton smiled without looking up and said, "And then?"

"I'll go to Fort Bliss. When they've mounted the detector on a vehicle, I'll go to the park and recheck places the previous investigators thought were the best bet."

Kowalski interjected, "I'll make sure that Fred has a marked-up map of the area."

"What about back-up, Kowalski?" Wheaton asked while studying a picture on the wall of himself and the vice president on a hunting trip.

"I agree with your suggestion that we should keep it low key this time around. Fred's cover will be one we used before. He's looking for a lost missile."

"Oh." The ambassador clasped his hands. "I had thought that he could say he was photographing the local flora for an article, and maybe a book."

"In a military vehicle with a large boom extending from it?" Kowalski asked.

"I suppose not." Ambassador Wheaton placed his hands flat on the table. "Of course, the bomb has probably rotted by now."

"Sir." Fred was unable to contain his surprise.

"You disagree?" The ambassador looked at his calendar again. "Mr. Schwarzmuller."

Fred ignored Kowalski's look, and said, "It seems unlikely in the dry desert air, Ambassador."

"That's what Kowalski said. We'll see. I agree with the proposal. Franklin suspects you may need some extra funds. I should be able to arrange that. Remember that I shall want regular reports." Wheaton looked at his watch, and pressed a button on his desk. A moment later, Mrs. Rogers opened the door.

"Is my material ready?"

"Yes, Ambassador. I've everything for Albuquerque in a file."

"Thank you." Wheaton sounded irritated.

Kowaski exchanged glances with Fred. "What's the occasion, Ambassador?"

"Bishop Orpheus John, whom we have discussed before, is holding a fundraiser for our gubernatorial candidate. He asked me to attend. The vice president will be there."

"Have a good time." Kowalski signaled for Fred to follow him and they left.

When they were safely down the corridor, Gene said, "Oh, God. I wonder what that asshole's going to say to the bishop."

"Or, what the bishop's going to say to him," Fred added.

"No point in worrying. We need to get you off to Wisconsin. First, we need to speak to that other political misfit, Franklin Jackson."

"Why do we have to see him?"

"He handles requisitions."

Franklin Jackson's office, on the fourth floor of the building in which Gene was housed, boasted a large window, a huge wooden desk and a sofa. African carvings stood on the floor and on side tables. His framed degrees in law and accounting were surrounded by photographs of Jackson with various political and business notables. "Gene, great to see you," Franklin Jackson enthused as they entered. "And this must be Frederick Schwarzmuller. A pleasure to meet you, sir." He rose from his chair, all five foot six of him, and came around his desk extending his hand.

Different from the ambassador on the surface, Fred thought, glad that Gene had warned him that the act was a carryover from Jackson's job as a lawyer for a tobacco company.

"You're request came in yesterday." Jackson said to Kowalski. He picked up a folder. "Borrow a prototype…a little unusual. I've been trying to understand how to proceed."

"Can't we use a standard requisition?" Kowalski asked quietly.

"Question of liability, Gene. We can't have the government being held liable for damage." Jackson appeared pleased that he had discovered an obstacle.

"I understand that Frederick—may I call you Fred…?" Jackson didn't wait for an answer, "will be taking this device to the wilds of West Texas."

"Franklin, Fred plans to use it, not blow it up," Kowalski snapped.

"That's a relief," Jackson said sarcastically. "Nevertheless, I am not comfortable signing for this without a clear statement from the company relieving us of all liability. And I have just heard that company may not do that."

"Do I need to talk to the ambassador?"

Jackson cut off that possibility quickly. "No need. We discussed it before, and he agrees that it would be unwise to borrow the device in these circumstances."

"So we have a Catch-22. The company may not lend the device unless we accept liability, and we won't accept liability."

"It appears so."

Fred, seeing Kowalski clench his fists out of Jackson's sight, decided to intervene. "Could we purchase the detector?"

"In principle yes, Fred: however, we would need the funds in hand, and for an item of this cost it would take time to go through channels."

"What channels?"

"Basically…me…and the ambassador."

"But the ambassador asked us to do this." Fred failed to hide his frustration.

"I don't think it's wise to criticize Ambassador Wheaton," Jackson said.

"I wasn't. I'm trying to understand why he asked us to do this if it wasn't possible."

Fred was about to say more when Kowalski signaled him to stop.

"The ambassador does want us to do this. I think he may have mentioned it to the president. Is there some other avenue?" Kowalski asked.

Jackson pursed his lips and looked thoughtful. "There is one way, lease to purchase. That way, if the item were damaged, we would buy it. This approach would allow us time to put a purchase order through the system." He paused. "I'm assuming that Fred does not destroy the device within the next three months."

Kowalski looked hard at Jackson. "And you would sign for this?"

Franklin Jackson smiled. "Not exactly. Since you would have to guarantee the purchase within your funding, you would be the principal signatory. I would initial to show that I agreed that you had the funding. You do have it, don't you?"

"I think so. The ambassador said he could provide funds if needed."

"Good, that's settled. Send the paperwork to me when it's complete." Jackson closed the folder and picked up the phone. "I have to make a call. As always, nice to see you, Gene. A pleasure to meet you, Fred."

As they left office, they heard Jackson say, "I can make our tee time. Don't leave without me."

When they returned to Kowalski's office, Fred mused, "He and the ambassador had it all arranged, didn't they?"

"Of course. The whole charade was to get me to take responsibility in case something goes wrong. You be careful you hear!"

"Yes, sir," Fred made a clownish salute.

Kowalski stared for a moment, then reached into his desk drawer, pulled out papers, and handed them to Fred. "You'll pick up the map at Fort Bliss. I've got a report in here on the detector. Read it. I'm sure the company will give you a briefing…which reminds me about our first meeting. Try not to be flippant. Okay?"

"I'll try, boss."

"Good. Now I've got to calculate how much money I'll need from the supreme asshole."

As Fred was leaving, he remembered a question he had. "Can you remind me what that vanished engineer from Sandia did?"

Kowalski's expression became grim. "He was an expert on the design of safety systems and triggers for nukes."

Fred's chest tightened. "Oh, God."

* * *

After nine days of relentlessly chasing paperwork through the system, Kowalski managed to get the final approval for the detector. The following day, Fred left for Wisconsin. He arrived in the evening and checked into a motel. After unpacking, he sat on the bed and surfed through television channels, catching the tail end of a news item that showed the Hollywood sign that Miguel and he had put on Sandia Mountain. Memories of Albuquerque flooded back, mostly of Millie. He decided that this would be a good time to call her.

"It's me, Fred," he said when she answered.

"How's Austin?"

"Wee-ell, I'm not exactly in Austin."

"Are you in Albuquerque?" Millie sounded hopeful.

"No. Madison, Wisconsin."

"Oh…. What are you doing there?"

"On business for a temp job. How are you doing?"

"Okay, I guess. Like you, temp jobs, mainly." Millie sighed. "You should have been here a few days ago. The vice president came. I met him."

Fred responded as if he hadn't known about the event. "Wow. So that's why our Hollywood sign was on TV."

"The bishop organized a fundraiser in the Convention Center. *Bye Bye Oscars* was the theme at the party." She giggled. "I went as Monique."

"Lucky V.P. How did the bishop use the movie?"

"After the dinner, Bogdan, Lola, Chuck and I did a skit with the Oscar statue and the bomb, and Sebastian showed clips from the movie."

"Wish I'd been there."

"You were; in a couple of scenes standing in for Chuck."

God. I hope the ambassador didn't recognize me, Fred worried. "Meet anyone else interesting?"

"The candidate seemed nice enough. A number of guys tried to hit on me."

"Not surprising, in Monique's outfit."

"Yeah." Millie sighed again. "Sebastian and cast members got to sit at dinner with some of the dignitaries. I was next to this real jerk, ambassador somebody or other."

"What did he do?"

"Squeezed my knee and said he was concerned about my security."

"What a shit," Fred muttered.

"I managed to drop my coffee in his lap. He had to go to the men's room to clean up. He was walking kinda funny when he returned. Sebastian lectured me about being more careful, but it was worth it."

"Good for you. So the ambassador missed the movie clips." Fred tried not to sound hopeful.

"No. He got back in time." Millie paused. "He and Sebastian were talking about it when I left."

Fred lay back and worried. What had the ambassador and Sebastian been talking about? What the hell, if the ambassador had recognized him, he'd hear about it.

"You still there, Fred?"

"Sorry, just wishing I'd been with you."

"Keep in touch."

"I promise."

"Take care," Millie said.

Fred thought he heard her blowing a kiss before she hung up.

Millie sighed as she put the phone down. She closed her eyes, picturing Fred's smiling face. What had Fred asked? Something about the ambassador seeing the clips. There had been something. What was it? Well, if it came back to her, she'd tell him the next time he called.

19.

The following morning, Fred headed south on Route 51 through the outskirts of Madison to an industrial area. The company, Fusion Solutions, was situated just beyond and to the back of a Health Center. He parked in front of the newly painted blue building, and went to the front office. While he was signing in, a door behind the secretary's desk opened and a bespectacled, bearded man walked in. "I'm Doctor Harold Klevan, and you must be Mr. Schwarzmuller," he said, holding out his right hand.

Doctor and mister. Not an auspicious introduction. "I'm Fred. Pleased to meet you."

Klevan opened the folder and handed a form and a pen to Fred, saying, "You'll need to sign this proprietary information form, Mr. Schwarzmuller, before I can brief you. Later you'll sign a receipt for the equipment."

Worried that his purchasing department had fouled up, Fred said, "I'm not taking it with me."

"No, one of our technicians will drive it to El Paso. Fort Bliss, it says here. He'll assemble the system and check out the detector for you before handing it over."

"Phew, for a moment."

Klevan looked over his glasses. "We'd hardly let you carry tritium onto a plane," he said as Fred signed the form.

After Fred had signed, Klevan handed it to the secretary and said, "We'll go to the assembly area, Mr. Schwarzmuller."

Klevan used a key card on the door and ushered Fred through. "We have to watch out for industrial espionage and radiation, and we have a radioactive material—tritium," he volunteered. "Can't be too careful."

The door led into a corridor with offices. Klevan took Fred into a high bay area.

Their first stop was a bench at which a technician was inspecting pieces of equipment.

"Joseph here will be delivering the equipment to Fort Bliss," said Klevan, pointing. "This is Mr. Schwarzmuller."

Joseph held out his hand. "Pleased to meet you Mr….."

Fred shook his hand. "Fred."

"Joe." Joseph smiled and returned to work.

"That's real neat," Fred exclaimed, looking at a spherical, open-wire basket. He reached down and picked it up. "Make a good softball." He pretended to pitch it toward a poster board.

"What do you think you're doing?" Klevan snapped. "Put it down. Now Joseph'll have to clean it again."

"No problem," said Joe, grinning.

"Sorry. I wasn't thinking."

"Obviously not." Klevan shook his head. "What you just mishandled is an inner molybdenum electrode that fits concentrically inside a second electrode—this steel sphere." He pointed to two halves of the sphere. "It's a vacuum chamber.

You can see the supports for the molybdenum wires. In operation, we apply a high voltage between them."

"Why molybdenum?" Fred asked.

"To handle the power," said Klevan, adding, "When we apply a voltage, the wires glow white hot."

"And this is what produces the energetic neutrons?"

"You're getting ahead of me." Klevan pointed to the first of four poster boards.

The first board had a heading: "Using Fusion Neutrons to Detect High Explosives." A list of topics appeared below the heading:

Fusion neutron production by Inertial Electrostatic Confinement (IEC).
History of IECs.
Interaction of neutrons with high explosives.
Fusion Solutions portable explosives detector.

Underneath the list was a cross-section of the assembled pieces that Fred had just seen.

Klevan indicated the first line. "The basic operation of an Inertial Electrostatic Confinement device is really simple. We evacuate the sphere and put in a small amount of fusion material—heavy hydrogen in common parlance—either deuterium or a mixture of deuterium and tritium." Klevan stared at Fred as if to make sure that he had his full attention. Then he took a deep breath and continued. "Deuterium and tritium are the heavier isotopes, i.e., types, of hydrogen. Deuterium occurs naturally as one part in 6,500 of all hydrogen. Tritium is radioactive and decays. It's made by bombarding lithium with neutrons."

Fred, who had been thinking longingly about how good a Moon Pie would taste, said, "That I do know." Then, thinking back to the accelerator he'd seen in the cathedral, he failed to suppress a shiver.

"Are you cold?"

"No, just remembered something unpleasant about accelerators."

"I see. As I said, we apply a high voltage to accelerate the ions toward the center of the two spheres. A few hit the wires, but the rest converge on the center, collide and some of them fuse and produce multi-megavolt neutrons—that's MeVs."

"The point being that MeV neutrons can penetrate a long distance, even through metals," Fred added.

"I had planned to get to that," Klevan said sharply as he moved to the next poster board. It carried a photograph showing a bright glowing spot inside the wire sphere. "With deuterium, the fusions produce 2.45 MeV neutrons. With a mixture of deuterium and tritium we get even higher energy neutrons, 14 MeV."

"So tritium's better if something is buried deeper?"

"Obviously." Klevan's eyebrows twitched. "In fact, you should be able to detect material down to at least five feet in earth with the tritium."

"Who came up with this idea?"

"Philo Farnsworth, inventor of the basic technology for television. He had the idea in the 1950s. In the '60s it was pursued further by Robert Hirsch at Illinois University who demonstrated that you could make interesting numbers of neutrons. It fell out of favor for fusion as other approaches showed more promise. Then different applications, such as explosives detection led to a renewed interest in Japan at Kyoto University, and here in the States at Illinois and Wisconsin. We've combined the best features of all of their work." Klevan pointed at a second photograph that showed a sphere with steel projections and cables arranged symmetrically on the outside. "Here we have added individual ion accelerators to boost the yield."

Fred peered at the photograph, trying not to think about Moon Pies. "With those bits sticking out of the detector, it looks like an old-fashioned naval mine."

"Hardly." Klevan turned to the next board. "Explosives Detection. This isn't the only possible application, Mr. Schwarzmuller. We're also looking into making a small system for production of radioactive isotopes for medical purposes," he explained before turning to the table under the title. "The key point for explosives detection is that the neutrons interact with elements, such as nitrogen, carbon, oxygen, hydrogen, and chlorine, and produce energetic gamma rays. The signature of the gamma signal from a detector can be used to identify the presence of explosives. Any questions?"

Fred, who already knew most of what Klevan had told him, did have one concern. "Yes. Is the detection automatic in the system we're borrowing, or will I need to do some analysis?"

Klevan snorted. "You're lucky. We just completed the electronics and software to give you a simple readout. It will even include an estimate of the type of explosive. We've programmed in quite a number of them." Klevan looked closely at Fred. "I hear that you'll be testing for unexploded ordinance. I was also informed that you want us to add a detector for delayed neutrons from uranium. Why is that?"

"Fort Bliss has some areas it would like to clear," Fred replied smoothly. "They're also concerned about depleted uranium. It's used in some armor-piercing shells, you see."

Klevan raised his eyebrows. "Part of the 'War on Terror,' I suppose."

Fred could tell that Klevan wasn't convinced by the cover story, but answered evenly, "Fort Bliss is an artillery base."

"My company is pleased to help. This final board shows a schematic of our system. The IEC and the detector are mounted on telescopic booms. The power supplies can be put on a vehicle."

"Do you use the vehicle's power?"

"No, we prefer to use our own batteries, charged by a portable diesel generator. On their own, the batteries have enough charge to run the whole system for about twenty minutes. Note that the high voltage won't come on until the IEC boom is extended beyond fifteen feet. While there is neutron shielding on the backside of the source, we need distance to reduce the neutrons coming back to the operator. It's also smart to have extra shielding on the vehicle, if you can stand the weight."

"What about personal-shielding...like the apron for dental X-rays?"

"Good idea. Joe, please make a note of that." Klevan did not wait for a response, but continued his discourse. "You'll be using the deuterium-tritium system so you have to be more careful," Klevan added pointedly. "You're too young to be losing vital capabilities."

Fred saw an instant image of Monique von Minx. "Thanks. Can I see the equipment now?"

"Sure. One other thing, we pulse the source of radiation. That makes it easier to detect the real signal above any noise. Follow me. We have a complete assembly in the lab over here. I'm not going to take you in. We'd have to give you a radiation badge and check to see you didn't pick up any contamination. You can see the operation through that lead glass window." Klevan indicated a small window above a desk that held a rack of electronic equipment. "Sit at the table."

Fred sat and, through the window, saw a telescopic arm reaching out over a ten-foot-square wooden box filled with sand.

"Our own little desert," Klevan said, smiling mirthlessly. "Your job is to find the explosive that I've buried somewhere."

"So we're using the tritium device?"

"Not this time, just deuterium. Tritium's too expensive. Let me show you the controls and the detector read-out." Klevan reached over Fred's shoulder and flicked a switch. One by one, a series of lights came on indicating the sequence of evacuation of the sphere, introduction of gas, and readiness of the power supply.

"Everything else is controlled from this portable computer keyboard in front of you," Klevan said. "Switch it on. It'll ask you for a password. Type in Farnsworth."

Fred followed the instructions and a series of icons appeared on the left side of the screen.

"Now, move the cursor to that icon of a building and click it. You'll see an example of what happens when an explosive's detected."

Fred clicked the icon. Bells pealed and a colorful animation of a large explosion appeared. Seconds later, the word Semtex came onto the screen. "Wow, that's great."

"Our computer programmer came up with it." Klevan's voice dripped disapproval. "Next, before we apply the high voltage, I want you learn how to move the IEC arm over the box. In the system that you'll get, the detector is also mounted on the

240

arm. It can move a few inches, and automatically positions itself for optimum signal."

"How do I control the arm?"

Klevan pointed at the computer screen. "Click the boom icon, and when the program comes up, click Go. A small, radiation-hardened, video camera mounted back on the boom will show you a picture of what's in front of the source. The cursor indicates where the source is pointed. Move the cursor to move the source."

Fred followed the instructions and a picture of the sandbox appeared. He moved the cursor. The boom jerked forward.

Klevan grabbed Fred's arm. "For heaven's sake, don't rush it. Pretend that this is your first date."

This comment triggered another image of Millie. "Sorry. What happens if I ram the source into something?"

"The final movements of the boom are powered hydraulically. There's a pressure sensor on it. The minute the pressure exceeds a preset level, the boom freezes in place. It will not move again until you punch this icon." Klevan pointed at an icon marked retreat. The apparatus will then recover from your mistake."

"What if I want to push it closer?"

Klevan looked disapproving, but answered, "Click the retreat icon twice and the boom will continue forward again. I strongly recommend that you do not use such a maneuver."

"When I moved my head, the view looked odd," Fred said.

"That's because there's a mirror. We try to avoid line of sight even with the lead glass in that window. Joe will bring a lead glass window to Fort Bliss."

"The IEC's that dangerous?"

"At full power with 14 Mevs, and one pulse per second for an hour, you'd likely die."

"Wow! I'll be real careful."

After a couple more attempts Fred was able to move the source smoothly over the box. As he panned over a far corner, the bells pealed again and a colorful picture of a huge explosion appeared. Seconds later, the word Semtex came onto the screen.

"Good, you found it," Klevan said.

"Is it really Semtex?"

"Of course not. We don't use real explosives inside the building. You found a surrogate."

"Does that mean I could get false readings?" Fred asked.

"Occasionally, maybe. But you can always crosscheck by clicking that icon that says 'Second Opinion.' It'll look at the data using a different algorithm. Usually sorts out the bad guys. Better to be safe than sorry…particularly in your case."

And up yours, too, Fred thought. "Should I try again?"

"I think that will be enough." Klevan removed Fred's hand from the keypad. "You will need to do another run through with Joseph at Fort Bliss. In the meantime, please study the manual."

"I have a question."

Klevan tilted his head expectantly.

"The area I just covered was very small," Fred said. "How far can I raise the unit off the ground, and still get a useful signal?"

"Good question. I'd intended to mention it, when I got distracted by your baseball stunt. Obviously, it depends on what's there and how deep it's buried. I think you should start with the unit five feet off the ground, with the beam pointing down and slightly away from you. That way you'll be scanning roughly ten feet out from the unit. If you get the slightest indication of a hit, lower the unit and try again. The strength of the bell sound is proportional to the signal.

"Thanks, I'll remember to do that."

They returned to the office. As Fred signed for the lease, Klevan said, "Remember that this is a lease to purchase. If any damage is incurred...." He did not elaborate.

"Don't worry, I'll look after your baby," Fred replied.

Klevan appeared doubtful, but shook Fred's proffered hand before leaving.

"Do you need directions to the airport, Mr. Schwarzmuller?" the secretary asked.

"No thanks. I'm not leaving for a couple of days. But you could tell me how to get to the City County building for Dane County."

The secretary took a map from a pile on a filing cabinet and marked the route from her building into town. Fred followed her instructions and easily found the parking area near the county building on Martin Luther King Boulevard. A sign in the lobby directed him to the records office in Room 110. There, he discovered that he would have to fill out an application form before being allowed to look into the records; giving the full name of the person whose birth, date, or marriage he wished to investigate. He started with Georgie's wedding, and wrote in Georgina Williams. He remembered that Gene had worked out that the bishop's second child would now be about thirtyish. If Georgie had married while still at university, say age eighteen, the marriage would have been around 1991 to 1992. The clerk accepted his form and directed him to a side room. The recent records were displayed electronically. Fred scanned through them but could not find a match.

He tried again, looking for Georgina John. No luck.

He went back to the main counter. "I'm trying to find a marriage certificate for a Georgina John. It's not working."

The woman behind the desk smiled. "Are you sure she was married in this county?"

"Yes. At least I think so."

"If you need help, the man in the office next door can do a search. It costs $7.00."

"Thanks. I'll keep trying."

She reached into her drawer. "Here's a list of common reasons for failure. The most common is that you have the wrong surname for the woman."

Fred couldn't remember the bishop's real surname without success. He telephoned Gene Kowalski. "I'm in the Dane County records office. I can't find Georgie. What would her surname have been?"

"Jenkins," Gene replied quickly. "How did it go with the detector?"

"Fine. I'll tell you about it later." Fred closed the cell phone and tried Georgina Jenkins. Bingo! In October of 1991, Charlotte Georgina Jenkins and Henry Albert Williams were married in the registry office.

Fred returned to the counter. If Georgie was as dangerous as he and Gene suspected, he needed to check one other thing. "I'd like to look at deaths," he said.

"That must have been a short marriage?"

"I guess it might have been...for him."

"You'll need to fill out another form then."

Fred completed the form, putting in Henry Albert Williams, 1992.

This time he found the answer quickly. Henry Williams had expired, or had been helped to expire, on Christmas Day, 1992. Nice present for someone, he thought. Fred completed his notes. On his way out he asked the clerk where he might find obituaries.

"So the groom died," she commented.

Fred nodded.

"You could look at old copies of the Wisconsin State Journal."

"I've got a map." Fred pulled it out of his pocket and handed it to her. "Could you mark where the Journal's building is, please?"

"Sure."

Armed with the information, Fred drove to the newspaper's building on Fish Hatchery Road. The woman at the front desk directed him to the reading room, where back copies were filed by year and month. Fred found December 26, 1992. No obituary, but there was a brief comment on an unfortunate death in the student apartments:

> *Henry Williams died in an apparent electrocution on Christmas Day. His wife, Charlotte Williams, explained to police that an electric heater, used to warm their cold bathroom, had fallen off a shelf into the bath.*

An accompanying photograph showed the grieving widow. It was Georgie with long blonde hair and no dark glasses.

Fred scanned the following days' papers. On January 5th, another brief article said that the death of a Henry Williams had been referred to the coroner.

In the January 10th paper, he found a summary of the coroner's report:

> *In the case of the death of Henry Williams, unusual markings on the neck prompted police to request an autopsy. The coroner concluded that the markings were made partly by*

the electrical cord from the heater that had fallen into the victim's bath. But, in addition, there were bruises that appeared to have been made by fingers. In explanation, the distraught victim's wife said that during her husband's convulsions, the cord had become wrapped around his neck. The other bruises must have occurred when she tried to remove the cord. The police decided not to investigate further.

Fred envisioned Georgie's face as her hands squeezed on Henry's throat. She'd strangled Henry, probably during violent sex. Deliberate or not, who could tell. Fred assumed that the electrocution had been arranged to provide a cover story. This reminded him how Georgie had laughed when she told him that Agincourt's previous assistant had been electrocuted in a bath. She had most likely committed two murders. How many more?

Fred found what he was looking for in the paper of January 16th; a photograph accompanied the obituary. Oh, God. The face staring out at him was of a clone to Chuck and…to himself. He felt as if he had committed incest. Had Georgie? He sighed and read:

Madison - Henry A. Williams, age 24, of Milwaukee, died from electrocution on December 25, 1992, ending a promising potential career as a nuclear engineer. Henry Williams was born in Milwaukee on March 13, 1968, the son of Charles Williams and Mary Jane (Tynan). He completed his undergraduate degree in nuclear engineering at the University of Wisconsin- Madison in 1990, and was pursuing a PhD in that field when he died. He is survived by his wife, Charlotte; his brother, Edward; and sister, Emily. Private family services will be held.

Fred went to the desk, and paid the fee to obtain photocopies of the articles he had read.

"It'll be a few minutes," the woman said.

He took the opportunity to go outside and call Gene.

"I got it." Fred said when Linda put him through. "Her real name's Charlotte Georgina Jenkins."

"Good work," Gene said.

"Oh, and she used to be blonde. The photo wasn't very good, but it looks like she has pale eyes, probably blue."

"What about the husband?"

"He died. Supposedly electrocuted when a heater dropped in his bath, but the way it happened my guess is she strangled him. Rough sex." Fred regretted the comment the moment he made it.

"Why do you think that?"

"There were finger marks on his throat. She claimed the electrical cord was tangled around his neck and she tried to get it off."

"You don't think that's plausible?"

Embarrassed by his slip of the tongue, Fred blurted out, "She tried it on me."

"Fred, you've got to be more careful. Investigating suspects and gathering information is okay up to a point. Again, you're not James Bond.... Nor for that matter is anyone else," Gene cautioned.

"I'm learning. I also believe she used the electrocution to hide what she'd done. Later, she may have done it again to get rid of Agincourt's assistant. That's how she got her present job."

"A true daughter of the bishop."

"Oh, and another thing, I reckon it was Georgie who searched my room, and mixed up the black and blue socks. Either she's colorblind or she kept her dark glasses on."

Fred heard the sound of clapping.

"Clever deduction," said Gene. "Wait a second. I need to get something." When he returned, he said, "I've started a new section in my file on Reverend Orlando Jenkins. Please send me copies of whatever you've found."

"Already made," Fred replied promptly. "Let me tell you about the detector. I have at last met Bond's Q—Dr. Klevan, who has no sense of humor, but he did a good job explaining the detector, and gave me a detailed manual to study. I even got to try out the detector. Neat device."

"So you're off to El Paso tomorrow?"

"The system won't arrive for a week, so I thought of dropping by to see my parents in New Braunfels first," Fred replied tentatively. He had been pumped on adrenaline ever since breaking into the crypt. Being the next Gene Kowalski, on a mission was all very well, but he felt edgy. He needed the calming influence of home and family.

"Good idea. I suspect you'll be stuck out in West Texas for quite a long time."

20.

As the plane turned into its final approach, Fred looked out of the window at the city spread out across the desert landscape. El Paso, population approximately 600,000, altitude 3,800 feet the advertisement had said, and home to Fort Bliss. How did anyone come up with that name? Not the servicemen and women who entered its gates, he guessed. As he passed through airport security, he scanned the crowd, and spotted a stern-looking soldier holding a sign with his name on it. Fred smiled and went up to him. "Fred Schwarzmuller reporting for duty, Sergeant."

"Collins, sir. Welcome to El Paso." The master sergeant's face showed no pleasure in the greeting. "I'll be working with you. Follow me."

Collins took Fred to a staff car, and then looked pointedly at the passenger doors. Fred got into the front seat.

"Has the equipment arrived yet, Sergeant?"

"Yesterday, sir. The technician has started unpacking it."

"I heard we'd be mounting it on a Jeep."

"There's been a change of plan," the sergeant replied. "We need something bigger so that you can stow everything under cover when you're driving. We don't want people seeing the equipment when you're out on the open road or parked for the night."

"So, what'll it be?"

"A modified Hummer. You may need the clearance underneath, too."

At the base, Fred received a photo-ID badge. After they had dropped off Fred's bags, they went to the workshop where the Hummer was being outfitted.

Joe, from Fusion Solutions, and an Army technician were working on the back of the Hummer. "Great to see you again, Fred," Joe said.

"Did you have a good trip?" Fred asked.

"It's a long way from Madison, but I enjoyed I-25. Never seen the Rockies before."

Fred peered into the stripped-down bed of the Hummer. "How's it going?"

"As you can see, we took the lid off. It'll be replaced with a canvas top, fixed to supports that will be rolled back electrically. In that position, the cover and supports will be over the operator's position and the front seats." Joe nudged Fred in the ribs. "Keep the sun off your bald spot."

"Thanks. Did Dr. Klevan think of that?"

"You're joking. The boss doesn't deal with human issues." Joe looked thoughtful. "He's better than he seems, Fred. Can't help having been born with pompous genes."

Fred grinned. "I suppose not."

"We've installed your operator's bench seat facing back so you'll be in front of the controls. There'll be a table in front of the bench with the electronics under it and the laptop computer on top. You can slide the laptop across the table. That way you'll always have a good view of the mirror showing the boom and the IEC. And we've nearly finished the mounting brackets for the boom." Joe pointed at the rear floor of the vehicle.

"Great, it looks like I'll be able to swing the boom out to either side."

"Yup, and out the back, too. When not in use it'll fold into the Hummer for storage, alongside the computer."

"When will everything be ready?"

"We've got to mount the deuterium gas cylinder, the sealable box for the tritium bottle, and the tank to recover the off gases. Then there's the table, electronics, power supplies and generator. Oh, and the mirror. It'll move with the boom. Couple of days, I reckon...," Joe glanced at the other technician, who nodded agreement, "and radiation shielding."

"Can I help?" Fred asked, hoping the answer would be yes. He might need to fix something when he was away from the base. Of course, Joe did not know about that.

"Umm, I don't know."

"I've nothing else to do," Fred pleaded.

"It'll get him off my hands," Sergeant Collins said gruffly.

"Thanks, Sergeant."

"Fine with me then," said Joe. "You can help right now. Put those safety glasses on and hold this bracket while I drill the holes."

* * *

Two days later, the Hummer was ready. The sergeant drove Fred to the test area.

"Remember that Joe thinks this is an abandoned part of the artillery range, sir," Collins said. "We've salted the area with eight shells, defused in case you have a problem." While he was smiling, his tone of voice implied he expected that to happen.

The test area consisted of a rough piece of ground next to a service road. Strings on short pegs had been used to map out a ten-foot grid on an area about a hundred feet on each side.

The sergeant parked his Jeep at the nearest corner, next to the Hummer. "It's all yours, sir," he said, indicating that Fred should get out.

Fred mentally compared the length of the boom—about fifteen feet—with the scale of the area. "Am I allowed to drive on the test area?" he asked.

"Your call, sir."

By this time, Joe and the Army technician had left the Hummer and walked over.

"Here are the keys, Fred." Joe said. "This one's the Hummer. This turns on the generator. This one opens the portable computer. Your password is Gallant Eagle."

"What?"

Joe chuckled and whispered, "They chose it. Typical army crap. I wanted Explosive Truffle Pig."

"Are you coming with me?"

"I have orders to leave you alone, unless you screw up." He reached back and produced a bundle of small red flags and handed them to Fred. "Drop one where you think you have something."

Fred did a quick count. "Why are there fifteen and only eight targets?"

"The army wanted it to see if you get false readings. Good luck to both of us." Joe and the other technician left to join the sergeant in the Jeep. Collins drove a short distance and turned the Jeep to face the test area.

Fred climbed into the operator's seat and studied the test area. He decided that he would drive fifteen feet from one side, with the unit five feet off the ground, as Klevan had suggested. This would allow a first check of a ten-foot-wide strip at the edge of the area. When he had dealt with that strip, he would turn around, switch the boom to the other side and repeat the process, continuing until he had covered the whole area—ten trips in all, plus a more detailed search whenever the bell rang.

Fred turned on the generator, booted the computer, and followed the prompt to enter his password. Shortly after he had flipped on the control switch, the series of lights indicated that the system was ready. He extended the boom fifteen feet, then got into the driver's seat and moved the Hummer so that the IEC unit was over the corner of the test area. Fred adjusted the rearview mirror down so that it showed the computer screen. He then reached over the back seat and turned on the high voltage.

Satisfied that everything was working, he drove slowly alongside the test area.

Nothing! What did that mean? Were the shells buried deep? Fred decided to retrace his path with the IEC at three feet off the ground. Not a single bing.

Fred raised the IEC to five feet and tried the second strip. Ten feet in, he heard a faint peal and the screen lit up briefly. He stopped the Hummer quickly, backed up a few feet, and clambered over the back of the seats into the control position. Carefully, he lowered the IEC and watched the cursor on the screen as he panned over the area around where he'd received a signal. The bell pealed loudly, the colorful explosion appeared, and "Explosive D" appeared on the screen.

"Bingo." Fred was about to jump out of the Hummer and drop a flag under the IEC, when a message in large red letters appeared on the screen, "Turn off the IEC!"

"Thank you, Dr. Klevan," Fred muttered as he switched off the high voltage.

Another message appeared, "Next time, REMEMBER!"

Fred approached the IEC cautiously, and tossed the flag onto the ground. When he turned to go to the Hummer, he saw Joe giving him a thumbs-up sign. He waved back. The sergeant's face was expressionless.

Over the next seven passes, Fred recorded ten more signals. Careful testing established that only seven were genuine. He dropped a further seven flags. "That's the eight," he said to himself. "Time to go home." As he started the Hummer up, he recalled the look on the sergeant's face when he had explained that they had salted the areas with eight shells. That did not mean that there couldn't be more. Fred drove slowly to the end of the strip, finding nothing. He turned the Hummer around and started the last traverse. In the final corner he received a large signal, checked it out and dropped the ninth flag.

"Congratulations, sir," said the sergeant as he stepped out of the Jeep. "You found the ninth shell. I lost my bet with Joe."

"Thanks, Fred. We owe you one. I can drive back a happy man."

"When are you leaving, Joe?" Fred asked.

The sergeant turned to Joe. "You agree he can handle it?"

"Absolutely. Couldn't have done better myself."

"Then you'll be leaving as soon as you're ready." The sergeant's answer brooked no argument. He looked at Fred, and said, "This afternoon, we start the serious stuff, sir."

"Right." Fred hadn't expected to be moving out so soon, but, on reflection, concluded that it would be good to get on with the main mission.

"Pleased with yourself?" the sergeant asked.

"I guess so." Fred wondered what was coming.

The sergeant smiled wryly. "You shouldn't be. I won the second bet I made with myself."

"What was that?"

"That you wouldn't check out the area of your first pass with the Hummer."

"But that wasn't in the test area," Fred expostulated.

"Mr. Schwarzmuller, I never told you it had been cleared." The sergeant pointed at the Hummer. "Never assume that an area is safe unless you know that it is. Go back and check it. I'll drive."

"He got you there, Fred," said Joe. He and the other technician were grinning.

Fred went to the Hummer and rotated the boom so that it stuck out from the back. Sergeant Collins turned the Hummer around, and after Fred had switched on the IEC he backed slowly along the original path. Two thirds of the way down the path, Fred heard a booming sound and a picture of a hydrogen bomb test lit up the screen.

"Depleted uranium, sir,' said the sergeant. "Next time, be more careful."

As he and the sergeant watched Joe drive off, Fred remembered to ask the question that had been bothering him, "Sergeant, my boss, Gene Kowalski, said that I would get a marked-up map of the area when I got here. Do you know anything about it?"

A brief flicker of a smile crossed Sergeant Collins' face. "I have the map in safekeeping, sir. We'll go over it now, and then you'll show me how to use the detector."

"We. Where will we do that?" Fred tried not to show his surprise, but could not resist adding, "And why?"

"Out on the range. There's an area we'd like to clear, and I'll be coming with you."

Fred gaped. "Nobody told me."

"Gene made the request. I only just got permission."

"So you know him?"

"I met him thirty-one years ago when we first tried to find the bombs. He asked for my help on later searches. You don't know the terrain. I do."

Fred was relieved. Secretly, he had not relished spending weeks alone out in the boonies. "You'll be a great help, and I could do with the company. Look, can we stop this 'sir' business. It makes me feel uncomfortable. I'm Fred."

The sergeant snorted. "Better than Rock Rump."

"How did you know that?"

"As I said, Gene and I go back a long way. He told me all about *Bye Bye Oscars* and the bishop."

"Scary guy."

"Yes, and after Gene contacted me, I started searching again, on weekends," the sergeant said. "It's been sort of a hobby. Recently, I saw the bishop out there. He's still looking for the second bomb. Now, let's go to my office and look at the map."

At the office, Sergeant Collins spread a map on the table. "We have always assumed that Old Tex didn't have access to a vehicle. Which means that his maximum range from where he found the bombs, and before he was seen at the Salt Flat cafe, would have been about twenty miles." He pointed at the road, marked 62/180, that went east from El Paso through Salt Flat to a junction with Route 54, just south of the Guadalupe Mountains National Park. "The favored area is bounded to the north by the park's high mountains, and by route 62/180 to the south and to the east, where the road meets 54 and heads up by the park."

"What about east of the road, and down 54?"

Collins looked irritated. "Over the years Gene and I have looked, but the main area alone covers four hundred square miles—twenty miles east to west, and twenty north-to-south. But Gene has always been convinced he didn't cross route 62/180."

Fred reacted quickly. "I wasn't criticizing, Sergeant, just trying to understand. So, you really think they could still be where you've already looked?"

"Yes. The next question everybody asks is, 'what about in the main part of the park?'" Collins looked resigned at having to give an explanation.

Fred nodded.

Collins pointed at the northern part of the map, and said, "Most of it is too high, going up to eight thousand feet. Tex's old burros would have had trouble handling the inclines with a heavy load." Collins looked to see if Fred was satisfied. Fred nodded again.

"Tex had a reputation for being secretive. We don't think he would have taken the bombs into the lower parts like Pine Spring and McKittrick Canyons. Too many tourists."

"But you did look at the lower foothills to the south of...." Fred indicated peaks on the map. "El Capitan, Guadalupe, Shumard, and Bartlett mountains rise out of the desert?"

"Yes. Gene's convinced he hid the stuff in Bone or Shumard Canyons, but we haven't found anything."

"What about farther west into the salt flats?"

"We thought about that, but decided that it's too exposed." Collins started to fold the map. "One other thing, Gene's certain that Tex hid one bomb beside this dirt road that cuts northwest across from 62/180 north to the Williams Ranch at the base of Bone Canyon. We found a rectangular hole." Collins let Fred study the map for a few seconds before folding it. "Let's eat."

That evening, after eating in the mess with the sergeant, who had still not divulged his first name, Fred returned to his room and plopped on the bed. His thoughts turned rapidly to Millie—only 300 miles to the north. Out of habit, he went outside before punching in her number. After a minute she answered.

"How's it going?" he asked.

"Where are you now, Anchorage?"

"Ha, ha. El Paso."

"Going to be there for long?"

"Leaving tomorrow. Got to get back to Austin." Fred felt uncomfortable with the lie.

"Rats. I'm between jobs. I could have driven down to see you."

"What about your mother?"

"She's having a good spell, and keeps telling me I need to get out more." Silence. "She likes you."

"How about you?" Fred hoped Millie could hear how he felt.

"You shouldn't have to ask."

Encouraging words, but he needed to move on to the subject that was partly behind his call. "Anything new on Oscars?"

"I bumped into Bogdan at the supermarket. He told me there'll be a big premiere downtown next week. Sebastian will announce it tomorrow."

"Are you going?"

"I think so. Bogdan said I needed to brush off my von Minx outfit."

"You don't sound happy."

"I'm not." Millie sighed. "Every time I wear those clothes, all the testosterone-heavy jerks think it's an invitation to make a pass."

"Worked for me," Fred said quickly without thinking.

After another silence, Millie said, "I'm not even sure I'd wear them for you."

Fred was about to reply when he heard a voice behind him call out, "Mr Schwarzmuller."

He turned to see the sergeant approaching, holding a folder.

"What did he call you?" Millie asked.

"It was someone else," Fred said quickly. "Sorry, I've got to go. About the outfit, I live in hope. I'll call you next week. Take care of yourself." Fred felt silly, but smooched the air into the phone anyway.

"Girlfriend, huh?" The sergeant sniffed and held out the folder. "These are the maps. Study them tonight. I suggest we go to the crash site first. I've got the tents and supplies loaded. Breakfast at six, sharp. Don't be late."

"Yes, sir." Fred Made a civilian "salute," but the sergeant was already striding away.

* * *

"It's all done, Lancie. *Bye Bye Oscars* is ready for primetime." Sebastian Agincourt sat back in his chair and puffed on a large cigar. If he had been more limber, he might even have put his feet on his desk.

"What are you going to do now, Bas?" Lance said, getting up from a couch that still retained the odd wisp of its plastic wrapping, and pointedly moving toward the open window to avoid the stream of smoke wafting over the desk.

"Not exactly sure, but the bishop said something that gave me an idea."

Lance looked questioningly.

"Middle East. There's a lot going on. Maybe a remake of *Bactrian Camels*."

"You mean like nuking the Mojave, but it would be in the Sinai?" Lance's tone of voice implied that he didn't like the idea. "How about the Negev desert? Better still Jerusalem. That'd get their attention."

"Who?"

Lance sneered. "The people with the funny hats."

"Them, and the Christians and the Muslims," Agincourt snorted. "They all hang out in that place."

"Guarantee an audience."

"And a *fatwah*, and whatever the Jews and Christians do to you when they're offended."

"Penance, Bas. Not so bad. You could lose some weight."

"Well it would be ecumenical." Agincourt puffed on his cigar and expelled a cloud of smoke in Lance's direction. "To be fair, we should also look at nuking a few other places…Baghdad, that place in Saudi Arabia, Teheran, you name it."

"But what if we've only got one bomb, and…?" A worried look crossed Lance's face. "Silly me, we can find a way to get more. Let them nuke each other."

"I'll think about it. Who'd be the backers?"

"I could talk to the bishop."

"Yeah. But he might not like evaporating Jerusalem."

"I'll ask."

"And we need a new title. Something catchy."

"How about *Religious Camel Armageddon*?"

"Nah, lose the camels." Agincourt blew more smoke. "We'll talk later. Lola'll be here in a minute to see my new couch."

"I wondered what it was for," Lance said as he went to the door.

21.

At 9:30 the following morning, after an eighty-mile drive from the base, Fred and Sergeant Collins reached Salt Flat on U.S. Highway 62/180.

"Next time we come through we'll eat there," Collins said, pointing at the Salt Flat cafe. "It's a favorite of Gene's."

After they had crossed the salt flats, Sergeant Collins turned left onto a dirt road.

"I thought we were going straight to the park," Fred said as they passed the remains of a small house, with only the chimney standing.

"Gene wanted you to see where the reverend lived. This abandoned building ahead was his first chapel." The sergeant drove another few hundred yards and parked.

Fred jumped out and took a deep breath. "Fresh air, like being at the seaside," he said. "If you made a lake I'd want to go swimming."

Sergeant Collins joined him. "I agree there's something about the air here," he said. "Fred, now that I'm not in uniform, you can call me Hank."

Fred, who had started toward a sign that had fallen next to a bushy plant with large, white trumpet-shaped flowers, looked around in surprise. "Sure, Hank." He lowered his hands.

'Don't touch the Jimson weed," Hank bellowed. "You might be allergic."

Fred gingerly picked up the sign. Faded letters spelled out the words Our Lord's Redeemer. "The reverend/bishop likes the idea of redemption, doesn't he?"

Hank snorted. "I'm not sure I'd like the bishop's idea of redemption."

"You know, Hank, seeing this place, stuck in the middle of nowhere, makes me wonder how the reverend got the funds to move up to that cathedral."

"Talk to Gene. He mentioned something once about rumors that Old Tex had some kind of a hoard. On the subject of Old Tex, come over here. There's nothing left to see in the chapel."

Hank led Fred to the cemetery. It contained three illegible wooden markers, and a dent where an open grave had apparently filled in over the years.

"Gene says that when he came here looking for Old Tex, he saw a hoist and a tarpaulin draped over this hole," Hank said. "Later, when you told him about the viewing coffins and the skeleton in the cathedral, he realized that the bishop must have already trapped Old Tex in one of them."

"Pity Gene didn't look."

"Yeah, in hindsight." Hank pointed to the north, where the jagged face of El Capitan, rising to over 8,000 feet, was outlined against the sky like the prow of a giant warship. "Let's move on. I reckon the other bomb is somewhere between here and those mountains."

Going north on the main road, a mile beyond the junction with Route 54, they passed a dirt road with a rusted metal gate on their left. "When we come back we'll take that road," said Hank.

"Where's it go to?"

"That's the road to Williams Ranch that I showed you. Our best guess is that Old Tex stashed the bombs somewhere not too far from the road. During our second search we found a hole that could have concealed the bomb that Gene believes the bishop took. Unfortunately, the higher ups didn't agree. We'll go to that site later."

Three and a half miles farther on as they climbed toward Guadalupe Pass, Hank turned into a rest area. "I'm parking here. Where we're going to hike is too rough for the equipment in the Hummer. The truck with the bombs came off across the road at that next bend. At five thousand feet, it's high enough to get freezing rain while the lower altitudes just get wet."

Hank turned on an alarm, locked the Hummer, and they crossed the road.

"Back in the '70s, visitors had made a tiny trail through the brush when they went off the road to take a leak," Hank said. "I reckon that the hijackers thought they saw a side road, made a snap decision and, by the time they realized what they'd done, it was too late."

Fred and Hank came to a sharp drop-off into an arroyo.

"Down there," Hank said as he and Fred scrambled down, scaring a jackrabbit in the process. "Can't see much now. We picked up everything we could find."

When they reached the bottom Hank took Fred's arm and pointed at a small depression. "We found an old big tooth maple here…gone now. Gouge marks on a lower limb indicated that Old Tex had rigged a pulley to lift the bombs onto his burros. Hoof prints into the arroyo showed him coming from the north, then showed him heading south, but soon petered out when he reached drier ground."

"So he could have hidden a bomb in this arroyo."

"That's what we thought at first. In the early days we spent most of our time searching around here. Later, we found that hole I mentioned, south of here near some soaptree yuccas."

Fred scratched his head. "I'm surprised you couldn't track down where he'd been."

"Fred, you're seeing this place in summer. In winter, the weather can get real bad. The tracks got washed out."

"In that case, I hope we get this sorted out soon."

They walked to the Hummer in silence.

When they reached the road to the Williams Ranch, Hank turned off and stopped in front of a gate locked with a padlock.

"How do we get in?"

Hank handed Fred a key. "I got the spare from the Park Service some time ago. Lock it up after I've gone through."

After he had opened and then locked a second gate, Fred got back into the Hummer. Hank turned and said, "The place where we think the first bomb was buried is about two miles on. We'll go there first."

On the way, Fred scanned the view through the windshield. "It's real bleak—cactus, gravel, nothing moving. I can't see what Tex could have found to prospect for around here."

"There's more here than meets the eye. Many of the animals come out at night. But I agree, everybody we talked to reckoned he'd become senile. Gene told me that when Tex was younger he used to travel all over West Texas and New Mexico, looking for Indian artifacts, and gold." Hank shrugged. "Maybe he stashed what he found somewhere up in the mountains. There could be caves. Oh, that other track joining us on the right is the old Butterfield Stage Route. We'll follow it northeast for a few miles."

At the next bend, Hank stopped. "Look on the left."

Fred followed Hank to where a couple of small trees and yuccas lined a dry creek bed. To the side of them was a pile of rocks and a dip in the ground.

"The hole's filled in now. It used to be sorta rectangular; just the size for a bomb crate."

Fred lifted a rock and peered under it.

"Watch out for rattlers!" Hank yelled out. "Our best guess was that he buried the other bomb under a pile of rocks, too."

"And you didn't find anything?"

"Right. And one of my men got bitten by a Mojave rattler. Nasty."

"What kind of detectors were you using?"

"Metal detectors."

"Assuming that you actually checked the right place, either he buried it too deep, or something obstructed the signal."

"I suppose so," Hank replied cautiously.

"If he did have a cave, it would be the place to look."

"We thought of that, but even checking with the locals and the park rangers we never found Tex's hidey hole."

"What if the second bomb is underwater? Wouldn't a layer of water cut the signal to the detector?"

Hank laughed derisively. "What water?"

Fred ignored the jibe. "You said there was freezing rain when the truck crashed. There would have been run-off water, and low places where it collected."

"True…at the time. But we came back in the spring and summer. I don't see it as a problem." Hank disagreed, but to Fred he sounded thoughtful.

Fred decided to push the point. "The Williams Ranch must have had water."

"I think they had a well," Hank said uncertainly.

"Okay. That means there could be areas under the shadow of that escarpment where water seeps out." Fred pointed at El Capitan. "In the canyons, I'd guess." Fred looked at the map.

"The map shows Bone Canyon and, farther over, Shumard Canyon."

"I remember, now. They used a spring in Bone Canyon."

"There you go."

"We scoured that area, Fred. First, I'd like to search along the road. Use the new detector and see if you can spot something we missed. If we don't find anything, we can do the canyons tomorrow or the day after."

"Fine with me. Hank, I don't plan to use the tritium unless we get a hint of something using the deuterium. Okay?"

"Makes sense."

They spent the next two and a half days checking sites that had been looked at before, plus a few that Fred suggested because they were in creek beds or marked by a tree or a saguaro cactus.

"I wish we could have the bells pealing and the explosion just once," Fred said wistfully, after they had investigated yet another drab-looking pile of rocks. "Rattlesnake hits on the IEC don't count."

Hank chuckled. "Those little suckers sure get pissed off by the buzzing sound, don't they?"

"What do we do now?"

"Camp out near the ranch house and start on the canyons tomorrow. We won't be able to take the Hummer into some of it. We'll walk and use the metal detector I brought."

They completed their drive up the rise to the Williams ranch house, and pitched their tents on a flat area that gave a stunning view of the salt flats in the distance.

"The land doesn't look good enough for a ranch," Fred said.

"I've heard that it was, before the various owners brought in a longhorn herd, and then sheep and goats," Hank said. "Overgrazing and a drier climate led to what you see—grass replaced by mesquite and acacia: Too bad." His face looked as if this had been a personal loss for him.

"And all we've seen are mule deer, jack rabbits, and roadrunners. Sad," Fred added.

"There's elk up near the park headquarters, and I've heard talk about mountain lions and black bears, too." Hank stared out into the distance. After a moment he continued. "Why don't you give Gene a call?"

Fred pulled out his cell phone and called Gene's office.

Gene answered. "How are you doing, Fred?"

"Nothing to report, I'm afraid."

"What do you think of the scenery?"

"The mountains are great, but it's pretty desolate when you get out of sheltered areas like the canyons; creepy at night. I'm glad you got Hank to come along." Fred dragged a toe on the dusty earth making a circle.

"He's a good man." Gene sounded tired. "Fred, I'd like to hear what you've covered, but first I need to bring you up to speed on the investigation. The agent I mentioned, Dan's his name, monitored the power input to the cathedral. You were right. Except for a quick drop when they switch the lights and air conditioning up and down, the power level is constant. Ergo, they're powering the tritium production."

Fred finished the two eyes and the smiley mouth. "Glad that worked out. Anything else?"

"Charlie talked to the guy who delivers office supplies, bribed is more accurate, into letting him help. They're making a delivery today. All he has to do is get in, quickly take photos and get out. God, I hope it works."

"Should work." Fred decided to change the subject. "By the way, I've a question that's been nagging me for a long time."

"Fire away."

"What is your theory about how the bishop managed to raise the money to build the cathedral?"

"I got to thinking about that, too, after you made it clear that the bishop and Reverend Jenkins are the same person. I looked at our notes on Old Tex. We found out that he occasionally sold Indian artifacts to raise money. My belief is that he had a hoard somewhere of everything he'd collected over decades of roaming the Southwest. Possibly, he even found Spanish stuff. Either way, some of those Indian artifacts can be highly valuable to collectors."

"It looks like the bishop found the hoard."

"Reckon so. I suspect that Tex tried to buy his freedom."

"It obviously didn't work." Fred erased the smiley face. "What did you do then?"

"I had a friend to check out sales of Indian artifacts. He found out that an unknown seller has been systematically unloading high quality material for the past twenty years; millions of dollars, Fred, plus interest on investments. I reckon that would do it."

"Couldn't you find out anything about the seller?"

"I tracked the stuff back to a dealer in Mexico. But that's it."

Fred thought for a minute. "If it had been me, I would've moved the stuff south of the border, too."

"That's what seems to have happened."

"One other thing, Millie told me the premiere for *Bye Bye Oscars* will be in Albuquerque next week."

"Hmm. The bishop's not wasting any time," Gene muttered. "I'll call you tomorrow, and let you know what happened at the cathedral. For now, let me talk to Hank."

Early the next morning, Fred and Hank headed up Bone Canyon checking for a signal from the dry creek bed and every unusual outcropping or pile of rocks. Finally, concerned that the Hummer would become stuck, they stopped.

"We'll walk the rest of the way. It's a short distance," Hank said. "I don't think Tex could have gotten much farther."

They reached a point where the slope rose steeply up to Guadalupe Mountain—the end of their climb. Fred sat on a rock, staring down the canyon, seeing patches of white, yellow and blue where desert flowers nestled in crevices. After a while, he said, "I don't think this is working. You made a good point about where Tex would take his burros. That hole you showed me is a clue, and I still think that water may be involved. I'm really disappointed that the Bone Spring area didn't show anything. We need to get into Tex's head."

"We've all been trying to do that for twenty years. Gene thought he was onto something with lone trees, but it didn't work out." Hank stood and kicked a stone down the canyon. "Anyway, let's try Shumard Canyon."

As they headed past the ranch house, a park ranger came off the veranda and motioned them to stop.

"What are you doing, gentlemen?" He paused and peered at the Hummer.

Hank ran the window down, and held out his hand. "Good to see you, Jack."

"Oh, it's you, Hank," the ranger said. "I didn't recognize the new wheels." He peered into the back of the Hummer. "Fancy equipment, I see." He grinned. "Still looking for that alien missile?"

"Yeah. This stuff has a bigger range than my old metal detector. Fred here knows how to operate it."

"Nice to meet you, Fred. Now I've said this to Hank before. Y'all be careful where you drive. This territory's pretty fragile."

"Yes, sir," said Fred. "I'd noticed."

"Have you seen our friend around recently?" Hank asked.

"Some time ago. He seemed very interested in the hilly area to the northwest below Bartlett Peak. Spent a lot of time there."

"We'll check it out.

"You alien missile hunters never give up, do you? Good luck." The ranger returned to the shade of the veranda.

"He doesn't believe the missile story, does he?" Fred asked. "And what was that stuff about aliens?"

"That goes back to the original hunt. These days I tell people we're conducting a geological survey. Aliens were something we added for fun in the early days; connection to Roswell, up the road. The Park Service still doesn't know what we're looking for. Let's keep it that way."

They spent the rest of the day searching Shumard Canyon. They met hikers and mule deer on the El Capitan trail that wound up the canyon. Both eyed them with curiosity. The hikers seemed satisfied with the geological survey story. The closest they came to success was a faint signal from under a pile of rocks in a flat area that abutted a steep slope. They moved the rocks and found a cache of unused rifle bullets buried in the dirt.

"Damn," Fred said. "I was about to put in the tritium." He picked up a bullet and studied it. "I wonder who put them here."

"Some kid maybe."

Fred scanned the area. "You know, Hank, if it wasn't for the trail nearby, I would say this would be a likely place. But, somehow I can't see Tex hiding the bomb so close to where hikers are wandering about."

"I agree. But it does look good with all the rocks piled up right next to the canyon wall. We spent a lot of time here in the old days looking for a cave."

"What do you want to do with the bullets?"

"Leave them." Hank chuckled. "Give the bishop something to find." He lifted a rock.

Fred dropped the bullet into the pile and helped him cover the cache.

The rest of their search was equally futile, and they pitched their tents by the El Capitan Trail.

Fred's cell phone beeped while they were eating chicken tetrazzini. In Fred's opinion, one of the army's better Meals Ready to Eat (MREs).

"Hello, boss. How did it go?" Fred asked.

"We're in trouble," Kowalski replied. "My guy's disappeared. I called his cell. Someone picked it up, but put it down the moment I said, 'How did it go, Charlie?'" Gene sounded distressed.

"Anything I can do?"

"Yes. I suppose you haven't found anything."

"Right."

"Go back to El Paso. Rent a car and go to Albuquerque. See what you can find out about Charlie. I'll get you a hotel, and there'll be a package waiting for you with info on Charlie and what he planned."

"Okay. Can I go see Millie?"

"Umm," followed by a silence. "Better not. In fact, you need to disguise yourself a little. It's better if nobody recognizes you."

"What about the Oscars premiere?"

"I'd forgotten about that." Another silence. "I'm curious about who's going to attend. Call me tomorrow about the hotel." Gene hung up.

"We're out of here," Fred said. "I've got to go to Albuquerque. We need to leave as soon as we finish supper."

"Problems?" asked Hank.

"Yes." Fred did not elaborate, and Hank did not look as if he expected him to.

22.

Fred inspected his room in the Howard Johnson Express; not bad. How did the hotel make a profit at the government rate? He opened Gene's envelope that had been waiting for him at the front desk. The key fact that emerged from the notes was that the new agent on the case, Charlie, had managed to persuade a Jesus—appropriate name—Gonzales to let him carry supplies into the storage area at the cathedral. Jesus worked for the Rio Grande Office Supply company. Gene had told him to try the company first and see if they knew anything. Fred pulled out the phone book, found their number and called it.

When a woman answered the phone, he said, "I'd like to speak to Jesus Gonzales, please."

"Who are you, sir?"

Fred glanced at the HBO program. It highlighted the movie *Titanic* and gave the names of the stars and the director. Leonardo DiCaprio was too obvious. "I'm James Cameron," Fred said. "It's about some insurance we were trying to work up."

"You haven't heard then?"

"Heard what?"

"It's terrible. A hearse crashed into his truck off I-40 east. Everything burned up. My boss was asked to identify Jesus and the other body in the truck." The woman sounded distraught.

"Oh, God. So Jesus wasn't alone?"

"That's right. But we don't know who the other man was. Jesus worked alone. Maybe he picked up a hitchhiker."

What to do now? Find out more about the second body. "I hate to intrude at this difficult time, but could I speak to your boss?"

"Let me ask him. James Cameron, insurance you said?"

"Yes, Titanic Life."

She put him on hold for a couple of minutes, before saying, "I'm putting you through."

"Maria says you've some insurance for Jesus," her boss said. "His family'll sure need it."

"Not exactly, sir. We'd been discussing insurance. He hadn't returned the form." Fred hated to continue the lie, but saw no other way to get information.

"I'm afraid that if he had the papers in the truck, they would have burned up. I'll get Maria to look in his locker. Hang on a minute."

When the boss came back on the line, Fred said, "Maria said that you were asked to identify another body."

"Yes, and I don't want to ever go through that again," the boss said. "I have no idea who Jesus had with him."

"Maria said your truck was hit by a drunk driver?"

"That's what the witnesses thought. This hearse was careening all over the place before it hit our truck. A drunk driver and no skid marks. The attendant at the morgue said he'd never seen anything quite like them."

"How so?"

"He called them drunken zombies; like they were mainly bones. He insisted on showing me the remains of the van. God, it was bad. They must have been carrying gas as well as the tequila, and drugs."

That's it. Assuming this was the bishop's doing, he would have needed two bodies to satisfy whoever had sent the snooper. The other bodies had to be from the crypt. Two sets of bones and one nearly decomposed corpse. Eliminate the remains of five dead men with one fire. Fred felt please with himself for working out and let out an involuntary "uh huh."

"Sir?"

"Sorry, I'm trying not to picture it," Fred said quickly. The feeling of elation at figuring this out dissipated quickly with the realization that it meant that Charlie was dead.

Fred heard voices. "Maria can't find anything. Poor Jesus. Give me a phone number so I can call you if anything comes up."

Fred looked at the open phone book on the bed, gave a number at random, and hung up. He grabbed his cell phone and called Gene.

"He's in a meeting, Fred," Linda said.

"Please get him out. This is urgent."

"Okay. I'll put you on hold," Linda said. After a minute, she came back on the line. "He's with Franklin Jackson. It may take a while. I'll get him to call you back."

Forty minutes later, Fred's phone played a couple of bars of *County Lineman*.

The moment Fred answered the phone, Gene said, "Sorry to keep you waiting, but I didn't want to talk to you from Franklin's office. What did you find out?"

"A hearse, probably carrying gasoline, hit the delivery truck. Everything burned up. Five bodies in total: I'm assuming that they were Jesus Gonzales, Charlie, and probably the three bodies from the crypt."

"Damn. It was staged." Gene said. He continued reflectively. "The bishop moved fast. I had visions of Charlie in a viewing coffin."

"Me, too." Fred thought hard for a moment before asking a question he didn't want to ask. "Do you want me to go back inside the cathedral?"

After a minute Gene responded, "No, I can't risk it. You stay and see who goes to the premiere. You are disguised, I hope."

"Dark glasses, plastic wads to fatten my face—those cotton wads I used before get real uncomfortable—and I haven't shaved."

Gene chuckled. "You actors are so ingenious."

"I really do look different." Fred affected a heavy accent. "And I sound like Marlon Brando in *The Godfather*."

"Yeah. Well, good luck." Gene chuckled. "I'll talk to the local police and find out what they know about the crash. Then I'll try to get the ambassador to agree to a search of the cathedral. In the meantime, I'd like you to go there and see if there's any unusual activity…from a distance. I'm worried that the bishop may decide to close down his operation."

"Sure." Fred was happy to have something to do while he waited for the night of the premiere. It would keep his mind off Millie.

"Good luck. Oh, and stay away from Millie."

Damnation, Gene must have read his mind. Fred went into the bathroom, put in the plastic wads and donned his baseball cap. He put binoculars, a camera, and a bottle of water into his backpack and headed for his car. On the drive east on I-40, Fred thought about the best place to observe the cathedral; deciding on a hill that gave a fair view of the back of the buildings and the exit from the parking lot by the workshop. He parked in the place he had used when he checked out the basement. He walked up the hill and settled in the shade of a scrubby tree to wait for something to happen.

Fred looked at his watch. It felt like more than an hour had passed. His right leg tingled. He wiggled his butt, without success, trying to find a softer piece of ground. The only good thing about the discomfort was that he hadn't fallen asleep. No sign of activity. Just as he was about to put the binoculars down, a large van pulled off the road and went into the workshop's lot. A second van followed. Fred's heart raced. This was it. Moving time, but he couldn't see what was being moved. It took him only a moment to decide that he would be better off sitting in his car, ready to follow the vans when they left.

Fred waited down the road from the cathedral. The two vans pulled out an hour and a half later, heading west. Fred followed them into downtown Albuquerque, where the driver surprised him by going to Agincourt's studio. He saw Georgie and Chuck walk up to the vans, and had no choice but to drive past. He parked out of sight on a side street and waited for the vans to move out.

Another half hour went by before the vans left. Georgie was in the first van with Miguel, Chuck in the second with Carl. Fred followed them to the Convention Center, parked and walked as close as he dared, wondering what they would unload. "I should have guessed," he muttered to himself as Carl and Miguel, helped ineffectively by Chuck, placed the large Oscar statue, the Hollywood sign, and other props from *Bye Bye Oscars* onto the loading dock. To Fred's surprise they also removed props from some of the bishop's movies.

So much for that, Fred thought. He returned to his room and called his office. After he had reviewed what had happened, Gene said, "The bottom line is that we don't know if the bishop moved his bomb operation out. I'll have to wait for Wheaton to agree to do something. Damn that man."

"What did you find out?" Fred asked.

"I talked to the police. The coroner was very puzzled by the remains in the hearse; called it the Flying Dodge Van. The police think that the crash looks fishy, but don't plan to do anything. Apparently, they assume that some drug dealer was hiding drugs in a coffin, and the bodies—bones really—were there in case they got stopped and searched. They're just happy with the idea they have fewer drug dealers around. Of course that doesn't explain who the hell was driving the hearse. What do you think?"

"Radio control," Fred said. "Might explain why the witnesses saw the hearse driving erratically."

"The police did check Jesus Gonzales' itinerary. The truck made two other deliveries after the cathedral. So it's hard to make a connection to the bishop." Gene said, clearly disappointed.

"Bummer," Fred said, suddenly remembering what had bothered him. "Where did the hearse come from? Was it the bishop's?"

"No. I asked that," Gene replied. "It was stolen a day earlier from a mortuary."

"I suppose Miguel and Carl could have made those other deliveries," Fred said.

"Yup. And I talked to the ambassador. Told him what you had seen in the cathedral: the bodies, the accelerator, the bomb crate. I pretended it had been seen by Charlie. The ambassador's going to the premiere. Surprise, surprise. He wouldn't discuss the bishop. I told him it was urgent, but he insisted I wait until he gets back to his office next week. He wants other people to hear what I want to do." Gene added bitterly, "What am I going to say to Charlie's wife?"

"I could check—"

"No, Fred. I don't want to tip off the bishop, in case he hasn't cleared the bomb stuff. When Wheaton agrees to do something, we can include looking at the props he moved to the Convention Center. I don't want to lose another agent. Take care."

* * *

From his position in the second row of the crowd on the far curb, Fred watched the procession of celebrities alight onto the red carpet. Upright viewing coffins containing mutant jellyfish models flanked the doors into the Center. The bishop must be very confident there won't be a search, Fred thought. He's giving us the finger.

"She's on *As the World Turns*," a woman next to him said excitedly, as a blonde beauty on the red carpet waved.

"Wasn't he on 'Oprah'?" another woman exclaimed, looking at the blonde's escort.

The Agincourt aficionados, dressed as characters from Agincourt movies, whooped and hollered when Lola Paramour and Bogdan Mirnov appeared. The two stars walked with uncertain steps. But when Lola turned and waved regally, losing her balance, Bogdan was still able to catch her gracefully.

"Way to go, Boggie," Fred yelled without thinking. He regretted his action immediately because the following group consisted of Georgie, still in dark glasses, and Chuck. Georgie spun around and scanned the crowd. Fred ducked down. He wanted to leave but couldn't move in his densely packed group without becoming obvious.

He looked up in time to see the white-suited bishop with Ambassador Wheaton and a woman, presumably Wheaton's wife, disappear through the doors. Following them, Lance and a male friend minced down the carpet. Millie came next, wearing her Monique wig and a stunning red sheath dress, to be greeted by a chorus of wolf whistles. She turned and waved to the crowd.

Sebastian Agincourt brought up the rear, strutting with a gold-topped cane a pace ahead of a flustered-looking, plump woman. He was magnificent in a flamboyant opera cloak and a broad-brimmed black fedora. She wore an ill-fitting black evening gown that might well have been selected randomly from the studio's wardrobe.

Fred had just decided that he could risk moving closer, when he saw Carl and Miguel come out of the Center. They ducked under the rope holding back the spectators. Fred glanced to his right to see Carl coming toward him. He decided that if he moved Carl would spot him, and he edged close to a family group.

"That Monique von Minx is something else, ain't she?" he said to the husband, noticing that Carl was only fifteen feet away.

"Who?"

"The one with the long black hair," Fred replied just before Carl reached them.

The man looked quickly to see if his wife was paying attention. "Yeah. I wouldn't mind a piece of that."

As he passed, Carl peered at the man and moved on.

"A piece of what, honey?" The wife laughed.

"You heard?"

She patted his arm. "It's okay. I don't blame you. She's beautiful, but she probably has two or three guys like you before breakfast."

"Millie's not like that," Fred said without thinking.

"Millie who?"

"Sorry, I was thinking of somebody else."

"Whatever." She took her husband's arm. "Come on, honey. It looks like the show's over. Let's get the kids home."

Fred waited until more of the crowd was moving to join the throng of people as they went to the nearby parking garage. He looked surreptitiously for Carl and Miguel. Finally, to his relief, he spotted them talking in front of the Center. Carl went in, while Miguel walked down the road away from Fred.

Fred returned to his motel, stopping to get a hamburger, and a Dr Pepper. He fell asleep in bed with the TV still on.

* * *

Millie stepped aside quickly as Carl and Miguel rushed past her. She overheard Lance say to his companion, "I wonder what they're up to?"

No concern of hers. She carried on toward the bishop. Who was he talking to? That odious ambassador. She kept her head down and passed them quickly to join Bogdan and Lola, who had found a bench to sit on.

"Lovely to *shee* you, my dear," Bogdan said. "*Pleesh* join us." He tried to make room, but was unable to move Lola. "'Fraid, Lola's a little squiffy."

Lola looked up, bleary eyed. "Is that the tarty girl *Sebashitia*n used to replace me in Oscars? I should have done it, you know." She wiped her eyes, smearing mascara.

"It's Millie," Bogdan said in a stage whisper. "Lolly, Lolly you look like a racc…hic…oon."

"What? I thought her name was somethin' von Bitch."

"Ah, three of the stars chatting about the movie," a voice said.

"*Who'sh* he?" asked Lola.

"Television, Miss Paramour," the interviewer said. "Do I sense that you are not happy that Miss von Minx was cast to play in the remake of *Bye Bye Oscars*?"

"You bet— "

"*She'sh* delighted," Bogdan said quickly. "T*hish* is a great movie. Dare I *shay* it, even better than the *firsht* version. *Shebastian* Agincourt has really matured as a director."

"Mature is not a word I've heard associated with Sebastian before," the interviewer said cattily.

"Have you ever seen any of his movies?" Millie asked.

"Well, yes, uh, when I was in school."

"Good. Well, we all hope you enjoy this one. I had a great time. I'm sure Lance Dupree will be happy to tell you more about it." Millie turned away.

"I have another question—"

Bogdan looked hard at the interviewer's crotch. "You're boasting." He said.

"What?"

"Zip."

"Oh, oh. Camera off." The interviewer reached down and left.

"Was he really unzipped?"

"No, I just wanted to get rid of the *odioush* creep," Bogdan said. "Lola's not in good shape. Can't have it on TV." He stood. "Please help me. Take her to the bathroom before we go in." He pulled a silver flask from his pocket and took a swig.

"I didn't mean it," Lola said when Millie had finished repairing her make-up. "I'm a stupid bitch sometimes."

"It's okay. Sticks and stones—"

"You see. I've been with him since I was seventeen. I love him, and he doesn't want me much anymore."

Millie put her arms around Lola and hugged her. "You ready now?"

"Yes, dear. Thank you."

Millie helped Lola negotiate the aisle between Oscar's props into the auditorium, and sat her down just as the lights dimmed.

A spotlight focused on the bishop as he appeared through a trapdoor in the stage.

"Jesus Christ," Bogdan muttered.

"Maybe he is," retorted Lance, who was sitting in front of them.

"My dear friends," the bishop said, interrupting further conversation. "Welcome to an exciting evening when you will see the premiere of Sebastian Agincourt's epic movie *Bye Bye Oscars*. I will not label it two, because it replaces the older version." The bishop raised his arms and his voice rose. "Yet again, Hollywood, that bastion of impropriety, will get its *rust jewards*." He pointed at the audience "Will Sebastian and his cast members and crew please stand."

"Help me up, old dear," said Bogdan. "I feel a bit shaky. You'd better, hic, *shtabilize* Lolly, too."

Spotlight's homed in on Chuck, Georgie, Lance, Loraine, the make-up artist, and the swaying threesome of Millie, Lola, and Bogdan. The audience clapped politely.

The bishop waited until the applause subsided before saying, "We are also honored to have with us, the mayor and council members of Albuquerque, the chief of police, and a special guest, Ambassador Wheaton. The ambassador has been a key figure in our fight to overcome the forces of evil and the satanic Muslims since the horrific events of 9/11. Please all stand."

When the applause had died down, the mariachis and honor guard from the cathedral marched onto the stage, taking up positions on each side of the bishop. They were joined by mutant alien jellyfish.

The bishop lifted his arms. "Please all stand for our National Anthem."

"I'm not *shure* I can *shtand* much more of this," Bogdan said when the singing finished. "I need a pee. Look after Lolly. I'll be back later." He brushed past Millie and staggered up the aisle.

The mariachis, honor guard, and jellyfish left the stage. The bishop walked to the trapdoor elevator and disappeared from view, saying, "Now, what you've all been waiting for, *Bye Bye Oscars*." The screen came down to show the opening titles.

At the end of the movie, which was more entertaining in an absurd way than Millie had expected, she went quickly to her car. Seeing Fred in the film had made her realize how much she missed him. Sebastian had tried to persuade her to stay for the party, but she didn't want to be groped by drunken men, and needed to get home to her mother.

*   *   *

"It was Fred Howard, Bishop," Carl said as he reached him in the foyer of the convention center. "I looked for someone like the man our janitor saw. A good disguise, but I know how tall he is, the shape of his head, ears, and the way he stands. He was pretending to be with some family."

"What did you do?"

"Told Miguel to circle around the parking garage to where he could see the exit. He saw Fred drive away."

"What about the car?"

"El Paso County plates. Probably a rental. Miguel couldn't get close enough to see."

"El Paso." The bishop looked thoughtful. "That means he's been looking for the other bomb. We must do something about that. I need to get to my seat." He started to walk away, turning to say, "Everything ready for tomorrow?"

"Yes, Bishop."

"Good. Let's see what Kowalski makes of this." He smiled a wintry smile.

23.

"He's ready for you, sir," Mrs. Rogers said, the moment Kowalski entered Ambassador Wheaton's outer office. "Go on in. Mr. Hessman is already here."

"Our legal counsel?" Kowalski asked.

She tilted her head and pursed her lips. "'fraid so."

Not a good omen. Kowalski knocked and entered the ambassador's office.

"Ah, Kowalski. On time I see. Have a seat." Wheaton pointed at a formally-dressed, rotund man sitting in one of the two chairs in front of his desk. "You know Victor, I think."

Kowalski walked over to shake hands. "Good to see you, Vic."

Wheaton pressed his palms together and looked intently at Kowalski. "I, uh...we are very interested to hear again your arguments as to why I should approve a search of the Redeemer Fountain Cathedral."

"Did the premiere go well, Ambassador?" Kowalski asked smoothly.

A flicker of irritation crossed the ambassador's face. "Yes, indeed, but we can come back to that later. For now, I need to hear your rationale for this, this dramatic action."

"As I told you before, I am convinced that Bishop Orpheus Jones is the alias for the Reverend Orlando Jenkins who I met twenty or so years ago in Salt Flat when we were looking for the stolen *nuclear* weapons," Kowalski said.

The ambassador stared at him intently.

Kowalski working hard to control his irritation, said, "I believe he found one of the bombs."

"Why only one?"

"Because my contacts tell me the reverend, now the bishop, is still searching for the second one."

"Assuming that they are the same person. Continue."

"I am also very concerned that, in recent years, two people with knowledge of nuclear weapons disappeared."

The ambassador opened a file on his desk and turned a couple of pages. "They would be the technician from Pantex, and the engineer from Sandia National Laboratory?"

"Yes, Ambassador."

"I asked the FBI to check on them." Wheaton drummed his fingers on the table. "The word I got back was that both had problems; marital, financial, and so on. They probably ran away to escape responsibilities or they committed suicide."

"Strange that they've not been seen since…dead or alive," Kowalski retorted.

"What else?" The ambassador turned another page.

"My agent in Albuquerque measured an unexplained use of electricity, even when the lights and air conditioning were turned down. He also searched the cathedral. What he saw convinced me that the bishop has the bomb and is preparing to use it."

Wheaton turned more pages and ran his fingers across the last one, his lips moving. "This is the agent who you now say is dead?"

Kowalski nearly answered no, but held himself in check. "Yes, Ambassador, he died in a truck accident last week after he had gone into the cathedral basement to take photographs. The circumstances of the accident are very suspect. There were five bodies, or sets of bones, and—"

"The implication being what?" the lawyer asked, opening a folder on his lap.

"The bishop got rid of the—"

"We'll come back to that." Wheaton turned back a page. "And the reason your agent didn't take photographs on his first break-in is that he was nearly discovered."

"Yes."

"So we have no photographs of:…" the ambassador counted on his fingers, "a crate for a hydrogen bomb, an accelerator with a brown gas cylinder—believed to be deuterium—a room with glove boxes, presumed to be used for tritium separation; and three bodies in viewing coffins in various stages of decay, supposedly now burned up in what you claim was a staged crash."

"Unfortunately, not."

"Unfortunate indeed, Kowalski." The ambassador snapped the file closed. "You have, without authority, deployed an agent to investigate Bishop Jones. You have authorized illegal break-ins. And you have no evidence to support these actions."

"I have my agent's reports, Ambassador."

The ambassador raised his eyebrows, and said dryly, "An agent who cannot verify them."

"I have other—"

The ambassador interrupted, preventing Kowalski from blurting out Fred's role. "Let me tell you something. *I*...did my own investigation."

"Sir?"

"Before going to the premiere, I called Bishop Jones and asked if my wife and I could have a tour of this cathedral you have told me so much about."

"You what?" Kowalski was too stunned to continue.

"The bishop was delighted to oblige. He even invited the other honorees at the premiere, and the press to accompany me."

"So you saw the inside of the cathedral?"

Wheaton looked smug as he said, "As well as this precious basement of yours."

Guessing what was coming, Kowalski suddenly felt cold, and tired. "And you saw?"

The ambassador held up his hand and counted off his list of findings. "One, a room in which they store coffins. Two, the bishop informed us that it is the last place before burial or cremation for the deceased...hence the bodies; a room with electrical equipment...an arc welder, and various furnaces." He paused, apparently for effect. "Three, a work area used to make props for the bishop's movies, er...." He looked at his notes. "No accelerator or brown deuterium gas cylinder...oxy-acetylene, yes. Victor, please show Mr. Kowalski my photographs."

Kowalski waved the counsel away. "I believe you, Ambassador. After you, so subtly, warned the bishop—adding to whatever he found out from our agent, before he killed him—the bishop moved out everything incriminating."

"An agent you sent without approval, Kowalski," the ambassador snapped. "And how do you know this?"

Kowalski swallowed hard before answering, "Because, when I realized my agent had disappeared, I sent Fred Schwarzmuller to check. He—"

"Counsel, please note this further infraction," the ambassador said. "On my orders, Schwarzmuller was searching for the missing bombs. Incidentally, nobody else accepted Mr. Kowalski's view that one of the hidden bombs had been found. All rotted, probably."

When Kowalski looked as if he was going to respond, Hessman held up his hand, and said quietly, "Mr. Kowalski, do you agree that these actions of assigning an agent to investigate Bishop Jones, authorizing break-ins, and sending Schwarzmuller to Albuquerque were all your doing?"

"Yes, but Fred saw — "

"Props from *Bye Bye Oscars* and other movies to be shown at the premiere." Wheaton looked triumphant. "The bishop showed them to me. They included viewing coffins, and the so-called stolen-bomb crate made by his staff for the movie."

"The bishop covered every angle, didn't he?" Kowalski commented bitterly.

"Kowalski, your continued criticisms simply serve to prove that you have a personal vendetta against this fine gentleman." Wheaton turned to Victor Hessman. "You see what I mean, counselor?"

Hessman nodded and made more notes.

"Now to the final claim: glove boxes. Yes, they are actually chemical fume cupboards and I saw them. The bishop is environmentally and safety conscious. In the course of their work, his technicians use various corrosive and toxic materials. The bishop, at vast expense, purchased state-of-the-art equipment to protect them." Wheaton spread his hands. "What do you have to say to that?"

Kowalski sat in silence.

Wheaton placed both hands flat on the desk, and looking pleased with himself, said, "Well?"

Gene glanced at Hessman before replying, "Counselor, I would like you to take down what I am going to say for the record."

"I think I have told you everything, Victor," Wheaton protested. "Do we need this?"

"I would like to hear the story in Mr. Kowalski's own words, for the record," Victor Hessman replied firmly. "Please go on, Mr. Kowalski."

Kowalski continued, choosing his words carefully. "In 1981, a truck containing two nuclear weapons was stolen. It crashed in Guadalupe National Park. James Buchanan, known as Old Tex, found them and hid them. He told his pastor, the Reverend Orlando Jenkins, about his find. I don't know how he did it, but the reverend got Old Tex to tell him the whereabouts of one bomb. Before we could interview Old Tex, he was run over. By the reverend or simply bad luck, I don't know. I have a photograph of what I believe to be his bones in a viewing coffin." Kowalski handed the photograph to Hessman.

Hessman looked closely at the picture. "Where was this taken?" he asked as he handed the photograph back.

"In the crypt of the cathedral, by my agent."

"The one who is dead?" Hessman waited while Kowalski stared at the ceiling. "Mr. Kowalski, I asked a question."

"Sorry, Mr. Hessman, I was thinking about Old Tex. Yes."

"Anything else?"

"I am also reasonably sure that the bishop got hold of the Indian artifacts that Tex had collected over the years. The sale of these artifacts formed the basis of the fortune the reverend used to establish the Redeemer Fountain Cathedral after he had become Bishop Orpheus Jones."

"You have no proof of these allegations," Wheaton interjected, rising to his feet. "The bishop explained his finances to us. He is entirely supported by his very large congregation."

Hessman motioned for the ambassador to sit. Wheaton, looking angry, obliged.

"My agent attended the bishop's services. The bishop rails against the movie industry and Hollywood in particular. I believe that the bishop plans to explode his bomb at the next Oscars ceremony."

Wheaton started to rise, but slumped back when the lawyer raised his hand. "What facts do you have to support that claim, Mr. Kowalski?" Hessman asked.

"A number of things. First, the bomb is over thirty years old. You can go on the Web and find out that the tritium in the primary of the bomb will have decayed sufficiently to reduce the blast very substantially. Hell, it's discussed in Clancy's novel, *The Sum of All Fears*. So the bishop knew he needed to replenish the tritium, hence the accelerator and deuterium, etcetera, used to produce it. Second, he needed expert advice so that his technicians, Carl and Miguel, could safely dismantle the bomb to the level where they could replenish the tritium."

"Tell me again how he got this advice?" Hessman sat with his pen poised.

"I believe that he somehow persuaded Herman Johnson, a technician from Pantex—the weapons assembly and disassembly plant near Amarillo—to help him. My information is that Mr.

Johnson was a religious fanatic holding similar views to the bishop."

"You have proof?"

Kowalski shrugged. "No, but I believe that a second coffin in the cathedral contained Mr. Johnson's body."

"Why?"

"A label sticking out from under the coffin had the word Amarillo on it."

"Hmmm. Go on."

"Third, all of these weapons have safety systems. He apparently tried to get an engineer from Sandia, Sigmund Hertz, to help."

Hessman looked puzzled. "What do you mean tried?"

"I believe that Hertz died before providing the information."

"So, even if your fantasy were correct, there would be no way for anyone to detonate the bomb," Wheaton gloated.

"Unfortunately, my agent concluded that they had worked around that problem."

"This information all came from the dead agent?"

Kowalski hesitated. "Yes, Mr. Hessman."

"Let us assume for the moment that all of your beliefs are true. Can you clarify the connection to the movie *Bye Bye Oscars*?"

"The movie came to the attention of Homeland Security when we were told that Sebastian Agincourt would be remaking the movie with a nuclear device replacing the mutant alien jelly fish of the original." Kowalski paused while Hessman completed his notes. "We investigate all mention of nuclear devices."

"I am not acquainted with this movie." Hessman looked amused. "What exactly is the role of these…mutant…alien jellyfish?"

"They are enamored of the color red and eat the red carpet and everybody on it, before returning to the sea at Venice Beach."

Hessman's face showed disbelief as he wrote down the information, and asked, "So, who lets off the bomb in the new version, in which I assume there are no jellyfish, mutant or otherwise?"

"I had heard there wouldn't be jellyfish in the new version. But, at the last minute, they reappeared."

Hessman lifted his pen. "Why?"

"The bishop wanted Sebastian Agincourt to wrap up the movie."

"Why…?"

"He needed to have the premiere quickly, release the movie, and get publicity to justify getting a sketch about Agincourt's work into the next Oscar ceremony. So he used old material," Kowalski blurted out.

"Incredible." Hessman jotted down more notes. "What exactly is the bishop's connection to the movie?"

"At first, I thought it was because his son, Charles Jenkins, was starring in it."

"Jenkins! There you go again!" Wheaton exploded.

Hessman glared, the ambassador looked down at his desk and flicked at it with a finger.

"Then I heard that the bishop had arranged for his workshop to make props to be used in *Bye Bye Oscars.*"

"A generous gesture, apparently?" Hessman questioned.

"The movie is semi-pornographic. It seemed like an odd thing to do."

"Oh, I see." Hessman underlined Kowalski's last words.

"More recently, it turned out that the bishop was contributing to the script and even rewrote the ending." Kowalski had been about to add something but was distracted by Wheaton's now insistent tapping.

"To speed up production?" Hessman asked, staring hard at Wheaton, who raised his hands as if to say it wasn't me.

"I believe so. Finally, I learned that it was the bishop who had funded the whole enterprise."

"From your dead agent, I suppose," Wheaton snapped.

"Yes."

Hessman looked hard at Wheaton before asking, "And all of this has led you to believe that the bishop plans to make this fantasy plot a reality at the next Oscars."

"Yes."

"Mr. Kowalski, I am going to read you my notes. Please interrupt if you feel that I have misstated your views." Hessman turned back the pages of his legal pad, and read from them.

A good job, Kowalski reluctantly admitted to himself when Hessman finished.

Hessman handed the pad to Kowalski, and said, "Please read the notes carefully, and if you agree, sign and date each page. The ambassador and I will also sign them. Mrs. Rogers will make copies for you and the ambassador. You can pick up your copy when you leave."

When Kowalski had finished signing, Wheaton called Mrs. Rogers in and she took the pad.

"Mr. Kowalski, I am going to give you my opinion of your findings or, more accurately, your views," Hessman said. "You paint a vivid picture of an evil mastermind plotting a ghastly event. It sounds very much like the plot of one of Mr. Agincourt's movies, which of course it is. But your interpretation of the *facts* is only one possible interpretation. The ambassador believes that there is a much simpler explanation."

Kowalski held out his hands. "Mr. Hessman, I feel responsible for an agent's death. All I want is the authority to do a thorough search of the cathedral and other property the bishop may have. I can confirm that there are traces of tritium in the cathedral, also I can get the DNA from the bones found in the wrecked van and truck tested."

Hessman shook his head. "In the absence of any concrete evidence, including no proof that the bishop is this Reverend Jenkins, there is no legal basis to do what you request. I understand that you have been pursuing this matter for over thirty years. Frankly, you seem obsessed with the issue. You need a rest." He stood. "Ambassador, I think we've beaten this to death. I have another meeting to attend."

Wheaton also rose. "Thank you for your sound advice, Victor." He turned to face Kowalski, clasping his hand in a prayer-like gesture. "Gene, I have talked to Human Resources, and the counselor and I have discussed your situation. We all agree that you are overstressed. As a valued employee, and for your own health, I am placing you on administrative leave for three weeks. At the end of this period, you will report to Human Resources, which has arranged for you to chat with our resident psychiatrist. I am sure he can help you. I'm taking you off this case, permanently. If you attempt to go around me, I will throw the book at you for illegally deploying an agent—one who is now dead."

Kowalski knew that the ambassador had him by the balls. He felt the bile rise from his stomach. He stood and put his hands on the desk, shoving his face toward the ambassador's.

Victor Hessman reached out and pulled on Kowalski's sleeve. "Mr. Kowalski, you are in no position—"

Wheaton backed away. "Oh, and I will ask Franklin Jackson to assume your responsibilities," he said quickly, moving behind his chair.

"That does it. You ignorant piece of shit!" Kowalski stood and slammed the desk with his fists. "God damn it, man, one of these bombs operating at full power will destroy everything inside a circle six miles in diameter."

"My experts agree with your earlier comment that, because the tritium will have decayed, only the primary would work," Wheaton retorted angrily.

"Great. Assuming the bishop hasn't succeeded in replenishing the tritium, that would make it only equal to Hiroshima or Nagasaki. Total destruction up to a mile from the blast center. What are you or Franklin Jackson going to do when Hollywood disappears?"

Wheaton looked at Hessman and raised an eyebrow, but did not respond.

Mrs. Rogers handed Kowalski an envelope as he left.

* * *

Fred rolled over on his bed at Fort Bliss and picked up the ringing cell phone. "Fred here."

"The reason I called is to let you know that I'll be on vacation for a few weeks." Kowalski laughed dryly.

"Great, but how come?"

"The ambassador has decided that I'm a basket case and put me on administrative leave."

"You're kidding?"

"No. He set me up. Asked the bishop if he could get a tour of the cathedral. Of course, the bishop agreed, and fed him answers to all the obvious questions."

"How did he explain the power lines and the accelerator?"

"What accelerator? You mean the welding equipment and furnaces," Gene replied wearily.

"Oh, shit. So it's just his word against yours and mine."

"Not really. He had our legal counsel with him, Victor Hessman. He insisted I tell my side of the argument in detail. Wrote it down, and then read it back to me."

"Did you get to see what he'd written?"

"Yes. It was a fair account. I signed it. But when you listen to what I said, you could conclude that I am a paranoid idiot. Which is more or less what they said to me: obsessed, overstressed and overworked. Wheaton has banned me from the case, permanently."

"But I know you're right. Can't I go to them?"

"I nearly told them everything you'd done, but didn't want to mention you. I concluded that whatever I said, Wheaton would distort it for personal and political reasons. Wheaton's got me on having an agent check on the bishop without authority, and breaking-in."

"What about Hessman?"

"Hard to tell. He joined Homeland Security at the same time as Wheaton and Franklin Jackson. I don't want to risk telling them." Gene paused. "Incidentally, you're now working for Jackson. He knows you were in Albuquerque last week. You may get a call. Be very careful what you say."

"What are you going to do?"

"As I said, take a vacation." He chuckled. "Patsy's real excited about going to Amarillo."

"It sounds like you're not giving up."

"Damn right I'm not. One of the arguments they made was that I hadn't proved that Bishop Johns and Reverend Jenkins were one and the same person. I'm going to show them."

"Gene, I'm so sorry. Good luck."

"You, too." Gene hung up.

Fred lay back on the bed. He had never acknowledged it before, but Gene had been like a father figure. Encouraged by him, he had done things he never would have believed possible a year earlier: understudy in a movie, breaking into a cathedral, dating a murderess, hunting for a stolen hydrogen bomb. My God, he had played the kind of role that every kid dreams of, "Shaken not stirred," "Make my day," "Now, this is a knife." With Gene out of the picture, Fred didn't feel like James Clint Crocodile Schwarzmuller anymore. The mission to find the second nuclear weapon and prevent the bishop from eliminating a large chunk of Los Angeles was now his.

24.

Fred did not have to wait long for Franklin Jackson's call. It came early the next morning.

"I don't know if you've heard what has happened, but our good friend Gene will be taking some time off," Jackson said in what Fred took to be a deliberately soothing tone. *The shit.*

"What's the reason?"

"People...Human Resources, Ambassador Wheaton think he's been overworking. A rest will do him good."

Fred briefly held the phone away from his ear, sickened by the unctuous voice.

"Are you there, Fred?"

"Yes. Sorry, a fly landed on my nose." Fred made a slapping sound.

"The point is that I will be running the section, pro tem. I am trying to get up to speed on all our activities, so I would like you to come back to L.A. immediately. Rashona will set up a meeting. I'll put you through to her."

"Who's Rashona?"

"My administrative assistant. Linda's taken another position."

They didn't waste time in eliminating all corporate memory.

Another voice, female, came on the line. "Fred, I'm Rashona. I checked flights and can get you here in the morning. Mr. Jackson can see you at two."

Fred mumbled, "Can't wait."

"I'll ticket you, and you can pick up an Avis rental car at LAX. Have a nice day," she cooed.

It would be a long time before he could have a nice day. Fred rolled off the bed and went to find Hank.

* * *

Franklin Jackson and Rashona Maclain were now the names on the sign outside what had been Gene Kowalski's office. Fred's eyes misted as he grasped the door handle, and went in.

"You must be Fred," said the large woman behind the desk.

A cartoon figure from a 1940's, Duke Ellington record album cover, Fred thought, remembering a picture on one of his father's old LPs, and adding in surprise, "Rashona, you don't look Scottish."

"Not an original comment," she snorted. "And I'm not related to the senator, either. It's spelled different."

"Sorry."

She acknowledged his apology with a dip of her head; apparently satisfied that she had put him in his place. "Have a seat. Mr. Jackson will be with you in a minute."

"Do you have Linda's new phone number?"

Rashona punched keys on her keypad, and scanned her computer screen. Without a word, she wrote a number on a piece of paper and handed it to Fred.

Fred put the paper in his wallet, and picked up a pamphlet on Homeland Security. The minute slowly became ten minutes.

Fred's eyes closed as a picture of a radar dome morphed into a Moon Pie.

"Mr. Schwarzmuller, Fred, he's ready for you," Rashona interrupted his second bite into the phantom pie.

"What? Sorry I must have dozed off." Fred dropped the pamphlet on a side table, and went into Jackson's office.

"Wonderful to see you again," Franklin Jackson gushed, rising out of his chair to motion Fred to be seated.

The office had a different atmosphere. The old-fashioned furniture that had followed Gene up through the ranks had been replaced with those of a decorator's image of a modern executive office. Franklin Jackson's desk and chair appeared to have been raised slightly above the level of the seats that faced him. Photographs of Jackson meeting various celebrities covered one wall—senators, congressmen, the vice president, business leaders.

Surprised by the changes, Fred blurted out, "I thought you were taking over temporarily?"

"I don't think Gene will be coming back to this position." Jackson sounded conciliatory. "I put his stuff into storage, to await a decision on his future work. But now, to what will happen to you. The ambassador is clear in his mind that what occurred under Gene's tenure cannot occur again. For this reason, I have decided that all of the staff I inherited from him should retake basic training."

"Which training? In addition to the Human Resources courses and instruction on the role of Homeland Security, I took courses on dealing with terrorists, combat techniques." Fred chuckled. "And lock picking."

Jackson opened the file on his desk. "It also says here that you took a course from Gene Kowalski on nuclear weapons. I notice that this was well before the ambassador sent you to West Texas. Following that course you were assigned to Gene's section. The records that I have found are not clear on what you did up until a few weeks ago, when you went to pick up the new detector. Why did you take the course, and what were you doing during this long period?"

Fred thought quickly. "I did odd jobs for Gene; gofer really. When Gene decided to suggest to the ambassador that I resume his search, I've been studying up on the bomb affair."

"I see." Jackson's tone of voice suggested that he did not see. "Well, you won't need to take nuclear weapons again, and certainly not combat or lock picking. You will be repeating all the other training, with the addition of sensitivity training, and office techniques."

"Office techniques?"

"Yes, I need an assistant."

"Where will I take the training?"

"Rashona will give you the details. I'll see you when you get back." Jackson stood up indicating that the meeting was over.

When Fred came back into Rashona's office, she picked up a package and held it out. "It's all in here."

"Am I going somewhere nice?"

Rashona raised her eyebrows. "Depends what you mean by nice. How does Des Moines, Iowa for two weeks sound? You'll leave Wednesday."

"You're kidding?"

She smiled and returned to typing.

* * *

As he drove up to the cathedral, Sebastian Agincourt imagined shooting a scene. In his mind, the steeple became covered in scaffolding. Bogdan, playing the Phantom Hunchback of Albuquerque, screamed at the angry mob rushing from the parking lots to the steps. Agincourt skirted the imaginary stragglers, and parked in front of the administrative building. Maybe that could be the next movie after his epic about the destruction of the Middle East. Lance came through the door and waved him in.

"The bishop's interested, Bas." Lance grinned. "And he's got some ideas."

"Good."

Lance ushered Agincourt down the corridor to an ornately carved wooden door. When Lance opened the door, Agincourt caught a waft of Old Spice before he saw the bishop seated behind a huge Spanish desk. The office was decorated with

Native American and Spanish artifacts, a richly woven carpet covered most of the polished wooden floor.

"Welcome to my humble abode," the bishop said. "I was just reading the good book; gaining inspiration for our possible new venture."

"Wonderful decorations, Bishop. Worthy of a museum," Agincourt said, then pretended to blow his nose on a yellow silk handkerchief that he had sprayed with eau de cologne. "How did you obtain them?"

"A beloved donation from a very dear friend, many years ago." The bishop looked upward as if giving a blessing. "Now, please take a seat."

Agincourt perched on the edge of a tooled leather chair in front of the desk and looked up at the bishop.

"Sebastian, let me tell you my thoughts. At first I was not taken with the idea of eliminating Jerusalem, but then I recalled what happened to Sodom and Gomorrah when their people strayed from the path of righteousness. What is Jerusalem?" The bishop stood and raised his arms. His voice became louder as he intoned, "A one-time site of the Temple of Solomon, occupied now by a Muslim mosque and an Orthodox church. Situated in a *stogue rate* surrounded by infidels."

Lance rose and said, "Amen, Bishop. Amen."

"So you like the idea of nuking Jerusalem?" Agincourt asked then brushed the handkerchief over his face.

"Yes, but not just Jerusalem," The bishop said animatedly. "All the evil cities in the Middle East."

Agincourt looked puzzled. "But how would that happen? What's the plot?"

"The Israelis have bombs. The Iranians are developing them. If a bomb goes off in Jerusalem, the Israelis will retaliate, and they will mutually destruct." The bishop spread his arms triumphantly.

"I can see it, Bishop," Agincourt said. "But we'd need a lot of props to convince an audience we were in the Middle East. We could use material from my movie *Atomic Bactrian Camels of the Mojave*."

"We'll deal with that later, Sebastian. It may be easier than you think."

Agincourt nodded but secretly was not convinced. Get the funds first was a motto that had always worked. Worry about the details, like script, actors and sets, later. "What about a title?"

"I had wondered about using *The Lost Tribe of Israel*," Lance volunteered.

The bishop shook his head. "Close but it's not new."

Agincourt stroked his Van Dyke. "How about *The Last Tribe of Israel*? he said, looking hopefully at the bishop.

The bishop stared up at the ceiling as if waiting for divine guidance. "I like it. Now let us pray." He rested his elbows on his desk and bowed his head.

Agincourt bent forward, looking out of the corner of his eye to see the top of Lance's head. The bishop wasn't joking.

"Dear Lord, please guide us in this new venture to counter the evildoers and rid the world of dens of iniquity. As we will dispense with Hollywood, so will we eradicate those perverted centers of the Middle East. We ask this in the name of Jesus Christ, Amen."

"Amen," Lance and Agincourt added.

"Now, gentlemen, you must leave me to my devotions. We will discuss the funding at another time." The bishop picked up his Bible and started reading.

"What did he mean about dispensing with Hollywood?" Agincourt asked as he and Lance exited the building.

"A figure of speech, Bas. He meant in your movie."

"I suppose so. See you next week."

"Probably not. The bishop's asked me to do some things," Lance replied. "Look after yourself."

Agincourt got into his car, and looked up at the steeple. The Phantom was still haranguing the mob. That movie had possibilities. Would the bishop agree?

25.

"Well, I'm glad we got to see Palo Duro Canyon together, even if it is October," Patsy Kowalski said to Gene, after they had booked into their motel in Amarillo. "I suppose I'll mostly be on my own from now on."

"Sorry, hon, there's something I've got to check on. I'm going to show that bastard, the ambassador."

"And you can't tell me what it is?"

"Better you don't know." Gene Kowalski handed her a brochure. "Have a look at this and tell me what you'd like to do. I can drop you off tomorrow morning."

Patsy quickly scanned *Attractions of Amarillo*. "I'd go for the 72 ounce steak—free if eaten within an hour—if they'd allow me eight hours." She looked at the brochure. "Amarillo Botanical Gardens sounds better. I'll go there."

"Great. Do you want to come to the library with me, now?" Gene asked. "I've exhausted the Web and got a few leads. I'm hoping to find some local books to fill in gaps."

"Why not. There should be info on other things to do around here."

At the library, Patsy went immediately to books on Amarillo, while her husband looked up churches and chapels. Thinking back to his decades earlier brief encounter with Reverend Jenkins had led Gene to three conclusions: the reverend would not be associated with any of the major denominations—

Catholic, Episcopalian, Lutheran, or even Baptist. If he had a church, it would be on an isolated site, and the church might have some or all of the words, Lord's, Redeemer, and Fountain in its title. He might have set up shop on the east side of town near the Pantex weapons plant: nevertheless, Gene decided to ignore his guess and exhaust the other areas first.

When he and Patsy left the library an hour and a half later, Patsy smiled and said, "You look smug. What did you find?"

Gene put his finger to his nose and shook his head.

The next morning, Gene dropped his wife off at the Botanical Gardens, and headed west on Amarillo Boulevard. He spent a frustrating day interviewing ministers in out of the way, Christian fringe establishments. None of them remembered a Reverend Jenkins connected to a church name with a word on Gene's list. On the off-chance that Jenkins had changed his name to John before moving to Amarillo, he also asked about a Reverend John. John yes, but their descriptions did not match his man. He took a break at a Starbucks.

Halfway through his latte, he phoned Fred, and listened patiently while Fred unloaded. "A break won't hurt you. Even if it's in Des Moines...." "I agree the training's Mickey Mouse...." "What did you just say about the files...?" "Shit. That squares with what Linda told me yesterday. Good thing I removed a few files before they took over. It sounds like they're trying to get us all out of the way, and bury the case...." "No. I don't want you doing anything yet. Wait 'til I've finished here. I'll call you if, when I find something...." "You, too." Gene put the phone back on his belt and finished the latte. Des Moines. The bastards. He hoped Fred would keep his cool.

Patsy looked closely at Gene when he picked her up at the Gardens. "No luck, eh? Well, I had a great day. I met these two ladies who are doing the sights. We're going to the Panhandle-Plains Historical Museum tomorrow. They'll pick me up."

"Great. I'll be checking the north suburbs tomorrow." Gene replied.

"You still can't tell me what you're looking for?"

"Sorry."

When Gene returned to their motel room, Patsy glanced up from a brochure. "I don't need to ask, do I? Your face says it all. I bought some scotch. Let's have a drink before dinner."

"Bless you, Patsy, I thought I was onto something and spent three hours chasing it. Nada." Gene grinned. "I'm ready for a drink or three. You can drive."

"Thanks a lot." Patsy put her arms around him. "Not too much, though. Wanna fool around later?"

"You're on."

On Wednesday, Gene got up late. Patsy had already left with her new friends. He drove east on Route 60. Ten miles out of town he saw a diner and stopped for a coffee and donut at the counter.

"I'm studying churches and chapels," he said to the woman who took his order. "Are there any around here including a name like Fountain or Redeemer?"

She shook her head. "Don't reckon so. Mind you, I've not been this side of town long."

"Where do you think I could find out?"

"Might try the mechanic in the gas station or the Baptist chapel in St. Francis."

"Thanks."

"No problem." She cleared away his cup.

Gene approached the mechanic who was working on an old Chevy in the dilapidated service station. "Sorry to trouble you, but I'm looking for a chapel or church; Redeemer or Fountain something."

The mechanic wiped his hands with an oily rag and scratched his head. "You know it's *bin* ten years, but Fountain or Redeemer. There's a large chapel near St. Francis." He rubbed his nose, leaving an oily smudge. "It's not called that anymore. Something Baptist, now. Not far from the Pantex turnoff."

It sounded to Gene that his conclusion about the reverend having a chapel near the Pantex Plant—the manufacturing and disassembly center for nuclear weapons—had been correct. Consistent with his assumption had been that the Reverend moved to Amarillo to find technical help with the bomb. "Back then, was the pastor a Reverend Jenkins?"

"Can't say that I remember, exactly. But the reverend did come in here once. Not the kind of man you forget. Tall, scary blue eyes...biblical looking. I fixed his truck. Broken springs. Too much weight carrying coffins, he said."

"Thanks for your help." Gene decided against shaking hands, and waved as he went to his car. He had no problem finding the chapel. A neat, white, wooden building surrounded on three sides by a graveyard, sat about a quarter mile from the highway. A step up from Salt Flat for the Reverend Jenkins, he thought, guessing that this was where the reverend had spent some of the early proceeds from selling Indian artifacts. He parked next to a Ford Taurus and went looking for its occupant.

"Can I help you, sir?" a voice called from the graveyard.

Gene looked around. An elderly woman, wearing jeans, a checkered shirt and a large blue linen sun hat, was weeding near one of the graves. "Yes. I'm researching the Redeemer order of churches and believe this chapel used to be of that denomination."

"Lord's Redeemer. Order of churches! More like the Reverend Orlando John's private religion." The woman chuckled as she stood up. "We inherited many of his flock, a lot of them workers from the Plant. I think they were relieved to be rid of the fire and brimstone."

So, Orlando Jenkins had morphed to Orlando John and finally to Orpheus John. "You knew him?"

"Not really. My husband's congregation bought the chapel from him, when we needed a bigger house of worship."

"Do you know why he sold?"

"I'm not sure. It's been twelve years. I think Reverend John had greater ambitions. My husband might know where he went." She paused. "What's your interest?"

"I met him many years ago. A fascinating man. I was curious as to what happened to him."

The woman looked Gene up and down. Her expression suggested that she felt there was more to his story.

"What was the chapel like when you bought it?"

"In good shape, except the cemetery was overgrown. What you see was done by our garden club." She pointed at the neatly-mown grass and fresh flowers on the graves. "It was unkempt and strange when we came here; particularly one open grave with a hoist all covered with a tarpaulin."

"Did he explain why?"

"Said he liked to be prepared in case someone died."

A pattern was emerging, he thought: one open grave in Salt Flat, one disappeared prospector; two graves in St. Francis, add a disappeared technician. Three, after the bishop moved to Albuquerque—the Sandia engineer? "Thank you, ma'am. I may be back."

"I'll tell my husband you came round. What name shall I give?"

"Gene Kowalski, Ma'am."

As he was leaving, she called after him. "It's the Reverend John's wife I feel sorry for."

Gene turned. "Ma'am?"

"She became ill and went into a nursing home. A nervous breakdown, I heard. Frankly, I wasn't surprised. I think she's still in the home."

"Do you know where?"

"Sorry, I don't know, but somewhere around Amarillo."

Patsy, holding a scotch on the rocks, met him at the door to their motel room. "You're smiling, Gene." She held the glass to one side and kissed him. "Do you need this?"

"Sure, but I haven't finished. I may need your help."

"Are you going to tell me what this is all about?"

Gene sat down, took a sip of the scotch, and put the glass on the coffee table. "I reckon I'll have to, but you mustn't tell anyone."

"Cross my heart and hope—"

"To die." Gene finished her sentence. "That's what I'm scared of, Patsy. Maybe it's better not to involve you."

Patsy joined him on the sofa and cuddled up to him. "That bad?"

"Yes." Gene drummed his fingers on the table. "I need to find a woman in a local nursing home."

"It's come to that, has it?" Patsy giggled. "I'm not good enough for you?"

"Ha, ha. I've only met Mrs. Sarah Jenkins once…a long time ago. Thank God I kept my notes. She may have information I need."

Patsy sat up. "Sarah Jenkins. Wait a second. When we were first married, you went to some out-of-the-way town in West Texas." She paused. "Looking for a lost missile. You mentioned a strange preacher. I'll never forget his name. Orlando the Marmalade Cat. The Reverend Orlando Jenkins. Right?"

"Patsy, how come I was lucky enough to meet a smart woman like you?" Gene shook his head admiringly. "Pick any restaurant, we're going to celebrate."

Patsy put her arms around him. "Dinner can wait. I'm going to have a shower. You could join me, hint, hint."

"I always liked the quotation, 'A nod is as good as a wink to a blind man.' Lead me on."

In the morning, Patsy called the local nursing homes and sanitariums in alphabetical order. She struck gold in the P's, with a nursing home to the south of Amarillo.

After a long wait, a friendly sounding woman answered the phone. "Pleasant Valley Home, how may I help you?"

"My name's Patsy Jones. I'm with my husband, we're visiting from El Paso. We're trying to locate Mrs. Sarah Jenkins, my distant cousin. The last I heard she'd had a nervous breakdown and was going into a home."

"We have a Sarah Jenkins here. I'm sure she'd love to see you. She doesn't get many visitors. In fact, only her husband, Reverend Jenkins, and its been a year since I've seen him."

"Can we come round now?"

"Surely. But I should warn you, she's very weak and her memory is erratic."

"We'll be there in about thirty minutes."

Gene hugged her. "Where did you get the Jones from?"

"Another Welsh surname, I guess. Was it okay?"

"Provided they don't ask to see your driving license."

"I can always say it's my maiden name."

"What would I do without you, Patsy?" Gene's hug became more ardent.

"Later, dear, remember thirty minutes, and I want to get some flowers."

Gene drove south on Interstate 27 and turned left to Haney. The nursing home sat on a back road outside town.

"Poor Mrs. Jenkins," said Patsy when she saw the rundown old buildings. "It looks like a barracks."

They parked near a sign for the office, by the only door at the front of the building. Gene tried the door, locked. He shrugged and knocked.

The door was opened by a short, fat woman, wearing what might have once been a nurse's uniform. "I'm Mrs. Donald. You're the Joneses?" she said.

"Yes," Patsy replied. "Thank you for letting us visit on such short notice."

"No problem. I've been getting Sarah ready. I have to keep the door locked. Some of the patients like to wander." She motioned for the Kowalskis to follow her.

"So you must have known the Reverend Jenkins. I can never remember his first name," Mrs. Donald said casually.

"Orlando," Gene replied. "Funny, I can never forget it."

Patsy squeezed his hand, and gave him a knowing look.

Sarah's room was at the back on the first floor. Mrs. Donald unlocked the door. "Sarah, your cousin Patsy Jones and her husband are here to see you. Look at the pretty flowers they've brought you."

The frail woman sitting up in bed stared at them blankly as they entered the room. "I don't know you," she said with surprising clarity.

"Don't worry, dear." Mrs. Donald patted Patsy's back. "She says that to me sometimes."

Thank God, Gene thought.

Mrs. Donald pointed at two chairs by the bed. "I'll leave you alone to get reacquainted. It may take a little time. Let me take the flowers, I have a vase somewhere."

"Orlando sends his love, Sarah," Patsy said.

Sarah's mouth twisted. "Orlando doesn't come to see me anymore. He's got what he wants."

"What's that?" Patsy asked.

"My children."

"How many do you have?"

"Two." Sarah reached over to the side table, scrabbling at the base of the lamp. "They've gone."

"What are you looking for?"

"My photographs." Tears formed in the corner of her eyes. "He took them."

Patsy reached over and comforted her. "Gene, is there anything we can do?"

"Maybe," Gene replied, thinking rapidly. "I've got a photo in my briefcase that might do. I'll get it."

He returned with a photograph, and handed it to Sarah.

She wiped her eyes and as she looked at the photograph a broad smile appeared. "My little Charlie. Oh, how can I thank you?" She slipped the photograph down the front of her nightdress, and clasped it through the cloth. "Orlando'll not get this one."

"I'm sorry I don't have a photo of your other child."

"Wouldn't want it. She's like her father," Sarah snapped.

Gene decided to try another tack. "Sarah, we have met before," he said. "At Salt Flat at your church. I was looking for James Buchanan...Old Tex. Do you remember?"

Sarah peered at him then lay back. "I don't want to think about Old Tex. What Orlando did to him was ungodly." Her mouth quivered, she closed her eyes, and her breathing became labored.

"What happened?" Gene asked.

Patsy glared at him and shook her head.

At that moment, Mrs. Donald returned with the vase of roses. She saw Sarah's face, quickly placed the oxygen feed into Sarah's nostrils, and turned on an oxygen cylinder. She said, "I think you'd better go now. I should have warned you that she's easily upset. Come on dear, let's give you some oxygen."

As they were leaving, Mrs. Donald added with a smile, "If you're able to come back, Sarah does love chocolates."

"We'll come by tomorrow, on our way to the airport," Patsy replied.

"Whose photograph did you give her?" Patsy asked as they got into their rental car.

"Charles...Jenkins, it was his face that reminded me about Salt Flat; Chuck Steak now. He looked just like his father did those many years ago." Gene accelerated out of the parking lot. "Well, not exactly. His face is weaker, but those very pale blue eyes. Like a mechanic out near St. Francis said to me, scary."

* * *

The following day, Mrs. Donald opened the front door as Patsy approached the building. "Oh, you brought chocolates. Sarah will be so happy. I'm afraid she's not in a state to see you, but I'll see that she knows who brought them."

Patsy smiled and handed over the box. "That's fine. We need to get to the airport."

"Now you have a good flight, y'hear," Mrs. Donald called out as Patsy reached the car. She returned to her office, put the chocolates on her desk and picked up the telephone. She was sure the reverend would be happy to hear that their cousins had visited Sarah.

* * *

Immediately after he had finished talking with Mrs. Donald, the bishop picked up his cell phone and dialed. When the person on the other end answered, he spoke, "Can you talk?"

After waiting for a minute, he continued, "Okay, I've got two jobs for you. Remember I mentioned Agent Eugene Kowalski?" He listened for another minute. "Right. He and his wife went to Amarillo and talked to your mother."

He paused. "They're somewhere in L.A. If you can't find them in the telephone book, give me a call. I have a source."

His face turned hard, and his breathing quickened. He stood and, as if on the pulpit, declaimed, "*Shey* have *tinned*. I want them gone. Make it look like an accident."

He listened again. "Good, now, I also hear that you mother is really tired. Go and help her to sleep, permanently." He looked at the picture of his wife on the wall while listening to the response.

"I'm glad you agree she's become a liability." The bishop put the cell phone back in its case and returned to working on his Sunday sermon.

26.

Fred was on his way to class, when his cell phone rang. He looked at the caller ID, and ducked into an empty corridor.

"Got a minute?" Kowalski said.

"Sure. Proper Conduct while working for Homeland Security doesn't start for another five minutes. How did it go in Amarillo?"

Gene chuckled. "Proper Conduct. What a joke. Jackson's really sticking it to you. That'll teach you to toe the line. Anyway, I hit pay dirt, or I should say Patsy and I did."

"You told Patsy what we're doing?"

"A little, I hope not too much. Anyway, Bishop Orpheus John was the Reverend Orlando John in Amarillo. He had a chapel near the Pantex plant. I talked to the bishop's wife…poor woman. It's clear Georgie is their daughter."

"What happens now?"

"I need to get all my notes together, and write a coherent report that doesn't sound like I'm insane. I'll have to mention you."

"No problem. We don't have a lot of time. Who are you going to send it to?"

"The heads of all the relevant agencies, and the chairs of congressional committees that have oversight on security."

"The press?"

"No. Some of the material is classified." The phone went silent for a moment, before Gene continued. "If anything should happen to me, go talk to Linda. She knows where my other files are."

Fred's voice rose as he responded. "You're kidding, aren't you?"

"No, and watch your back. The bishop's crazy. Enjoy your course."

*   *   *

"Gene, the gas company called and said they need to fix our meter. Somebody will come by this afternoon. I said okay. I told the lady I'd be playing bridge at Fanny's, and gave her the number so that I could let them in the house. She said that after they'd fixed it, they would need to check all the appliances to make sure everything was okay. Just thought I'd let you know."

Gene listened to the recorded message, shrugged, put down the telephone, and returned to filling in a form for Human Resources. The idiots wanted a year-by-year account of everything he had worked on since 1980. The woman who had given it to him had said that it was essential information if they were to slot him into a suitable position.

When Gene reached his home in Huntington Beach, Patsy met him at the garage door. "How did the gas thing go?" he asked.

"Fine. Such a pleasant young woman, sounded just like some of those girls in Texas."

Gene kissed her and said, "Amazing isn't it, jobs women do today."

"Good thing, too." Patsy laughed.

"Huh!" A sudden image formed in Gene's mind of a woman with a Texan accent, whose mother did not like her. "What did she look like?"

"Mousy looking, but I think there was a shapely figure under her overalls. As they say, she'd probably clean up well. Very safety-conscious, asked me to step outside while she checked the appliances. I took the opportunity to go out and get a bottle of a new Chardonnay. When you've got your drink, I'll have a glass." Patsy headed down the corridor before he could argue. "I'll be in the kitchen. Talk to me while I get dinner ready. It's a barbecued chicken. I need to warm it up. You could peel the potatoes."

Gene followed her and laid his briefcase on the kitchen table. Working on his letter summarizing what he knew about the bishop's plan could wait until after dinner.

Patsy handed him the bottle of Chardonnay from the refrigerator. "Can you open it, please?" She put the chicken onto a roasting pan. "The potatoes are on the counter by the sink. I'll put the oven on." She walked to the range.

"What color eyes?"

"Pale blue. Very striking."

Oh God, a woman with pale blue eyes who did not want Patsy to see her check the appliances. Gene grabbed Patsy's arm and started to drag her away from the stove. Her hand twisted and turned the oven knob. It was the last thing Gene saw before the blast rammed them and the kitchen door over their neighbor's fence.

When the fire engine, ambulance, and police arrived, they found the Kowalskis, clasped in each other's arm, floating on their kitchen door in their neighbor's pool; charred and unconscious but alive.

"Never seen anything like it," said the first medic on the scene to the woman who was in the pool preventing the door from tipping over. "What happened?"

"There was this huge bang, and I saw Gene and Patsy fly through the air and land in my pool," she said. "Good thing I was on the patio. I was worried they'd slip off and drown."

"You did well, ma'am. We'll take over now." The medic jumped in the pool and helped the woman maneuver the door into the shallow end.

Because of Kowalski's position with Homeland Security, the FBI performed a very careful analysis of the disaster. They did not have an explanation for how enough gas could have accumulated to cause such an explosion. The belief was that gas might have leaked into the wall cavity. They did not recognize the pieces of the simple igniter that had been primed by a radio signal and triggered when any knob was turned on the stove. The tiny remains of electronic components, in the area where the kitchen had stood, were interpreted as coming from household electronics—a television set or digital clock. Given this information, the ambassador and Franklin Jackson refused to believe Kowalski when, on recovering consciousness, he insisted it had not been an accident. They held to their position despite the fact that the gas company denied having sent anybody to the area

*   *   *

The lecturer droned on about the insensitivity of some people to the importance of affirmative action. As far as Fred could tell, the speaker had a limited view of the area. In answer to a comment from his audience, he had been dismissive of the view that the biggest problem was the appalling treatment of women in many parts of the world. A faint musical sound alerted Fred to an incoming call. After disturbing the *Bye Bye Oscars* set, Fred had muted *Happy Days Are Here Again* to a whisper. He glanced at the number showing on the little screen. Franklin Jackson's office.

A second call flashed the same number as Fred reached the door.

"Am I boring you Mr. er…Schwarzmuller," the speaker asked.

Fred wanted to say worse than boring, but restrained himself. "Insistent calls from my boss. Excuse me."

He waited until he was outside to answer. "Fred here."

Rashona sounded upset. "Franklin Jackson needs to talk to you. I'll put him on."

Fred wondered what the sanctimonious creep wanted.

Another few minutes passed before Jackson came on the line. "Howard, I have bad news. Very bad news. Eugene Kowalski and his wife, Patricia, have been severely injured."

The landscape became blurred. Fred managed to blurt out, "How?"

"Gas explosion. As far as we can tell, it was an unfortunate accident."

Fred nearly broke the telephone he was clutching it so hard. "You don't think it has anything to do with Gene's investigation?"

"That fantasy. Heavens no." The sound of a suppressed snort followed.

"Are Gene…Patsy expected to recover?"

"Yes, but I'm afraid it'll take a long time. I doubt that he will ever return to work."

Fred caught himself before telling Jackson about Gene's findings in Amarillo. "It doesn't strike you as a strange coincidence?"

"If you know anything, you'd better tell me. I'll talk to you when you come back. When is that?"

"Next week, but I could come earlier."

"Not necessary." The phone went dead.

In a daze, Fred walked back to the meeting room. He stopped before he got there, no way he could concentrate on the course, particularly, this course. He needed to clear his head and turned around and went outside. It was cold and drizzling, but he barely noticed. He had been able to handle his assignment because there had been Gene supporting him in the background. Even when Gene had been put on leave of absence, his reassuring presence was still there. Now, everything was up to him and he didn't know what to do.

"Fuck. Fuck. Fuck." he railed at the sky. The drizzle mixed with his tears and ran down his cheeks. His focus turned to the bishop, and from there to Georgie. It had to have been Georgie. Thoughts of revenge flashed through his mind—strangulation would fit well, electrocution in her damn hot tub, a burning car wreck. "I'll do it," he said. Only to realize that he couldn't. The only thing he could do was to try and get someone else in authority in Homeland Security to take the bishop's insane plan seriously.

What had Gene said? "Fred, if anything should happen to me, talk to Linda; she knows where my other files are." That was it. Now where was her new phone number? In his briefcase that was in the meeting room. Damn. He headed back inside, at last feeling cold and wet.

The speaker looked at Fred with curiosity when he entered the room, and appeared to be about to comment. Fred glared and shook his head. Water dripped down his neck as he rifled through his briefcase looking for Linda's number, finding both it and a Moon Pie. What the hell. He removed it, tore of the wrapper and ate small pieces surreptitiously, while pretending to listen.

When the interminably boring session ended, he went to his room and called Linda.

"I just heard the news," Fred said. "We need to talk."

"Anytime. Where are you?" Her voice sounded shaky.

"Des Moines. Training."

"When will you get back? I'm scared."

"Friday night about seven. I'm flying into LAX on United."

"I'll meet you there, near the baggage claim. Got to go," she whispered. "Someone just came into the office."

Fred was about to say that he always traveled light and wouldn't check anything, when she hung up.

*   *   *

Fred passed by the side of the security area, and followed the signs to the baggage claim area. He waited with other passengers from his flight by the carousel. There was no sign of Linda. After what felt like an interminable wait, bags started to arrive. Fred fretted while, one by one the passengers picked up their bags and left; still no Linda. He was about to give up, when a group from another flight appeared. Linda was with them. She came over to him with her scarf-covered head down, carrying a large shopping bag.

"I was getting worried," Fred said.

"I saw you arrive and waited to see if anyone followed you."

"That bad?"

"I don't know." She sounded scared. "Franklin Jackson grilled me for hours."

"What did he want?"

"I think he was trying to find out whether Gene had done more than he'd admitted to the ambassador."

"So—"

"I didn't tell them about you. I've got your files here. They only got the duplicate set that has you working for Gene in L.A."

"Did Jackson believe you?"

"I don't know, Fred." A tear ran down her cheek. "I just...."

Fred put his arm around her. "Let's get a coffee. There's a place upstairs."

When they were seated at a corner table, away from other customers, Linda handed Fred a thick manila envelope. "This is your real file, and Gene's summary of everything he knows about the bishop and the-you-know-whats."

"Thanks." Fred took the envelope and put it on his knees.

Linda eyes became teary, and she gripped the edge of the table hard. "I can't believe what happened. Patsy is such a sweet lady, and he's the best boss I've ever had." She took a Kleenex from her bag, blew her nose and dabbed her eyes.

"Have you been to see them?"

"Yesterday. They were taken to the Hoag Memorial Hospital in Newport Beach. Gene sounded very weak. There was a man from Homeland Security in the room. Gene made it clear we shouldn't talk about…you know. But he managed to let me know that he's looking forward to seeing you when they leave him alone. He says best if you wait for him to contact you."

"What do you know about the explosion?"

"Some of the people in the office said it looked suspicious to them. Jackson arranged a meeting and the ambassador and the fire and police investigators and an FBI expert came and spoke to all of us."

"What did they say?"

"The guy from the fire department said he'd not seen many cases like it—gas getting into the wall space like that—but it did happen occasionally. The police officer agreed, said it looked like the explosion might have been triggered by someone turning on the oven. The FBI guy said they found shattered electronics but that it looked like it came from a TV."

"That's it?"

"Well, not exactly. One of the neighbors told them she'd seen a woman, wearing what looked like gas company clothes, working on the outside. The gas company said that they'd not had any crews working in the area, and it wasn't meter-reading time."

Fred's stomach clenched. "Any description of the woman?"

"Small, athletic-looking I think, and brown hair." Linda looked at Fred sharply. "You look like you know something."

"There's someone who fits the bill, and she's a killer."

"Oh, Fred, how awful, and all because Gene was doing his job." Linda started to cry again. "What can we do? I'll have to go to the Westwood Cemetery and talk to Marilyn. She always gives me good advice."

"I need to go through Gene's material and see if there's anything new. The ambassador's already rejected the basic case; partly because Gene chose not to tell them about me until he'd tied the bishop to the reverend in Salt Flat. I can tell people what I saw. Problem is I don't know who to trust. Gene mentioned a department lawyer, Victor Hessman, maybe he could help. Do you think you could find out his background?"

"I'll try." Linda wiped her eyes and attempted a brave smile. "At least I'll feel that I'm doing something."

She pushed her coffee cup away and stood. "I've got to go. My babysitter will turn into a pumpkin if I don't get back soon." She hurried away.

"Take care," Fred called after her. He sat for a while finishing his coffee, thinking about how to proceed. He decided to do nothing except make more copies of Gene's files until he'd heard about Hessman. He put the envelope in his bag. As he left the cafeteria, he felt someone take his arm. He turned to see a man in a dark suit.

"We'll carry that for you, Mr. Schwarzmuller," the man said. A second man came up on his other side.

"Wait a second! Who are you?" Fred said, but he knew the answer.

"Homeland Security. Please come with us. Mr. Jackson wants to talk to you."

27.

One agent remained with Fred in Rashona's office, while the other agent carried his bag into Jackson's office. After forty minutes, the second agent opened the door and motioned for them to come in. Jackson was sitting behind his desk looking pensive, but smiled broadly when Fred entered. A second man stood to the side of the desk, under a photograph of Jackson with the vice president. Jackson motioned for the agents to leave.

"Fred, I would like to say that I am happy to see you," Jackson said unctuously. "But these are not happy times. I have asked our attorney, Victor Hessman, to attend our discussion. It will be recorded and transcribed. He pointed to an area microphone on his left. Victor, it's all yours."

"Mr. Schwarzmuller, it appears that you were not totally forthcoming with us about your activities." Hessman picked up the files that Linda had given Fred. "These files indicate that you were in Albuquerque for most of the time we were told you were here in L.A., but they do not say what you were doing there. We would like a detailed account of what you did after initial training up to the time you went to Wisconsin."

"Mr. Kowalski assigned me to work on the movie *Bye Bye Oscars*."

"He what?" Jackson exclaimed. "What on earth did you do?"

"I was understudy for the lead actor, Chuck Steak, and I helped make a copy of the Hollywood sign." Fred looked to see of anyone was going to say anything. Seeing nothing, he continued. "Mr. Kowalski picked me because I had done some acting and with hair dye I looked like the actor Chuck Steak."

"Exactly what were you assigned to do in this role?"

"See if there was more to the movie than simply a remake of the original, because it now involved a nuclear weapon."

"Were you aware that the FBI had already looked into that, and," Hessman referred to some notes, "concluded that the movie was as idiotic as the original?"

"Yes."

"Why then did Kowalski not accept that report?"

"One of the faces in the FBI photographs reminded him of someone he had met years earlier when he was looking for the stolen bombs."

"Who?"

"Chuck Steak. His real name is Charles Jenkins. He's Bishop Orpheus John's son. Mr. Kowalski saw the resemblance."

"Can you clarify the connection of Jenkins and John?" Hessman asked quietly.

"The bishop was previously known as the Reverend Orlando Jenkins. His chapel, when Mr. Kowalski met him in 1973, was in Salt Flat, near where the bombs disappeared. He—"

Jackson held up his hand, and snapped, "Did Kowalski have proof of this?"

"Not until recently. Before he and his wife were blown up, they went to Amarillo and found that the reverend moved from

Salt Flat and set up a chapel near the Pantex site. He had changed his name to Orlando John."

"Kowalski was in Amarillo to check on the bishop!" Jackson exclaimed. "We stopped that investigation. It will not look good on his record."

Fred started in surprise. "What?"

Jackson's voice rose as he answered, "Flagrant disregard for orders."

"Franklin, he's severely injured in hospital," Hessman said softly.

"Oh, yes.... Did you say Pantex?" Jackson looked thoughtful.

"Yes. Mr. Kowalski believed that the reverend kidnapped a technician to gain information on bomb assembly and disassembly."

"But no proof?"

"Right, but the bishop's wife admitted that the bishop had tortured Old Tex."

"His wife is where?" asked Hessman.

"In a nursing home in South Amarillo; I imagine the information is in Mr. Kowalski's notes."

Hessman looked at Jackson and shook his head. "I didn't see it. Is there another file?"

"I don't know."

"Let's get back to what you did," Hessman said. "I assume that Mr. Kowalski asked you to investigate the bishop."

"Not at first. He didn't even tell me about Chuck. He simply asked me to keep my ears open and report anything unusual."

"And?"

"Nothing at first, but Sebastian Agincourt was looking for something to make Albuquerque look like Hollywood. I suggested a copy of the Hollywood sign to be put up on Sandia Mountain. He liked the idea and agreed that I could help build it in the bishop's workshop." Hearing no question, Fred continued. "The workshop is against the basement wall of the cathedral. I noticed steel tracks on the floor leading through double doors into the basement.... They could be used to move heavy equipment. Also, I walked around the whole complex and saw substantial power lines going into the cathedral. I wondered what they were for."

Hessman glanced at his notes. "I gather the power is needed for lighting, air-conditioning, heating, and running the workshop. You have some reason to think differently?"

Fred thought for a moment, uncertain whether he should admit that he had broken into the cathedral. "Maybe, I can come back to that later. You asked me why Mr. Kowalski was convinced that Bishop John and the Reverend Jenkins were the same person. One reason was the spoonerisms."

Jackson, who had been doodling on a pad, looked up. "Spoonerisms?"

"Mixing up the first letters of two words; and named after the Victorian clergyman, the Reverend William Archibald

Spooner, who was noted for having this problem," Hessman interjected, with a rare smile, "My favorite is *shining wit*."

"Shining wit," Jackson looked puzzled for a second. "Oh, I see what you mean."

"The reverend and the bishop both do spoonerisms when they're excited," Fred said. "I went to a Sunday service. During his sermon the bishop said, '"Am I guilty of *talling* into their *frap*?'"

"Very entertaining," Franklin Jackson said sarcastically. "But hardly enough to prove anything."

Hessman consulted his notes again. "I don't think this discussion is getting anywhere. My notes say that, recently, when Ambassador Wheaton asked the bishop where he came from, the bishop volunteered that he'd come from Texas and admitted that he had changed his name."

"Why wasn't I told?" Jackson said angrily.

So Gene hadn't been told either. Fred waited for the answer with interest.

Hessman pursed his lips.

"Come on, Victor. If you don't tell me, I'll go to the ambassador."

Hessman nodded toward Fred. Jackson made a dismissive gesture. Hessman shrugged and said, "The bishop told the ambassador that when he decided to move on from his time at Salt Flat, he changed his name to Orpheus John. More distinguished than Orlando Jenkins, he felt. It's not a crime to change your name. Anyway, the ambassador decided that there was no need for anyone to know."

"Mr. Kowalski talked to the bishop's wife," Fred said, angry at the smug look on Jackson's face."

"And?" Hessman asked.

"She told him the bishop had tortured Old Tex. She also said that their daughter was as evil as the bishop."

"Do you have any record of this conversation?"

"No, Counselor. It's what Mr. Kowalski told me over the phone."

"Unfortunate." Hessman consulted his notes again. "Mrs. Jenkins died last week."

Fred had a sudden vision of Georgie. "How? Electrocution?"

"No." Hessman replied. "She had emphysema. Needed oxygen. Apparently, the supply ran out. It was like she had suffocated."

"So, no evidence again," Jackson muttered. "Back to this daughter you mentioned. You made a very strong accusation. What has she got to do with this case?"

"Georgina Jenkins, married name Williams. Known as Georgie. She's assistant to Sebastian Agincourt. His former assistant died in an apparent electrocution."

"Apparent?" Jackson asked. "You have proof it wasn't an accident?"

"No, but her husband died the same way."

"How do you know this?"

"I checked the records when I was in Madison."

"Did Kowalski ask you to do this?"

"Yes." Fred made a quick decision, and added, "I think she caused the explosion."

"Do you have any proof?" Hessman asked dryly.

Fred shook his head. They had him again. The only thing he had left was what he had seen in the cathedral. He started to say something, "I have—"

Franklin Jackson interrupted him. "It's Kowalski all over again: a lot of talk and no proof. The next thing you'll say is that you believe this story about an accelerator and tritium production, and the bomb hidden in the Oscar statue. The ambassador decided not to take any chances. We looked in every single prop from the bishops' workshop. Nada, Fred. Nada!" He sat down, looking triumphant, as if daring Fred to contradict him.

Hessman looked irritated. "You were about to say something, Mr. Schwarzmuller?"

"Nothing important," Fred replied, relieved that he hadn't blurted out what he knew. "You don't think that the ambassador may have tipped off the bishop that Mr. Kowalski was on to him?" he asked mildly.

"No," said Jackson. "What an idiotic suggestion. Gene Kowalski had it in for the bishop for reasons I cannot fathom. You seem to have been dragged into this mess. The question now is what to do with you."

Fred tried again. "You're not concerned that Hollywood may disappear next February, and there's still another bomb out there?"

"Fred, as far as we know there are still two lost bombs, and we have arranged to provide extra security. Everything going into the Kodak building will be checked thoroughly, on the faint chance that there's something in what you claim," Jackson retorted. "That satisfies me, and it should satisfy you."

"What'll I do now?" Fred asked.

"I have discussed that with the ambassador, and with Human Resources. We all agree that, because you were only following orders, you will remain in your present position reporting to me. But there are conditions. You may not contact or in any way bother the bishop. You must stay out of Albuquerque. And you must not discuss this case with anyone. If you do, I will have you locked up. Is that clear."

"Yes…, sir. What then? Stay here in L.A?"

"Until after Christmas, when you will return to Texas to continue the search for the bombs." Jackson emphasized the plural. "You may go now."

When he reached the street, Fred remembered that his car was still at the airport. "Shit." he muttered. He stopped and flagged down a taxi.. What to do? The bastards had an answer for every issue he could raise. He knew they were wrong, but who would believe him if he told them what he had seen in the cathedral. He could hear them. "Was it well lit?" "Do you have photographs?" Only a poor picture of Old Tex's bones. "How do you know who that is?" The bishop had given them an answer for everything. Maybe their security checks at the Oscars would be enough. He realized that dealing with the bishop was now his mission—alone. He didn't know what to do, except talk to Hessman. If he went to the press, the Feds would throw him in jail. His stomach hurt. Think about something else. Moon Pies. He grimaced. No, not even Moon Pies. Millie. He had an image of her dressed as Monique von Minx. He smiled for a second. But he wasn't allowed to go to Albuquerque. Maybe she'd come to El Paso when he returned there. That'd work. Tomorrow afternoon he'd talk to Linda. See what she'd found out about Hessman.

* * *

Fred, remembering that Linda went to Marilyn Monroe's grave when she was worried, called Linda. "Marilyn," Fred was all he said, when Linda answered the phone.

"I think you have a wrong number," she replied and hung up.

Fred stood in the alcove that contained Dean Martin's crypt, and scanned the people wandering around the Westwood Memorial Cemetery; an activity that had engaged him for the forty minutes since six o'clock. He hoped that Linda had understood his message.

"I've been checking to see if anyone followed me," a voice said from just outside the alcove. "I think we're okay." Linda appeared from around the corner. "Let's go to Marilyn."

"These all yours?" Fred asked, pointing at the array of floral tributes and photographs on the ground under Marilyn Monroe's plaque.

"No, silly." Linda's smile vanished quickly. "Is there a problem?"

"After I left you, the goons from Homeland Security picked me up," Fred said quietly.

"Oh, Fred, how terrible. Am I next?" Linda looked distraught.

"They reamed me out, but said that I was only acting under orders. I'm sure they'll say the same to you."

"You think?"

Fred made an effort to sound more confident than he was. "If we still work for them they have control."

"Yes. Did you tell them what you saw in the cathedral?"

"I was going to, when they told me they'd checked everything out. That's more than they told Gene." Fred paused. "Which brings me to Hessman. He might be the guy to talk to. What did you find out?"

"The word is he's a company man, but I didn't hear anything bad." Linda snorted. "He has a reputation for being honest, unlike Franklin Jackson."

"What to do?" Fred said. "I can't just ignore what I know. I guess I'll have to tell him everything."

"This may help." Linda searched in her handbag and produced a small envelope. "Gene wanted me to give you this. Good thing I decided not to bring it yesterday. The key is for a safety deposit box at a bank. The address is inside. He said to use it only if you're in real trouble." She paused. "Why don't you wait until you've talked to Gene before contacting Hessman."

"Yeah. I should," Fred replied. Thanks for your help. Now...I need a drink. Want to join me?"

"Fred, I've got to get home. But first I'd like to chat with Marilyn."

As Fred walked away, he heard Linda talking earnestly to the memorial plaque in the wall.

28.

In the morning, Fred retrieved the papers from the safety deposit box. They contained all the details of Gene's thirty-one-year quest to find the nuclear weapons. Gene explained how he had asked Fred to break into the cathedral and included details of what Fred had found, and a copy of the photo of Old Tex. Gene also described what he had found out in Amarillo.

Fred wrestled with what to do, finally coming back to what he had said to Linda. He made copies of the papers, with the intention to mail one set to his parents. Realizing that their mail might be checked, he dropped the plan. Instead he found a bank nearby and paid for a safety deposit box.

That evening, he called Millie. "It's Fred," he said when she answered.

"Where have you been?" Millie asked.

Her voice brought back memories of the delicate perfume she used. "All over the place. I was in El Paso. Then they sent me on training to Des Moines. Now I'm in L.A. until after Christmas."

"Any chance you'll be coming to Albuquerque?"

Fred replied carefully, "It's a little difficult at the moment. My company needs me here. I'll be back in El Paso around the end of January…. Maybe you could visit?"

"Or you could come to Albuquerque," Millie retorted sharply. "Mother's not doing well. I can't leave her."

"I'll see what I can work out. I hope your mother gets better."

"So, I may see you?"

"Yes." Fred tried to sound convincing.

*   *   *

Fred remained in a state of limbo because, through Linda, he continued to hear that Gene was not yet in a fit state to see him. He began to look forward to returning to Fort Bliss, as one pitiful task followed another: preparation of a computer data base of agency vehicles and their maintenance schedules, training on a new filing system that he then had to explain to the division's secretaries, back to Des Moines for more sensitivity training after he had snapped at Franklin Jackson in frustration. Jackson kept him busy with one mundane task after another.

Finally, in the first week in December, Gene called and suggested that they meet. He and Patsy were living in an apartment in Huntington Beach while their house was being rebuilt. Fred drove over immediately and parked in front of their building. As he was approaching the entrance, he noticed an unmarked van with tinted windows parked in a corner of the lot, facing him. He could not tell if it was occupied. He found Gene's place on the ground floor and rang the bell. After a couple of minutes, he heard shuffling sounds and the door opened. He looked up expecting to see the erect figure of Gene, but a stooped old man with a scarred head and wisps of hair, his right arm in a sling, faced him. "Gene." Fred could not stop his involuntary gasp.

"Not easy is it, but I'm getting used to seeing my reflection in the mirror." Gene's mouth twisted as he attempted a smile. "Come on in."

He led Fred into a sparsely furnished small living room. "What's left of our stuff is in storage." He explained, clearly embarrassed by his situation.

"The key thing is you survived." Fred said quickly.

"You heard how we ended up?"

"In the neighbor's pool. Incredible."

"We were lucky, I guess. The water cushioned our fall. But I still have these nightmares of being adrift in the ocean, with a burning sensation…like The Ancient Mariner."

"At least you survived," Fred said. "How's Patsy doing?"

"Coming along." Gene replied. "She apologizes for not getting up, but she's not ready for company yet. Now, tell me what's happening."

"First, there's a van outside. It looks out of place."

Gene chuckled and his gray eyes looked sharp for a moment. "My bodyguards. I put odd notes in the trash and get neighbors to send large parcels of junk to obscure addresses. Keeps them busy."

"Is this place bugged?"

"Doubt it. More likely they're trying to pick up speech from laser light reflecting off vibrations on the window." Gene turned on the television to a soap opera. "Give them something to listen to. Now, what's happening?"

Fred explained how he had been taking dumb courses and doing odd jobs for Jackson.

"What else?"

"It's shit not being able to do anything about the bishop. Jackson's made it clear what will happen if I say anything. The only thing I've come up with is to ask Victor Hessman for help."

"Hmm. I guess you have no choice." Gene looked pensive. "I think he's honest. Look, you've inherited the mission, son. Use your judgment. The bishop has been very clever in using the Oscar's sketch to get air time. People are going to believe that anything I say is either all part of a publicity stunt or the ranting of a nut case. In the meantime, what else are you going to do? I never got to send material to committee chairs."

"Jackson' sending me back to El Paso after Christmas. Hank and I will try and find the second bomb before the bishop does." Fred stood and paced for a moment before facing his ex-boss. "I feel helpless."

Gene shrugged. Gene winced and his head sank. "Sorry I need to rest, can you get me down the corridor?"

Fred helped Gene to his feet and walked with him to a bedroom door.

"Give my regards, to Hank," Gene said weakly, and pushed the door open.

When Fred left, the van had gone. He drove back to his apartment, hoping that *As the World Turns* had drowned out his discussion.

He half-watched another soap opera, before picking up the phone and calling Victor Hessman. "I need to talk to you, privately," he said.

"I will have to record our conversation," Hessman replied.

Fred began to regret his decision, but images of Hiroshima and Nagasaki came to mind He couldn't act as if the whole thing was a fantasy. "Okay."

"I had the feeling you weren't telling us everything," Hessman said when Fred entered his office. He switched on a recorder. "What made you decide to talk to me?"

"There is a bomb. The bishop plans to blow up the Oscars. Like Gene, I can't just let it go. Look what happened to him. They may come after me." Fred looked to see if there was a reaction.

Hessman continued to stare at him. "I keep seeing images of Hiroshima," Fred said.

"Strangely, so do I," Hessman said. "Go ahead. Tell me what you know."

Fred handed over Gene's package. "These are all Gene Kowalski's notes on the investigation. In them, you'll find out that I was the person who broke into the cathedral. I saw the viewing coffins and took the photograph of Old Tex. I heard the

363

bishop talking to them. I am pretty sure that the other two bodies were the Pantex technician and the engineer from Sandia Lab. I heard the bishop say that he had gotten enough information to finish refurbishing the bomb."

"Why didn't he see you?"

"I was hiding under a table, and it was dark."

"My God. What else?"

"I saw the accelerator and the deuterium bottle. I saw the glove box and electronic lab. I'm convinced they were making tritium, and redoing the electronic trigger for the bomb."

"Kowalski mentioned a bomb crate."

"I saw one but didn't have time to photograph it."

Hessman sat back and rubbed his face with his hands. "What exactly do you expect me to do with this information?"

"Tell people higher up what's happening."

"Do you mean the ambassador and Franklin Jackson?"

"You're kidding!"

Hessman smiled. "Not totally, but I see your point." He fiddled with a pen for a moment before continuing. "I won't be able to keep you out of this."

"I know."

"I need time to plan this out, but I will do something," Hessman said. "I have a contact in D.C. who may be able to help. It'll probably be after Christmas. He's on travel." Hessman held out his hand. "I think it will be best if you don't call me again, in case the wrong people find out. I'll try to get word to you. Be careful."

"Yes, sir. Thank you." Fred shook Hessman's hand and left. Feeling good about having found an ally, he found a store and bought a Moon Pie and a Dr. Pepper. Life was looking up.

* * *

Around the middle of December, Fred noticed that Sebastian Agincourt would be a guest on a late night show. Not surprising, *Bye Bye Oscars* had been an instant success, joining the original as an excuse for a late night party. Raucous gatherings performed the countdown scene. A rap song, *Three, two, one, boom*, rose to the top of the charts and led to a new dance— somewhere between the lambada and the conga.

He stayed up to watch. When Sebastian waddled onto the set, the audience stood and counted down. The host joined and the first guest, Marlene Bountiful, a hopeful starlet, joined in. Sebastian shook the host's hand and embraced Marlene, who pressed against him, and whispered loudly enough to be picked up by a microphone, "I'd love a part in your next movie."

The host arched his eyebrows, went tut-tut with his fingers and said, "*Bye Bye Oscars*, Sebastian, wow! What can I say?"

"It's going well."

"Wow! I hear there'll be a retrospective of your work at the Oscars. Can you say anything about it?"

Sebastian looked coy. "Nothing finalized yet, but we're all hopeful."

"Will they do the countdown scene?"

"It's being discussed."

"That'd be so awesome," Marlene gushed, patting Sebastian's hand.

Sebastian raised her hand to his lips, and kissed it. "You are so kind."

"When you two have finished canoodling." The host's eyebrows arched. "Ten, nine, eight…I'd like to get back to the interview."

Laughter as the audience joined in the countdown.

The host waited until they all reached one, then said, "Can you tell us anything about your next movie, Sebastian?"

Sebastian squirmed in his seat. "I'm not—"

"Oh, come on, you're among friends."

"Please, Sebastian," Marlene put her hand on his knee

"It's in the early stages. I've a first draft of the script."

"*Bye Bye Oscars Three. Bactrian Camels Two.* Does it have a name?" The host raised his arms appealing to the audience to help him. They responded with cheers.

"*The Last Tribe of Israel*," Sebastian said quickly.

"Wow! A provocative title. What's the story?"

Sebastian's pudgy face broke into a grin and his Van Dyke beard quivered. "When I've made it you'll find out."

"Ladies and gentlemen, Sebastian Agincourt." The host clapped and the audience stood. "My next guest—"

Fred switched off the set. *The Last Tribe of Israel.* What did that mean? Another script from the bishop? Millie might know or could find out. He lay back and had happy thoughts about her as he fell asleep.

*   *   *

Three days before Christmas, Fred phoned Millie. "Merry Christmas," he said when she answered.

"Where are you?"

"Austin, with my parents," he said from New Braunfels.

"That's a shame. I wanted to give you a big kiss for the wonderful present. It came two days ago."

"Hey, you already opened it."

"I just couldn't wait." Millie giggled.

Fred remembered agonizing in one jeweler's after another trying to find the right present. "Are they okay?"

"They're lovely. The only thing that worried me was whether you could afford such pretty sapphire earrings."

"I raided my piggy bank."

"Oh, Fred." Kissing sounds followed.

"I loved the tie you sent me." Fred tried to lie convincingly. He never wore ties. "How's your mother doing?"

A big sigh, followed by. "Not well. I had to put her in a nursing home."

"You're on your own for Christmas?"

"No, Lance and his friend are coming over, and we're invited to Sebastian's for drinks."

"Great. Incidentally, I saw Sebastian on TV. He mentioned a new movie, *The Last Tribe of Israel*. Have you heard anything about it?"

"No. I'll ask Lance." Millie sounded puzzled. "I'm looking for a new role. I was hoping Sebastian would ask me."

"Well, if you hear anything."

Millie chuckled. "I'll let you know."

Fred decided to go for broke. "Millie, we don't have much of a romance, do we? I mean...."

"I wish I knew what you meant, Fred." Millie sounded thoughtful. "I need time to get to know you. Except for being on the set together we've hardly done anything."

"That's what I mean."

"But not what I meant." Millie now sounded irritated. "Get it through your head. I'm not Monique."

"It came out all wrong. I really like you, and want to see you, but I'm in a difficult position. Can't explain."

"Well, when you can, call me."

"In the New Year." Fred kissed the telephone, and closed it.

* * *

"Franklin wanted to see me?" Fred asked as he went into Rashona's office.

"No, I did." Rashona smiled. "Franklin's already gone." She pushed a manila envelope on her desk toward him. "These are your travel orders for the next training course."

"What about going back to Texas?"

"Not sure, 'xactly, but I don't think it'll be until the second week in February."

"I was beginning to wonder if Franklin had changed his mind."

"No. It was a problem at their end." She pointed at Fred's left arm, which was curled behind him. "Something wrong with your arm?"

"No." With a flourish, Fred presented her the bouquet of roses he'd been hiding. "Merry Christmas, Rashona."

Rashona hung her head. When she looked up, her eyes were shining. "Fred, they're beautiful. But, I don't have anything for you."

"No problem."

She emerged from behind the desk, a small version of Aretha Franklin. "Let momma give you a hug." She embraced Fred until he thought that he would faint from the pressure of her massive breasts and her pungent perfume. "You look after yourself. Have fun in Des Moines." She pecked his cheek and released him.

"You're joking."

"You'll find a way." She smiled roguishly.

29.

Des Moines in January was hell. Not only was the course boring, but Hessman had still not been able to deal with their problem, although he claimed that he was making progress. Fred remained in a state of numbness until, on a cold Sunday in the second week in February, he returned to Fort Bliss. Thank God. A chance to do something. After picking up a badge, he called Hank Collins. "I'm back, Hank. I'm on my way to my room. Same place as before."

"I'll be right there, Mr. Schwarzmuller. We need to talk," Hank replied.

Surnames, we're back on the base, back in the army. "Right, Sergeant Collins."

Hank didn't waste any time getting to the point after they had shaken hands. "What happened to Gene and Patsy? The bishop?"

Don't comment on how bad Gene looked. "Recovering slowly. As for the bishop, I think his daughter, Georgie, set up the explosion."

"Have you discussed this with your management?"

"Yes, and they didn't believe Gene about anything, and they didn't believe me."

"Shit. Why not?" Hank pounded the side of his Jeep.

"I'm sorry. I can't discuss it. My assignment is to find the bombs."

"But you think the bishop's already got one? You're not going to do anything?"

Fred thought about what else to say before adding, "There is one guy who is trying to do something, but I haven't heard from him." Fred looked away. "My hands are tied. I think Homeland's doing everything it can."

Hank shook his head. "Orders. Damned orders. I'll see you first thing in the morning." He left.

Embarrassed by the pathetic answer he'd given, Fred watched as Hank left. Gene gone and no way he could see to punish the guilty. Then, what about the Oscars? Did the bishop really plan to blow up the ceremony? He only had one bomb. Maybe he planned to use it in the *Last Tribe of Israel;* another of his scripts, so Lance had implied to Millie. For someone as bigoted as the bishop, the Middle East would be a more likely target than Hollywood. God, he was having weasel thoughts again. And why hadn't he heard from Hessman. He picked up his cell phone and dialed.

"Anything happening?" Fred said when Hessman answered.

"I talked to my contact in D.C.," Hessman replied. "He referred me back to the ambassador."

"Oh, sh...."

"The ambassador's still not convinced about the bishop. Frankly, he doesn't want to ruin his chance to go to the Oscars ceremony. It's all he'll talk about."

"You're kidding?"

"No. And his wife's got a fancy new dress. It's that bad."

"Do I need to come back to L.A.?"

"Better not. I'm going to keep on working on him. Stay cool." Hessman hung up.

An early morning mist clung to the peak of El Capitan when Fred and Hank reached the park gates. Sunlight reflected off the rocks at the base of the mountain.

Hank stopped the Hummer. "Beautiful. It nearly makes me forget what we're here for. Gene loved this view," he said pointedly.

"Where do you want to start?" Fred said, changing the subject deliberately.

Hank looked straight ahead. "You can't ignore what happened, Fred. If there's something you can do, for God's sake do it."

"I don't see anything I can do that would make a damn bit of difference, except to find the second bomb before the bishop does. Okay?"

Hank shrugged. "Okay. Well, I think we've beaten Bone and Shumard to death. Let's try farther to the northwest beyond the

El Capitan trail…fewer hikers. More likely Old Tex would have hidden something there."

"What if we don't find anything?" Fred asked.

"Have a go at Guadalupe Canyon and Glover Canyon."

"Outside the park?"

"Sure. Those crates were quite heavy, but anywhere within ten miles or so of where the truck crashed is fair game."

*   *   *

"Bishop, good to see you. Please have a seat." Ambassador Wheaton beamed at the gaunt figure in the white suit who had just entered his office.

"My pleasure, too, Ambassador. I dropped by to tell you that all the arrangements have been made for you and your dear wife to join my son and me at the Oscars. A chauffeur will pick you up in a limousine. We can confirm the time later."

"Wonderful. So your son will be there?"

"Yes, he has a lead role in the movie. And he'll be appearing in a *Bye Bye Oscars* sketch at the ceremony."

"Good for him." Wheaton clasped his hands in front of his nose and adopted a serious tone. "Bishop John, I apologize for having to put you through such a trying time. But, when someone raises an issue we have no choice…." He waved his hands deprecatingly.

Uneven white teeth flashed briefly between the white beard and moustache. "I fully understand, Ambassador. It's your job.

May the unfortunate person who made the accusations go with God."

Wheaton unclasped his hands and looked at the photograph of the vice president on the wall. "I probably shouldn't tell you this but there was a gas explosion and the investigator and his wife...." He made a sweeping motion with his hands and sighed.

"I see." The bishop bowed his head as if in prayer. "God moves in mysterious ways." After a brief moment of silence, he looked up. "So, one way or another, I can assume this is the end of it."

"Yes, Bishop. We have made various reassignments. The matter is settled."

"Good. Now, I must go to help organize a fundraiser for a local congressional candidate. I will leave you to your important work. May the blessings of the Lord be with you."

A few minutes after the bishop had left, Wheaton called Victor Hessman. "Victor, I just heard something that should reassure you about the Oscars business." He listened for a minute. "Yes, I know you have concerns, but I was just talking to the bishop. Both he and his son will be attending the ceremony. He's obviously very proud of his son. I can't see the bishop sending him to his death." Wheaton paused again and listened. "Look I've arranged for a bomb squad and a detachment of fully-armed troops to be standing by near the garage. At the slightest hint of a problem, I'll send them in." He listened again. "Glad you agree. Anyway, the bishop will be there, too." He put down the phone, turned toward the photograph of the president and saluted.

*   *   *

"A whole week and not a single hit." Fred clicked the icon and started retracting the boom. "We're missing something."

Hank Collins nodded. "I agree. Somehow we have to get into Old Tex's mind."

"Yeah. What would he have thought about when he found the bombs?"

"We need to discuss it, but I need a break." Hank said. "Let's go into Carlsbad and find a bar. We can discuss Old Tex's thought process over a couple of beers."

Fred took a swig from his cold mug of Pearl. "So if you were Old Tex what would you have done?"

Hank clasped his mug and looked into the golden liquid. "Get out of there as quickly as possible. Old Tex was a pack rat. I'm sure he had lots of hidey holes for his treasures. He'd likely go to the nearest one that was big enough to conceal a crate."

"Then go to the second one and then…?"

Hank scratched his head. "I remember Gene telling us that Old Tex had been seen at the Salt Flat Cafe, not long after the crash. The next time anyone saw him was when they found what the reverend claimed was Old Tex's body down 54 toward Van Horn." Hank took a sip of beer. "Boy, we wasted a hell of a lot of time searching around that Route 54."

"What do you think Gene would do?"

Hank looked up from his beer. "Gene always says…said." He lifted his glass and finished the beer in one go. "I'll get a couple more." His beer mug hid his face as he turned away.

When Hank returned, he said, "Gene was convinced that the reverend took the first bomb. He reckoned that the second one would be between the crash and that bend in the trail we looked at."

"You're not so sure anymore?"

"Right. We never paid much attention to the area behind the chapel."

"What about near the Salt Flat Cafe?"

"That neither. Gene reckoned that Old Tex would not have buried it where people might see him." Hank sipped his beer. "Maybe Gene was wrong."

"How about we search the chapel area up to the Williams Ranch, next, and then the two canyons? If there's nothing up there, we can work our way over the salt flats to the café."

"Agreed. I need to get back to the base tomorrow. We can go out again Monday, if the weather's okay."

*   *   *

Fred was having breakfast on the Monday morning when Hank dropped by. "Bad weather is on the way. They're predicting freezing rain," Hank said. "I'm afraid we'll be stuck here for a couple of days."

"I'll think of something to do," Fred replied. "Polish the Hummer. Reread the manual."

"Good. It may be longer, if it gets really wet." Hank walked toward the door. "Either way, the commandant needs me to do a job for him. How about we try again next Monday, same time?"

"Okay." A whole week with no commitments, Fred thought. He wondered what Millie's was doing? In their weekly telephone calls she had told him that her mother was now permanently in a nursing home, and her life had become easier.

Fred phoned Millie only to get her answering machine. "I'm not able to come to the phone," Millie's voice said. "Please leave a message."

Damn. "Hi, Millie, it's Fred. I may have some time off this week. I thought we might get together if you're not working full time, and if the roads aren't covered in ice. I miss you," he said, having made a quick decision not to mention where he could meet her.

Fred spent the rest of the day with the Army technician to improve the operation of the boom. Its motion had become jerky, which turned out to be due to a faulty hydraulic hose. The technician replaced the hose and Fred took the time to refine his control of the boom. One of the problems he'd encountered was an overly sensitive pressure sensor. He called Klevan.

"The pressure sensor on the boom freezes up if I brush the head against a plant. Can I reset the device, and keep it moving?"

"Has it prevented you from doing your job?" Klevan asked brusquely.

"Not exactly, but it's a real pain."

"It's possible, but I'd prefer that you didn't mess with anything." Klevan paused. "I could send Joseph down, but it would cost you."

Fred considered quickly how Franklin Jackson would respond to a request. "I don't think I could authorize that."

"You can double click on the boom icon to override the sensor. But, Mr. Schwarzmuller, please remember that you will be responsible for any damage." Klevan said sharply. "Don't—"

"Don't worry. I'll look after your baby. Have a nice day." Fred hung up.

A few hours later he phoned Millie again. This time she answered and sounded happy to hear from him. "I'd love to see you," she said. "I'm free on Friday."

"Friday'll work. There's just one thing." Fred paused. Mustn't piss Millie off. "Uh, I can't explain, but I can't come into Albuquerque. Could you meet me in, say Socorro?"

After a long silence, Millie said, "I don't understand, but I suppose I could. Are you in trouble?"

"In a way. The people I work with don't want me to...."

"Is it something to do with *Bye Bye Oscars*?"

"Sorta. I really don't want to talk about it."

"Okay. How about we meet at the San Miguel Mission on El Camino Real at ten? I'll have to leave by two to visit mother."

"Great. I'll be there at ten." Fred closed the phone. Bless Millie. His previous girlfriend would have bitched and bitched. Now, if only she would play Monique von Minx for him, everything would be perfect. He mused on this happy thought as he sipped a Dr Pepper, and watched television; another National Geographic program about the growing volcanic island in Thera Bay in the Meditteranean.

* * *

A bitter wind stirred up the dust as Fred drove down El Camino Real. He spotted Millie in jeans, boots, and an anorak standing outside the mission door; hugging herself and stamping her feet to ward off the cold. She rushed up to his car and embraced him the minute he got out.

"I'm freezing," she said, brushing cold lips and a red nose against his cheek.

"We need to share bodily warmth. It's a line from a James Bond movie," Fred replied. "And I hoped it was because you needed me."

Millie snuggled against him. "I do, really, but I don't see you very often, and if you can't come to Albuquerque, where—"

"Trysts in cheap neon-lit motels out in the boonies," Fred replied. "It works for me."

"Fred, be serious." Millie pulled back and shook her head. "I'm not Monique."

"I know, but allow a guy his dreams." He grinned, considering the limited choices they had, and asked, "Where do you want to go?"

"I've never been inside the mission. There's also a museum of some kind." Millie buried her head on his shoulder, and said in a muffled voice. "I need time to get used to you again. I've lots of questions. I'll save them for lunch."

Fred paid little attention as they toured. He made polite comments, and thought how gorgeous Millie looked with her pink cheeks and sparkling eyes. Reality returned when they sat down for lunch in the café on Manzanares Street.

"What do you really do for a living, Fred?" Millie asked.

Fred took a bite of his organic sandwich, while deciding how to reply. If things were going to work out with Millie, he had to trust her…at least a bit. "I work for Homeland Security," he said, tired of pretending to be was someone he wasn't.

Millie nodded thoughtfully. "That would explain a lot. Is Fred Howard your real name?"

"How does Frederick Howard Schwarzmuller grab you?"

"Schwarzmuller. That's what that man called you over the phone. You lied." She smacked his hand.

"I hadn't decided to tell you, then."

"Mildred Howard. Mildred Schwarzmuller. I'll sound like Arnold's great aunt. Yuck." Millie made a face. "So, what do you do?"

"Investigate things."

"*Bye Bye Oscars*!" Millie was incredulous.

Fred nodded. "Sorta."

"It's not the movie, exactly, is it? I remember you asking me a lot of questions." Millie studied Fred carefully. "You were investigating the bishop, weren't you?"

"Millie, I've said enough."

"Getting information; is that the only reason you dated me?"

"No, and I was really disappointed when you kept turning me down."

"I told you why…my mother."

"I thought you were making an excuse because you didn't like me."

"I liked you, but I've been burned by people coming onto me because of roles like Monique." Millie sighed. "They assume too much."

"I don't, anymore." Fred changed the subject. "How's your mother doing?"

"Not well. She hasn't got long."

"What will you do when—"

"Leave Albuquerque. I'm getting offers from Hollywood." Millie sipped her Diet Coke. "In fact, Sebastian wants me to be in the Oscars sketch. It would be a great showcase—"

Fred held onto the table, and pretended interest in a flyer advertising an upcoming Celtic music session in the café.

"What's the matter?" Millie looked scared.

"I wonder if that would be a good idea," Fred said, keeping his voice even while he tried to create a plausible argument as to why she should not attend. "Being seen as Monique might cause people to typecast you."

"Good point, but…but anyway I turned him down. I won't leave my mother, not now."

"I think you're doing the right thing," Fred said, trying to keep his voice even and relieved that Millie appeared to accept his comments at face value.

"You're in El Paso. Where are you working?"

Fred had an answer prepared. "Fort Bliss, learning about explosives," he replied.

"Don't get hurt." Millie finished her drink.

"When will I see you again?" she asked as they left the café.

"I'm tied up until after the Oscars. The following week should work. I'll call you."

They drove back to the mission where Fred picked up his car. Millie's farewell kiss was long and loving. Fred toyed briefly with the idea of asking her to stay. Her body said she might like to, but he knew she would turn him down. *I need to keep an eye on Mom,* she would say. He watched wistfully as she drove down the road toward Albuquerque.

* * *

Hank pulled the Hummer off the road and headed down the track to where the Reverend Jenkins' chapel had been. He stopped just beyond the cemetery, looked north toward El Capitan, and said to Fred, "If Tex buried the second bomb between here and the Williams Trail, I think he would have come west off the trail, along the base of Quail Mountain, and down here by Cone Peak."

"Makes sense. I'll get the detector set up." Fred pushed the button to retract the canvas hood. As it came back he looked up at Cone Peak. "Are we just going to look at the dry stream beds or do we need to go up the hills?"

Hank looked thoughtful. "The burros must have been pretty tired by the time they got here. I think he would have stayed on the flat. We'll only go up if we see some unusual feature; a cairn or a clump of shrubs."

For three and a half days Hank and Fred systematically worked their way to the Williams Trail and back; gradually moving east from the mountains toward the main road. At night, they slept in the Hummer, turning on the engine periodically to use the heater and stay warm. On their first few circuits, they walked up to check odd features on the rock-strewn mountainsides, but found nothing of interest. Finally, they made a detailed search around the chapel and where the reverend's cabin had been.

"Waste of time," Fred sighed.

"Not really." Hank gave a rare smile. "When we eliminate an area it helps us to find the real place. This afternoon, we'll start north up Guadalupe Arroyo, and if that doesn't work we'll try Glover Canyon."

"And then?"

"Down the road to the Salt Flat cafe," Hank replied firmly.

"What if the bishop's already found the second bomb?"

"Fred, the ranger told us he'd seen him recently," Hank said with irritation. "Like us, he's still looking."

"Sorry. I'm worried about what the bishop's going to do with the first bomb."

"I know. Gene reckoned the bishop was going to nuke the Oscars—"

"You don't agree?"

Hank scratched his head. "It sounds too Mickey Mouse." He laughed. "What I mean is, surely he'd use it for something more dramatic; take out Washington or I don't know."

Fred thought for a while before responding. "Good point, but…." An image of the cathedral flashed through Fred's mind. "He's raised heaven and earth to get a remake of *Bye Bye Oscars* and an Agincourt retrospective into the ceremony."

"Is there anything you can do?"

"I'm stuck." Fred said the words, thinking that the words sounded pathetic.

"Tell you what; on Sunday we'll go back to that bar in Carlsbad. Get them to turn on the Oscars on their TVs. If you're right, I'll buy the drinks. Hell. I'll even get you a Moon Pie. If I'm right, you buy."

"Done. I pray you're right," Fred said. They shook on the deal. For a moment he was tempted to say, "Can it, I'm going back to LA." But what would he do when he got there?

Two and a half backbreaking days later with jolting rides in the Hummer, they were finished with the canyons, tired and frustrated. "All we've done is scared jack rabbits and rattlers, and crushed unsuspecting plants," Fred muttered. "You know, maybe the detector isn't working."

"Easy to find out," Hank replied, reaching for his bag. He pulled out a government-issue pistol and handed it to Fred. "See if you get a signal."

Fred took the pistol, paced out five yards and placed it on the ground. He returned to the Hummer, turned on the detector and extended the boom. The bells pealed out as he lowered the detector.

"Satisfied?" Hank asked.

"Yup. It's Friday, let's get a drink."

A sign outside the bar showed a crudely drawn picture of a mutant alien jellyfish next to a mushroom cloud. The advertisement said, "Oscar party every night this week."

"And I wasn't sure they'd show the ceremony at all," Fred said, bemusedly.

Hank grunted. "I'd better park away from the building. I don't want some drunk messing with the Hummer." He pulled over into a neighboring lot.

Inside, the bar was crowded and noisy. A few of the customers, anticipating the main event, were wearing *Bye Bye Oscars* costumes; including two women as poor versions of Monique von Minx.

"Like a Jimmy Buffett concert," Hank said.

"No parrots. You a fan?"

"Ever since *Margaritaville*."

The TV sets showed the red carpet and celebrities arriving for the 2005 Oscars ceremony. Fred and Hank found a table away from the rowdies at the bar. When the waitress appeared, they ordered loaded nachos and a pitcher of beer, and watched the program in silence.

"You never told me what you were doing before you came here with the detector," Hank said as he finished his second beer.

"I worked on the remake of *Bye Bye Oscars*."

Hank stopped in the middle of unlocking a nacho chip from the congealed mess that remained on his plate. "You're kidding. Doing what?"

"I was a stand-in for the lead, Chuck Steak."

"Hmm, sounds like a porno movie star's name." Hank poured himself a beer. "Get any action?"

"No. Agincourt needed someone to do the scenes Chuck screwed up. No screwing for me." Fred looked at his plate. "I'm still hungry. Want some *sopapillas*?"

"Why not. That's all you did?"

Fred signaled to the waitress. "The props for *Bye Bye* were made in the bishop's workshop. I—"

"How do you know that?" asked the waitress, who had just arrived.

"I had a bit part in the movie, and helped make some of the props," Fred replied unwisely.

The waitress put two fingers to her mouth and let out a piercing whistle. The noise in the bar subsided. "Folks. This gentleman here is in the new *Bye Bye Oscars*."

"Yeah sure," a surly looking man yelled. "And I played opposite John Wayne in *The Alamo*."

"What part of the Mexican Army was that?" a drunken voice yelled back.

"Up yours."

"Were you really in it?" a quiet woman's voice asked.

"As a double for Chuck Steak."

"Can I have your autograph?" She handed Fred a bar menu.

Fred made a signing motion with his hand, and the waitress handed him a pen, saying, "Did you want to order something?"

"*Sopapillas*—"

"And another pitcher," Hank added, watching in amusement as a crowd of women clustered around their table waiting to get Fred's signature.

By the time Fred had finished signing, the waitress had brought their order.

Fred sipped his beer and watched an earlier Oscar ceremony disinterestedly.

Hank quickly downed two more beers. When the pitcher was empty, Hank said, "I've had enough fun. Let's find somewhere to camp." He stood and held onto the table. "Not too far, I need to sleep this off."

"You want me to leave my fans?"

"Your fans? You should have seen your face." Hank was laughing as he weaved toward the door.

"I'll see you out there. I need to make a pit stop," Fred said.

When Fred left the bar, the emcee was introducing the presenters for best animated feature. He walked to the Hummer. The cold air made him dizzy for a moment or two, and his eyesight became blurry. He saw Hank's figure hunched over in the passenger seat. He obviously wants me to drive Fred thought, and slid into the driver's seat."

"I'll go to that rest area back toward the park. You asleep?" Fred asked. Hearing no response, he prodded Hank, who rolled over against the passenger door. The light from a street lamp illuminated the red flow congealing on his throat. His face wore an uncharacteristic grin.

"You should have had less beer, Hank," said Fred sadly as he reached for his cell phone.

Georgie's voice came from the operator's seat. "Don't try anything, Fred. I've got a gun pointed at your guts."

"How long have you been watching us?" Fred asked, trying to gain time to figure out what to do.

"Last couple of weeks."

"I should have expected it," Fred said bitterly.

"Wouldn't have done any good," Georgie giggled. "You're all so stupid we'd have got you anyway. Now put your hands behind your back."

Fred ignored her until he felt the gun pushed hard against his spine. Fred complied, and Georgie quickly snugged a plastic tie to bind his wrists.

She pointed the gun at him and said, "Now get in the back and lie down on the seat, facing away from the driver."

Fred managed to do it with difficulty. Georgie scrambled past him into the front. He was tempted to bite her, but reckoned she'd enjoy it and use the opportunity to hurt him.

After a minute, Fred heard the engine start, and felt the Hummer move.

"Where are we going?"

"Back to the park." Georgie cackled. "You're going to show me how to use this thing, and tell me where to look."

"No way."

"I can hurt you real bad, Fred, and I will if necessary. Dad'll be here late Sunday."

Fred shivered, remembering what the bishop did to his victims. Stall for time. "So it's you and me alone until then?"

"No, Miguel and…never you mind will be here tomorrow night."

"Since I haven't a chance, where's the first bomb?"

Georgie giggled. "I'm not telling."

"Everything'll be searched. They'll find it."

Georgie laughed. "And what are they going to do?"

"Disarm the damn thing," Fred retorted.

"Sure, and ten seconds later…boom!" Georgie punched Fred in the side to bring home the point. "Do you think Carl's stupid? Now, you concentrate on how you're going to help me find that second bomb before Dad gets here. Maybe I'll finish you off before he arrives. And you'll be grateful. Think viewing coffin."

30.

Fred woke, aching from a restless night lying in the back of the Hummer. His hands, still cuffed, had gone to sleep. He sat up, and through the windshield saw a shaft of light break out of the clouds and hit the face of El Capitan. The clock on the dashboard read 7:32, El Paso time, and less than thirty-five hours until the start of the Oscars ceremony. He looked down and saw red smears on the passenger seat and door—all that was left to show what had happened to Hank.

"Georgie, I need to pee," he shouted. Silence. Fred managed to roll over onto the driver's seat, but couldn't open the door. "Georgie!"

The door opened and Fred fell forward. "I heard you. Get out," Georgie said.

Fred slid out of the Hummer and stood with difficulty, facing Georgie. She was not wearing dark glasses. He turned to show the plastic tie. "You'll need to take this off."

Georgie's pale blue eyes scanned him coldly. "No." She reached down, unzipped his pants, and pulled his penis out. "Do you need help, Fred," she said stroking expertly.

"Fuck off! What have you done with Hank?"

"Nasty. He's out of sight off the road. I dumped him last night. Now get on with it." She climbed into the Hummer.

Fred saw that Georgie had driven them into the park close to where Gene believed the first bomb had been. He considered making a run for it, but concluded that, with his hands trapped behind his back, he wouldn't get very far. Back to plan B: show Georgie how to operate the detector, and con her into going to a particular site where he might be able to get an advantage. With the bishop and his men on his way, there wouldn't be much time.

"Is there any food other than Moon Pies?" Georgie asked with irritation as she started unloading the bags that were in the back of the Hummer.

"Food locker in back. Army rations."

She came over, pushed Fred's penis back and zipped him up. "Drinks?"

"Water, orange juice, and Dr Pepper." Fred wrestled with how to phrase a question to find out how much time he had. No, not a question, but a statement that Georgie would react to. "I don't see how the bishop's going to get here without being caught. When the bomb goes off, Homeland Security's going to be looking for him," he said snidely.

"A lot you know," Georgie sniggered. "Dad'll be miles away before he triggers the bomb. You don't need to know how."

"You won't get away with it."

"Shut up while I get the food ready."

Georgie ate her meal in between asking questions about the detector. When she had finished, she said. "Now you're going to tell me where to go."

"I'd be happy to tell you where—"

"No time to be smart," Georgie snapped flipping open her switchblade.

"A drink and a Moon Pie first."

Georgie motioned as if she were going to stab him, then made a face, tore off the wrapper and held out a Moon Pie.

Before answering, Fred leaned forward and finished the Pie in four bites. He then took two swallows of Dr Pepper from the bottle that Georgie put to his mouth. "Well, Hank and I reckoned Old Tex hid the second bomb near the chapel."

"Bullshit! I saw you check it out. Nada!" Georgie put the point of the blade against Fred's wrist and pushed.

Fred groaned as Georgie worked the point against his wrist join. How many false answers before she believes the one I've chosen, he wondered? "Then you also know that we looked at Guadalupe and Glover Canyons?"

"Of course." She twisted the blade.

Fred let out an involuntary yelp. "Then you won't be interested in trying Bone and Shumard, I guess." Fred tried to make the idea uninteresting.

"No." Georgie pulled the knife away. Blood dripped on to the ground. She closed it, peered closely into Fred's face, and shoved the knife into her back pocket.

Fred looked back, trying not to blink. His mother had always known when he was lying. She would say, "That innocent face doesn't work on me, Freddie. Now tell me the truth."

"You're lying," Georgie snapped. "You don't want me to go there. Dad always reckoned the second bomb was near the Williams ranch. His detectors weren't good enough to find it. She picked up her cell phone and dialed. "I got it," she said triumphantly. "Piece of cake. You on schedule?" She listened to the answer. "Great. We're going to check out Bone and Shumard. What? You're getting faint, Dad." She shoved the phone into her pocket. "Damn. No charger. Where's your phone, Fred?"

Fred considered ignoring her but that would delay things. "In the glove compartment."

She retrieved it and dialed. "I found another phone. Oh, and the bomb's not near the chapel—they checked. I agree, if the canyons don't work out, that leaves just one place to try tomorrow. Love you. Bye."

Georgie started toward the Hummer then stopped and clicked on the phone. "It records the numbers you dial, right?" She didn't wait for an answer, dropped the phone on the ground and stomped on it until it was in tiny pieces.

She turned to Fred. "Get in the Hummer, we'll try Bone first." She picked up the uneaten food packages and drinks and put them in the Hummer, leaving the remains of their breakfast on the ground. "Let's go."

"The FBI checked all the props at the Conference center, after the bishop cleared out the cathedral. Why didn't they find the bomb?" Fred asked as they reached the canyon.

"You're all so stupid," Georgie said dismissively. "All that stuff was at the casino." She parked near the Williams ranch house. "Now, show me how this thing works."

While Fred talked, Georgie took notes on the back of the instruction manual, and left it and the pen by the computer. She spent until early afternoon checking out Bone Canyon. Fred hoped they would get to Shumard Canyon in time, but said nothing because he knew Georgie could misinterpret any attempt to get her there.

"Godammit, there's nothing here," she said wearily.

"How about lunch," Fred asked. "Can I get out? My butt's sore."

"S'pose so. When we get to Shumard."

At the base of the canyon, Georgie found some spaghetti and meatball rations and fed herself, giving a meager amount to Fred.

When they had finished, Fred said, "Why do you wear dark glasses?"

Georgie laughed, "That's a weird question from someone in your position."

"I know, but it's been bugging me since I first saw you."

"If people on the Oscars set had seen my eyes they might have made the connection to Chuck and dad."

"Why not contacts?"

"Fashion statement and I don't like contacts."

"Oh. How about a Moon Pie and Dr. Pepper?"

"Sure." Georgie stood. "It can be your last meal when we find the bomb. Get back in the Hummer."

Three hours later, as they approached Fred's chosen spot, he asked, "How many people have you killed, Georgie?"

Georgie smiled a sly smile. "Only Hank."

"Come off it. What about your husband Henry? Was he the first?"

"How do you know about Henry?"

"I checked on you. Electrocution, huh. Rough sex, I bet."

"He was a wimp. Like you."

"A wimp who looked like your brother and me, right?" Fred sneered.

"My brother wouldn't do it anymore," Georgie said bitterly. "Threatened to tell Dad."

"Then Agincourt's assistant. Same trick."

"Dumb bitch deserved it." Georgie swerved the truck from side to side, causing Fred to bang against the passenger door, and sending a shooting pain through his wrists. "Who else do you think got it?"

"Those two guys burned in the truck crash in Albuquerque, and the three bodies from the cathedral."

"That wasn't me. Carl and Miguel fixed it."

"But you caused the explosion that crippled Gene and Patsy Kowalski."

Georgie chuckled. "I was very clever, wasn't I?"

"He was my friend."

"Tough shit!"

"You killed your own mother, too. Why?"

"She threatened to tell Dad about me and Chuck. Anyway, Dad said it was time for her to go," Georgie said matter-of-factly. "She talked to your boss." They reached Fred's chosen area. "We'd better find something soon, it's getting dark," she muttered, adding, "You're next, and Dad's pissed off with Chuck."

"Does Chuck know about the bomb?"

"Of course not. He's stupid." Georgie stuck her tongue out and smiling, said, "Know who we'll be offing then?"

"I've no idea."

"You're little friend Millie. Would you like to hear what I plan to do with her?"

Fred tried to stay calm. "Not really. Are we looking for the bomb or not?"

"I'm going to tell you before—"

The bell pealed and Georgie slammed on the brakes. The IEC swung gently above the pile of rocks that Hank and Fred had stacked over the rifle bullets. "Is that it?" She started to get down from the Hummer, but stopped. "Got to turn off the neutrons. You were hoping I'd forget, weren't you?"

Fred shrugged. Actually, he'd been about to tell her. It wasn't part of his plan to get free.

Georgie closed down the detector and pulled it back a few feet.

"Want me to help you?" Fred asked casually.

"Yes. No, you're up to something. You stay where you are." Georgie took the Hummer keys and stuffed them into the back pocket of her jeans, walked over to the rocks, and started to throw them aside.

Fred immediately swiveled to where he could release his seat belt, and then sat up quickly, in case Georgie looked back. She did, smiling at seeing him apparently stuck in the Hummer. Fred waited until she was crouched directly in front of the detector, leaned over the seat and picked up the pen with his teeth. He stabbed at the boom icon again, and again, and again until he heard Georgie scream. He clicked it two more times for good measure and then sat up. Georgie was pinned to the ground by the protrusions on the IEC source; frantically scrabbling with her hands to get free.

Fred opened the passenger door and got out. He approached Georgie carefully in case she was faking.

"You bastard, I'll get you for this. And that bitch Millie. Let me up."

Fred squatted down behind her, facing the Hummer. He dug into her back pocket and found the switchblade. He decided to cut the plastic tie before trying to recover the Hummer keys.

"Fuck off." Georgie tried futilely to reach back and grab them.

Fred reached the Hummer, opened the knife and jammed the haft into the back of the front seat with the blade projecting. He sat and rubbed the plastic tie against the blade. After nicking his wrists a few times, he managed to cut the tie. He returned to Georgie and extracted the keys. She pawed at the ground trying to free herself.

Fred was about to comment when he heard the faint noise of a vehicle. He stood on the hood of the Hummer and looked down the canyon toward the Williams Ranch Trail. The reflection of sun off a vehicle suggested that Miguel was coming. Fred had planned to drive away, quickly enough that Georgie wouldn't be able to get up in time to catch him. He decided that would give his position away and his loaded up Hummer might not be able to outrun the bishop's vehicle. He had one gun, Georgie's. He hadn't seen Hank's, probably with the body. With his damaged wrist he wasn't convinced that he could win. That and the thought of what Georgie might do to Millie led to another option.

"What are you going to do?" she yelped.

"You'll find out," Fred replied. He turned on the tritium, flicked the icon and, as the IEC started pulsing at once a second, the bell rang again and again.

"Are you trying to kill me?"

"That'll depend on how long you're stuck here. Half hour, you'll be uncomfortable; hour, fifty-fifty chance you die; an hour and a half, you're toast."

"Fred, turn it off," Georgie pleaded.

"You shouldn't have attacked Gene and Patsy, and threatened Millie."

"I'm going to freeze," Georgie screamed.

"The neutrons will keep you warm until your Miguel or your dad gets here." Fred reached into the Hummer and filled a bag with food, drinks, Hank's binoculars, and extra clothing, before setting off down the El Capitan Trail as if he were heading south. After he was out of sight, he circled back to pick up the El Capitan Trail above the Hummer, where it headed east and north. In Fort Bliss, he had studied the map and had a clear picture of the trail's route to the Park headquarters. The sounds of the IEC faded away as he climbed up the canyon. By the time he reached the point where the trail went east at the base of the El Capitan cliffs, snow flurries were gusting against his back and visibility was diminishing. He pressed on another two miles, put on extra clothes, cleared rocks in a gulley to make a depression as he had been trained and hunkered down for the night.

As the first rays of the morning sun hit the rocks above him, Fred got up and shook off the blanket of snow that had covered him. He glanced at his watch—7:12—and just over eleven hours to the Oscars. Fred pulled the binoculars from his bag, and staying down scanned the valley below for signs of Miguel. When he looked beyond the Williams ranch, he saw two vehicles—Hummers—partially obscured by a hill, driving south from Shumard Canyon. That meant that Miguel had found Georgie.

He wondered who was driving the second Hummer—if not Georgie, who?

Fred rummaged through the bag and found a Moon Pie. He chewed on it thoughtfully while trying to convince himself that he was right to fry Georgie. From what Dr. Klevan had told him, if the IEC had run for more than hour, before it either stopped running or someone turned it off, Georgie would die a lingering death. Even at half an hour she would be in trouble. The thought that that was what James Bond would have done, made him feel better.

Bond would also have a plan to stop the bishop. Georgie had said something about there being only one other place to try if the bomb wasn't in Bone or Shumard or near the chapel. Near the Salt Flat Cafe, the final place he and Hank had decided to investigate. If only he had a cell phone. Better get a move on. He took a swig of Dr Pepper and headed toward the park headquarters.

The path became icier as Fred made his way around El Capitan, and he had to move slowly. A fall here would leave him helpless. The sun swung past due south and was turning west by the time he reached the park's visitors' center. The parking lot was iced over and he center was closed. Fred peered through the front door, seeing a welcome desk, books, and a display about the park. He banged on the door until a light came on and he saw a figure approaching.

The door opened. "How the hell did you get here, and where from?"

"Shumard Canyon," Fred said, realizing that it was Jack, the ranger that he and Hank had met back in the fall.

"The missile hunter." Jack laughed. "Is Hank with you? You guys never—"

"I need your help," Fred interrupted him.

Jack's face changed abruptly. "I can believe that, looking at you. What can I do?"

Fred decided he had to be straightforward. "Look, I'm not a missile hunter. I'm with Homeland Security, and Hank's dead."

"What! How?"

"Someone connected to the bishop. One or more of his men came last night. That's why I'm here. I need to use your phone."

"The main phone line's down. Come in back. We've got a cell in the office."

"How about driving out of here?"

The ranger looked uncertain. "We could try, but the road's iced up. I don't think we'd get far. I'll get the phone."

At the door, he turned around. "I bet you're freezing. There's coffee back here."

When they returned, Fred noticed the clock on the wall read 9:30. "Is that clock right?"

"Yes. We're on mountain time," Jack replied, handing over the cell phone.

404

Fred called Franklin Jackson's office. Rashona's voice on the answering machine said, "We're either out of the office or on another call. Please leave a message at the beep."

Fred looked at the battery signal. Still some charge left. He dialed 9-1-1. The line was busy. "Shit!"

"If that was 911 you're probably out of luck. With this weather they'll be inundated with calls for help," Jack said. "Sorry, I can't find the charger."

"Yeah. Have you got a phone book handy? Can you look up the area code for El Paso? And I need a pen and paper."

"It's 505, I think." Jack pulled a notepad and pen from his pocket and handed them over.

"Fort Bliss, please," Fred said when the operator answered. He wrote down the number and then dialed it quickly. When the operator answered, Fred said, "I don't have much time. Please write this down and tell the commandant. This is Fred Schwarzmuller. Hank Collins has been murdered...." "Yes, murdered...." "I'm not joking...." Your commandant knows what Hank and I were doing in the park. Please hurry...." "Get the commandant out of his meeting...!" "Please tell him to call Victor Hessman in Homeland Security and ask him do to some things for me." Fred rattled off his request. "Also ask him to send troops to the Salt Flat Café...there's a second bomb...." Yes, Salt Flat. I'm at the Guadalupe Park headquarters. Can you...."

The line went dead. "Damn! I hope she got it right."

405

"All this time you guys were looking for bombs? Nukes?" Jack asked.

"Yes, and you mustn't tell anybody. Is that clear?"

Jack nodded. "No problem, I prefer the missile and aliens story."

"So do I," Fred said wearily. "I guess we'll just have to sit and wait." Fred lay back on the couch and dozed off.

The sound of a helicopter woke Fred from a light sleep. The clock on the wall read 2:15. Less than five hours to the ceremony. He rushed to the window and watched the helicopter land in the parking lot.

A moment later, a soldier came through the door. "Mr. Schwarzmuller?" he asked.

"Yes. Did—?"

"I'm Captain Wilkes," the soldier interrupted, adding with a trace of anger, "First, you need to explain to me what you meant about Hank Collins getting murdered."

Fred replied, "He and I have been out here looking for a…lost missile. Do you know what I'm talking about?"

"I've heard rumors. Hank dealt with the commandant and Homeland Security on this."

"I work for them. Hank was killed by Georgie Williams, the daughter of Bishop John. He, his daughter, and some others have also been trying to find the missile. I think I know where it is. That's why I told your operator that people needed to get to the Salt Flat Cafe."

The captain looked troubled. "The commandant's out of town. By the time I heard about this, the message was to pick you up and then go to Salt Flat."

"Damn. Let's go." Fred put on his coat. "Can I talk to the commandant from the helicopter? He needs to warn Homeland Security."

"He's gone somewhere, but I know he spoke to someone in LA."

Fred shrugged. "That'll have to do." He turned to the ranger. "See you, Jack. Thanks for your help."

Fred looked out of the passenger seat window as the helicopter approached the Salt Flat Cafe. The sky was clear and the wind had died down. A Hummer sat in the scrub, about two hundred yards from the café. "Can you land here?" Fred asked, pointing.

"Sure. Not too close though." The pilot turned the helicopter in a gentle arc and set it down in the café's parking lot.

The second they landed, Fred jumped out and ran toward his Hummer. It was in a direct line with the silhouette of El Capitan. He could see that the boom was deployed over some low scrub. Closer in, he saw a rectangular hole in the ground in front of the IEC. "Too late," Fred muttered. Only then did he wonder whether Miguel was still around. He returned to the helicopter.

The captain watched him with a wry smile on his face. "Sir, next time wait for me."

"Sorry. They've got it. Let's check the Cafe."

The café owner was sweeping up when they entered. "I'm sorry we're closed," she said.

"Not a problem," Fred reassured her. "Were some people around here earlier? Maybe in uniform?"

"Yes. Actually, two of them. One of them didn't look like a soldier, if you know what I mean." She giggled as she put one hand on her hip and minced away.

Could it have been Lance Dupree? Possible if *The Last Tribe of Israel* was anti-Semitic. Fred dismissed the thought and asked, "When did they leave?"

"About an hour or two ago."

"What direction?"

"East, I think." She scratched her head.

Why would they do that? Fred wondered.

She shook her head slowly. "Funny thing though. I thought I heard a plane take off shortly after they left."

"Is there a landing strip here?"

"Not really. But we've had people land right nearby on the Dell City Road, when they've had a problem. Even right outside the cafe once."

"Thank you, ma'am. Captain, we need to go take a look."

Soon after they took off, Fred spotted a second camouflaged Hummer. "Should have spotted it we came in," he muttered. "Concentrating on the café."

As they were landing, Fred said, "We'd best not touch anything. People like that could well have booby trapped it."

"Right, sir." The captain pointed. "See these three other tracks. They had a plane here."

Fred did a quick mental calculation. Since Miguel brought their Hummer, someone else must have been the pilot.

The captain walked toward the helicopter, saying, "I need to call base, find out what they want to do with you."

After listening for a while, the captain put down the headset. "I'm to take you to the airport. There's a plane waiting. ETD is three forty."

Only three hours until the Oscars starts, Fred thought. "Where am I going?"

The pilot grinned. "La La Land, sir. Seems appropriate."

31.

Two and a-quarter-hours after leaving El Paso, Fred's Citation jet landed and pulled up to the terminal at Burbank Municipal Airport—4:55.

As Fred stepped out of the plane, Victor Hessman rushed up. "Come on, I've got a car over there," he said, pointing.

"A car? No helicopter?"

"Don't want to create a scene, someone may be watching."

"Did the ambassador agree to my requests?" Fred asked as they sped across the tarmac.

"In parts. I told him you had heard that the bomb would go off ten seconds after someone tried to disarm it."

"And?"

"He didn't like your solution, but agreed that the troops should have armor piercing weapons, including an anti-tank gun," Hessman said as they reached the government vehicle.

"I assume he's ordered the bishop's arrest," Fred said as they climbed in.

The car left. Hessman shook his head. "No, he kind of accepts that the bishop has a bomb, but he's not convinced it will work. 'Probably rotted,' he said. And he's still not convinced that the bishop plans to use it."

"Why in hell not?"

"Because both the bishop and his son will be at the ceremony."

"And if the bishop and Chuck leave?"

"I hope he'll agree to do something."

"Shit. We don't even know where the bomb is and he's—."

"I agree. It's crazy, but our hands are tied," Hessman said abruptly. "I don't know how to argue with the fact that security checked out all the props…thoroughly. Nothing."

"That means it's somewhere else." Fred said, "So, can I get in to see him?"

"No. He left explicit instructions." Hessman clasped Fred's arm. "Doesn't want a scene in front of all those important people at the ceremony. We're to stay outside with the troops."

"How will we know when we move?"

"He'll call me on his cell phone."

"God save us from amateurs." Fred scratched his head. "Will we be able to watch the ceremony?"

"Yes. They've set up a TV in a command vehicle on Orchid Avenue, behind the Hollywood and Highland Center."

Two trucks carrying National Guardsmen were parked next to the command post vehicle. When Fred entered the vehicle, television monitors were showing areas in and around the Hollywood Center. A soldier was sitting at a panel controlling the movement of the cameras. The regular television broadcast showed Ambassador Wheaton, immaculate in a tuxedo, escorting an elegantly dressed blonde woman. They were followed by Chuck and the bishop. In the background, a Lincoln stretch-limousine was leaving the front of the Kodak Theater.

"Bishop Orpheus John, the backer of *Bye Bye Oscars*, and now playing Moses, has arrived," said the commentator. "That's a first for the Oscars."

"Are you sure?" asked his co-host. "What about Charlton Heston?"

"He only wore a white robe and carried a staff in the movie."

Hessman tapped Fred on the shoulder. "That young guy with the bishop. He looked a bit like you."

"Chuck Steak, star of *Bye Bye Two*," Fred said.

Further comments were interrupted by the commentator saying, "Look, here's Sebastian Agincourt, creator of the cult hit *Bye Bye Oscars*."

"Who's that?" asked Hessman, as a bouffant head of hair appeared after Agincourt, her extensive exposed cleavage wobbling as she got out of the limo.

"Sebastian's squeeze, Lola Paramour," Fred replied.

Finally, Bogdan Mirnov stepped out. He took Lola's arm and the two of them wended their tipsy way down the red carpet behind Agincourt. The crowd roared with delight as they careened into an interviewer. Bogdan reached out for support, snagging Lola's dress. The top slipped down, revealing a Howard Hughesian support system. She let go of Bogdan and hauled her dress up, causing them both to fall over.

"Shades of the Super Bowl," the commentator quipped as the camera panned to where the bishop and Chuck were standing by two large model Oscars near the entrance to the theater.

"Made in the bishop's workshop," Fred said.

"We took them apart," said a captain. "And everything else. I hope we weren't wasting our time."

By the time Fred had finished an expurgated version of why they had been called in, the opening ceremonies were over. The command post was silent except for Sunny Jamaica on TV, who raised his arms and said "And now, what you've all been waiting for, the *Bye Bye Oscars* retrospective. Take a bow, Sebastian."

The camera shot panned to show Sebastian Agincourt standing triumphantly, his arms raised above his head. Fred saw that the bishop and the ambassador were sitting beside him.

The audience cheered as a troupe of dancers, who looked as if they had come off the set of *The Ten Commandments*, rolled an oversize Oscar onto the stage.

"Show us the bomb." a diva with a powerful voice shouted.

Her demand was echoed around the theater.

"Patience, folks, all in good time," Sunny Jamaica replied, motioning with his hands to quiet the audience.

"How can we have a good time when you're celebrating this crap?" a famous director muttered, loud enough to be picked up by a microphone.

The camera swung to show Agincourt jumping to his feet.

"Picky, picky. Professional jealousy," he shouted.

The dancers performed semi-erotic gyrations to the *Bye Bye Oscar*s theme music. Chuck Jenkins playing Charles Innocent playing Chuck Steak minced onto the stage. He was followed by a Millie/Monique von Minx look-alike.

Oh, my God, thought Fred. It wasn't a look-alike, it was Millie. The room started to spin.

"Are you okay, sir," Hessman asked, steadying Fred.

"Millie shouldn't be here. I've got to do something," Fred replied distractedly as he watched the dancers cavort in front of the Oscar, before together pushing a button on the back of the model. The Oscar peeled open revealing a fake-looking bomb with fins and a large red-lit countdown clock.

"Ten, nine," someone shouted from the audience, drowning out Hessman's response.

"Wait for it," Sunny shouted. "I have the honor."

Chuck and Monique cavorted wildly around him as he moon-walked around the bomb, pretending to start the countdown.

Two mutant jellyfish waddled on from stage left and joined the dancers. The first jellyfish removed its disguise, revealing a Lance Dupree mask, and moved toward the statue.

Sunny grabbed the alien's arm. "Not yet!"

"Disgusting," the bishop shouted as he stormed down the aisle and ran onto the stage.

Sunny spread his arms, appealing to the audience. "Who the hell—"

"Quiet, you parasite!" roared the bishop.

The TV commentator laughed. "It looks like the organizers didn't tell Sunny about this." He paused. "Great theater." The camera panned to show the audience roaring its approval. The orchestra started playing the *We'll Meet Again* song that graced the end of *Dr. Strangelove or: How I learned to Stop Worrying and Love the Bomb*. Fred could not resist a grin. Some of the audience sang along.

The bishop lunged for the button.

"It's my gig," said Sunny, getting there first. "Ten, nine,…"

The audience joined in. "Eight, seven, six, five."

Fred covered his face with his hands as the chant continued.

"Four, three, two, one."

Nothing.

Fred peeked from between his fingers to see Sunny Jamaica pointing at the audience. A camera adjusted quickly to show Agincourt, Lola, and Bogdan. "I'll get you for this, Sebastian," Sunny shouted.

Agincourt's face showed surprise. Next to him, Ambassador Wheaton stood up looking upset and pointing at the stage.

"Too late, ambassador," Fred muttered.

The camera panned back showing the bishop with arms raised, and holding a remote control.

"Moses on Mount Sinai," the commentator said quickly.

"The Lord will rain *frimstone* and *bire* on *Godom* and *Somorrah*," the bishop screamed.

The last image on the screen was of his index finger punching in a code.

As Fred walked to the door, a message appeared on the screen: Sorry, folks. We'll be back to *Bye Bye Oscars* as soon as possible.

"Great stunt," one of the soldiers said.

"I didn't hear an explosion. Millie's safe. We're still here," Fred muttered. As he spoke the screen lit up, and Sunny Jamaica said, "To our TV audience: We got you, folks."

The bishop and Chuck, standing on either side of the comic, raised their arms in triumph to a standing ovation. They disappeared to the side of the stage. After a commercial break, the camera panned the audience and Fred caught a quick glimpse of the ambassador, holding a cell phone and talking earnestly to Chuck, as Chuck took the bishop's seat.

"Chuck's still there. Where's the bishop?" Fred said to himself. Suddenly, he remembered what Georgie had said, "You're next, and Dad's pissed off with Chuck. Know who we'll be offing then?" Chuck was expendable. The bishop had gone.

"Can you replay the people arriving at the theater?" Fred asked.

"Which part?" said the soldier at a control-panel.

"Just before Ambassador Wheaton arrived."

The soldier pushed a button and the Oscars scene scrolled back. He stopped the scene as the ambassador's limo pulled up. The chauffeur got out, and for a moment faced the camera.

"It's Carl." Fred shouted, realizing as he said it where the bomb was. "The bomb's in the limo. We've got to take it out. We may have ten minutes or less. The bishop won't trigger it until he's out of the blast zone. Where's—?"

"How do you know?" the captain asked.

"Where's the limo? I'll tell you on the way."

"Around the corner on North Orange Drive, sir," said a soldier.

"You go with the troops," Hessman said. "I'll call the ambassador and get people looking for the bishop and Carl, and clear the area outside the Center."

"What if the ambassador doesn't agree?"

"As the senior Homeland Security man at the scene, I'm in charge, Fred," Hessman replied. "I've had enough of this crap. Use your judgment."

As they raced down Franklin Avenue, the captain asked, "So, why are you sure?"

"Months ago, I was working in the bishop's machine shop," Fred said as he trotted beside the captain. "I saw Carl working on an engine block. The bishop has one of those white Lincoln limos."

"But it won't run."

Fred thought quickly, seeing an image of the bishop's Lincoln with the brake drums removed. "At a guess, Carl put in batteries and electric motors on the wheels. Good enough for a short distance."

They reached the corner of Franklin Avenue and turned onto North Orange Drive, to see lines of limousines parked on each side of the road all the way down to Hollywood Boulevard.

"Clear everyone out!" shouted the captain. "Look for a white stretch Lincoln."

"Without a driver," Fred added.

They found the bishop's car a hundred yard back from Hollywood Boulevard.

"Before we take it out, explain something to me. All the limos were searched." The captain sounded worried.

"Including the one with a senior Homeland Security man inside?"

"Unfortunately, Ambassador Wheaton's limo only got a quick scan." The Captain sounded convinced. "What do you want us to do?"

"Get two squads to keep people away so that no one can see into this road," Fred replied. "You, the anti-tank guy and I will go back up to Franklin Avenue, to where he can get a shot through the headlight into the engine block. It's our only chance."

The captain gave the orders and then they raced up the street. The three of them crouched behind a limousine and the soldier placed the anti-tank gun on the hood pointing at the bishop's car.

"Ready when you are, sir," he said.

For a moment, Fred panicked. They hadn't received approval from the ambassador. "I've had enough of this crap,"

Victor Hessman had said. So had Fred and Millie was in the complex across the street. "Go for it!"

Fred heard the roar of the anti-tank gun as he ducked down. The explosion shook the car and the sky lit up. Pieces of limousines rained down for what seemed like minutes.

"Jesus Christ," the captain shouted. "That was more than an anti-tank shell."

"High explosives in the bomb," Fred said. "We've got to get out of here. Let the decontamination squad work the place over." Thank God, the shell had destroyed the trigger mechanism before it could operate. As he peeked over the hood, the captain's cell phone rang.

"Just in time," said the captain, ashen-faced. "The ambassador agreed."

Fred scanned the rising smoke, and the scene of devastation. A large hole marked the place where three limos had been parked. All the other twenty or more vehicles were smoldering wrecks, and there wasn't a pane of glass left in the nearby buildings. "Good thing. There are going to be a lot of unhappy limo and business owners."

* * *

Two days after the attempted bombing of the Oscars ceremony, Fred was released from a military hospital. There, he, the captain and the marksman had been decontaminated, and treated for lacerations and broken bones. Fred had emerged relatively unscathed with nothing broken. A Homeland Security driver met him as he signed out, and took him downtown for a de-briefing at the building that housed the ambassador's office. Victor Hessman met Fred at the door to the meeting room. "We weren't quick enough; the bishop got away."

"How?"

"The FBI searched the whole complex soon after Wheaton agreed that there was a problem. They found the bishop's robe and a mess of white hair in a restroom, backstage. Who knows what he looked like when he left the building."

"Damn. But at least we stopped the bomb. What about Miguel, Georgie and whoever was with them?"

Hessman scratched his head. "The only thing that I heard was that radar picked up a plane heading across the border just about the time that you were picked up at park headquarters. But it was before anybody realized they had to do anything."

"I'll suggest they check on medical facilities in Mexico," Fred said. "Georgie'll need treatment for radiation exposure."

"I thought you were joking when you said you'd turned on that detector thing."

"Hell no! She crippled the Kowalskis and threatened the woman I love."

"Good grief." Hessman looked surprised by Fred's vehemence. "One other thing, what do you think the bishop plans to do now that his minions have the second bomb?"

After a long silence he said, "The only clue I have is that Sebastian Agincourt was planning a new movie. I'm guessing that the bishop was behind it. The bishop and Lance Dupree wrote the script for the new *Bye Bye Oscars*. Agincourt said his new movie would be called *The Last Tribe of Israel*."

"Holy sh...." exclaimed Hessman, shaking his head before taking Fred's arm briefly. "I need to warn you, before you go in. You're going to find it tough in there. The ambassador's taking credit for preventing a disaster. He also claims that Franklin Jackson did not inform him of all the facts."

"What about the ambassador being cozy with the bishop?"

"He claims he was deliberately leading the bishop on." Hessman chuckled. "The ambassador's a pompous idiot. He was amazed to hear the explosion occur as he gave his approval, never worked out that you didn't know."

"I suppose I should find that funny," Fred grunted. "But, Jesus Christ, how can he take credit? He was the problem!"

"Let me put it this way. You know how the president likes to give nicknames. Well, now he has one for James Wheaton—Jimbomb. The word is he'll get a medal and may be in line to take over Homeland Security. Jackson will be shunted sideways, but will keep his grade; the price the ambassador paid to keep Jackson's mouth shut."

"What if we publish Gene's notes?"

"I thought of that, but the administration has taken a position on this case—the new 9/11 that justifies all their efforts." Hessman smiled ruefully. "They've picked a hero, and a villain—Al Quaeda—and hidden the fact that there was a real nuke."

"How will they explain the need for cleaning up the spattered plutonium and uranium?"

"Franklin Jackson put out the story that it was a dirty bomb," Hessman replied. "We all know that isn't true, but it may be better if the public doesn't find out the truth. As far as they're concerned, one bit of nuclear crap is the same as another. The administration and chairs of the key congressional committees have agreed to keep it that way. You may not say anything about this matter."

"I still think we—"

"Keep your cool. Be glad that Gene's and your efforts saved the country from an absolute disaster." Hessman put his hand on Fred's shoulder. "We can't win. Frankly, I'm concerned what some people might do if we tried to expose the truth. But I made sure the ambassador knew there were documents that would come to light if anything happened to us. We need to get on with our lives. Take some time off. You deserve it. Oh, Gene sent a note."

Hessman fished in his briefcase and extracted a card. It showed a picture of a beach in Hawaii. On the back, Gene had written. Fantastic, I watched on TV. Now get the second Nuke. Signing off, Gene.

Fred looked at his toes to hide the tears of frustration. An image of Millie flashed into his head. He'd go to Albuquerque as soon as his de-briefing was done. "Okay, I'll be quiet. Let's get it over with."

Epilogue

Fred, feeling strangely nervous, carried the large bouquet of roses to Millie's front door. He rang and waited. Strange, Millie's car was in the driveway, but there were no lights on in the house.

Georgie's bitter face flashed before him. "You bastard, I'll get you for this. And that bitch Millie." That's what Georgie had said.

Fred swallowed hard, crept around the house, and carefully opened the gate into the backyard. He peered through the windows but did not see anything. As he approached the back door, a sinking feeling was followed by fear as he heard a noise. Someone was coming. He moved to the side of the door and crouched down. The door opened. Fred looked up to see high heels, elegant legs, black stockings, black lace panties, and a garter belt.

"What on earth are you doing down there, Fred?" asked Monique von Minx.

Made in the USA
Columbia, SC
14 February 2019